The Outbreak

Preface

This is the second book in the *For Those In Peril* series. I know that there will be many who are champing at the bit to find out what happens to Rob and his crewmates (the characters from the first book), but before that can happen, I need to introduce a new cast of characters, and provide a first-person view of what it's like to be in a city as it's being overrun by 'the infected'. Rest assured, though, Rob and the others will reappear in the third book in the series.

Just like the first book, for this second one, I have drawn on my own life experiences to write it. Much of the sailing side of things is based on the time I spent working on a number of whale-watching vessels on the west coast of Scotland in the 1990s. They were fun days as I learned not just about sailing, but also about how different my native land looked when viewed from the sea rather than from the shore.

However, I've also drawn on the experiences I had while I worked for a few years, off and on, as a professional juggler, plying my trade as part of a double act on, amongst other places, Buchanan Street in Glasgow, Scotland's largest and most cosmopolitan city. Thus, much of the back story of Ben, the narrator of this book, is based on my own, although, while at one point it was a distinct possibility, I never did take the job I was once offered working on a whale-watching vessel in the Azores. Maybe if I had my life would have turned out more like Ben's (or at least Ben's life up to the point where this book starts).

During my time as a juggler, I worked with Gordon, who was a few years older than me and who was, for about ten years, a permanent fixture on Buchanan Street, regularly drawing crowds of several hundred people as he performed his show (or *our* show when we worked together). While all the characters in this book are entirely fictitious, some elements of one of the characters (Tom) were inspired by him. While he is no longer around, I think if he was, he'd have got a kick out of being remembered in this way. Of course, he would also have told me that I'd got him completely wrong, but then again, Tom isn't meant to be Gordon, they just happen to have some characteristics in common (although I won't tell you which ones).

As always with writing any book, there are plenty of people to thank. These include Stephen Burges, Michele Airns, Jennifer Learmonth, Chris Parsons, Emily Lambert, Lilian Lieber and Barry Nicholls for their comments on early drafts. Thanks also to Chloe Burges for answering my questions on how to treat a pneumothorax with the types of everyday items usually found on a boat. In addition, I would like to thank Anna MacLeod and Gale Winskill (*www.winskilleditorial.co.uk*) for their editing and proof-reading skills.

Finally, the biggest thanks of all must go to Sarah for her patience as I developed the basic plot for this book, for her editing advice and for her support throughout the writing process, and throughout my life.

The real-world locations where the fictional events of *The Outbreak* take place.

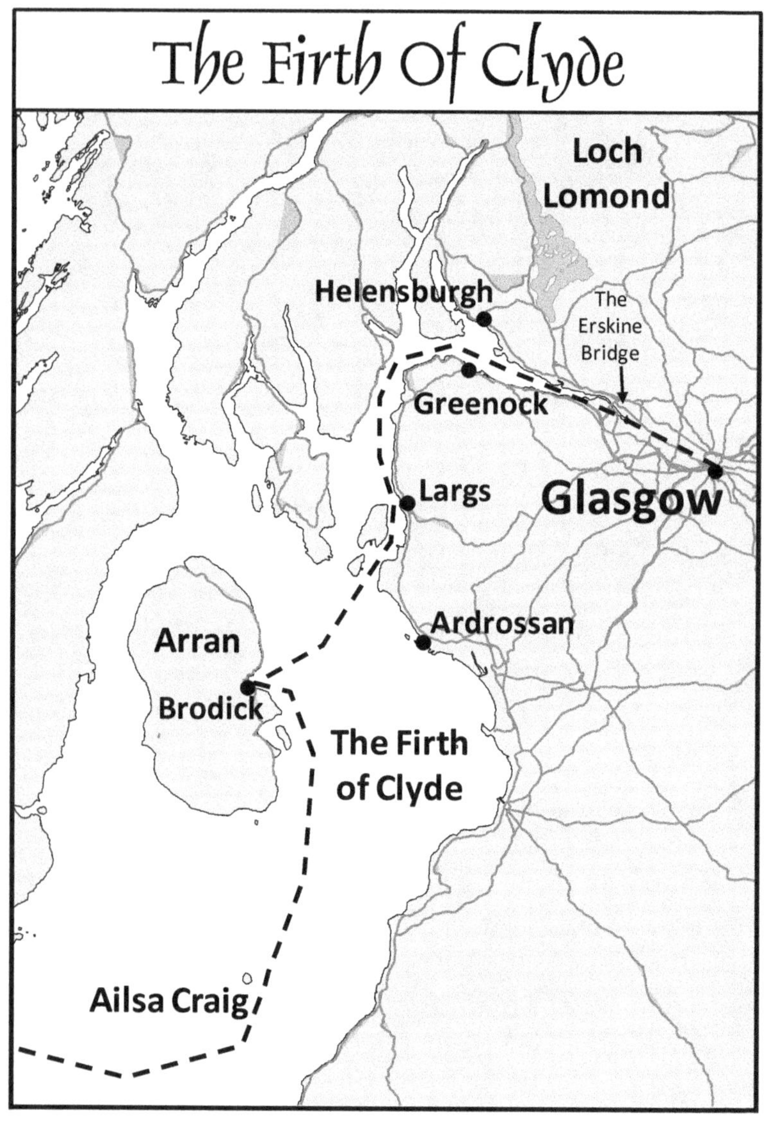

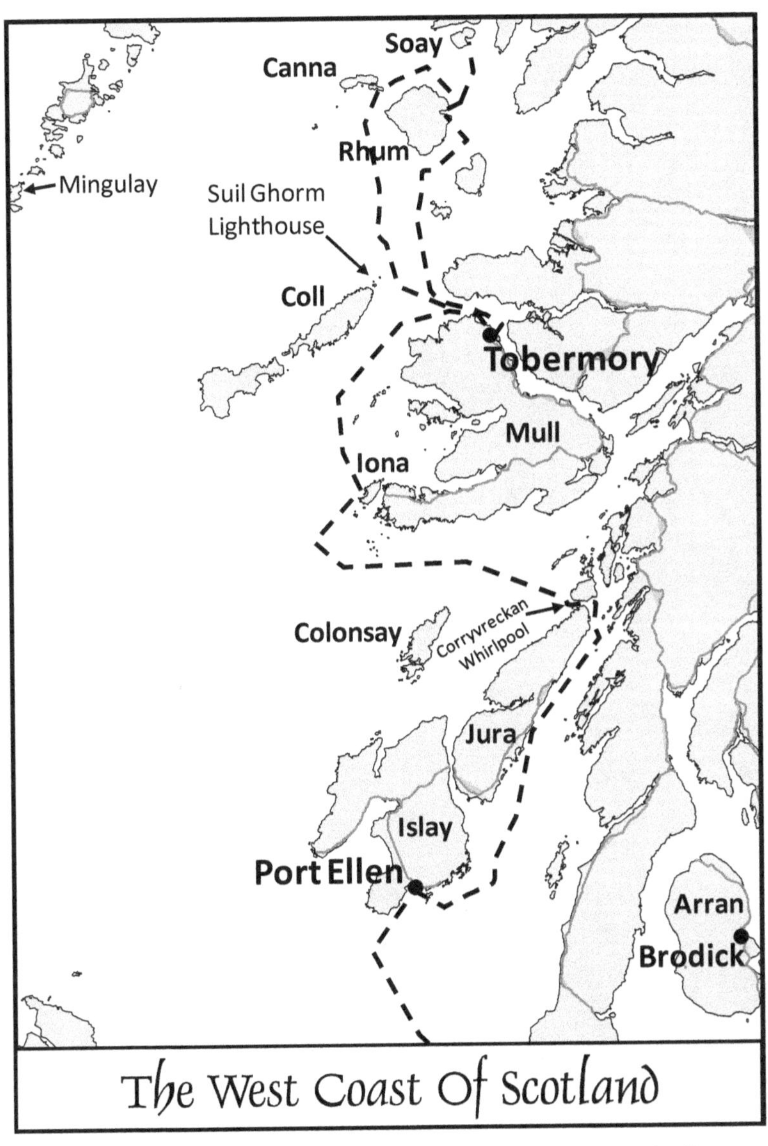

The West Coast Of Scotland

For more information about these locations, including interactive maps, visit *TheOutbreak.ForThoseInPeril.net*.

*What if the end comes, not with a whimper or a bang,
but with a scream?*

Prologue

General McDonald burst through the door without bothering to knock. 'Sir, that was the Americans; it's official: Miami's been overrun.'

'I know. I'm watching it happen.' The Prime Minister nodded to the large television on the wall of his private office, a grim look on his face. On the screen, CNN was showing grainy footage from a security camera on what seemed like a permanent loop. 'I don't think they're going to be able to contain it. If this thing can bring down Miami, imagine what would happen if it reached London.'

The General turned to the TV. On it, hundreds of people were surging through downtown Miami, attacking anyone they could catch. The footage froze for a second and then the mob stormed down the street again. After watching it a third time, he turned back to the Prime Minister. 'The Americans, they're sure all this is down to this new virus?'

'They've not made it public yet, but they're 100 per cent on it.' The Prime Minister puffed himself up. 'I heard it from the President himself.'

'And there's no cure?'

The Prime Minister rose and walked over to the General. 'No.'

'No treatment?'

'No.'

A thin layer of perspiration started to form on the General's forehead. 'There's no vaccine?'

'I've got people looking into it, but it doesn't seem like there's anything viable.' The Prime Minister strode back to his desk. 'And even if there was, people probably wouldn't take it: they'd be too scared of what it might do to them. You've got to remember … it was a vaccine that caused the virus to mutate in the first place.' With a sigh, he slumped into his chair. 'Anyway, it's all academic. At the rate it's now spreading, there isn't enough time, even if there was something promising we could work on.'

General McDonald moved over to the window and leant on the sill, gazing at the people walking along the street several storeys below. 'In that case, we need to start thinking about ourselves. We need to close the borders; we need to do all we can to make sure the virus doesn't get in.' The General turned back to face the room. 'And we need to do it now.'

The Prime Minister sat silently for a full minute, hands together in front of his face, the tips of his index fingers touching his lips, before he spoke again. 'You're right, it's our only choice. How long will it take?'

The General glanced at his watch. 'It can be done within the hour.'

'Right,' the Prime Minister placed his hands on his desk and levered himself to his feet, 'I'd better make an announcement before everyone starts to panic.'

He was halfway to the door when the General cleared his throat. The Prime Minister froze as General McDonald started to speak again. 'There's something else we need to discuss …'

The Prime Minister turned, the anger clear on his face. 'You really think this is the time to be discussing anything else?'

'Yes.' The General stiffened. 'We need to decide what to do if the virus gets in.'

The Prime Minister took a pace towards the General

and bellowed, 'But you said closing the borders would stop that from happening!'

General McDonald had to stop himself taking an involuntary step backwards. 'No, *sir*, I said it'd minimise the risk. There's a big difference between the two.'

The Prime Minister remained where he was, his face contorted by fury and confusion as he tried to work out how best to respond. After a few seconds he gave up and walked back to his seat. When he spoke again, it was in a resigned tone. 'So what are the options?'

The General swallowed nervously. This was the moment he'd been dreading. He knew what they'd have to do, but he wasn't sure he could convince the Prime Minister to agree to it. 'There's only one viable option, sir.'

'If there's only one bloody option,' anger rose in the Prime Minister's voice again, 'why do we need to discuss it?'

General McDonald did his best to sound self-assured, but inside his stomach was churning. 'Because of what it would mean we'd need to do.'

'And what would that be?' The Prime Minister spat the words out.

'If we get an outbreak ...' The General's eyes flicked subconsciously from the Prime Minister to the television and back again. 'If we get an outbreak, we'll need to seal the area off. We let no one in.' He locked eyes with the Prime Minister. 'And no one out.'

'No one?' The Prime Minister sounded incredulous.

'Absolutely no one.' There was a steeliness to the General's voice now. 'No matter what.'

The Prime Minister closed his eyes momentarily, almost as if he was readying himself for the answer he knew was coming before he even asked his next question. 'People aren't just going to sit there quietly while something like *that*,' he jabbed a finger towards the TV, 'happens. They're going to try to get out. What will you do then?'

The General leant on the desk, bringing his face close the Prime Minister's. 'We treat them as *unfriendlies*, sir'

'What on earth does that mean?' The Prime Minister shot back.

The General could feel the warmth of the Prime Minister's breath on his face. All the nervousness he'd felt about raising his plan with the Prime Minister was now gone, replaced by something closer to confidence. He looked the Prime Minister in the eye once more. 'We take them out.'

The Prime Minister pulled back in disgust. 'You're talking about killing people? British citizens on British streets?'

'Yes.' The General straightened up. 'It's the only way to contain something like this.'

'Bloody hell!' The Prime Minister put his head in his hands and rubbed his eyes. This wasn't why he'd gone into politics. He might have expected to send troops to keep the peace in a far-off tropical jungle, or to keep the right people in charge of a strategically important scrap of desert, or maybe even the illegal detention of some would-be terrorist or other, but never this.

He thought about it for five minutes, wrestling with all the possible outcomes, knowing that if he made the wrong decision it would dog him for the rest of his career. If he agreed to the General's plan and it turned out things weren't as bad as they seemed right now, then he'd always be the Prime Minister who'd ordered the shooting of British citizens. Even if it didn't actually happen, it would still get out that he'd given it the green light and his career would be over. Yet, if he vetoed the General's plan, and things went wrong, he'd be responsible for everything that happened as a result, and his opponents would never let anyone forget it. Finally, he spoke. 'Okay, get it set up. Do whatever you need to do.'

The Prime Minister got to his feet and strode towards the door once again. When he reached it, he turned and addressed the General one last time. 'But it's your head on the block if anything goes wrong.'

'Bloody politicians!' the General muttered under his breath, as he pulled out his mobile phone and selected a number. When it was picked up at the other end, he said only four words and hung up. He leant against the desk, staring at the TV screen, hoping against hope they'd never need to implement the order he'd just given.

***

'Ladies and gentlemen, we're starting our descent into Glasgow International Airport. If you'd like to fold your tables away and return your seats to the upright position, we should be on the ground in about twenty minutes.'

Michael did as he was told, but as he shifted in his seat, he could feel his shirt, soaked with sweat, sticking to his back. Despite the dryness of the air in the cabin, his skin felt clammy: he hoped he wasn't getting ill, that this wasn't the first sign of the infection. He glanced down at his arm. Even though he couldn't see them, he could feel the scratches burning underneath the makeshift bandage. If the homeless man who'd attacked him had been infected, then he would be, too. Yet, there was a good chance that the man hadn't even had the disease. After all, there were only a few pockets of infection here and there in the US, and the Government was managing to keep a lid on it, unlike the situation in Haiti or the other islands to which the disease had spread so far. Maybe the man who'd attacked him had just been drunk or high; there was no way to know for sure. He'd simply sprung out of nowhere and lunged at Michael as he'd tried to get into his car. Michael had managed to push him away and scramble behind the wheel, but the question lingered in his mind: why had the old man attacked him?

He pushed these thoughts from his mind because it didn't matter; he'd be on the ground in a few minutes and then he could see about getting some treatment for whatever was going on. Michael glanced at his watch. It was just over twelve hours since the man had attacked him and if he was infected, he didn't know how much longer he'd have before it was too late. Maybe there was someone at his work he could call who would know what to do: they'd created the disease after all, so they might know how to cure it, or at least stop it getting worse; that was if he even had it.

Michael had always known running a field trial so early in the development phase of the vaccine was risky, but they'd heard rumours that one of the major pharmaceutical companies was working on something similar. Even though they were a multinational business, they still couldn't compete with big pharma. If they didn't get their vaccine on to the market first, they'd be pushed out, meaning years of research, and more importantly, millions of dollars, would have been wasted. That's why he'd given the go-ahead for the trial in Haiti, despite the inherent risks he knew it would bring.

No one could have foreseen this, though; that the vaccine would cause the rabies virus to mutate, to become more virulent, but less pathological. It no longer killed; it just drove people mad, made them violent: all they wanted to do was to attack others, kill them, tear them apart. It was the virus doing its best to ensure it was passed on; the virus was taking control of people, turning them into machines, to make as many copies of itself as possible and then infect others. It was no surprise — that's what viruses had evolved to do — only their vaccine had somehow caused it to change. They'd thought the siRNA molecule they'd created would make the virus more susceptible to the immune system, allowing the body to fight it off on its own. Instead, it had made it stronger, almost indestructible. This hadn't happened in the lab mice, or the monkeys, or the pigs; it had only happened when they'd tried it for real on humans. There was no way anyone could have predicted this, and by the time they'd realised what was going on it was too late: the mutation had happened and it had started to spread.

****

Michael lay on the bed in his hotel room, staring at the widescreen television, watching the disaster in Miami as it continued to unravel before him. For once, rolling news was living up to its billing: things were happening so fast that new reports really were needed every hour. No one was quite sure how it had happened, but somehow hundreds of people infected with the disease had suddenly appeared near the port. They'd rampaged through the city, attacking people; not killing them, just bringing each one down long enough to infect them before moving on to the next fleeing target. The infection had reached a tipping point and was now spreading like wildfire. The Governor had sent in the National Guard, but there was nothing they could do, not with so many people being infected so quickly. Michael knew diseases;

he knew this disease: there was only one way this was going to go now and it wasn't good.

Despite the air-conditioning in the room, Michael was still sweating heavily; the scratches on his arm still burned and his body was starting to ache. He tried to tell himself it was just a reaction to what he was seeing on the television, but deep down he knew it was the infection. The only question left now was what was he going to do about it? If he'd still been at home, he could simply have taken his gun and blown his brains out; messy, but quick. But he wasn't, he was in Scotland. He'd only ended up in Glasgow because it was the first flight out of the US he'd found when he arrived at the airport the previous afternoon. He was hoping for somewhere more exotic, but he figured Glasgow would be a start. He knew people would come looking for him as soon as anyone outside of the company found out he'd been the one to ignore the risks and give the okay for the trial. He knew he had to get out of the country before that happened. By the looks of things, it was just as well he did or he'd have still been in Miami, watching all that was happening there in person, rather than on TV from half a world away.

As he was leaving Glasgow airport, Michael had passed a convoy of armoured vehicles heading towards it. He'd heard on the cab driver's radio that Britain was closing its borders and sealing itself off in the hope of stopping the disease getting in. Now, in the safety of his hotel room, he wondered how many other countries would follow suit. He laughed grimly to himself: little did they know it was already too late; the virus was already here; he could feel it coursing through his veins. It had been almost eighteen hours since he'd been infected and Michael knew he didn't have much time left. He knew he had to kill himself before he turned and infected anyone else. That way, at least he'd do some good.

He thought about how he could do it. He didn't want to cut himself; that would be too difficult. Hanging was off the cards; there was nowhere in the hotel room he could suspend himself from. He went over to the window and considered jumping, but he was only two storeys up and that wasn't high enough. Then it dawned on him: an overdose. Quick, painless and it would be easy enough to get hold of the drugs to do it. He could leave a note saying he was infected, warning people to dispose of his body properly. That would work. All he had to do now was to go out and purchase the painkillers, and hope that he had enough time to return to his room before the disease finally overwhelmed him.

***

The mounted policeman nudged his partner and pointed down Argyle Street. 'Effin' drunks,' he looked at his watch. 'Just gone midday an' he's aff his heed already.'

'He's better dressed than your average Jakie, though,' his partner replied.

'Bein' rich don't stop you bein' an alkie, does it?' He watched the man stagger a few yards further and then collapse. A knot of people quickly gathered round to gawk. 'I suppose that's the cue for one of us to get involved.'

'Usual way?'

Rock, paper, scissors had been their way of deciding who got to do any unpalatable tasks ever since they'd first been teamed up. 'Yep.'

'On the count of three.' They held out their fists. 'One, two ... three.'

'Bugger! That's the fifth time in a row you've won. How the feckin' hell are you doin' that?' Still grumbling about his run of bad luck, the policeman slipped from his horse and gave the reins to his partner. He spoke into his radio, calling for an ambulance as he walked towards the small crowd. When he got there, he knelt down beside the man; he was unconscious, but still breathing … just. The policeman put a hand on the man's neck: his skin was red-hot and his pulse was racing. Then the policeman noticed something unexpected: there was no smell of booze. Usually drunks reeked of the stuff, especially when they'd had enough to pass out. As he stood up, a thought flashed through his head: maybe the man was sick rather than drunk. It couldn't be the disease the Prime Minister had talked about on the news that morning, the one from Miami, could it? He hesitated for a moment and then reached for his radio again; better to be safe than sorry.

Suddenly, the man's eyes snapped opened. His breathing was now slow and steady: something had changed. The man sprang to his feet and lunged at the policeman, clawing at his face and throat, sinking his teeth deep into his neck. The policeman punched his attacker as hard as he could, sending him staggering backwards into the surrounding onlookers. A woman screamed as she jumped out of the way and the man seemed to notice the bystanders for the first time. He leapt onto the nearest one, pushing her to the ground and biting savagely at her face. In an instant, there was pandemonium, with people tripping over each other as they tried to scatter. Distracted by all the movement, he broke off his assault on the woman and went for a middle-aged man who'd fallen and was now scrabbling to get back to his feet. He was only on him for a moment, just long enough to bite and infect him, before he went for another, then another, bringing each one down before moving on to the next.

In all the confusion, nobody noticed the injured policeman slump to the ground, his wounds searing with pain as the infection took hold. Suddenly, he was burning up, his heart was pounding, his breathing growing shallow. He tried to work his radio, to get a warning out, but he was losing coordination in his fingers; his eyes drifted out of focus and slowly his world faded to black.

***

'Sierra six-one to base. Sierra six-one to base. Man down, I repeat, man down. We need backup. We're on Argyle Street. There's a man, he's gone berserk; he's attacking everyone.'

The voice on the radio crackled with a mix of panic and confusion, and it was clear to all who were listening that something serious was happening. 'Scott's down. He's been injured. I think he's unconscious. Hang on, no it looks like he's okay. He's getting back up.'

The voice sounded relieved, but only for a moment. 'Shit! He just bit a woman ... Now there are more of them. People are just attacking each other.'

Fear replaced panic in the voice. 'It's just like on the news; it's like what happened in Miami!'

Those listening heard the transmission key being released, only to be pressed again a fraction of a second later. 'I'm getting the fuck out of here!'

Chapter One

I stared down the length of Buchanan Street. It was amazing to think how much it had changed since I was a kid. Back then it had been little more than a cut-through from one shopping street to another, but now it was awash with posh boutiques and fashion-hungry shoppers. Even the steps I was sitting on were new, built on what had literally been a bomb site in my youth. Now, in its place, stood a concert hall where the more cultured could come to listen to operas and orchestras, but for most, it was a place to rest from the hustle and bustle of the street, eat lunch, meet friends or just watch the crowds going by. I glanced at my watch; it had just gone quarter past twelve, but the street was already packed and, as usual, Tom was late.

I'd met Tom not far from this very spot, just after I'd graduated from university. He was working as a street entertainer and helped me turn juggling from a hobby into a lucrative money-spinner. For the rest of that summer we worked a patch halfway down the pedestrianised street, performing our show four or five times a day, and earning enough money to ensure that I didn't have to think about getting a real job right away. Soon, I'd wasted a couple of years. Well, not really wasted, as I'd had a lot of fun, but it wasn't something I wanted to do forever and I thought I should at least try to make use of my marine biology degree.

Tom wasn't pleased, but he understood, and whenever I was in town I'd make sure I made time to catch up with him. He was still working our favourite spot, and every now and then he'd persuade me to join him in a rerun of the old show. Whenever I did, I was reminded both of how much I enjoyed it, and why I didn't want to do it for the rest of my life: it was just too nerve-wracking, especially the finale which involved flaming torches, blindfolds and some unsuspecting volunteer we'd dragged from the audience.

As an alternative to juggling, I'd taken a job as the resident expert for a whale-watching company in the Azores. I'd intended it to be a stepping stone to a research career, but as my first summer there wore on, I realised I'd found my niche in the world and that I wanted to stay. I'd worked my way up until I had the knowledge and the connections I needed to start my own company. Ten years later, I was living the dream: I spent my summers on the west coast of Scotland, taking tourists out on my forty-five foot sailboat to see minke whales and other local wildlife, while I wintered in the Canaries doing a similar thing, but with different whale species.

Like the birds, each spring and autumn, I'd migrate between my summering and wintering grounds. And each time I passed, I'd stop off in Glasgow to meet up with Tom. A couple of days of drinking too much and talking over old times twice a year were enough to keep our friendship going.

The day before, I'd sailed up the Firth of Clyde on the west coast of Scotland, past the lighthouse on Ailsa Craig, keeping clear of a red, white and black ferry as it made its way from Ardrossan on the mainland to Arran, the southern-most of the inhabited islands in the Firth, and on past the cooling towers of the Hunterston power station. As I turned eastward into the river itself, the land closed around me. The residential town of Helensburgh was to the north, while the more industrial Greenock lay to the south. Ahead, the span of the Erskine Bridge stretched from one side to the other, a hundred feet above the water. Few people ever approached Glasgow this way these days, but for me, passing under the bridge always meant I was home, even though it would be several more hours before I'd reach the city itself.

As I sailed on, I was eager to see what had changed in the six months since I'd last visited. Glasgow had been making a concerted effort to redevelop a river front that had once been dominated by shipyards, and there was always something new. This time, it was the sleek metal lines of a new museum squatting beside the water. I saw that the tall ship I usually tied up next to had been moved down to a new berth beside it, meaning that I'd have the floating pontoons just west of the city's exhibition centre all to myself.

By sunset, I'd settled in and phoned Tom to tell him I was back in town before arranging a time and place to meet the next day. After that, I turned on the TV: things had been getting pretty weird in the last couple of weeks, and I wanted to see what the latest news was. What I found out wasn't good. It seemed they'd finally confirmed this new virus everyone had been talking about was, in some way, linked to the violence that had been bubbling up here and there in various US cities, and to the unrest that had been erupting across the Caribbean. Nobody seemed to know how it had got into the US, but rumours suggested a contaminated drug shipment out of Haiti. Yet, that didn't quite seem to fit with the way it was spreading, especially in the islands. I was just about to switch it off when they cut to some breaking news, and I watched in horror as Miami descended into chaos, live on air and right in front of my eyes.

Sometime in the night I must have fallen asleep, because I

woke in the morning to find I was still sitting in the saloon. The television was still on and the news was even grimmer than before: Miami, it seemed, had been overrun. It was still unclear what had happened, but all indicators pointed to it having something to do with the disease; the one they were calling the 'Haitian Rabies Virus'. It seemed that it was now jumping from person to person, being passed on when infected people attacked others. The Governor of Florida was trying his best to reassure everyone that they'd get things back under control, but his eyes and the slight quiver in his voice told a different story. They were sending in the National Guard and trying to enforce some sort of quarantine, but it was too little too late.

At nine, the Prime Minister came on. He looked like he hadn't slept and his usual air of self-confidence was noticeably absent. He stumbled over his words, but his concern and his intentions were clear: Britain was sealing its borders to stop anyone who might be carrying the disease from getting in. I knew other countries would follow Britain's lead, but I wondered if it would work: if people were pushed hard enough, they'd always find a way in. I hoped the Americans would somehow get it under control before it spread much further, but it seemed unlikely. It was dark in Miami by then, and all that could be seen on the live news feeds were flames leaping high into the air.

Just after eleven, I remembered I'd agreed to meet Tom at twelve and tore myself away from the news to walk the mile or so along the riverside to the city centre. As always, I was struck by how much Glasgow had changed over the years. When I was young, the riverside had been little more than a wasteland of abandoned shipyards, but gradually it had been transformed. Now, both sides of the river were cluttered with oddly shaped buildings, clad in metal and glass, which housed cinemas, media companies and conference facilities. These seemed to sprout and multiply with every passing year, and I could see the steel skeleton of the latest addition rising up into the sky.

Further on, I passed under the bridge which carried the railway lines to all points south and turned north, crossing Argyle Street and walking up Buchanan Street itself. I looked at my watch: I'd arranged to meet Tom at the steps of the concert hall in fifteen minutes' time. Usually, a walk up Buchanan Street would have been a leisurely stroll, while I gazed at the sandstone architecture and watched the people moving around me, but this time it was different; I couldn't get the thoughts about what had happened in Miami out of my head and I was so distracted that I almost walked into a pair of mounted policemen as they plodded in the opposite direction.

When I reached the top of the road, I climbed the steps and sat down to wait, my eyes drifting lazily across the people on the street below. Mostly, they were shoppers, but here and there were gaggles of foreign exchange students talking excitedly in languages I couldn't understand. Further down the street, I could hear someone playing a guitar, while closer to me a man in a dark suit prattled on about God through a tinny PA system. Around me, on the steps themselves, some were eating an early lunch, or maybe it was a late breakfast. Others, like me, were waiting for someone and would glance at their watches every now and then. A few feet away, some teenagers were hanging around the base of a tall statue, the boys trying to climb on to it, the girls laughing and taking photos of each other on their phones. I wondered how many of them had seen what I'd seen on the news. They all seemed so calm while I was churning up inside, worrying about what would happen next. Maybe they'd been reassured by the Prime Minister's announcement at breakfast time, but for me, all it had done was reinforce just how worried those in the know must be.

I saw Tom in the distance. He'd just emerged from the underground station further down the street, a battered suitcase in one hand and a hand-rolled cigarette in the other. I knew the case would contain his equipment: juggling clubs, flaming torches, three large machetes and a bottle of paraffin. As he passed a living statue dressed as a vaguely familiar character from Scotland's past, he dropped some loose change into his hat. It was a ritual I knew well: Tom always thought it was good luck to start the day by giving another busker some money, and that he'd get more in return for doing so. He'd do the same on the way home as a thank you to the universe for another successful day.

Once he was closer, I could see that, as ever, little had changed. Unlike me, he still sported his long hair, currently tied back in a ponytail, but then again, despite being a few years older than me, he could still get away with it. The beard was new, but it was little more than stubble, so it was hard to work out if it was a fashion statement or just laziness. He wore the same black leather biker jacket he always did and dark jeans. Again, he managed to carry off this youthful, rebellious look, while others, including myself, had been forced to smarten up as we grew older.

Tom waved distractedly as he clambered up the steps and sat down beside me. 'Sorry I'm late. I got caught up in the news. You see what's been going on in Miami? It's fucking mental!'

'Yeah,' I stifled a yawn. 'I was up most of the night. I

couldn't take my eyes off it.'

Tom took a draw on his cigarette and turned to me. 'You know about this kind of thing. Can you explain all this virus stuff to me?'

I shook my head, 'I'm a marine biologist, Tom, not an epidemiologist.'

'But you know more about this sort of thing than I do.' He took one last drag on his cigarette and dropped the end onto the step below before grinding it out with the toe of his boot. He slowly blew out the last of the smoke, waiting for my answer.

I thought for a moment or two before I replied. 'I really don't know much about this kind of thing, but it seems to be something different from anything that has ever happened before.'

The disease had first appeared in Haiti, where a vaccine trial had been taking place. It had all seemed manageable at first, meaning that it had earned little more than a footnote on the evening news. When it first leapt to Miami and on to other US inner cities, the reporters started investigating and asking awkward questions. Contaminated drugs were blamed at first, but then it started spreading from person to person as they attacked each other. Still, it had all seemed like something that could be dealt with, and as I'd watched the news broadcasts while I sailed north from the Canaries, it looked like there was little to worry about, particularly not where I was heading. All the experts reckoned the outbreak would burn itself out eventually.

Then Miami happened, and it was while watching all that go down that it had started to dawn on me that this wasn't something that would simply go away if we waited long enough ... this was something which was here to stay.

'Ben, are you listening to me?'

'Huh?'

I turned round to see Tom had taken out his tobacco tin and was rolling another cigarette. He looked up at me. 'I asked what you thought about what happened in Miami last night.'

'I think it's a mess, and I'm not too sure if there's anything they can do about it, not now; there are just too many people who are infected or who've been exposed. The system's not set up to deal with something this big. I'm just glad that it's over there and we're not.'

Tom placed the cigarette he'd just made between his lips as he prepared to light it. 'So you think the PM was right to close the borders?'

'Damn straight! I think it's probably the first time in his life he's actually done the right thing at the right time. It's the only way we can stop it coming over here, at least for now.'

Tom took a long draw on his new cigarette and blew a steady stream of smoke into the air. 'Maybe if they can keep it out long enough, someone will be able to come up with a cure.'

'I doubt it.' I leant back on the steps, watching the people around me. 'They've been trying to cure rabies for 150 years, and they've got absolutely nowhere. Once you start showing symptoms, that's pretty much it.'

'Shit!' Tom paused for a second and we both stared off down the street. 'Did you see the footage where the man got ripped apart by those children?'

I had; I think everyone had by then. A reporter had been standing in the street doing a piece to camera somewhere in Miami when some kids appeared out of nowhere and set upon him. The oldest was maybe about ten, the youngest was dressed in Spiderman pyjamas and couldn't have been older than four or five at the most. The cameraman dropped his camera and ran, but it had carried on broadcasting live to the world. The reporter tried to fight them off, but there were too many of them. Eventually, he stopped moving, but the children kept on attacking him. The network finally pulled the plug when they'd started eating him, but not before everyone watching saw the oldest child tear open the man's abdomen and pull out his intestines.

I looked beyond the end of the street, across the Clyde and out to where a group of wind turbines turned slowly on the distant hills. There seemed to be no way the virus could be stopped now; it had grown too big and spread too far. I wondered how the world would cope, and how long it would be before it found its way through the closed borders and into Britain.

I took a deep breath. 'Look, Tom, I think this is it: the big one. Sooner or later it's going to turn up here and we need a plan for what to do then.'

'What d'you mean?' There was a confused tone to his voice.

I turned to him. 'We need a strategy, just in case. We need to think of a place to go where we'd be safe. Somewhere like ...'

I never finished the sentence. Something had caught my eye: a riderless police horse galloping at full speed up Buchanan Street, scattering people left and right as it went. Once it was nearer, I could see it was foaming at the mouth and dripping with sweat from the exertion. It turned left and headed up the next street. From behind, I could see what looked like blood smeared down its right side. The horse made it across the first road, but at the second a speeding taxi smashed into it, bringing the animal crashing down onto the vehicle. Tom leapt to his feet. 'What the hell was that all about?'

'No idea.' I jumped up, too, 'I wonder what spooked it.'

'And where's the policeman who should have been keeping control of it?'

While everyone else around us was still staring at the accident, and the people rushing to help, I turned to look back down Buchanan Street. All seemed normal and you'd never have guessed that a runaway horse had just galloped along its length. Then, at the far end, something changed. At first, I couldn't really see what, but something was different.

'Hey, Tom, look down there.' I craned my neck, trying to get a better view. 'D'you see anything odd?'

Tom did the same. 'What d'you mean?

'Down at the far end, by Argyle Street.' I pointed to the spot I was talking about. 'Something doesn't seem right.'

At the bottom of the street, everyone was pushing and shoving against each other, as if they were trying to get away from something.

'Ben,' Tom dropped his half-smoked cigarette onto the ground, 'I don't like the look of this.'

Suddenly, a wave of people started surging towards us. Soon, it seemed like the entire lower half of the street was moving as one. Then I noticed something odd. While everyone in the approaching crowd was running, some, it seemed, were chasing and grabbing at the others.

I thought flashed into my head. 'Tom, we've got to get off the street right now.'

'What? Why?'

'I think the virus is here.'

'How?'

'I don't know, but look at the crowd. See that person there?' I pointed to the man I meant. 'And that one there? Look how they're acting! I think they're infected.'

'Shit!' Tom eyes darted across the crowd. 'Are you sure?

Before I could say anything, the man seized an elderly woman and pulled her to the ground. As the pair struggled, they disappeared from sight amongst the crowd, but soon the attacker was back on his feet and had chased down someone else.

'Frickin' hell!' Tom ran his hands through his hair. 'Ben, what're we going to do?'

I glanced round. At the top of the steps was a series of doors; I knew we had to get off the street and we had to do it now.

'Let's get inside.' I ran up the steps. Behind me, Tom grabbed his case and followed. The first door I tried wouldn't move, nor would the second. I kept going, eventually finding one on the far right which opened. Once inside, I locked the door behind us and looked round to find a flight of stairs leading upwards. We raced up them, all the time glancing back over our shoulders. At the top, we emerged into a restaurant filled with empty tables set for lunch.

A blonde waitress in her mid-twenties appeared through what I presumed was the door to the kitchen and hurried towards us, shouting. 'Hey, we're not open yet. You need to leave.'

I pushed past her and ran up to the windows which stretched from floor to ceiling. From there, I had a clear view down the length of Buchanan Street.

'I said: we're not open yet.' The waitress strode towards

us. 'Are you deaf or something?' Finally, she reached a point where she could see the street below. 'Hey, what's going on out there?'

The stampeding crowd had now reached the entrance to the underground station. I searched for the people who were chasing the others, but I couldn't find them. I wondered where the infected had gone; maybe I'd got it wrong. Then I realised it wasn't that they'd disappeared, it was that almost all of them were now infected.

I tried to say something, but I couldn't find the words. Instead, I just stared, paralysed by fear and disbelief at what I was witnessing.

As the crowd reached the statue in front of the steps, the people lingering there, watching the aftermath of the crash further up the next street, finally realised what was happening around them and they scattered. Some ran up to the locked doors, while others sprinted along the street to the right. As I watched, the first of the infected reached the steps and raced up them, while the rest followed those who'd fled up the next street. One man climbed up onto the statue's plinth and started to pull a woman up after him, but before she was beyond its reach, an infected grabbed her legs. There was a tug of war between the two, with the woman screaming in the middle. Then another infected grabbed hold, then another. The man refused to let go of the woman even though I could now see her guts spilling out onto the street. He tried to keep his footing, but there wasn't enough space and he slipped, falling into the mass of infected people which were now feeding on the woman's remains. They set upon him, clawing and tearing at him until he'd been pulled apart and scattered across the street.

There was a noise behind us and I turned to find the waitress talking rapidly into a mobile phone. I didn't recognise the language, but from the way she spoke, I could tell she was as confused and horrified by what was happening outside as I was.

I returned my attention to the window: the crowd was starting to thin as the main mass passed us and headed away up the next street, those who had the disease pursuing those who didn't. Here and there, small knots of infected squabbled over bodies, pulling at them with their hands and teeth, feasting on those they'd killed. After a while, even those stragglers had dispersed in search of others to attack, leaving the street devoid of life. Nothing moved, and if it wasn't for the bodies scattered along its length, it would have been impossible to believe what had just happened. Yet it had, and I was struggling to take it all in. I just didn't understand it: where had the disease come from? How had it made the leap across the ocean? Was it just Glasgow or was it in other places in Britain, too?

It took a few more minutes of standing there, transfixed by the devastation, before I managed to get my brain back into gear. 'Tom, we've got to get out of here. We've got to get out of the city while we still can. You think we could make it to my boat?'

Tom was still gazing down at the street. 'Where are you tied up?

'Down by the conference centre.'

'I don't know.' Tom looked at me briefly before returning his attention to what was happening outside. 'It's a long way to go.'

We both stared out of the window, but nothing moved.

Tom was the first to act. He stepped forward and leant

against the glass, looking from side to side. 'Where've they all gone?'

I moved forward to stand beside him. 'I guess they must have chased the crowd as they ran away.'

Tom was now eyeing up the far end of Buchanan Street. 'If we can make it to the river front, I think we should have a pretty clear run from there down to where your boat is. There won't have been many people down there at this time of day.'

Suddenly something struck me. 'Have you got anything we could use as weapons?'

'What?' Tom looked confused. 'Why?'

'Because if we run into any of *them*, we'll need to be able to defend ourselves.'

'You mean like …?' Tom's voice faltered; he cleared his throat. 'You mean like *kill* them?'

I shifted uneasily; I didn't like the idea of it any more than he did, but if we did meet any infected, we'd have little choice: it would be them or us. 'If we have to.'

'Jesus!' Tom was as white as a sheet. For a moment he stood still, then he knelt down and opened his case, 'I've got these.' He pulled out the large, curved machetes he used as part of his act. They weren't sharp, but they were still formidable weapons.

I picked one up, and ran a finger along its length. 'They'll do.'

By then, the waitress had turned off her phone and spoke to us for the first time since the crowd had rampaged up the street, her voice trembling. 'What're you going to do?' There was a trace of an Eastern European accent in her voice.

'You saw what happened in Miami last night?' I glanced across at her and she nodded. 'Well, the same thing's happening here. We need to get out of the city as quickly as possible. I've got a yacht down on the river. If we can get to it, we can get out of here. D'you want to come with us?'

She glanced at her phone and then out the window before coming to a decision. 'Yes.'

'What's your name?'

'Iliana.'

I held out my hand. 'I'm Ben and he's Tom.'

She looked at Tom as if seeing him properly for the first time. 'Hey, I know you; I've seen you before. You're the juggler, aren't you?'

Tom gave a slight bow, used to people recognising him like this, 'That's me.'

I turned and stared out of the window again: still nothing moved.

'Right,' I took a deep breath and felt my body start to shake as I thought about what we were about to do. I looked at Tom and saw he was shaking too. I did my best to calm myself. 'Let's do this.'

Chapter Two

We made our way over to the stairs and crept slowly down to the entrance. I peered through the window in the door; there were bodies on the flag stones just outside, lying like rag dolls, limbs at odd angles, covered in blood. Many had chunks of flesh missing from their arms and faces, and one had a leg missing. My eyes searched around, stopping when I saw it lying several feet away. Despite the carnage, there was no movement.

As quietly as possible, I unlocked the door and inched it open. I adjusted my grip on the machete I was holding and nervously stuck my head outside. Everything was still. I crept forward to the edge of the stone steps where I could finally see not just down Buchanan Street, but also up the street to the right; it, too, was littered with bodies. Off in the distance, I could make out some movement, but nothing closer. I beckoned the others to follow and together we picked our way along Buchanan Street, alert to any signs of life.

As we passed the dead lying in the street, I couldn't help but stare. Some bore deep wounds and had clearly been killed by those with the virus; others had bruises and broken limbs, and looked more like they'd been trampled to death in the stampede. We reached the steps at the entrance to a shopping mall and I glanced through the glass doors: bodies were piled at the base of the escalators, some having fallen from a great height. Above them, I could see others hanging over handrails, held there by the mass of people that had pushed up from behind in a desperate bid to escape. In amongst the bodies, there were movements from those trapped in the crush, or who'd been so badly injured they couldn't get up again. Then I saw him: a man dressed in loose-fitting chinos and an open-necked Oxford shirt, both of which were soaked in blood, chewing on the face of a teenage girl. From the way she was lying, I could tell both her legs were broken, but the fall hadn't killed her; she was trying to fend him off, but she was no match for him and he buried his teeth into her flesh again and again. Knowing there was nothing I could do to help and unable to watch any longer, I turned away, feeling the bile rise in my throat as I did so.

Then I felt the ground tremble beneath my feet. It was something I'd felt hundreds of times before and I knew exactly what it was. I looked at Tom. 'You feel that?'

'Yeah.'

'You think the underground's still going?'

'Must be.'

The tremors stopped as the subway train pulled into the station which lay directly below us. Then I heard a sound, so faint at first I wasn't sure it was real, but as it grew louder and louder, I became certain it was. It seemed to be coming from the glass-covered entrance to the station thirty yards further down the street, and sounded like distant thunder.

Iliana gripped Tom's arm. 'What's that?'

Not having an answer, Tom and I shrugged. Suddenly, I realised I could hear screaming and shouting mixed with the noise itself. Then the first person burst onto the street, running as fast as he could. He glanced back and stumbled over a body lying in front of him. He scrambled to his feet, without even bothering to look at what he'd tripped over, and started running again. Another person appeared, but this one looked different: he was dishevelled, with blood dripping from a wound on his left cheek. He chased after the first man and was quickly followed by another and then another. Soon, people were streaming from the entrance, and it was clear they were infected. As one, we turned and raced up the street and back to the stone steps. At the top, I stopped and looked back: the man was still running, but the infected were closing in behind him.

'Oi, up here,' I waved as I shouted. He saw me and changed direction. Iliana was already inside and Tom was holding the door open as he yelled at me. 'Ben, you've got to get back in here now.'

'We can't leave him out here; they'll kill him!' Turning back to the man, I saw he was at the bottom of the steps, with the first of the infected only a few yards behind. I sprinted over to Tom, and got there in time to see the man reach the top just as the heads of the pursuing infected came into view. He made it to the door with only moments to spare and we slammed it shut, but before we could get the lock turned, the infected hit the door like a freight train. The force threw us backwards and clawing fingers appeared around the edges. Tom and I pushed as hard as we could against the door, but it wouldn't move: the fingers of the infected were stopping it from closing.

Shaking with fear, I turned to Tom, 'What the hell d'we do now?'

He looked at me, terrified. 'Use the machetes?'

I felt the weight of the long metal weapon in my hand, and I gripped it tightly, wondering how things could have changed so fast. I swung the blade and sliced off half a dozen fingers; blood spurted across the walls and the floor. I swung it again and again until the door was clear and we could finally get it closed and locked.

Tom and I sank to the floor, both of us breathing

heavily. Iliana had her phone out again and was desperately tapping away, while the man was sitting on the bottom of the stairs with his eyes fixed firmly on the door behind me. I felt it move, but the lock seemed to be holding. I surveyed the severed fingers that lay strewn across the floor. Suddenly, I felt sick.

'How'd you end up with that lot chasing you?' Tom's voice trembled with fear. I looked at the man properly for the first time: his face was ashen and he couldn't have been more than eighteen at the most. He turned to Tom. 'What?'

Rather than push him to relive what he'd just been through, I held out my hand. 'I'm Ben. This is Tom, and that's Iliana.'

The teenager stared blankly at me for a second before taking it. 'I'm Daz. Well, Darren really, but everyone calls me Daz.' He paused for a moment. 'You guys got any idea what's happenin' out there?'

'Did you see what went down in Miami last night?' Tom got to his feet and glanced through the window in the door. The infected could sense we were inside and were still clawing at it, blood from the stumps of their fingers smearing the glass: even their injuries didn't slow them down.

Daz's eyes drifted towards the floor. 'Yeah.'

Tom avoided making eye contact, too. 'We think the virus which caused that is here.'

'Fuck!' A puzzled expression appeared on Daz's face. 'I thought they'd closed the borders or somethin', so that couldn't happen.'

'I guess they were too late.' I thought about this. It was odd. Of all the places for the virus to suddenly appear, the centre of Glasgow seemed one of the most unlikely. I could see it happening at Heathrow, or Gatwick, or even somewhere like Manchester Airport: they all had plenty of connections to the US, but as far as I knew Glasgow only had two direct flights: one to Newark, and the other to Miami. That's when it struck me: the morning flight from Miami would have arrived just before the borders had been closed; someone on that flight must have been infected and they must have made it as far as the city centre before they turned.

'So how'd you end up being chased by our friends out there?' Tom nodded his head towards the door as he looked at Daz.

'I stayed over at a pal's last night in the West End an' was just headin' into town for a bit before goin' home. I got on at Hillhead an' sat down in the first carriage. I was just textin' this girl I met the other night, tryin' to get her to go out for a few drinks later when we pulled into the next station. There was this young boy lying on the platform with people crowdin' round him. Before I could see what was goin' on, the train had moved past. Looking through the doors which connect all the carriages, I could see a fight breakin' out at the far end. I thought it was just a bunch of Neds messing' around, an' I went back to my phone. At the next station, I looked up again and saw the fightin' had spread to the next carriage. I could see people strugglin' with each other an' that.'

Daz took a deep breath and looked quickly at each of us in turn, as if he was checking we were ready to hear what he had to say next.

'We moved off again, but I kept watchin'. Just as we arrived in Cowcaddens, a man burst into my carriage and tried to force the door shut behind him. He was covered in blood an' was shoutin' somethin' I couldn't quite make out. Everyone turned an' stared at him, an' the train lurched forward; he lost his footin' an' fell onto the floor. The door burst open again an' these people just started pourin' through. Except they weren't actin' like people, they were actin' like animals, attackin' anyone they could get their hands on. They were covered in blood an' one of them was rippin' into some poor woman's face.'

He shook his head, as if trying to rid himself of this image. It was a few seconds before he carried on.

'As everyone started to crowd towards my end of the carriage to get away from these people, I was squashed up against the door. Just before the first of them got to me, I felt the train slow an' I realised we'd pulled into Buchanan Street. The doors opened an' I was pushed onto the platform by the people behind me. The same thing was happenin' at the other doors an' soon there were all these people on the platform. I scrambled to my feet an' started runnin' up the steps. I heard this sound behind me, an' I looked back an' saw all these people chasing me, their faces screwed up with anger an' blood on them, on their hands an' all over their clothes.'

There was a loud bang as one of the infected threw itself at the door with enough force to cause it to shudder alarmingly. Daz jumped as a look of panic flashed across his face, but when he realised we were still safe, he steadied himself, closing his eyes for a moment before speaking again. 'When I got to the top of the stairs, I ran into the first turnstile, but it didn't move so I jumped over it. Then I heard a crash and I glanced over my shoulder. It seemed that the turnstiles weren't working for them either an' instead of leapin' over them, they were just pilin' up against them; the ones in front being crushed by those comin' up after. I slowed down, thinkin' I might've gotten lucky, but one of them made it through by climbin' over the bodies of the others ahead of it. Then another made it, an' another.

'I sped up again an' headed for the escalators, takin' them two at a time. I could hear the people comin' up behind me, an' the noises they were makin' were echoing off the walls around me. It was pure terrifyin'.' His voice faded out and he took a deep breath before carrying on.

'Anyway, I think you pretty much know the rest from there.' Daz was staring down at his shoes. He slammed his fist into his thigh. 'Fuck! I can't believe this is happenin' here.' He looked up. 'What the hell're we goin' to do?'

I could hear the infected still hammering at the door behind me. 'Well, we can't go back out there.'

Tom stared at me. 'Are you saying we're trapped in here?'

Iliana looked up from her phone. 'We could try the other door. It leads onto the street by the bus station. We might be able to get out that way.'

'Sounds like a plan to me,' Tom grabbed his machete. Which way?'

'Up here!' Iliana shoved her phone into her pocket and raced up the stairs. We followed as she led us through a maze of empty corridors. I wondered where everyone was, but then I realised it was still too early for the concert hall to be open, or even for many of the people who worked there to have arrived. Eventually, we reached a solid-looking door and Iliana stopped. She put her hand on the handle, then hesitated before withdrawing it again. 'What happens if they're out here, too?'

Up to this point, none of us had considered this possibility. I pressed my ear to the door, but heard nothing. I eased it open as quietly as I could and peered through the gap. The street looked deserted and there were no bodies in sight. It looked like the horde of infected hadn't passed this way. I glanced back at the others. 'I think we're in luck.'

'What're we going to do once we get out there?' Iliana sounded scared.

'We need to get out of the city as soon as we can. We need to find a car or something … anything,' I hesitated for a moment, 'Ehm, any of you happen to know …?'

'Know what?' Daz looked at me enquiringly.

'How to steal a car?' I glanced round nervously as the others shook their heads.

'What are the chances?' Tom snorted. 'Four Glaswegians and none of us knows how to nick a car!'

I stifled a snigger, knowing Tom was just trying to lighten the mood. 'Not really the right time, Tom.'

I opened the door a second time, and risked poking my head out. I could see a portly middle-aged man in a business suit prowling round a car, slamming at the windows as he tried to get in. As quietly as possible, I pulled my head back in and turned to the others. 'D'you want the good news or the bad news?'

Tom put his ear to the door, trying to work out what was going on outside. 'What's the good news?'

'I think I've found us some transport.'

Tom pulled away from the door. 'And the bad news?'

'There's an infected man between us and it.'

Daz glanced at me. 'What d'you mean?'

'There's a woman out there sitting in a Range Rover, so she must have the keys. The trouble is there's one of *them* trying to get to her. We'll have to deal with him before we can get to the car.'

'How're we going to do that?' Tom asked worriedly.

I looked down at the machete I was still clutching in my right hand; it was already covered in blood from where I'd severed the fingers of the infected as they'd tried to get inside. The very thought of what I was about to suggest made me feel like I was going to throw up. I swallowed hard. 'I guess we could use these.'

'And do what exactly?' Tom was staring at me.

'Take it out, you mean?' Daz was staring at me, too.

Iliana gulped, disbelievingly. 'You're going to kill someone?'

'Yes.' I closed my eyes, wondering if I could bring myself to do it. 'I don't think we have any other choice.'

Tom shuffled his feet nervously. 'Have you ever done anything like that before?'

'No.' I stared at the ground. 'Have you?'

Tom shook his head.

As we looked at each other shiftily, I heard the sound of breaking glass outside followed by a roar. I opened the door and stuck my head outside; the fat man had broken through the front passenger window of the Range Rover and was trying desperately to reach the woman in the driver's seat. He was, however, sufficiently rotund that he couldn't fit through the window and she remained beyond his grasping hands. As I watched, she swivelled round in her seat and started kicking him as hard as she could. Soon there was nothing left of his face but a mass of blood and broken bones. Finally, he stopped moving and lay still, half in and half out of the car.

I turned back to the others. 'Looks like we won't have to deal with him after all.'

They looked at me questioningly, but before they could ask, I turned and ran out of the door; seconds later, I heard them follow. I was halfway to the Range Rover when I noticed a distant sound; I glanced round to see a crowd running towards us. By the way they were moving, I had no doubt they were infected. When we reached the Range Rover, Tom and I tried to pull the lifeless body from the window, but the man's bulk meant he was tightly wedged. Up the road, the infected were rapidly closing on us. I called out to the others, 'Daz, Iliana give us a hand!'

While Iliana grabbed one of the man's legs, Daz remained staring at the approaching crowd. 'What?'

'Daz, we need to get this body shifted.'

Daz turned and gripped the man's jacket. With all four of us pulling and the woman pushing from inside the car, we finally got him free. The infected were now only fifty yards away.

The woman pointed out of the broken window. 'The keys! I need the keys. I dropped them in all the confusion.'

I scooped them up and tossed them to her. She caught the keys with her outstretched hand and hastily shoved one of them into the ignition. She turned it, but the engine didn't catch. She looked up. 'Are you getting in or what? We need to be ready to go the moment I get the engine going. It's always a bit temperamental, especially when it's cold.'

We didn't need to be asked a second time. Tom pulled open the front passenger door and jumped in while Daz, Iliana and I piled into the back. It was only once we were inside that I realised the woman wasn't alone: a young boy was clinging to her side and she had one arm wrapped protectively around him; huddled in the back behind the driver's seat was a teenage girl, tears streaming down her face as she shook with fear. The woman turned the key again: still it didn't catch. 'Damn thing never starts when you really need it to.'

I stared wide-eyed through the windscreen: the nearest

of the infected would be on us in seconds. The woman glanced up, but she didn't panic; pumping the accelerator, she twisted the key for a third time and the engine spluttered into life. 'Finally! Now let's get the hell out of here.'

She slammed the Range Rover into gear and floored it. Without even blinking, the woman drove straight into the mass of infected charging towards us. Even with the SUV bearing down on them, they kept coming; not even trying to get out of the way. Blood sprayed across the windscreen as we hit the first one, and I felt the car judder as we drove over its body. There were so many of them ahead of us, I worried they might be able to bring us to a halt. If that happened, we'd be dead in seconds. Looking round, I saw we were just coming up to a crossroads. I leaned forward and pointed. 'Turn right here.'

As the car skidded round the corner, narrowly missing another one coming in the opposite direction, Iliana was thrown against me, pushing me hard into the door. I reached around, searching for a seat belt, but with four of us crammed into the back seat, I couldn't find one.

'Where're we heading?' The woman yelled over her shoulder.

'If we can get onto Great Western Road, we should have a pretty clear run out of the city. Turn left there,' I pointed again, 'and then keep left at the next junction.'

The woman braked hard and shifted the SUV down a gear as we overtook an empty bus on the inside, before throwing us round the next corner. She shifted back into a higher gear and accelerated again. As we left the city centre behind and crossed the bridge over the motorway, I glanced down, wondering if I'd made the right decision; the road below was packed with stationary cars, and infected were streaming between them. Some people got out and tried to run, but were dragged to the ground before they got more than a few feet; others stayed inside and locked the doors, but the infected simply smashed through the windows to get to them.

We reached the east end of Great Western Road and I saw the route ahead was blocked with traffic. 'Shit! How're we going to get passed that?'

I felt a jolt as we mounted the kerb and I was thrown upwards, my head slamming into the roof. There was just enough room for us to squeeze between the shop fronts and sandstone tenements on one side, and cars parked along the side of the road on the other. As we sped along the pavement, forcing panicked pedestrians to dive out of the way, I looked into the cars that were jamming the road; the people inside seemed to have no idea of what was happening in other parts of the city. We passed a junction where one car had rear-ended another; the passengers standing round as the drivers exchanged their insurance details. Given the circumstances, this seemed rather pointless, but they had yet to find out why.

Ahead of the accident, the road was clear and the woman steered back onto the tarmac and slowed down. She turned to Tom, 'I'm Claire, by the way; this is Jake.' She smoothed the hair of the small boy clinging to her side. 'And that's Sophie.' She nodded to the teenage girl in the back seat: she was no longer crying; instead she just looked terrified, not only by what was going on outside, but by having these strange people, who'd appeared out of nowhere, waving machetes and wearing bloodstained clothes, in the car with her.

Tom leaned across from the front passenger seat and shook Claire's hand. 'I'm Tom.' He twisted in his seat. 'That's Ben, Iliana and Daz.'

I waved when I heard my name. Tom carried on. 'How

did you end up with the big guy attacking you?'

'We were just picking up some tickets for a concert we're going to next weekend, and it took longer than expected, and then Jake needed to go to the toilet. When we finally came out, it seemed like everyone, all the people and the traffic, had just vanished. We were about halfway back to the car when the "big guy",' she looked at Tom, 'as you so eloquently called him, appeared. I could see almost immediately that there was something wrong with him; I think it was his eyes. Anyway, he started running towards us and I knew we had to get to the car as quickly as possible. I fished out my keys and pressed the button to unlock the doors, but Jake slipped and I dropped the keys as I picked him up, so we got into the car in time, and got the doors locked, but I couldn't drive away. God knows what would have happened if you lot hadn't come along when you did.'

I caught Claire's eye in the mirror. 'From what I saw, you were doing pretty well on your own.'

We drove by grand sandstone buildings and the glass palace of the Botanic Gardens and then, as we passed over the brow of a small rise, for the first time I could see the hills that lay beyond the city. They looked so close and my spirits soared: surely we were going to make it out. We dropped into a dip and then up over another rise.

'Shit!' Claire jammed on the brakes and we skidded to a halt. The road ahead was filled with queuing traffic. 'What's this all about?'

I leaned forward, trying to get a better look. 'Must be the lights at the next junction.'

After a minute of just sitting there with nothing happening, Tom noticed something odd. 'How come there's nothing coming the other way?'

Now he mentioned it, I realised I hadn't seen a single car pass in the opposite direction for a while.

'This can't be good.' I opened the rear passenger door and stood on the SUV's sill. I was high enough up that I could see down to where several police cars, their blue lights flashing, were parked across the road, just on the far side of the junction. Beyond that, the road was clear as far as I could see.

I called down into the Range Rover. 'It's the police. It looks like they're setting up a roadblock.'

I heard another door open and saw Claire appear on the other side. She stared down the road.

I watched her reactions: she didn't seem surprised; instead, it was more as if she was trying to work out what to do next. I nodded towards the police cars. 'What d'you think that's all about?'

Claire glanced back at me. 'I guess they're trying to contain the outbreak before it spreads too far.'

'But why are they setting it up around here? We haven't seen any infected for a good couple of miles.'

Claire stared off down the road again. 'I'm guessing they're doing it here exactly because the infected haven't reached this point yet. Anyway, whatever the reason, I don't want to be stuck on this side of it.'

Ahead, at the crossroads, a police van pulled up and two uniformed men got out. I saw them pointing to the road which led off to the right and I realised it must still be open, at least for the moment.

'We've got to go!' I shouted to Claire. 'Pull onto the other side of the road and turn right at the junction.'

We both dropped back into the SUV and slammed our doors. As Claire pulled out and accelerated down the opposite carriage way, I noticed Jake was now sitting on Tom's knee. Tom had slipped his seat belt on and was holding Jake tightly to stop him being thrown around. We were at the crossroads in seconds and with the policemen waving at us to stop, Claire turned right and then stood on the brakes again: two police cars were already blocking the road ahead.

'There!' Iliana pointed over Claire's shoulder to where a narrow lane led past a row of blonde sandstone town houses. Claire revved the engine and pulled the car to the left, throwing Iliana against me once again. We sped down the street, running parallel to the main road, separated from it by a grassy bank and a low stone wall. Soon, the lane ran out, but a wide pedestrian path led back down to the road. The Range Rover juddered as we leapt onto the kerb for the second time. After a few seconds, Claire jerked the wheel to the left and pulled us onto the road again, well beyond the roadblock.

'Woohoo! That was way cool; like a video game or somethin'.' Daz squirmed round so he could see out of the rear window. 'No one's chasin' us. I think we got away with it.'

As we raced along the deserted road, I noticed the trees which now separated the two carriageways were just coming into blossom. I'd always loved driving along this road in spring when the cherry trees were in full bloom: on a sunny day, it could beat almost anywhere in the world, but today, all I could think about was getting out of town as quickly as possible. We passed under a railway bridge and immediately ran into another queue of traffic. Claire didn't brake. Instead, she bounced over the kerb and we sped down the pavement once more. Suddenly, the unmistakeable silhouette of a tank emerged over the top of the cars ahead of us. As we got nearer, I could see machine guns mounted on armoured jeeps and heavily armoured soldiers manning a barricade spread across the road ahead.

'No wonder they didn't bother following us; it looks like they're pretty serious about containing this thing.' Claire adjusted her grip on the steering wheel. 'Hold on.'

I grabbed onto the handle above the window and felt Iliana brace herself against me. Ahead of us, a metal barrier blocked our way; on the other side of it, a slip road curved off to the left, away from soldiers. If we could somehow get to that, we could at least keep moving. Suddenly, there was the sound of gunfire and the windscreen exploded. Ducking down, I looked through the shattered glass; at the right-hand end of the main barricade, three men in army uniforms, machine guns raised, were firing at us.

Despite the gunfire, Claire kept the accelerator pressed to the floor as I felt more bullets slam into the car.

'Why the hell're they shootin' at us?' Daz was crouched as low in the seat as he could get. Before I could answer, Iliana's face exploded and Tom screamed. 'Fuck, I'm hit!'

The teenage girl crammed in beside Daz screamed too.

'Sophie, are you alright?' For the first time Claire sounded panicked.

'She's fine.' Daz called out. 'She's just scared.' There was a moment's pause as he swallowed. 'I think Iliana's dead, though.'

Claire looked across at Tom. 'What about Jake?'

'He's fine,' Tom winced with pain. 'It's just me that got hit.'

Claire turned her attention back to the road ahead just

as the Range Rover crashed through the barrier. The car skidded and Claire had to fight hard to keep it under control. I felt the SUV slide across the tarmac and we side-swiped the barriers on the far side, causing Iliana's body to rattle back and forth between Daz and me, sending blood flying in all directions. Claire wrestled with the steering wheel, managing to keep us moving in the right direction. She glanced at Tom's shoulder. 'Don't worry, it looks like it's only a flesh wound, but we'll need to get some pressure on that pretty quickly so you don't lose too much blood.' She turned to me. 'Are we out of their range yet?'

I nervously inched my head upwards until I could see out of the back window: the soldiers were no longer in sight. I breathed a sigh of relief. 'Yeah.'

'And they're not following us?'

'No.' I wondered why this was. Maybe we were still inside the cordon they'd set up to stop people leaving the city. If that was the case, we'd need to find another way out.

'Good.' Claire stood on the brakes. Tom yelped as he was thrown against his seat belt and Iliana's lifeless body slammed into the back of his seat. The car screeched to a halt and Claire jumped out. She pulled open the back door. 'Sophie, you need to take Jake.'

The teenage girl got out and took the small boy from Tom, kissing his head and stroking his hair before climbing back into the car. I glanced at him. He seemed listless, almost as if he was unaware of all that was going on around him.

'You,' Claire pointed at me, 'get that body out of there and then help me get him,' she pointed at Tom, 'into the back seat.'

I opened the passenger door, stepped out and reached back to the car. I grabbed Iliana and pulled, but she didn't move. I changed my hold to get a better grip and tried again. This time I managed to drag her lifeless body out of the car and there was a sickening thump as it hit the ground. I glanced down and saw that Iliana's blood, mixed with flecks of her brains, was now smeared across my jacket; I had to work hard to stop myself throwing up. Trying not to look at Iliana again, I helped Tom out of the front seat, while Claire disappeared round the back of the Range Rover. She reappeared a second later carrying a rectangular black bag.

'Get him in here.' She pointed to the back seat, and then she looked up at me. 'D'you know how to drive?'

'No, not really; not cars at any rate.'

Claire turned to Daz, 'What about you?'

'Yeah.'

'Good. Get up front and let's get going again.'

Daz slid behind the wheel as I clambered in the passenger side. I heard Daz fiddle with the seat, moving it back and forth until he was comfortable. All the time I was watching Claire: she'd torn Tom's shirt open and was pressing a thick white pad she'd taken from her bag against a ragged wound in his right shoulder.

'Why aren't we moving?' Claire glared at Daz as she worked on Tom.

'Where're we headin'?' Daz looked from Claire to me and back again.

I thought for a second. 'Try the tunnel. We might still be able to get out that way.'

The Range Rover leapt forward as Daz floored the accelerator. I turned my attention back to Tom and Claire. She seemed to know what I was thinking. 'Don't worry. I know what I'm doing.' She smiled at me. 'I'm a doctor.'

'Fuck! More polis.' Daz was pointing ahead, where three police cars were parked — lights flashing but empty — across the road leading to the tunnel that I hoped would take us under the River Clyde and out to Glasgow's Southside. At first, it seemed like our path was blocked, but then I saw they'd been positioned too far forward and there was a way for us to get past. 'Daz, take that slip road to the left and then turn sharp right. We can get round them.'

'Gotcha!' Daz barely slowed as he followed my instructions and soon we were on the road that led down to the tunnel. With no other cars around, Daz was able to push the Range Rover to the max and we were doing about eighty when we shot into the darkness. As a kid I remembered playing a game where you had to try to hold your breath from one end of the tunnel to the other. Going at the legal maximum of thirty, I'd never managed it, but at the speed we were going now, it would have been easy.

Ahead, the tunnel descended and then turned slightly to the left. The sound of the engine roared against the concrete walls and was thrown back through the broken windscreen. Suddenly, I saw something ahead: blue lights from some unknown source flashing in the gloom. A second later, first one police motorcycle, then two more, shot round the bend and passed us in the opposite direction. I turned and watched them disappear up towards the entrance, wondering what they were doing coming through the wrong side.

'What the hell's that all about?' Daz slammed on the brakes and we skidded to a halt: a sea of shadows danced on the tunnel wall, thrown there by some unseen light. Then they came into view: a mass of people charging towards us, their yells and screams echoing all around. There was no mistaking it: these were infected.

'We need to get out of here!' I shouted.

Daz looked across at me, scared and starting to panic, as he struggled to find reverse. 'I'm trying!'

By the time he finally found it, the first of the infected were only a few feet from the car. He stood on the accelerator and the engine screamed as we shot backwards, doing a speed that the reverse gear was never designed to do. At first, it seemed like the infected were able to keep up, but slowly the gap between them and us widened. By the time we reached the entrance of the tunnel, we were well clear of them, but I could still hear the noise they made as they chased after us.

'Where now?' There was an urgency in Daz's voice as the car continued to shoot backwards.

'What about your boat? You said it's at the exhibition centre, that's not far from here, is it?' Tom was leaning forward, his shoulder tightly bandaged.

'Okay, that sounds like a plan.' I glanced round. 'Daz, aim for that slip road there.'

Daz stomped on the brakes and then put the Range Rover into first gear. He pulled sharply on the steering wheel as he accelerated, spinning it round. We bumped across the central divide and shot up a slip road which curved back on itself as it rose above the entrance to the tunnel; below, I saw the infected emerge and scatter. Soon, we were speeding along a broad dual carriageway, heading back towards the city centre. Our side of the road was empty, but the other was jammed with cars held up by yet another police roadblock. Some of the drivers had got out of their cars and were arguing with the policemen. They were so intent on shouting at each other that they didn't notice the first of the infected sprinting towards them. In seconds, they'd been pulled to the ground, and as more infected streamed between the idling vehicles I turned back to face the front, knowing what was about happen and not wanting to see it.

Daz was squirming round, trying to figure out what was going on behind us. 'How far're we goin'?'

I leaned forward to get a better idea of where we were 'There's a pedestrian bridge over the road. We can use that to get across to where the boat is.'

Daz squinted through the windscreen. 'Where?'

'There! Right there!' I pointed ahead to where a narrow metal bridge spanned both carriageways of the road we were on. The other side was still filled with cars, while ours remained clear.

Daz hit the brakes, bringing the Range Rover screeching to a halt. I looked back at Tom. 'Are you okay to run?'

Tom stretched his shoulder tentatively. 'Yeah, I should be.'

I turned my attention to Claire. 'You good to go?'

She nodded. 'Where're we heading?'

'Just over the bridge, and then it's about fifty yards to the boat. You can't miss it; it's the only one there.'

'Let's go!' Claire grabbed her black bag and leapt out of the car, quickly followed by the rest of us. Daz helped Sophie over the metal railings which ran along the side of the road, while Claire lifted Jake across. As we started to run up the sloping ramp of the bridge, I heard a shout and turned to see Claire begging Jake to run, trying to make him understand the urgency of the situation, but he just stood there, staring vacantly at her. I stopped and waited for her as she grabbed Jake's hand, trying to pull him forward, but still he refused to move. I heard a crash in the distance and then a scream, and I looked round to find people running between the cars on the other side of the road. They didn't appear to be infected, but they were running from something, and I had little doubt as to what it was. 'Claire, infected! You'll have to carry him.'

Claire scooped Jake up and within seconds she was level with me; together we ran after the others. At the top of the ramp, the bridge turned sharply to the right, taking us out over the dual carriageway. To the left, was a railway line and a stationary train. Within its carriages, I could see people wrestling with each other: blood splashing onto the windows as people fought for their lives.

Turning away, I saw infected on the road below us, chasing people down and attacking those they caught; screams and snarls mixing with the sounds of idling engines. By the time we were halfway across the bridge, I could see Claire was struggling to keep up. I held out my arms. 'Here, I'll take him.'

As she passed Jake to me, I could feel his body was limp and his skin was warm and clammy. As we ran on, his head bounced against my shoulder as he drifted in and out of consciousness.

Claire and I caught up with the others at the far end of the bridge where another ramp led back to the ground. Some of the infected on the nearby road must have heard Claire yelling at Sophie, urging her on, because their heads snapped round, and within seconds, they were sprinting after us. As we raced across the car park to where the boat was tied up, I glanced round; we were well ahead of the infected, but they were closing fast, their screaming and howling audible even above the sound of the blood pounding in my ears. I tried to judge the speed they were moving at, and the distance we still had to cover, but the fear of what would happen if they caught us clouded my mind. All I could do was hope and pray we'd get there with enough time to not only get on board, but also get far enough away from the shore to be safe.

Chapter Three

'Tom, get that rope; Daz, help Claire!' When I felt we were close enough, I'd passed Jake back to Claire and raced ahead, reaching the boat seconds before the others. Once there, I ran along the dock and untied the front rope from its cleat on the pontoon. Following my orders, Tom did the same with the one at the back, while Daz leapt on board before turning to take Jake from Claire. Sophie was still a few steps behind and Claire waited to help her on board before climbing on herself.

As soon as the ropes were free, I looked back: the infected were only twenty yards away. As I pushed the front of the boat away from the dock, I shouted to Tom. 'Get on!'

He didn't need to be asked twice, and the moment he landed on the deck, I jumped on myself. I ran down the side of the boat and leapt into the cockpit. When I reached the wheel, I pressed the starter button, and breathed a sigh of relief when the engine immediately burst into life. I glanced over my shoulder: the first of the infected had reached the pontoon and were pounding along it. I slammed the throttle forward, causing the engine to scream in protest, and turned the wheel, taking the boat away from the dock. One of the infected, a man, perhaps in his late twenties, ran alongside and threw himself towards us, but we were just out of his reach. I watched as he fell into the water and sank from sight. Back on the dock, the rest paced back and forth, roaring with frustration at our escape.

As I manoeuvred the boat towards the middle of the river, I heard the sound of another, more powerful engine approaching at speed. Looking upstream, I saw a seaplane skimming over the water towards us. The pilot had the door open and was trying to dislodge an infected which was clinging to the left-hand float. The noise grew louder and louder as the plane grew nearer, heading straight for us. At the last minute, the pilot spotted us and must have pulled back hard on the stick because the plane rose sharply and unevenly. The weight of the infected had unbalanced the plane and I could see the pilot fighting both to control it and to avoid hitting us. I twisted the boat's wheel hard to the right just as the plane banked left and its wing-tip missed the top of the mast by less than a foot.

A hundred yards further down the river, the infected lost its grip and fell, twisting and tumbling, as if in slow motion, before splashing into the river ahead of us. Finally, free of its unwanted passenger, the plane evened out and climbed higher into the cloudless sky. I watched until it was little more than a white speck against the blue, wishing we could escape just as quickly. As it was, it would take us a good few hours before we'd finally be out of the city.

I looked at the others: Daz and Tom were staring after the aircraft, while Sophie had pulled out her mobile phone and was tapping at it furiously. After a few seconds, a confused look spread across her face. 'Why can't I send any messages?'

Daz turned to her. 'Dunno.' He pulled out his own phone and examined it. 'There's no signal on mine.'

'None on mine either.' Tom shoved his phone back into his pocket. 'Maybe the network's down. Everyone's probably trying to call everyone else at once to find out what's going on; must be jamming up the system.'

I was just about to join the discussion when I noticed Claire: she was bent over Jake, examining him closely. I watched him for a second, but he lay still, his eyes unfocussed, his breathing shallow and rapid. I put the engine into neutral, letting the current carry us downstream, and moved over to Claire. 'Is he okay? What's wrong with him?'

She said nothing, but pulled back the sleeve of his sweatshirt revealing a ragged wound which snaked across his pale skin.

'What's *that*?' Daz had joined us.

'It was when the man attacked the car, Jake was sitting in the passenger seat; the man grabbed him when he smashed through the glass. I thought I'd got him away in time.' Claire's eyes filled with tears.

'You mean ...?' Tom didn't finish the sentence, but he didn't need to.

Claire nodded.

'Wait, what?' Daz's eyes moved from face to face, 'What's up with him?'

'He's got the disease, hasn't he?' We turned to find Sophie standing behind us. 'He's going to die, isn't he?'

Claire wiped her eyes and straightened up, 'Yes, he's got the disease, but I don't think it's going to kill him.'

'So, he'll be okay?' Sophie sounded hopeful.

'No.' Claire hesitated momentarily. 'No, he won't; he'll become like that man who attacked us.'

Sophie's eyes widened. 'But, Mum, you're a doctor; you must be able to do something.'

'Honey,' Claire walked over to her, hugging her closely, 'there's nothing I can do.'

Tom and I glanced at each other uncomfortably.

'What's goin' to happen when he ...? You know, when he turns?' Daz didn't look at anyone. He just kept staring at Jake.

A realisation spread through my mind and I saw it occur to Claire and Tom, too. We were on a boat in the middle of the river with someone who would soon turn into an infected, and when he did, he'd attack us. He might only be a child, but in the close confines of the cockpit, we'd be unable to get away from him, and I'd seen on the news the previous night just how dangerous kids could be once the disease had overtaken them.

Claire let go of Sophie, and paced back and forth. She paused, staring at Jake for a moment, before setting off once more. 'Shit! Shit! SHIT!'

'Mum ...' Sophie stepped towards her, but Claire brushed her aside. She tried again. 'Mum, you've got to do something.' Tears were streaming down Sophie's face, 'Please!'

Claire stopped, a look of resignation creeping across her face. She turned to Sophie. 'There's only one thing I can do, honey.'

'Then do it!' Sophie urged her.

Claire took a deep breath. 'Okay.' She knelt down beside her doctor's bag, and with her hands shaking, she pulled out a syringe and a small glass bottle filled with a clear liquid. Wondering what she was going to do, I watched as she drew the liquid into the syringe and then held Jake's small hand. For a second she closed her eyes and just knelt there, like a statue; then she leaned forward, her dark hair brushing against his cheek, and kissed him on the forehead, murmuring softly, 'I'm sorry, baby, I'm so sorry.'

Claire kissed him again and then turned his arm over. She quickly found a vein and pressed the needle into his pallid skin: he didn't even flinch. She paused again, this time more briefly, before she pushed home the plunger, emptying the contents of the syringe into his body. As the rest of us watched, Claire pulled the needle out and leant forward. She picked Jake up and held him tightly against her body, her shoulders heaving up and down as she whispered to him. It took a few seconds before I realised the boy's breathing was slowing and soon it stopped altogether. I was confused for a moment, then I saw the word *Morphine* on the label of the now empty bottle and realised what she'd done. She laid Jake back down and stood up. Sophie was staring at her. 'Mum, what did you just do? What did you do to Jake? Mum?'

Claire pulled her daughter close once more and held her tightly. 'The only thing I could do for him, honey.' She wiped the tears from her face with her sleeve. 'The only thing.'

Sophie struggled free and pushed Claire away; she stared at her brother as he lay there, motionless. She ran to him and laid her head against his chest. After a few seconds, she glared at her mother. 'Oh my god, you killed him, didn't you? How could you do that?'

Daz, Tom and I stood frozen, not wanting to intrude on the family's moment of grief, but not knowing what to do instead.

Sophie and Claire were staring at each other, tears streaming down both their faces. 'I had to, honey. He would have become one of them if I hadn't. I couldn't let that happen to him. I couldn't. You didn't see the news last night; you didn't see what happened in Miami. I couldn't let him become like that. Please tell me you understand, please.'

Sophie looked towards Jake and then back to her mother. 'There was really nothing else you could've done?'

'Really.'

Sophie said nothing. Claire stepped forward and wrapped her arms around her, holding her tight, but I couldn't help noticing that Sophie didn't hug her back.

After what seemed like an age, Claire broke away and went back to where Jake was lying. As gently as possible, she picked up his body and carried it below. The rest of us followed, but we remained in the main saloon as she laid him out in the forward cabin. As we waited for her to return, I switched on the television, trying to find out more about what was going on, and just as I'd watched Miami fall apart the night before, I watched Glasgow go the same way. Many of the scenes were similar, but it was so much worse watching it happen to somewhere you recognised, that you knew, that lay all around you.

The official line was that people should stay inside and let the police deal with the infected, but no one was listening; everyone was trying to get out. In response, the army had put what they were calling a 'ring of steel' around the city, and were refusing to let anyone through. Just like the soldiers we'd encountered, they were heavily armed and there had been footage of them shooting into the crowds gathered at their barricades. The commanding officer claimed they were shooting at infected, but that wasn't what it looked like to me.

One of the news channels had got hold of a feed from a CCTV camera which overlooked Buchanan Street, and it was interspersing live footage of the near-deserted street, along which the occasional infected shuffled between the dead bodies, with repeats of the infected sweeping up it from earlier in the day. An hour of this was all I could take and I went on deck to try to think about what we should do next. By then, Claire had returned to the main cabin and she followed me up.

'So what's the plan?' There was an edge to Claire's voice that suggested she wasn't doing as well as she appeared.

'I don't know.' I looked out over the city. Smoke was twisting up from somewhere over by the university, while military helicopters circled above the centre and parts of the Southside. Occasionally, there were muzzle flashes from the machine guns which I could just make out protruding from open doors.

Claire cleared her throat. 'How about we just get out of here for now and work on a plan later?'

I turned back to her. 'Yeah, that'd work for me.'

There was a moment of silence before Claire replied, 'But we need to do something first.'

'What?'

She sniffed. 'We need to bury Jake. I want it done properly.' Her voice was trembling. 'It's the last thing I'll ever be able to do for him.'

'I'm sorry, Claire,' I glanced away, not wanting to meet her eyes. 'We can't do that; we can't go ashore.'

Claire raised her head and stared at me. 'You can do a burial at sea, can't you?'

'Yeah, but …' I stood up and walked to the back of the boat, 'but it's not something I've done before.'

'You can do it, though, can't you?' Claire implored me.

I turned her suggestion over in my mind. I knew the basics of what to do, at least in theory, and it really was the only option we had left. I let out a resigned sigh. 'Yes.'

Two hours later, we gathered on the deck as we continued to drift slowly downstream. In that time, we'd travelled a couple of miles, and we were now passing through the outer suburbs of the city. I'd wrapped Jake's lifeless body in some old sailcloth and weighted it down with a spare anchor. Since I was the closest thing to a captain we had on board, it fell to me to perform the ceremony. It wasn't something I'd ever thought I'd have to do and I didn't really know where to begin. I looked round at the others, trying to get some inspiration. Despite all we'd been through, it was only when we were safely on the boat that we'd had time to introduce ourselves properly. Daz was seventeen and came from Maryhill: not the best part of Glasgow, but by no means the worst. His real name was Darren, but his friends called him Dazzler, or Daz for short. He was just under six foot and skinny in an unhealthy kind of way, like he'd never eaten anything home-cooked in his life.

Claire and Sophie were from the more prosperous west end of the city. Claire's shoulder-length hair was a mess and her make-up was tear-streaked, but there was still a certain sense of refinedness and self-confidence about her. She worked at a local medical practice as a general practitioner, but before she'd settled down with a family, she'd spent time working in casualty departments across two continents, as well as numerous stints overseas with *Médicins sans Frontières*. This gave her a level of experience rarely needed when listening to middle-class mothers complain about their child's latest food intolerance, or giving well-heeled pensioners their annual flu vaccinations.

Sophie was fourteen, but tall for her age. Although she had the same dark hair as her mother, it was longer, hanging down over her shoulders, with a slight wave to it. Given all that had happened, she seemed to be holding up about as well as could be expected. Mostly she was angry and confused, but the enormity of what her mother had been forced to do and the realisation of what the disease would have done to Jake was starting to sink in. It didn't make it any less devastating, but it at least made it more understandable.

Claire was holding it together, too, but much of this seemed to be her professional persona, no doubt honed over years of working under stressful conditions. Daz just looked lost. He was clearly well out of his comfort zone, and he didn't seem to know what to do next. Physically, Tom looked the worst out of all of us. His shirt was torn where Claire had pulled it open, and it was soaked in blood from the gunshot wound. Yet, somehow he'd maintained his naturally upbeat attitude. It wasn't that he could see a bright side to everything going on around us, it was just that he was doing his best to try to stay positive despite everything.

In contrast, I was close to losing it. I kept reliving the events we'd witnessed and I was beginning to wonder whether we had any real chance of surviving for anything longer than a few more hours. I worried about family and friends I was leaving behind. Should I have done more to try to get them out of the city, too? Could I have done anything even if I had? There was still no phone signal and no way I could communicate with them. I just had to hope that they were lucky enough to have found a way out, just like I had.

I stared down at where Jake's body lay wrapped in sail cloth on the deck near the bow; it seemed so small and delicate. Suddenly, I knew what to say.

I took a deep breath, trying to remember the words. I couldn't recall them exactly, but I began nonetheless: 'Do not stand by my grave and weep, for I am not there.

'I am in winds that blow, I am the light glinting on

snow.'

I glanced quickly at Claire and Sophie's tear-stained faces, then across to where Tom and Daz were standing with their head's bowed and hands held behind their backs. I carried on. 'I am the sun on ripened grain, I am the gentle November rain.

'I am the song of birds circling in flight. I am soft star-shine and the moon shadow cast at night.'

I bent down and picked up Jake's tiny body. 'Do not stand by my grave and cry,'

Holding Jake across both arms, I crouched down and held him as close to the water as I could reach. 'For I am not there,' I let his body slip into the water, 'I did not die.'

I watched as the white sailcloth sank from sight, then I stood up and walked over to Claire, hugging first her and then Sophie. Daz and Tom followed suit. Moving back to the cockpit, I turned the engine on again and pointed the boat down the river. We were leaving Glasgow behind, and with a heavy heart, I realised it was unlikely I'd ever return.

As we headed west, Tom and Daz took turns scanning the banks of the river with my binoculars. Here and there small bands of people ran, some being chased, others just fleeing. Occasionally, there was the sound of a racing engine and the screech of tyres. Once, a convoy of camouflaged vehicles roared by, men in uniforms clinging to machine guns mounted on the back. Behind us, helicopters continued to fly over the city, moving in ever-expanding circles. I wondered if this tracked the spread of the infection: if so, it seemed to be moving fast. I looked across to where Claire and Sophie sat, holding each other, lost in their grief.

'Hey, Tom.' He turned to face me, 'How d'you feel about taking the wheel for a bit? I want to check on something.'

'Em, I don't really know how to drive a car, let alone a boat.'

'It's pretty easy. All you've got to do is keep us pointing in the right direction and not go too near the banks.'

'Still ...' Tom seemed reluctant.

'I'll do it.' Daz shot to his feet. 'I mean, how hard can it be?'

I hesitated; I didn't know Daz, or what type of person he was. He was young, but at least he was eager, and there wouldn't really be too much that could go wrong. It also wouldn't hurt to have someone else on board who knew how to drive the boat, just in case something happened to me. I came to a decision. 'Okay. Come stand here and I'll show you what to do.'

As Daz stepped behind the wheel, I moved to the side. 'This is the throttle here, but you don't really need to touch it at the moment. That's the rev counter; it shows how fast the engine's turning over. You want to keep it at about 3,000. The wheel's just like a car's; turn it in the direction you want to go, but try to only make small movements, not big ones. For now, you're just trying to keep us going forward in a straight line. If you want to see how well you're doing, you can look back at the wake.' We both looked over the stern, the wake lay in a straight line behind us, or at least it did until the point where Daz had taken the wheel: after that it snaked from side to side as Daz moved the wheel back and forth, trying to keep us on course. 'Any questions?'

Daz glanced around nervously. 'Where're the brakes?'

'Boats don't have breaks.'

He frowned. 'So how d'you stop?'

'You don't, at least not quickly at any rate. That means you've got to look ahead and plan your movements carefully.'

Concern spread across Daz's face; I patted him on the shoulder. 'Don't worry about that for now. Just keep us in the middle of the river and we'll be fine. There shouldn't be anything you can hit out here.' I watched him for a few minutes, making sure he'd got the hang of it; he was learning fast and already we were steering a much more consistent path. 'I'm going below. Call me if you need me.'

Before Daz could say anything, I disappeared down the companionway and into the saloon. The television was still on, but the sound was off. A worried-looking woman clutched a microphone as she stood on a near-empty road. Behind her, the door of the Prime Minister's residence at 10 Downing Street was visible. A small, but persistent, trickle of visitors came and went as the woman spoke. I picked up the remote and turned up the volume.

'So far there has been no word from the Prime Minister, but he is believed to be in discussions with military leaders and the heads of other European states. Meanwhile, the latest reports suggest that while the situation in Glasgow is getting worse, the army are still managing to contain the outbreak within the city itself. Everyone in the affected area is being told to lock their doors and stay inside as this is their best chance of avoiding the infection. This is also critical to the army's strategy as it allows them to identify those infected with the disease and neutralise them.'

'Neutralise them? That's a rather nice way of saying they've been given orders to shoot them on sight.' I turned and found that Claire had come into the saloon behind me. 'And since they can't really tell who's infected and who's not, it means that they're just going to shoot anyone they see. It's one way to deal with the situation, but a lot of innocent people are going to end up dead.'

'Surely they wouldn't do that, would they? Just shoot anyone they see.'

'The soldiers are going to do what they're told. They'll be scared; they'll be panicking; they're going to shoot first and ask questions later.' She crossed her arms as she stood beside me facing the screen. 'I've seen it before, when I was in Africa: when soldiers are faced with a threat like this, one where they can't tell the enemy from the innocent, one where they're so heavily outnumbered; they stop thinking and just do whatever they've been told to do.'

I was about to say something when the picture on the television changed. The woman had disappeared and instead they appeared to be showing a football match. Given the situation, this seemed odd. I turned my attention to it as a voice-over put it in context.

'This footage was recorded in Glasgow a few hours ago, at Ibrox football stadium, where the home team was taking on its local rival. It's still not clear quite what happened, but it seems that somehow someone with the infection got into the crowd. Younger viewers and those of a nervous disposition might want to look away now.'

Suddenly, the camera shifted from following the players on the pitch and zoomed in on an area high in one of the stands, where it looked like people had started fighting. The commentators could be heard tutting and criticising the fans. Then the violence started to spread, slowly at first, then faster and faster as more and more people became infected, turned, and then passed it on. Those who could, struggled onto the pitch, trying to escape the violence that was engulfing them. Others, those who were already infected, pursued them, pulling them down, tearing them apart. The camera kept having to pull further and further back to keep all of the action in the frame. By this time, the commentators where shouting over each other as they tried to understand what was going on. Then there was a crash and one of them yelled. A scuffle could be heard in the background, as well as swearing and screaming, and then the screen went blank.

A second later this was replaced by the live feed from Downing Street and the reporter was speaking again. 'That was the scene at the Rangers-Celtic match earlier today, and it shows how quickly the Haitian Rabies Virus can sweep through a crowd. This is the justification that the army are using for their shoot-on-sight policy for anyone who is known, or even suspected, to have the disease. Remember, there's no cure for rabies, no treatment once people start showing symptoms, and they are claiming that only if the number of infected can be kept to a minimum, can there be any hope of stopping this outbreak. A military spokesman has already warned that if this strategy doesn't work, more serious measures may have to be taken. Back to you in the studio.'

A man's voice cut in. 'Hold on, Michelle. "More serious measures"? Do you know what they mean by that?'

The woman held her finger to her ear and then glanced down at the bundle of papers she was holding. She shuffled through these, trying to find the one she was searching for. When she found it, she looked back at the camera. 'All we've been told is that the current strategy is to shoot any people who are infected, or who are suspected of being infected, on sight. If it looks like this strategy is failing, then they will reassess the situation and consider whether more serious measures need to be implemented.'

'That doesn't sound good.' Claire turned to me. 'How fast can this boat go?'

'About four miles an hour tops.'

Claire considered this for a moment. 'What are we doing now?'

'About three. Why? What are you thinking?'

'I'm thinking they aren't going to be able to handle this just by shooting people. There are too many already infected for that to be possible. Think about the size of that football stadium. There had to have been tens of thousands of people in it, and god knows how many of them are now infected.' Claire unfolded her arms and placed her hands on her hips. 'I'll bet they're already preparing to implement their "more serious measures" and I think the further away we are from Glasgow when that happens, the better.'

'Well, we should be coming up to the bridge any time now, and once we're under that, we'll be well clear of the city.' I'd just finished speaking when there was a shout from the deck.

'I guess I'd better get back up there.' I turned and climbed through the companionway and out into the cockpit.

Claire clicked off the television. 'I'll come with you.'

Up on deck, Sophie sat huddled in one corner, staring blankly into space. Daz was still at the wheel; Tom was standing beside him, peering through the binoculars. Both had concerned expressions on their faces. I looked down river, towards where the span of the Erskine Bridge stretched across the water about a mile ahead of us.

'What's up?' I glanced at Daz, but it was Tom that replied.

'There's something going on ... on the bridge. A lot of

people moving around up there, and ...' He swept the binoculars from left to right. 'And I think they've got cannons or something.'

Daz let go of the wheel and took the binoculars from Tom. 'Those aren't cannons; they're field guns an' howitzers, an' that sort of thing. That's some pretty intense hardware.'

I looked at Daz curiously. 'How'd you know that?'

Daz shrugged. 'I play a lot of computer games. Not much else to do most of the time.'

'What could they do with them?' I was concerned about what the army might be planning to use such large weapons for.

Daz bit his lip nervously. 'Blow this thing to pieces for a start.'

I assumed Daz was being flippant, but the very possibility had me worried. I took the binoculars from him and studied the bridge myself. There were three large guns, one at each end and one in the middle, all pointing up the river and towards the city; and that meant they were pointing towards us.

I handed the binoculars back to Daz, who ran them along the bridge, stopping at each gun in turn. 'Looks like they're still settin' them up. They won't be able to fire them yet.'

'You learned that from computer games, too?' Tom sounded sceptical.

'Nah,' Daz shot back, 'the Discovery Channel!'

'We'd better get a move on then.' I stepped behind the wheel and pushed the throttle up until the revs reached 4,000. The engine was now working flat-out; if I pushed it any harder, I'd risk damaging it.

Chapter Four

We'd crossed about half the remaining distance to the bridge when the first shots rang out. The sound was deep and rapid, and the bullets crashed into the water about thirty yards in front us, each sending a small jet of water into the air.

'Why're they firing at us?' Tom was crouching on the cockpit floor along with Daz. Claire had thrown herself across Sophie, trying to protect as much of her as possible, while I huddled behind the wheel.

I scanned the bridge ahead of us, trying to see where the gun was being fired from. 'Maybe they think we're infected. Here, Daz, take the helm. I'm going to see if I can get them on the VHF radio, tell them we're okay and not to shoot.'

As he stood up, the machine gun fired again; this time the bullets were much closer. Daz swore and threw himself onto the deck, wrapping his hands over the back of his head.

'Daz, you need to get over here.'

Keeping himself as low as possible, Daz crawled over to the wheel and crouched behind it.

'You can't see anything from down there. I'm afraid you're going to have to stand up and do it properly.'

Daz remained where he was. 'Are you mad? I'll get my fuckin' head blown off!'

'Don't worry. I think they're just warning shots; I don't think they're actually trying to hit us.' Just as I finished speaking, the machine gun fired again. The first bullets hit the water a few yards to our right, while the rest crashed into the foredeck, sending splinters of fibreglass flying into the air. I pulled the wheel sharply to the left, turning the boat as tightly as I dared. As soon as we were facing upstream, I straightened it up and headed back the way we'd just come. A fourth rally from the machine gun smacked into the water close enough to the stern that I felt the spray land on the back of my neck.

I glanced round the cockpit. 'All of you, get inside! Get right up front; it'll be safest there.'

Claire ushered Sophie down the stairs, and was closely followed by Tom; Daz didn't move.

'What about you?' He sounded concerned.

'Someone needs to keep us heading in the right direction.'

Daz remained huddled by my side. 'I'll stay, too, then.'

'There's no point in two of us being out here. Just get inside. Now!'

There was another burst of machine gunfire from the bridge. As I ducked down, I heard the bullets whistle overhead and smack into the water about ten feet ahead of us. It was all the encouragement Daz needed. He scuttled across the cockpit on all fours and disappeared down the companionway just as the machine gun fired again. I shrank down as low as I could get, trying to use the back of the boat to give me as much cover as possible. I didn't see where the bullets landed, but I heard the spray they threw up hit the side of the boat. I shifted the throttle forward causing the engine to scream as I pushed it well beyond a level that was safe; it wouldn't be able to run like that for long, but we needed to get as far away from the bridge as quickly as possible. There was another volley of shots, but they landed well short of us. I hoped this meant we were finally out of its range.

'Ben?' I looked up and saw Tom standing in the

companionway, trying to keep his head as low as possible. 'We've got a problem. There's water coming in.'

'How much?'

He glanced over his shoulder and then back to me. 'A lot.'

'Shit!' I thumped the wheel. 'Come up here and take the helm.'

Tom stayed where he was, looking petrified.

'Don't worry. I think we're out of their range.'

'You *think* we're out of range?' Tom repeated worriedly.

I shifted the throttle down so the boat was barely moving forward. 'Just keep us pointing upstream.'

Tom climbed slowly out into the cockpit, his eyes darting all around him. 'Won't they chase after us?'

'I don't think so. They're army; they won't have boats, and anyway, their job is probably just to stop anyone getting out. As long as we keep far enough away from the bridge, I don't think they'll bother us.'

Finally satisfied, Tom stepped forward and took the wheel as I ran past him and down into the cabin.

'Ben, up here.' Claire and Daz were in the front cabin staring at the side of the boat, while Sophie sat on the bed, her knees pulled up to her chest.

Even before I got to where they were standing, I could see the problem: the bullets had barely been slowed by the fibreglass of the deck and had gone straight through the hull. Each had left a ragged hole about an inch across in the side of the boat. I could see daylight through the ones which were above the waterline, while water poured through the ones below it.

Daz heard me coming and turned, his face etched with worry. 'Can you no' do somethin' about it?'

'Yes, I've got a repair kit somewhere, but given how much water's coming in, we'll need to move fast.' I watched the speed at which it was coming through the holes. 'By my reckoning we've got about fifteen minutes before we're in real trouble.'

Daz raised his eyebrows incredulously. 'We're no' in real trouble already?'

'No, not yet.' I glanced round at my companions and came to a decision. 'Daz, can you swim?'

'Aye,' he looked slightly confused, 'but why?'

'I've got plugs which can be used to block up the holes, but the only problem is that they need to be pushed in from the outside; and I'll need an extra pair of hands when I'm in the water.'

'I'm no' goin' swimmin' in the river; it's manky. You see what people throw in it?'

'Daz, I'm not asking. I'm telling: my boat; my rules.'

'Can't Tom go?'

'Not with that bullet wound in his shoulder, he can't,' Claire interjected. 'There's too big a risk of infection.

Daz realised he was fighting a losing battle. He held up his hands. 'Okay, okay, I'll do it, but what am I goin' to wear?'

'You've got underwear on, haven't you?' Claire said matter-of-factly. 'Just strip down to them.'

'But ...' Daz turned from me to Claire and back again.

Claire shook her head. 'Oh, don't be so bloody modest. I'm a doctor: trust me, you won't have anything I haven't seen before.'

'Come on, Daz, we've got to get the holes filled as soon as possible.' I went back through to the saloon and found the water was already up to the level of the floorboards. I opened one of the lockers under the seats and rummaged through it for the repair kit. Finding it, I pulled it out and ran up on deck.

Tom was crouched down against the back of the boat holding the wheel as low as he could. I ran my eyes nervously over the now distant bridge. 'Any more shots?'

'No.' Tom glanced over his shoulder. 'I think they've given up.'

'Good.' I slipped the engine into neutral and went forward to drop the anchor. As soon as it was in place, I stripped off and searched around for Daz. I found him standing in the cockpit beside Claire, wearing nothing but a pair of baggy boxer shorts and a sheepish expression.

'Right, Daz, up front and over the side.' I carried the repair kit forward and opened it, revealing a number of orange cones, each one about nine inches long and almost five inches across at their widest point. I'd never tried them before and I hoped they'd work as well as they were supposed to. 'Once you're in there, I'll hand these down to you and then I'll come in. Whatever you do, don't let go of them.'

Daz peered over the side and then jumped, entering the water feet first. He disappeared from sight and then resurfaced, spitting and huffing.

I looked at him. 'Bit cold is it?'

'Fuckin' freezin'!'

I chuckled and handed Daz the repair cones before lowering myself slowly over the side, giving my body a chance to acclimatise to the change in temperature. I took the first of the cones from Daz and ducked under the water. I felt around for a hole and when I found one, I jammed the cone into place. I repeated this again and again until all four holes were filled.

I called up to Claire. 'That should be it, but can you go

and make sure?'

She disappeared for a few seconds and then returned to the foredeck. 'There's no water coming in through the top three, but the bottom one's still letting a lot in.'

I dived down again and found the one that was causing the problem. I pulled it out and tried again, this time taking more care to make sure it was securely in place. I surfaced and Claire disappeared again; this time when she came back up she gave me the thumbs up. With no more coming in, the bilge pump would soon be able to clear out all the water which was already on board and we were safe. Well, maybe not safe, but at least we were no longer sinking.

'What now?' Daz looked enquiringly at the rest of us.

We were sitting in the cockpit, trying to work out what to do next. I'd tried calling the people on the bridge on the radio, but there had been no response. I was sure they could hear us, but that they were choosing not to reply. We were riding at anchor and I'd spent the last hour and a half repairing the holes in the deck and the side of the boat. The smell of epoxy resin drifted around us and I knew it would take a good few hours before anyone would be able to go into the forward cabin again because of the fumes. 'I don't know. We need to get beyond the bridge somehow, but I don't think they're going to let us through.'

'What if we waited for it to get dark. Could we sneak past without them seeing us?' Tom was watching me as he spoke, trying to judge what I thought of his suggestion.

I scratched the back of my head. 'I guess.'

'At least it's an idea,' Claire was clearly eager to be doing something, 'and it's better than just sitting here. I'm telling you, when their current strategy for containing the outbreak fails, they're going to try something more ...' She hesitated as she searched for an appropriate word. 'More, you know, drastic, and I think it would be best if we aren't here when that happens.'

Sophie looked up from her mobile phone where she'd been trying unsuccessfully, once again, to send out messages to her friends. 'More drastic?' Her eyes narrowed. 'Like what?'

'I don't know.' Claire shifted uncomfortably on her seat and although I could tell she had a pretty good idea of what, she clearly didn't want to say it in front of her daughter. 'But the sooner we get beyond the bridge, the better.' Before Sophie could respond, Claire stood up, 'I'm going to check the news; see if there's anything new.'

With that, she went down into the saloon where I heard her switch on the television and turn up the volume. While the boat was riding at anchor, there was little to do on deck, so I figured I might as well join her. When I got down the stairs, the same reporter was still on the television, camped outside 10 Downing Street. She seemed to be responding to a question from the studio. 'Well no, the current strategy — what General McDonald is calling "containment" — doesn't seem to be working. I've just heard that they've had to pull the cordon back again. It now encloses an area that's about five miles across and encompasses Glasgow city centre, the West End, Maryhill, and an area of the Southside which stretches for about three miles along the banks of the Clyde. The problem here is that each time they move back, the perimeter gets longer and more difficult to control. We've heard that a couple of checkpoints have already been overrun, either by infected or by people trying to get out of the city, and so far about forty soldiers are thought to have either been killed or have succumbed to the disease.'

A disembodied male voice broke in, presumably from back in the studio. 'So what are they going to do next? Is there another plan they can implement?'

'Well, there is ...' The woman hesitated and her eyes glanced to her left where an arm in a green jacket appeared briefly on screen before vanishing again. 'There is another strategy, but at the moment, I'm being informed that it's classified. What I can say, though, is that General McDonald is currently inside the building behind me,' she pointed a finger over her shoulder, 'discussing the alternatives with the Prime Minister with whom, I'm told, the final decision will lie.'

Claire changed the channel, first to one, then to another: all of them were showing the same live feed from Downing Street. She snorted derisively. 'Looks like the military's nobbled the press.'

I carried on watching the television; the reporter was half-turned from the camera, holding her finger to her ear. After a second, she looked up. 'I believe we can finally link up with a reporter at BBC Scotland's offices in Glasgow and see if we can find out a bit more about what's going on. Gavin, can you hear me?'

There was a crackling sound and the screen flickered before a new picture appeared of a man holding a small camera at arm's length. He was hunched down in the corner of a room which looked like it was an office rather than a studio. Then the man spoke. 'This is Gavin Kessington here at the BBC's Glasgow studio.' He glanced at his watch. 'It's now been six hours since the outbreak of Haitian Rabies Virus started in Glasgow city centre just a few miles from here, and I can tell you the situation inside the military containment zone is getting desperate. If you look outside,' he shifted the camera so the viewers could see out of the window behind him, 'you'll see there are many, many people milling around out there. I'm not certain, but I think they're all infected: I've seen them attacking people, killing them, even eating them. They show no mercy to anyone they encounter, but they're not attacking each other. There must be some way they know who's infected and who isn't.'

The female reporter's voice cut in. 'Have you seen the army at all? Are they doing anything to help?'

Gavin pressed his finger into his ear, as if adjusting an earpiece. 'I did see them initially, but that was when we were at the edge of the containment zone. Since they pulled back, I've only seen helicopters flying overhead.' He shifted his position. 'And now, it seems, even they've gone. When they were here, there didn't seem much they could do. There're just too many infected; they're everywhere.'

'And how are you holding up, Gavin?'

'I think the phrase is "as well as can be expected".'

'How many of you are there?'

'It's just me. Some of the people from my office tried to get out, but I think they got caught by the infected. There might be people in other offices but it's not safe to move around to find out. There are infected in the building itself. I'm not too sure how they got in, but I've seen them in the corridors. At the moment, I've got the door barricaded with a desk, and I just hope that will be enough to keep them out.'

'Okay, Gavin. Can we come back to you for an update in a couple of hours?'

'Yes.' There was a sudden crash and the man's head snapped to the left before returning to the camera. He spoke again, almost whispering this time. 'If I'm still here.'

With that, the picture switched back to the woman in Downing Street. She straightened her coat. 'That was Gavin Kessington reporting from Glasgow, where, if you're just joining us, there's been an outbreak of the Haitian Rabies Virus. This is the same virus that has been spreading slowly through the Caribbean and some parts of the US in recent weeks, and it is thought to have been responsible for much of the destruction we witnessed in Miami yesterday. The Prime Minister closed the country's borders this morning, and it's still not clear how the outbreak in Glasgow started. Now, back to the studio, where we will be discussing what we know about this emerging virus and where it came from.'

Suddenly, Daz poked his head into the cabin. 'Hey guys, I think you need to see this.'

Claire and I went back out on deck where Daz was now staring towards the city with the binoculars. There was a plane, just visible high up in the sky, circling slowly. I shielded my eyes with my hand as I watched it. 'What's up?'

Daz lowered the binoculars, looking concerned, and pointed at the aircraft. 'That is.'

I carried on watching the plane for a few seconds, and couldn't see anything worth being concerned about. 'I don't get it.'

'That's a bomber; I recognise the shape.' He lifted up the binoculars again. 'Why would they have a bomber over the city?'

I glanced at Claire and wondered whether this was part of some new strategy. As we watched, something fell from the back of the plane. At first, I thought it was a bomb, and I was relieved when I saw a red and white parachute open up. Whatever it was, it drifted slowly through the darkening sky towards the ground. As far as I could work out, it was going to touch down somewhere near the city centre.

'Shite!' Daz was tracking the object with the binoculars. He was clearly panicked.

'Daz, what's wrong?' I strained my eyes as I tried to work out what it was about the object that had Daz so worried.

'I know what that is.' Daz was breathing rapidly as he spoke. 'I've seen them before. It was in a documentary I watched. They used them in Afghanistan. Oh shit! OH FUCK!'

'Daz,' Claire was staring at him, 'are you going to tell the rest of us what it is, or do we have to guess?'

Daz took a deep breath. 'It's a fuel-air bomb. They're bombin' the city; they're goin' to incinerate the place ... an' everyone in it.'

'Hang on. Back up, Daz. What's a fuel-air bomb?' Tom sounded worried, but not as worried as Daz.

'It's like this really powerful type of bomb. It disperses fuel over an area an' then sets it on fire. It's so powerful, it's like a mini-nuclear explosion. It'll destroy the city an' burn down whatever's left.'

Now I could see why Daz was so concerned. 'What sort of range does it have?'

'Dunno.' Daz lowered the binoculars. 'A thousand yards; maybe two; somethin' like that.'

I felt myself relax. 'So we should be safe here then?'

'If that's the only one, yeah, but look ...' Daz pointed up. A second bomb had been dropped from the plane, this time closer to us. Over the next few minutes, four more bombs were dropped over different parts of the city and drifted slowly downwards, each on its own parachute; the nearest was going to come down about a mile from where we were anchored. Given what Daz had told us that could be close enough to cause us real problems.

As we watched, a shimmering cloud started to spread out across the sky from the first bomb. It descended towards the city, and then exploded. First, we saw the light — it looked like the very sky was on fire — then we saw the blast cloud sweep down and across the city. Finally, we heard it. Even from this distance it was loud; loud enough to make Sophie yelp and cover her ears. Above the detonation site, a large, black cloud rose high into the air.

By then, the second bomb had started dispersing its fuel across the sky, followed by the third and the fourth. Each ignited in turn, obliterating another area of the city and with it, both the infected and those who were still human. The fifth detonated and this time we not only heard it, we felt the blast front buffet us as it passed. The sixth was even closer and soon, it too, would explode.

I shouted to the others. 'We need to get inside!' I didn't know how much protection the cabin would give us, but it had to be better than nothing.

Daz went in first, followed by Sophie, Claire and Tom. Only once they were all in the cabin, did I scramble down after them. I was securing the hatch over the companionway when I saw the flash of light. It seemed like it was almost on top of us, but it took a moment before the blast front hit us. When it did, it felt as if the whole boat was being lifted from the water. Then it fell and there was a brief pause before the blast returned, heading in the opposite direction as the explosion sucked the oxygen from the atmosphere, creating a vacuum at the detonation site. The boat lurched beneath us and turned violently in the water, heeling over until the mast was almost level with the surface, throwing us, and everything else around us, across the boat. Sophie cried out as Daz crashed into her; Tom hit the side of the boat with a loud and sickening thud. I landed next to him, my shoulder smashing one of the small windows in the cabin roof. Water started pouring in, but before too much could enter, the blast had passed and the boat started to right itself. Again we were thrown around the cabin like rag dolls, crashing into tables and seats, and into each other.

Chapter Five

Gradually, the boat settled itself in the water and I could finally stand up again. My head was throbbing and I could feel something running down the side of my face. I touched it, confirming it was blood. I glanced round: Daz was struggling to his feet, while Tom lay in a crumpled heap. Claire lay nearby, with Sophie stirring next to her.

Tom seemed to be the most badly injured, so I went to him first. Kneeling beside him, I could see the dressing from his bullet wound had come off and he was bleeding again. There was also blood flowing down his face from a cut hidden by his hair and his arm lay at an odd angle to the rest of his body. I touched his neck with my fingers, feeling for a pulse; it took me a few goes to find it, but it was there. I checked his breathing: it was shallow and laboured.

'Is he ... you know ... dead?' Daz was standing over me.

'No, he's okay.' I stood up. 'Well, he's alive at any rate.' I stared at Tom, wondering what to do next. I had a rudimentary knowledge of first aid, but that was all. For the moment, I decided it might be best if I left him where he was and I turned my attentions to Sophie and Claire. Claire was still motionless while Sophie was now crouched next to her.

'Mum? Mum! Wake up, Mum!' Sophie was shouting, ignoring the fact that she was bleeding from a deep cut on her own arm, but Claire didn't move. I reached out and checked her pulse: like Tom's, it was there. I cast an eye over her; she had no obvious injuries and, apart from the fact that she was unconscious, she seemed uninjured. I looked up at Sophie. 'She's okay, I think.'

Sophie's brow furrowed with concern. 'Why isn't she moving then?'

'I don't know.' Then I remembered something. 'Where's your mum's bag? The big black one.'

Sophie sniffed. 'It was around here somewhere.'

'Can you see if you can find it? You'll need to be careful though, there's a lot of broken glass around.'

'Okay.' Sophie started searching through the debris scattered across the floor. I glanced round the cabin, looking for Daz and found him anxiously watching Tom for any sign that he might be coming round. 'Daz, can you help Sophie?'

Daz didn't take his eyes off Tom's unmoving body. 'Huh?'

'Can you help Sophie look for Claire's bag?'

Daz finally looked up. 'What d'you want that for?'

'Because she's a doctor. There might be something in it that will help.'

'Oh, yeah.' Daz started searching the cabin, too. A moment later, he called out. 'Found it!'

He handed it to me. I opened it and rifled through its contents, looking for surgical dressings and bandages. I found some and went over to Tom. 'Daz, come here. Hold this onto his shoulder; just push down, not too hard; you only need enough pressure on it to stop the bleeding.'

Daz knelt down and held the surgical dressing against Tom's bullet wound, while I searched through his hair. The wound wasn't deep, but it was bleeding heavily. I'd just taken another dressing and pressed it to his head when there was a moan from behind me.

Sophie was back over beside Claire, leaning over her. 'Mum?'

'What happened?' Claire was trying to sit up.

'We got knocked down by the blast.' I turned my attention back to Tom. His head wound was still bleeding, but the flow was starting to slow.

'Everyone okay?' Claire spotted Sophie. 'Honey, you're hurt. Where's my bag?'

'I've got it here. Everyone's okay, except Tom.' I watched him for a couple of seconds: his breathing was becoming erratic; his skin was pale; and there was a hint of blue around his lips. 'I think he's in trouble.'

'Let me have a look.' Claire shuffled across and I moved aside so she could examine him. Her face changed almost immediately from concern to panic. 'I think he's got a pneumothorax.'

'A what?' Daz was leaning over Claire, trying to see what she was talking about.

'A punctured lung. He must have broken a rib.' Claire's eyes darted around the cabin. 'I need some sort of tubing.' She turned to me. 'Have you got anything like that on board?'

I sprang up and opened one of the lockers. Its contents had been thrown everywhere, but I eventually found the rubber tubing I was looking for. I held it out. 'Will this do?'

'Yes. What about a plastic bottle? Have you got one of those?'

I moved over to the galley, picking my way through the shattered crockery that littered the floor. In one of the cupboards I found a water bottle which I handed to Claire. She poured some of its contents onto the floor, leaving it half full. Taking a scalpel from her bag, she cut the tubing in half, feeding one end of each half into the bottle; one right into the water, the other just above it. Using Elastoplast, she then bound them into position. 'What about duct tape?'

I found that quickly and passed it to her. She wrapped it round and round the top of the bottle until it was completely sealed. Next, she pulled open Tom's shirt and examined his chest. 'Have you got any alcohol? Whisky? vodka? Something like that?'

I raced back to the galley and returned with an old bottle of gin which had been floating around in the back of a cupboard for the last couple of years. 'Will this do?'

Taking it, Claire examined the label. 'Yeah, that'll work.' She unscrewed the lid and poured about half of it over her hands, the scalpel and the right-hand side of Tom's chest.

'What d'you do that for?' Daz was following Claire's every move.

'She's sterilising everything.' Sophie was standing behind Claire, watching her mother work on Tom. She glanced over at me. 'You're bleeding.'

'So are you.' I retorted and pointed to her arm. She looked down briefly before taking a surgical dressing out of Claire's bag. She applied it to her arm and then wrapped a bandage around it to keep it pressed tight against the wound. When she'd finished, she pointed to the nearest seat. 'Sit!'

I didn't move. 'No, not until I know Tom's okay.'

Claire looked up. 'There's no point in me sterilising him if you're just going to bleed all over the place. Let Sophie sort you out,' Claire smiled at her daughter. 'She knows what she's doing.'

I sat down and watched as Claire took the scalpel and cut deep into Tom's chest between two of his ribs. There was an audible wheeze as air escaped from the wound. Almost immediately, Tom's breathing started to become deeper and more regular; Claire let out a sigh of relief before turning to Daz. 'I need you to help me.'

Daz stood, staring, as if mesmerised by the blood oozing from Tom's chest.

'Daz, snap out of it and get down here!'

'What? Oh! Yeah.' Daz knelt down next to Claire.

'Take that bit of hose and pour some of the gin over it.'

Daz did as Claire told him.

'That's right. Now, while I hold this open, I need you to slowly feed the tube into it.'

With her fingers, Claire levered open the cut she'd made in Tom's chest, causing blood to rush out; Daz grimaced in horror, but he did as he'd been told.

Claire smiled encouragingly. 'Perfect. Now I need you to take that Elastoplast and use it to hold the tube in place.'

Daz wrapped the tape around the tube, securing it to Tom's chest. There was a noise from the bottle as air started bubbling into the water and colour finally started returning to Tom's face.

'That's the worst of it dealt with. Now let's get the rest of him sorted.' Claire ran her eyes over Tom's body. 'Looks like he's dislocated his shoulder. Daz, hold him down.'

Daz put his weight on Tom as Claire pulled and rotated his arm. There was an audible *pop* as it slid back into place. As Claire sorted out the dressings Daz and I had applied earlier, Sophie took some gauze from Claire's bag and tipped some of the gin onto it.

'This is probably going to hurt.' With that Sophie dabbed it onto my face. Pain shot through me like a lightning bolt and I jerked backwards.

'Sorry.' She drew back her hand apologetically. 'I'm trying to be as gentle as I can.'

She dabbed at the cut on my forehead again: it still

stung, but not as badly as the first time. After she'd cleaned the blood away, she opened the surgical dressing and applied it, using some of the Elastoplast to keep it in place. Claire glanced up. 'Good job there, Soph. Ben, you'll need to keep some pressure on it until it stops bleeding.'

I held my hand up and pressed the dressing to my forehead. I turned to Sophie, 'Thanks.' Then to Claire: 'why's he still unconscious?'

'I don't know.' Claire sounded concerned. 'Daz, Can you help me get him up?'

Together, they lifted Tom onto the seat on the other side of the table where he lay motionless.

Claire walked over to the galley and washed Tom's blood from her hands. 'There's not much more I can do for him now. We'll just have to wait and see what happens.

To take their minds off Tom's condition, Claire set the others to work, putting everything back where it belonged down below. I chose, instead, to go outside and make sure the danger had passed, at least for the time being. As I pulled back the hatch, the first thing that hit me was the smell of partially burned fuel and of thick, acrid smoke. Darkness was falling, but the eastern sky was ablaze as far as the eye could see. Tongues of fire leapt fifty or sixty feet into the air, consuming the city and all those who'd still been in it when the bombs had been detonated. Above the fire, thick black clouds were building, rising high into the air until they disappeared into the descending night. Grabbing the handheld spotlight from its bracket just inside the hatch, I moved round, checking the boat for damage.

Beneath my feet, the deck was coated with a greasy film which was mixing with ash falling from the sky, making it difficult for me to keep my footing. I was relieved to see that, despite the battering it had received, the boat seemed to be undamaged and the anchor was holding firm. I turned the key in the ignition, but the engine remained lifeless. Checking the batteries, I found the wires had been knocked off. I put them back in their rightful places and retried the engine. This time it turned over, but it didn't catch. Pulling up the covers of the engine compartment, I peered inside; the smell of diesel hit me almost immediately. Looking at the fuel tank, I saw the fuel line had come loose. I shimmied into the confines of the compartment and reconnected it, then tried the engine again, but still there was nothing. After three more attempts, the engine finally started. This was a relief: even though it was several hundred yards wide at this point, we'd have difficulty navigating in the confines of the river without the engine.

Not wanting to waste any more fuel, I turned it off again and was just about to go below when I heard something bump against the bow. I shone the spotlight onto the water and saw a large plastic dumpster floating past the boat. It had partially melted and fused to its lid was the burnt remains of a human arm. Shining the light upstream, I saw the river was filled with debris which had been blasted into the water by the explosions; some of the larger pieces still burned and smouldered. In amongst these floated charred and disfigured bodies, or parts of them, and as they drifted past, the smell of incinerated flesh lodged in my nostrils, making my stomach churn.

Suddenly, I glimpsed a movement. I pointed the spotlight forward and illuminated a large section of what might have once been a roof that was floating towards us; three figures clung to it, their singed clothes hanging from their bodies, their skin charred and blackened: yet, somehow they were still alive. As they grew nearer, they seemed to sense my presence and turned towards me, their eyes burning with anger and rage as they let out low, guttural growls. I called out to the others, 'Daz, Claire, get up here. We've got a problem.'

Daz stuck his head out of the cabin door. 'What? Claire's busy with Tom.'

'This is more important. I need both of you up here now. Sophie can stay with Tom.'

Daz disappeared and then a second later, first he and then Claire emerged from the cabin. By this time, the roof, and its unwanted cargo, were only thirty feet from the bow.

Daz took one look at the figures, and blurted out, 'How're they no' dead?'

Claire stared at them. 'Are they infected?'

'Yeah, I'm pretty sure,' I played the spotlight over them again. 'Look at the way they're moving; look at their eyes.'

Concern raced across Claire's face. 'Are they going to be able to get on board?'

'If they get close enough, yes.'

Daz gasped. 'What're we goin' to do if that happens?'

'I don't know.' I stared at the figures, trying to come up with a plan, but I couldn't. I turned to the others. 'Any ideas?'

Daz was the one that answered. 'Have you got any guns?'

'Only a flare gun, and that's not really a proper gun.'

'Can we no' just move out of their way?'

'No, there's not enough time to get the anchor up

before they get here.'

'Shit!' Daz was starting to panic.

As the roof drifted closer, the infected clambered unsteadily to their feet, but they found it difficult to stay upright on the battered and uneven surface as it bobbed up and down. One slipped, falling heavily onto the wood. By then, they were close enough that I could hear the snapping of bone as it landed. With much difficulty, it climbed back to its feet, its left arm dangling uselessly by its side, but it didn't seem to notice.

I looked around frantically, searching every inch of the deck, eventually landing on the boathooks which were tied, one on each side, to runners on top of the cabin. They were the closest thing to real weapons I'd thought of so far.

'Daz, take this!' I thrust the spotlight into his hand. I pointed towards the approaching infected. 'And keep it pointed at them.'

As I struggled to untie the first boathook, I heard the infected snarling and screeching as they floated ever closer. The moment boathook was free, I passed it to Daz before moving round to where the second was lashed to the cabin's roof.

I felt a shudder as the debris hit us across the bow, sending it spinning lazily down our left side as the infected clawed at the boat, desperate to get on board. I glanced at Daz; he stood, clutching the boathook in one hand, rooted to the spot with fear. Lit by the light Daz was holding in his other hand, I could see every line on the faces of the infected as they howled, mouths open, saliva dripping from their teeth. Up close, I could see they weren't as badly injured as I'd first thought; their hair and clothes were singed, but their skin was mostly blackened rather than burnt. As they scrabbled against the hull, their fingers drummed against the plastic, leaving dark streaks on the white paintwork. I turned my attention back to untying the second boathook, eager to have it free in case any of them made it on board.

There was a shout and I looked up to see the first infected had managed to grasp on to the guard rail and had pulled its upper body onto the deck. Daz was standing motionless, staring at it, but Claire had run forward and grabbed the boathook from him. She swung it hard at the infected, connecting with its head with a sickening thump. As she swung again, it took its hand off the rail and lunged towards her. She hit it hard across its neck and it slipped over the side; a splash telling me it had dropped into the water.

By then, the next had both hands on the deck and was hauling itself upwards. As Claire stepped forward to swing at it, Sophie appeared in the cockpit. 'Mum, what's going on?'

Claire turned, taking her eyes off the infected. 'Get back inside!'

Sophie craned her neck, trying to get a better view of what was happening, unaware of the danger we were in. 'But what's going on?'

'Inside, now!'

'But, Mum!'

'NOW!' Claire bellowed and Sophie disappeared down the companionway just as the third infected reached through the guard rail and grabbed Claire's leg with its one good arm. She yelled and tried to step backwards, losing her footing on the slippery deck. She landed on her back with a crash, but her attacker refused to let go. Instead, it started pulling her towards the edge of the boat, gnashing its teeth with anticipation. Claire's cry finally roused Daz and he leapt into action, latching onto one of Claire's arms, but it wasn't enough to stop her being dragged across the deck. Suddenly, there was a shout and Sophie appeared beside Daz, grabbing Claire's other arm, and together they were able to stop the infected pulling her any closer to its waiting mouth.

'Sophie, get back inside!' Claire shouted, but Sophie remained where she was, hanging onto her mother's arm with all her strength. 'No!'

'Sophie, it's too dangerous for you to be out here!'

'Mum, I'm not losing you, too; not after Jake; not after Dad.' Sophie was blinking rapidly, doing her best to hold back the tears that were threatening to overwhelm her. 'You're all I've got left. I can't lose you, too.'

Before Claire could reply, I heard a sound behind me and turned to find the second infected had made it onto the boat. It leapt towards me, its face contorted with anger and rage. I swung my boathook, catching it in the chest and sending it staggering backwards, but within a second it was attacking again; lips pulled back; teeth bared; blackened, grasping hands reaching towards me. I swung the boathook once more, this time aiming for its head. There was a sharp crack as my hit found its mark, sending the infected spinning onto the deck. At first I thought I might have broken the boathook, but as the infected scrambled around, trying to get back to its feet, I could see the noise hadn't come from my makeshift weapon. Instead, it had been the sound of my attacker's jaw breaking, and the left side now hung uselessly from its skull.

I advanced, hitting it over the head again and again until it finally stopped moving. Leaving it there, I ran back to where Claire was still being pulled one way by the infected and another by Daz and Sophie. I stamped on the infected's arm, hearing bones shatter beneath my boot. Still it held on, its grip like a vice. I leant over the guard rail and brought the boathook down hard on the top of its head, smashing it in two. Only then did it finally let go and Claire was able to scramble back to her feet. I ran my eyes over her. 'Are you hurt? Did it scratch you?'

Claire pushed up her trouser leg and I grabbed the spotlight from Daz and shone it on to her calf: it was badly bruised, but the skin was unbroken. I breathed a sigh of relief. 'That was close.'

'Way too close.' She turned to Daz and Sophie. 'Thanks. I don't know what would have happened if it wasn't for you two.'

Sophie wiped her face and threw herself at her mother, hugging her tightly, but Daz wasn't paying attention. Instead, he was pointing upstream into the darkness, his hand shaking with fear. 'There's another one coming!'

I scanned the water ahead of the boat with the spotlight; sure enough there was another infected floating towards us. This one was half-submerged and clinging to the smouldering trunk of a large tree. 'I think we'll be okay with that one. I don't think it's going to come near us.'

I cast the spotlight wider and further ahead; the debris was now coming thick and fast, and almost everywhere amongst it I could see the movements of infected, clinging to anything they'd managed to get a hold of.

'We need to get away from here.' I glanced up at the sky. 'With the city on fire, this is about as dark as it's going to get. I think we should try to get under the bridge again. D'you agree?'

The others nodded.

'Daz, go and start the engine. Claire, come with me

and help me pull up the anchor. Sophie, take the spotlight and keep moving it around. Yell out if you see any getting too close.'

Daz ran back towards the cockpit, but before he got there he stopped and nodded towards the body of the infected. 'Ben, what're we goin' to do with that?'

'Use the boathook; push it over the side. Whatever you do, don't touch it.'

As we approached the bridge for the second time, we could hear machine gunfire.

Daz hunched down nervously, ready to throw himself to the deck in an instant. 'Are they firin' at us?'

'I don't think so, look.' I pointed to where two large beams of light were sweeping back and forth across the water. All along the bridge, men were firing straight down, shooting at any infected they could see passing beneath; they were hitting some, but there were too many for the soldiers to be able to get them all and some still moved in the water after they had passed under the bridge.

'I bet they didn't think about that when they decided to bomb the city.' Claire spat cynically. 'I wonder when they'll realise it hasn't worked; that there are still infected out there? All they've done is drive them past their "ring of steel".'

I shielded my eyes as one of the spotlights swept away from the bridge and caught us in its beam. 'That's the least of our worries.'

Moments later, the deep rattle of the large machine gun started again. The bullets from it slammed into the water straight ahead of us in a tight cluster.

'Fuck!' I whipped the wheel to the right until we were heading upstream once more, trying desperately to avoid hitting any of the debris floating down towards us.

'Should we try again?' Daz peered into the darkness behind us, where the spotlight had returned to scanning the waters below the bridge.

'I don't think they're ever going to let us pass, not if they see us.' Claire was right. It seemed there was no way they would let us under the bridge if they saw us, and it seemed there was no way we could get past without being seen. We were trapped between the bridge and the remains of the city. To the east, flames still rose high into the air; above them, the sky was jet-black; not a single star was visible. As I watched, lightning flashed across the sky; the rumble of the thunder arrived a fraction of a second later.

Sophie stuck her head out of the cabin where she'd been keeping an eye on Tom, spooked by the unexpected noise. 'What was that?'

I wrestled with the wheel as I answered. 'Nothing to worry about, just a thunderstorm. How's he doing?'

'He's still the same; just lying there.' She turned to Claire, her forehead creased with concern. 'Is he ever going to get better?'

Claire glanced at me and then back to Sophie, 'I don't know, honey. I hope so, but I can't tell how badly he's hurt, not without taking an X-ray or an MRI scan.'

I stared ahead, trying not to let the worry show on my face. Sometimes, it felt like I'd known Tom all of my life, and now I'd lost everything else, I couldn't face losing him, too.

There was another flash, followed immediately by a crash that reverberated through the boat. Sophie flinched and disappeared back into the cabin.

'It's getting closer. I'd better go down. Sophie's never

been good with thunder.' Claire climbed down into the cabin leaving me and Daz in the cockpit.

Daz frowned. 'How come there's lightnin' all of a sudden? There wasn't a cloud in the sky earlier.'

I looked up. 'A fire that big starts to make its own weather. All that soot and ash in the air helps the clouds form and the heat gives it all energy.'

There was an almighty flash of light and then a crashing *boom* that I felt deep in my chest. 'The storm's drifting over us; it's going to get wet up here. Daz, if you go down below you'll find some waterproofs under the bunk in the front cabin. Get one for yourself and then bring one up for me.'

Daz got back just as the rain started to fall in earnest, but it wasn't normal rain: it was black and oily, and it clung to us rather than running off onto the deck. Whenever we moved, it slithered down our necks and worked its way up our sleeves, staining our faces and our clothes. With it, came fierce gusts that pushed and pummelled the boat, meaning I had to fight to keep it pointing in the right direction. I adjusted the throttle so that we weren't really going anywhere, just holding our position against the current. Around us, the waters were thick with burnt and melted debris. The smaller pieces weren't much of a problem, but I had to keep an eye out for larger ones and move out of their way if it looked like they might hit us.

With the detritus from the ruined city, came infected; some were so badly injured, they could barely move; others were almost unharmed. I wondered how this had happened: whether it was just the way the bombs had fallen or whether some had been shielded from the blasts while others hadn't.

Suddenly, a blackened and blistered hand, the tips of its fingers missing, appeared over the side of the boat.

'Daz, boathook.'

Daz grabbed his weapon and ran forward; there was a sickening crunch as he made contact, but it took several blows before the infected finally let go.

'Daz. There!' I pointed to the other side where another hand had appeared over the gunnels. Daz ran across, barely managing to keep his footing on the increasingly slippery deck, and laid into the new infected. Even as he did, more grasping hands were appearing out of the darkness that surrounded us. With Daz already busy, I let go of the wheel, grabbed the other boathook and ran forward, but before I could get there, the boat struck something in the water, the impact sending me spilling onto the deck. I struggled back to my feet, looking around desperately for my boathook, but it had skidded beyond my reach. With no time to retrieve it, I kicked out hard at a badly scorched head which appeared between the guard rails, sending it spinning into the river. I just had time to see it disappear in a swirl of inky black water before the boat juddered again as we hit yet more of the wreckage. I picked up my boathook and looked round to find Daz was back on the right side of the boat, bringing his makeshift weapon down onto the head of yet another infected, while Claire and Sophie had emerged from the cabin.

Sprinting unsteadily back to the cockpit, I threw the boathook to Claire and went back to the wheel. Claire immediately ran forward and joined Daz as he fended off the ever-increasing number of infected trying to get on board. Ahead, I saw the burned-out remains of a large boat drifting directly towards us. I turned the wheel to the left, trying to keep the movements smooth enough to avoid sending Daz or Claire over the side, and missed the wreckage by a matter of inches. Knowing we'd just got very lucky, I turned to Sophie. 'Take the spotlight and go up to the bow. I need you to keep it shining forward and shout if it looks like we're going to hit anything.'

'Okay.' Sophie, her wet hair plastered to the side of her face, trembled with fear as she tentatively made her way past where Daz was striking out at yet another attacker. As the lightning flashed again, illuminating Daz and Claire as they kept up their assault on any infected who tried to haul themselves on board, I wondered how long we could continue to hold them back. If it was just the storm, or the debris, or the infected, we could probably deal with it, but all three at once was just too much. We wouldn't be able to rest, not for a second, and we couldn't carry on like that for long.

Chapter Six

By dawn, the fires where Glasgow had once stood were beginning to subside and the storm had passed. We'd made it through the night, but we were exhausted. The infected had attacked us relentlessly, latching onto the boat as they were swept past us by the flow of the river. There were so many of them in the water that no matter how hard I tried, it was impossible to avoid them all. None had got on board, but only because we'd been constantly on guard against them. Now the sun was rising, we could see more clearly what was going on around us, and this made it easier to keep well away from any debris which had infected clinging to it. It helped that the wreckage was beginning to thin out, too, and finally I felt we could start to relax.

Suddenly, the engine spluttered and died. I checked the fuel gauge: we were out of diesel. There was no wind, so the sails were useless, and we began to drift slowly along with all the other flotsam and jetsam that surrounded us, towards the bridge.

Claire shouted back from her position on the left hand side of the boat. 'Why've you turned the engine off?'

'I didn't. We're out of fuel,' I called back.

Claire frowned. 'So what happens now?'

'The current will carry us down to the bridge, whether we like it or not; there's nothing we can do about it.'

'Can we no' drop the anchor?' Daz was making his way towards the cockpit along the other side.

'If we do that, we won't be able to move out of the way if anything big comes towards us, and we'd risk getting holed. If that happens, we'll end up in the water and we won't last long in there.'

'But what about the soldiers?' Sophie's voice trembled with fear.

I stared grimly downstream. 'We're just going to have to take our chances.'

We waited nervously as the bridge slowly grew larger, but Daz was the first to spot that things were different this time. 'Somethin's wrong.'

I shaded my eyes with my hand as I looked up at it. 'What d'you mean?'

'Last time, the soldiers were strung out along it; now they're all crowded in the middle.'

Sure enough, the men were huddled in the centre of the bridge and their vehicles had been rearranged to form barriers across it. They started firing; not at us, not into the water, but along the bridge itself. It took a moment to work out what they were shooting at, then I saw them, the infected, swarming onto the bridge from both ends.

Daz gazed upwards. 'The fire must've driven them out of the city.'

'The law of unintended consequences!' Claire snorted. 'Bet that was another part of their plan they didn't think through properly.'

'Claire, this isn't the time or the place for that.' I pointed to the bridge. 'Not when people are dying up there.'

Claire opened her mouth to say something, but thought better of it and remained silent. As we drifted closer, I watched the infected descend on the soldiers, clambering over their makeshift barricades and weaving between the vehicles. No matter how fast the soldiers fired, it made no difference; more infected simply replaced those that fell. As the bridge passed directly overhead, we could no longer see what was happening, but we could hear the guns, and the shouts and screams of the terrified soldiers high above us as they fought for their lives. Rather than face the inevitable, some chose to leap, but from that height they might as well have been landing on concrete and we heard them hit the water with a deep, bone-shattering smack as they disappeared from sight. Few resurfaced, but those that did were so badly broken that they were barely recognisable as something which had once been human.

By the time we reached the far side of the bridge, the battle was over, and the only movements were from the infected feeding on the bodies of those they'd killed. Despite their training and their weapons, it had taken less than five minutes for the soldiers to be decimated. There must have been several hundred of them there, and now they were all dead. If they couldn't hold off the infected, what hope did we have?

Once clear of the bridge, we did our best to clean the boat. The detritus from the city had been carried out to sea by the flow of the river and it had returned to its usual state. We sloshed buckets of water across the deck and scrubbed until the worst of the oily grime which coated every surface had been removed. Yet it remained grubby in comparison to the pristine white it had been before. Then we turned our attention to ourselves: we were as dirty as the boat, our clothes, even through waterproof jackets, were caked with the fallout from the bombs and stained with blood from the infected; our faces and hands were smeared with the greasy, sticky ash.

Making sure there were no infected nearby, we removed our waterproofs and took turns to drop into the river, finding the cold, clear water refreshing after the long, sleepless night. It quickly became obvious that while we could clean ourselves, our clothes were beyond saving and that the best option would be to discard them altogether. This wasn't a problem for me, but the others were faced with having to make do with the limited range of clothes in my wardrobe. Daz faired best, since we were closest in size, and Claire somehow managed to still look smart, even dressed in slightly oversized men's clothes. Sophie came out worst, being swamped by the shirt and jeans Claire picked out for her. Claire rolled up the legs and sleeves, and tied the front of the shirt in a knot: it improved the fit, but I could tell it was far from Sophie's usual style. She stood in the middle of the saloon, her arms held out to the side, glaring at Claire. 'I look like a scarecrow!'

Claire took a step backwards. 'It's not that bad.'

'I want my own clothes back!' Sophie yelled in response.

'You can't; they're just too dirty.'

'Can't we clean them?'

'Sophie,' Claire ran her fingers through her still damp hair, exasperated by her daughter's outburst, 'this is a boat; it doesn't have a washing machine. These clothes are your only option; you'll just need to make the best of it.'

Sophie said nothing. Instead, she turned and stormed off into the forward cabin.

As the morning wore on, the wind started to pick up, meaning we could finally use the sails. Claire stayed below with Tom, who remained unconscious, while Sophie and Daz helped me on deck. I showed them how to undo the sail ties and raise the larger main sail in the middle of the boat, then the smaller mizzen sail at the back. Sophie's strop over having to wear my clothes had passed, and having dug around, she'd found an old woollen jumper to cover the shirt. She was now making the most of it, pulling the sleeves down over her hands to keep them warm as she moved around the boat.

Once the sails were up, I demonstrated how to use the winches to crank them tight. Then I showed them how to unfurl the triangular jib at the front of the boat, and use the sheets to set it in the right position.

Both Daz and Sophie seemed to enjoy the challenge of learning how to do something new, and I guessed it took their mind off the events of the last twenty-four hours. I glanced at my watch just to double-check; I couldn't believe that only eighteen hours ago I'd been sitting on the steps at the top of Buchanan Street, watching the people go by. Now Glasgow was gone, and I couldn't see how anyone would be able to stop the rest of the country going the same way.

After teaching them the basics, I showed Daz and Sophie how to steer the boat under sail. Mostly it was about setting them just right so that it went in the direction you wanted it to, with little need to touch the wheel. By the time I disappeared into the cabin to get some food, they were taking turns, using the wake to judge who could steer the straightest course. To be honest, neither of them was doing particularly well, but they weren't doing too badly considering they'd been on the boat for less than a day.

Down in the cabin, I went over to where Claire was changing the dressings on Tom's wounds. She turned to me. 'I wish I had something better than gin to keep these sterile. I really don't want him getting an infection on top of everything else.'

I rubbed my chin nervously, feeling the roughness of

fresh stubble. 'How's he doing?'

'Really well,' Claire applied a new dressing to Tom's shoulder, 'apart from the fact he's still unconscious.'

I watched Claire as she worked. 'No sign of him coming round?'

'No.' Claire sounded glum. 'I'm beginning to wonder if that head wound is worse than I originally thought.'

'How much worse?'

'I really don't know, but worst case, he might be bleeding into his brain. If that's happening ...' Claire's voice faded out.

I stared down at Tom. He was someone who was usually filled with energy and life; always on the move: it was unnerving to see him lying so still. 'Is there anything we can do to try to help him wake up?'

'Not really; not without knowing exactly what the problem is. We've just got to wait and see.' Claire adjusted the position of the tube which snaked from Tom's chest. 'Have you seen the news this morning?'

'No, not yet. Anything positive?'

Claire picked up the remote and switch on the television. 'Judge for yourself.'

On the screen, a newsreader sat, stone-faced, behind a desk, shuffling through his papers as if he was searching for something. Eventually he found it, but he seemed to have to read it twice before he was ready to speak. He cleared his voice and began, 'This is the latest update we have. Er ...' He scanned his notes again. 'It seems that last night's attempt to eliminate the HRV outbreak in Glasgow has failed.'

Claire stood up. '"Eliminate the outbreak"? That's a great euphemism for killing half a million people. They're being careful not to say what they did; not a single mention of them bombing the whole city back to the Stone Age.'

I ignored her and kept my attention focussed on the television, but I couldn't help thinking that she was right.

'The virus has now moved beyond Glasgow and into the surrounding areas. General McDonald has announced a new strategy to try to contain the outbreak and limit its spread. Rather than trying to set up a cordon around the infected areas, they have established two lines of defence: one to the south along a range of hills known locally as the Southern Uplands; and another to the north. Naval blockades have also been set up in the Firth of Forth and the Firth of Clyde to prevent anyone infected with the virus from getting out.

'Meanwhile, the Prime Minister has been meeting with other European leaders and NATO commanders to discuss what needs to be done. In a statement released earlier today, he stressed that every effort is being made first to contain the outbreak and then to eliminate it.

'In related news, the outbreak of HRV which started in Miami two days ago is spreading rapidly across the US. Since the State and Federal Governments didn't initially realise the events in the city had been triggered by the virus, they only began to try to contain the outbreak yesterday. These belated attempts seem to have failed and there are reports of other major outbreaks in Atlanta and South Carolina. It's still not clear if the outbreaks in Miami and Glasgow are related, but it seems that a transatlantic flight between the two cities landed just a few hours before the HRV outbreak started in Glasgow, suggesting a link between the two. As a precaution, all commercial flights across the world have been grounded until further notice. However, there are already as yet unconfirmed reports of similar outbreaks in other cities as far apart as Rio, Hong Kong and ...'

I'd seen enough, and I turned off the television. The Government and the army had been more than ready to sacrifice Glasgow to try to stop the outbreak, and now it seemed they were willing to do the same with most of the remaining population of Scotland. There must be close to four million people living between the two defensive lines which had been set up, and it seemed there would be no way for anyone caught between them to get out. That meant there'd be no way to avoid the infection.

Suddenly, Tom moaned, moving for the first time since we'd been knocked down by the bomb blast. Claire sat down on the bench beside him. 'Hey, how're you feeling?'

Tom licked his lips. 'Where am I?'

Claire put the back of her hand on his forehead. 'We're on Ben's boat.' She lifted up his wrist and felt his pulse. 'Do you remember?'

Tom opened and closed his mouth slowly. 'Yeah.' His eyelids drooped and then closed. 'It's the virus, isn't it? We were trying to outrun it.' He opened his eyes and looked at me blearily. 'Did we get away?'

'Yeah, we got away.' I smiled at him, glad he was finally awake. 'At least, for the moment.'

'So what happened?' Tom made a feeble attempt to sit up, but Claire put a firm hand on his chest, holding him down. He didn't seem to have the strength to fight it. He cleared his throat and winced in pain. 'I remember watching the bombs come down ... then ...' A look of concentration spread across his face; after a few seconds he gave up. 'Then it all gets a little hazy.'

I folded my arms, thinking back to the night before. 'The last one landed a bit too close. We got hit pretty hard, but we made it through in one piece; more or less.' I pointed to his chest.

Tom glanced down and saw the tube coming out of his chest for the first time. 'What the hell's that all about?'

Claire walked over to the galley and filled a glass with water. 'You fractured a rib and it punctured your lung.' She went back to Tom and held his head up as he took a sip. 'I needed to drain the air out.'

Tom blinked slowly. 'I don't remember.'

Claire put the glass down beside him. 'You'll have lost your short-term memory when you got knocked out.' She put her hand on his forehead again, trying to judge his temperature. 'It's not unusual.'

Tom tried to sit up again and this time Claire let him, but he only made it halfway before the pain got too much and he slumped back onto the seat. He closed his eyes. 'My shoulder hurts.'

'I'm not surprised. You dislocated it.' Claire offered him another sip of water, but he batted the glass away.

'Did I?' With that Tom drifted off again.

I leant forward, concerned. 'Is that okay?'

'Yes, I think he'll be fine. He'll just need to rest.' The relief was clear in Claire's voice. 'Although I'm not looking forward to removing that tube and sewing up the incision without any anaesthetic; It's going to hurt like hell.'

'What's for supper? I'm starving.' Tom was properly awake now, his eyes following me keenly as I rummaged through the cupboards. As usual, there had only been me on the boat on the run up from the Canaries and I'd expected to be able to pick up more supplies while I was in Glasgow. This meant I didn't have much left on board, and certainly not enough to feed five people for any length of time.

Daz, Claire and Sophie sat around the table with Tom, all looking at me expectantly. We'd dropped the sails and were drifting with the current somewhere between the town of Largs on the mainland and the island of Cumbrae, which lay off to the west.

'Not much.' I inspected the contents of the last food cupboard I'd searched. 'All I've got is a couple of cans of baked beans and a packet of supernoodles.' I turned to the others apologetically, 'I meant to pick up some supplies yesterday, but I never got the chance.'

'Hey, food's food, isn't it?' Daz looked round, grinning, but he saw he was getting little support from the others.

'Well, it's all we've got, so it'll have to do, whether you like it or not.' I turned back to the cupboard and emptied it.

***

The following morning we lay off Brodick, a small ferry port on the island of Arran, and contemplated the shore. We needed supplies and we needed fuel, but we couldn't be certain if it was safe to go ashore. I hoped the islands out in the Firth might be safer than the mainland, but I had no way of knowing whether or not this was true. The news on the television wasn't much use. It was now filled with what amounted to little more than propaganda, and none of it seemed to match with our own experiences.

They still hadn't mentioned what had happened to Glasgow and they were still pretending that the best chance people in the infected zone had was to stay inside and keep themselves to themselves. I felt sorry for those who believed them: given what we'd seen so far, I figured that since they'd been abandoned by almost everyone, there was little hope for them. I just hoped they didn't realise it, not yet at any rate; I wanted them to live the briefness that would be the rest of their lives in hope. We knew the real situation, but at least with the boat it seemed like we had a way out. There was still talk of a naval blockade on the Firth, but we'd seen no evidence of it yet.

Brodick was little more than a cluster of shops, cottages and other buildings, but it offered the possibility of supplies close to the shore. It seemed likely that the ferries, which were its only connection to the mainland, would have stopped running before the outbreak reached the nearest mainland port, and it was possible that the infected which had been swept down the river after Glasgow was bombed hadn't made it this far before they finally drowned. I surveyed the land: nothing moved, but smoke circled up lazily from a couple of chimneys, meaning there was still life in the small community.

I dropped the anchor, and Daz and I set to work inflating the dinghy and fitting the engine. Once we had it in the water, we climbed in and puttered towards the shore. Soon, we were alongside the harbour walls and I tied the dinghy to a rusting iron ladder before we climbed up and onto the quay. Daz looked around. 'What now?'

'There's a shop up there,' I pointed to a small, white-washed building with boards advertising various newspapers on either side of the door, 'I guess we should try there first.'

As we walked along the dock, I surveyed my surroundings, worried about what we might find, but with the exception of the gulls which wheeled and circled overhead, everything remained still. When we reached the shop, we found it was closed. Daz was rattling the shutters, trying to judge how easy it would be to break in, when there was an explosion and the shop's window disintegrated in front of us. I spun round to find two men standing in the middle of the street, each armed with a shotgun.

I called out to them. 'Hey, don't shoot, we're okay. We're just looking for some food.'

The man on the right raised his gun and I saw his finger shift onto the trigger. 'Daz. Run!'

We sprinted for the dock as the man fired again, sending splinters flying from the door where we'd been standing just moments before. Back at the ladder, Daz climbed down first and I quickly followed, glancing back at the two men; they were now standing at the entrance of the quay, shotguns resting in the crooks of their arms: it seemed they weren't out to kill us, just to drive us away, and it had certainly worked. I jumped the last few feet into the dinghy, landing in it with a loud *whop*. I steadied myself before untying it, annoyed and a little worried that we were heading back to the boat with nothing to show for our efforts.

'They tried to kill you?' Sophie was shocked by Daz's retelling of the events on shore.

'I don't think they really meant to hurt us.' I was trying to bring a sense of calm back to the boat. 'I think they were just warning shots'

'Warnin' shots? Any closer an' they'd have blown our bloody heads off!'

'Daz, you're exaggerating.'

'Am no'!'

'Either way, why were they shooting at you?' Tom had raised himself slowly and painfully into a sitting position.

'I'm guessing it's because we're strangers.' I leant back against the cooker in the galley. 'They were probably worried we'd bring the disease to the island. Most likely they were just trying to keep themselves safe.'

Tom shrugged. 'I suppose you can't really blame them.'

'No, I guess not,' Claire stood up and paced around the cabin, 'but we still don't have any food.' There was a note of concern in her voice.

Looking at the clock, I realised it would be low tide in a couple of hours. 'I think I know where we can get some, but it's probably best if we move down the coast a bit first. We don't want to run into those men again.'

'Where?' Daz's stomach rumbled loudly as he spoke.

'You'll see.' I climbed up into the cockpit, leaving the others buzzing with curiosity about my plan.

A couple of miles down the coast, I found a section of uninhabited, rocky beach and dropped the anchor again.

Daz scanned the shore with the binoculars and then turned to me with a confused look on his face, 'Why're we stoppin' here? There're no shops,' he scanned the land again, 'or anythin'.'

I patted him on the shoulder as I passed him to ready the dinghy for going ashore. 'Not all food comes from shops, Daz.'

'What d'you mean?' He asked quizzically.

I took a bucket out of a deck locker and threw it into the dinghy. 'You ever watch Ray Mears?'

'Yeah,' Daz answered slowly, trying to work out where I was going with this.

'Well then, you should know there's plenty of food out there, if you know where to look for it.'

'What sort of food?' Sophie had come up behind us.

I smiled at her. 'Come with us and you can see for yourself.'

I climbed into the dinghy, followed by Sophie and then Daz, while Claire stayed behind with Tom. A minute later, the rubber dinghy was bumping onto the rocky shore and we were getting out. Together, Daz and I lifted the dinghy just beyond the water's edge, then I set to work showing the two youngsters where we could find things we could eat. 'There are limpets attached to the rocks, and mussels and periwinkles, too.'

Daz was confused. 'What the hell's a periwinkle?'

I pointed to the small black shells covering the rocks.

He scowled. 'But they look like snails!'

I laughed. 'They *are* snails.'

'I'm no' eatin' snails!' Daz sneered disgustedly.

'They're not as bad as you'd think, you know,' Sophie shot back. 'I had some once when we were on holiday in France. They're a bit rubbery, but they're okay. Jake didn't like them, though, they made him sick.' She stopped suddenly and looked down at her feet. Daz put an arm round her shoulders and hugged her tightly. After a few seconds, she broke away, wiping her eyes and sniffing, trying to hide how upset she was.

Daz tried to stop her moving away. 'It's okay to miss him.'

Sophie shook Daz off and, drying her face on the sleeve of the outsized jumper she was wearing, she turned her attention to the rocks, picking off the periwinkles and mussels before dropping them into the bucket.

Reckoning the best thing would be to leave her to it for the time being, I turned to Daz. 'There are other things we can eat here, too. See this green stuff? That's called sea lettuce and it's edible. And if you turn over rocks and pull back the seaweed, there'll be crabs and butterfish under there.'

This piqued Sophie's interest. 'What's a butterfish?'

'Here, I'll show you.' I leant down and shifted a large handful of seaweed, revealing the rocks underneath. Everywhere there was movement as the sea creatures which had been hiding beneath it skittered away from the unexpected burst of light. I picked up a small crab and dropped it into the bucket, before scooping up some eel-like fish about the size of my index finger which were flapping around between the rocks. I held them out to Sophie and Daz. 'These are butterfish. They're small, but they're really tasty when you fry them up.' I dropped them into the bucket and moved on to the next patch of seaweed.

Over the next half-hour, we moved slowly along the shore, spread out in a rough line, picking up more butterfish, crabs, mussels and periwinkles as we went. Suddenly, there was a shriek from my left; I turned to see Sophie stumble backwards and trip over a rock, sending her spilling onto the ground. Daz and I sprinted over to her.

I was the first to reach her. 'What happened?'

'Look!' Sophie pointed at what I'd presumed was a log. Examining it closer, I saw it was a blackened body: the skin burned from the skull and the features charred beyond recognition.

'Fuck!' Daz had arrived and was staring at the remains. 'Where d'you think *that* came from?'

I helped Sophie to her feet. 'I guess it must have floated down the river.'

'Hey, someone's comin'!' Daz was looking along the beach to where a figure was moving towards us. 'It doesn't look like they've got a gun or anythin'. Maybe they've got some real food they could give us.'

Daz waved and called out, but the figure didn't answer; it just started moving faster. That was when it hit me: if a dead body had been washed up here, then it was possible that some of the still-living infected we'd seen clinging to debris from the devastated city had also ended up on the same beach.

'Quick, back to the boat!' I grabbed the bucket and pulled Sophie after me as I stumbled as fast as I could over the uneven shore.

Daz stayed where he was. 'But what about them givin' us some food?'

I called out to him. 'Daz, I don't think that's a person … at least not anymore.'

Daz stared at the approaching figure. 'How d'you know?'

I shouted back. 'It's the way it's moving; it's just not right. Just trust me and get going.'

Sophie and I were almost at the dinghy, but Daz was still watching the figure. As it neared, it was increasing its speed, moving over the slippery rocks faster than seemed safe, and certainly faster than any thinking person would move.

'Daz, come on!' Sophie implored him.

He finally turned and ran after us. I dropped the bucket into the dinghy and started to man-handle it back into the water. A second later, Daz joined me. The tide had dropped further while we'd been on the shore and it was now a good ten feet from the water's edge. As we lifted the dinghy over the rocks, I looked over my shoulder and saw the figure was closing rapidly. 'Come on, Daz, put your back into it!'

'I'm goin' as fast as I can!' As he spoke, Daz slipped on

a clump of seaweed, dropping the dinghy and falling onto the rocks. I glanced back at the figure: it was no more than forty feet away and at the speed it was going, it would be on us in seconds. Daz scrambled back to his feet and started to lift the dinghy again. A few feet further on and he stumbled again. The infected was now close enough that I could hear its feet slapping against the rocks as it sprinted towards us.

Sophie cried out, clearly terrified, 'Ben, do something!'

Realising we'd never get the dinghy into the water before the infected got to us, I started searching for something I could use as a weapon. My eyes settled on the short wooden paddles I kept in the dinghy in case there was a problem with the engine. Pushing Daz and Sophie out of the way, I grabbed the nearest oar and turned just as the infected launched itself towards me, mouth open; face contorted with rage. I swung the paddle, catching it on the side of its head and sending it spinning to the ground. It snarled as it struggled back to its feet and threw itself at Sophie. Daz pulled her out of the way just in time and I hit it again, this time from the side. Again it went down, but only momentarily. It whirled round to face me, what was left of its badly burned clothes flapping in the breeze, and roared. Before it could move, I lashed out, the oar smashing into its left cheek. It tumbled onto the rocks, and I fell on it, hitting it again and again until it finally stopped moving.

As I tried to regain my breath I stared at what remained of the infected. I'd killed some the night Glasgow was bombed, but it had been too dark to see the damage I'd inflicted. Here, in the harsh light of day, I could see every detail: the head no longer looked human; instead, it was little more than a mush of flesh and bone fragments; there was blood everywhere, dripping from its body, running down my arms, spilling on to the rocks and splashed across the side of the dinghy. Even though I knew I'd had to do it, I was revolted by what I'd just done, but before I could react, there was a shout from Daz. 'There's another one!'

I straightened up. Sure enough, a second figure was now fast-approaching, and then a third appeared behind it. I dropped the blood-covered paddle, and Daz and I hurriedly lifted the dinghy the remaining few feet back to the water. The nearest figure was close enough that I could now see it had once been a woman and while the first infected looked like it might have been swept downstream from what was left of Glasgow, this one was too clean and well-dressed to have come from the city, which meant the infection must have reached the island.

Sophie and Daz scrambled into the dinghy as I pushed it away from the shore. When the water was deep enough, I climbed in and started the engine. As we motored back to the yacht, I surveyed the shoreline. There were now five infected converging on the spot where we'd been standing just moments before, pacing around, trying to work out where we'd gone.

'I wonder how they knew we were there.' Sophie was staring back at the beach.

It was Daz that answered. 'It was probably you screamin'.'

'No, it wasn't!' Sophie retorted defensively; then, with less certainty, 'Was it?'

She turned to me for an answer, but I didn't have one; I was too busy thinking about how close we'd come to being attacked and what I'd done in response. It had saved our lives, but it was something I'd never have thought I was capable of and I found it deeply unsettling.

Chapter Seven

Back on the yacht, I showed Sophie and Daz how to cook the sea creatures we'd collected by throwing them into a large frying pan along with some butter, olive oil and a couple of cloves of garlic I'd found in the door of the fridge. The mussels and the periwinkles went in first. As they were cooking, I killed the crabs and removed their legs and claws before tossing them in as well. Lastly, in went the butterfish: they were small enough that I didn't need to worry about gutting them first or removing any bones. Once the mussels had opened and the butterfish had crisped up, I emptied the contents of the pan into a large bowl and set it on the table in the saloon. I passed plates out to the others and we sat down to eat. Daz regarded the food with suspicion and seemed at a loss as to where to start; Sophie didn't seem too keen either.

'Come on, you two, it's just seafood.' Claire spooned a mix of mussels, butterfish and crab claws onto her plate as she spoke. She picked up one of the butterfish and after breaking its head off, she ate the rest in one go. 'You know, this is really quite good.' She eyed me curiously. 'How'd you know about this stuff?'

'I learned it as a kid. When we went on holiday, I'd sneak out in the morning, before anyone else was up, and go down to the beach. I'd collect stuff like this and then make a fire out of driftwood so I could have it for breakfast.'

Sophie was intrigued. 'How old were you?'

I thought back. 'Eleven, maybe twelve.'

'And you were allowed out on your own? Mum won't even let me walk home from school with my friends.'

Claire cracked open a crab claw. 'Things were

different back then.'

'I was allowed out on my own when I was a lot younger than that.' Daz took a tentative bite of one of the butterfish. 'Well, it wasn't so much bein' allowed out; more that my mum was usually so blootered she never really noticed.' Daz stopped suddenly, realising he'd revealed something about himself that he hadn't meant to. His face burned red and he shifted awkwardly in his seat.

I quickly changed the subject. 'How's the food?'

'It's no' bad.' Daz took another small mouthful, 'I didn't think I'd like it, but it's quite tasty really ... as long as you don't think too much about what it is.'

'Spoken like a true gourmet.' Tom laughed and then let out a yelp of pain.

'You need to be careful, Tom.' Claire scooped the inside out of a mussel and popped it into her mouth. 'I think maybe we should take out that chest drain later; it'll make it easier for you to get around, and the sooner you're closed up, the less likely it is you'll get an infection.'

I picked a periwinkle out of its shell. 'We can do it after lunch. It's not like we have anywhere else we need to be.' I looked at Tom. 'That okay with you?'

Tom shrugged. 'Might as well get it over and done with.'

'Okay, I'm not going to lie to you, this is going to hurt, and it's going to hurt a lot. I'd give you some of the gin, but I need what's left to keep everything sterile.' Tom was lying on his back on the floor and Claire was kneeling beside him. Laid out on a nearby towel was the last of her surgical pads, a pair of scissors, Tom's cigarette lighter, and a needle and thread I'd found in the drawer under the chart table.

'Ben, you'll need to hold him down so he doesn't move. Can you come down here and push on his shoulders? Daz, you do the same with his legs. Sophie, I'll need you to pass me things when I ask for them.' Claire looked round. 'Everyone ready?'

We all nodded.

'Here goes.' Claire gradually removed the dressing and started to pull the tube slowly out of Tom's chest. Tom didn't make a sound, but his face contorted and his body writhed in pain.

I glanced at Claire. 'Can't you go any faster?'

'No. It has to be slow and steady, or I'll do even more damage.' She continued to inch the tube backwards until it finally popped free, causing Tom to cry out.

Claire held out her hand. 'Needle and thread, please.'

Sophie passed them to her, and I watched as Claire threaded the needle and then bent it until it was almost at a right angle. Then she took the cigarette lighter and flicked it on, running the flame along the needle before she started to stitch the gaping wound closed. Each time the needle sank into his skin, Tom grimaced. Finally, Claire asked for the scissors and snipped the thread close to Tom's chest: the black stitches contrasting sharply with his pale skin.

'Not exactly my best work, but it'll do.' Claire wiped over the wound with some cotton wool soaked in gin before picking up the surgical pad and taping it in place. 'You can let him go now.'

That evening we sat silently in the cabin catching up on the news. Until we got more fuel, we had no way to recharge the batteries, but we still needed to know what was going on. So, while we still watched the TV, we only had it on for short periods at a time. It seemed the Government — or, as Claire pointed out, more likely the military — was trying to keep a tight control of all the available information, but enough was slipping out that we could see how bad things were getting. People were phoning in locations where they thought they'd seen infected and the news channel was plotting these on a map. The main concentration was still around what was left of Glasgow, but there were others well beyond it and there were several small clusters in Edinburgh, as well as further afield.

The army, it seemed, was in the process of pulling back yet again; this time as far as Hadrian's Wall in the south. Here, they were hastily erecting barriers to keep the infected, and anyone else, from getting past. To the north, they were still trying to keep the disease from spreading, but with no natural features to help slow the movement of people, there was little they could do. There was a short piece of footage showing a group of soldiers desperately trying to stop a large crowd fleeing along the main road to the north, but there were so many of them that the heavily armed men had no chance.

Even when they opened fire, it didn't stop the people pushing forward, forced by the weight of those behind them. Eventually, the soldiers were simply overrun and they pulled back, allowing the crowd to surge past. I don't think the people knew where they were heading and I don't think they cared: they just wanted out. From the grainy footage, you couldn't tell if any of them had been injured by the infected, but if they had, and were yet to turn, they'd carry the disease with them wherever they went.

While the disease remained confined to Scotland, its effects were already being felt elsewhere. There were reports of blackouts and panic-buying of food throughout the country. People in rural villages were setting up their own roadblocks and were stopping others passing through in the belief that this would mean they could keep the disease out. As one of them said, it had worked for the Black Death, so why wouldn't it work this time? Then there were reports of people being set upon and killed because others had mistakenly thought they were infected. It seemed that much of Britain was gradually slipping into anarchy, even though it was still unclear how far the outbreak would spread.

Other countries were facing similar problems. Most of the south-eastern US was now being abandoned to the infected, and it didn't seem like it would be long before the north-eastern states succumbed, and with them would go Washington, Baltimore, New York, Boston and about 200 million people. Further outbreaks were being reported as far apart as Vancouver, Montevideo and Sydney. In some places, it seemed the authorities were having some measure of success in keeping it controlled, but it took just one person who was infected, but had yet to show any symptoms, to slip through and it would flare up again. Both China and Russia were claiming they were free of the disease, but seismologists had detected nuclear explosions emanating from within their borders, suggesting they'd tried a similar approach to the one the British Government had adopted to try to extinguish their own outbreaks.

After fifteen minutes, Claire got up and turned the volume down. 'We need to start thinking about what we're going to do.'

Tom gazed at her blankly. 'What d'you mean?'

'We can't just float around here for the rest of our lives, can we? We need to work out where we can go; where it'll be safe.'

'Surely nowhere will be safe,' Tom retorted. 'This disease seems to be pretty much everywhere.'

'There must be some places that are safer than others, though.' Daz looked round at the rest of us.

'Maybe.' I thought about it for a few seconds. 'If we can get out of the Firth here, there'll be places where we could go to, like the islands off the west coast. There aren't a lot of people up there, and because they're islands, it'll be harder for the infection to reach them.'

Daz cut in. 'But there were infected on the island we were on this mornin'.'

'That's different; they came down the river after the city was bombed. Out on the west coast, the currents move in different directions; they won't carry the infected that far north.'

'I don't know.' Tom stared at the silent television as if waiting for an answer to appear. 'Maybe we'd be better heading south. If the defences at Hadrian's Wall hold, maybe they can keep the infected out. It'd be easier to get food and other things we might need. I mean, where are we going to find anything to eat on some remote little island?'

'That's a good point,' Claire interjected, 'I've not got much faith that they'll be able to keep the infected out, but if they can, we'd have a much better chance down south.'

'Yeah, I suppose you're right.' I glanced at the screen where the headlines were scrolling across the bottom of the picture. 'As long as they can hold the infection at the wall.' Like Claire, I had my doubts on this last point, but it seemed right to hope that it would work.

Daz turned to me. 'How d'we get there?'

'It's pretty straightforward, really. We could be there in a day or so,' I crossed my arms. 'But here's the thing: there's meant to be some sort of naval blockade precisely to stop people doing what we'd need to do. They've mentioned it a couple of times on the news. Given what happened the last time we ran into the military, I don't know what will happen if we run into them again.'

'But if the other option is to stay here, shouldn't we at least give it a go?' Claire's mind seemed set. I turned to Daz, Tom and Sophie. 'What d'you three think?'

Tom was the first to speak. 'I'm with Claire: we should give it a go.'

Next was Daz. 'Yeah, I guess. We can always try somethin' else if we can't get through.'

I turned to Sophie. 'What about you?'

Sophie was slightly nonplussed, not used to being asked for her opinion on such decisions. She looked from me to her mother and then down to the floor. 'Yeah, whatever. I mean, does it really make much difference where we are? Everything's pretty messed up anyway.' She looked up, her eyes glistening. 'Isn't it?'

Claire started to say something, but I held up a hand. 'Sophie, we've got as good a chance as anyone and probably better than most. I'm not saying anything's going to be easy, just that it might be possible.'

Sophie shrugged and leant her head against her mother's arm.

***

'Hey, Sophie, go and see if Tom's up yet.'

Now we had a plan, I was keen to get going as soon as possible. I'd got up at sunrise and, with Daz's help, I'd pulled up the anchor. By the time Claire and Sophie had emerged from the forward cabin, which they'd claimed as their own, we were already under sail and were making good progress. With nothing for breakfast, Sophie and Daz were openly grumpy, while Claire and I tried our best to hide the fact that we felt the same way.

It was just before nine when I spotted another boat; the first we'd seen since leaving Glasgow. As we neared, it became clear that it was just drifting with the wind and the currents, rather than moving under its own power. Tom still hadn't appeared by this point so I sent Sophie down to get him. She reappeared a minute later, looking worried. 'Mum, something's wrong with Tom; he won't wake up.'

'That's not good!' Claire disappeared down the companionway. Leaving Daz to steer the boat, I followed. In the saloon, Tom lay on the couch, his head moving listlessly from side to side as the boat rocked back and forth. Claire put her hand against his forehead and then pulled back the covers. She peeled back the surgical dressing, revealing that the skin around her stitching was red and inflamed.

'Damn!' Claire glanced up at me. 'He's got an infection.'

She opened her medical bag and rummaged through it. After a couple of minutes, she still hadn't found what she was looking for and resorted to emptying its entire contents onto the table before going through each item one by one. After she'd finished, she looked up at me again. 'No antibiotics. I usually carry some, but I must have forgotten to refill my bag last time I ran out. I don't suppose you've any on board, do you?'

'No, nothing like that.'

'In that case, we've got a big problem. I've seen

infections like this before. If we don't get him on antibiotics within the next twenty-four hours, he's unlikely to recover.'

Sophie let out a gasp. 'You mean he's going to die? Mum, there must be something you can do, isn't there?'

'Not without the right medicines.'

I stared down at Tom, and the redness that was radiating out from around the stitches. I couldn't believe he was going to die just because we lacked something as simple as a few pills.

'Ben, are you okay?' Claire was watching me, concerned.

'Yeah.' I swallowed. 'I'll be okay.'

Sophie's brow furrowed. 'Is there anywhere we can get some antibiotics?'

I slumped dejectedly onto the seat opposite Tom. 'Not without going ashore, and it would need to be in a town somewhere, which would be too dangerous. We almost got killed yesterday when we were on an empty beach. In a town, there are going to be infected everywhere.' I looked across and saw Sophie's bottom lip was trembling. 'Sorry, I didn't mean to upset you.'

'No, it's okay. It's ...' she sniffed, 'I was just thinking about Jake ... and about all my friends: they're all dead, aren't they? It's like I'm the only one left. We all had these great plans, the things we all wanted to do, and now they're all gone, and I'm stuck on this boat. I'm never going to get to do any of it, am I? I mean, this is it; this is my life from now on: sitting here, waiting for the people around me to die.'

As Sophie descended into tears, Claire held her tightly and gently stroked her hair. I left them alone in the saloon and returned to the cockpit, wondering where we could possibly get antibiotics from.

'Is everythin' okay?' Daz enquired.

'No, not really.' My voice sounded flat.

'What's up?'

'Tom's got an infection. Claire reckons if he doesn't get some antibiotics soon, he's probably going to die.'

Daz put his hands behind his head. 'An' Claire's no' got any?'

'No.'

'Where're we goin' to get some from then?'

Looking off into the distance, my eyes fell on the drifting boat: it was now only about 500 yards away, and a thought struck me. I wondered if there might be some antibiotics on board. After all, it wasn't unusual for sailors to keep some in their first-aid kits just in case. Even if there weren't any antibiotics, it was worth checking just to make sure, and there might even be some food we could scavenge.

'We're going to try there.' I took the wheel from Daz and turned it to the right. I readjusted the sails and soon we were converging on it. It was a yacht, about ten feet shorter than ours. It looked in good condition and there was no evidence of any damage. I wondered what had happened to the crew: it wasn't the first time I'd found an unmanned boat drifting around at sea, and it was something most sailors had either encountered or heard stories about. Sometimes you found out what happened; sometimes you didn't; it was just a part of life at sea. The rules were also clear: once a boat became unmanned, it was very much a case of finders keepers.

Getting alongside a drifting yacht while under sail would be difficult, so once we were close enough I chose, instead, to heave to and use the dinghy to ferry myself across. I didn't want to waste what little petrol we had left for the outboard motor, so leaving Daz in charge, I paddled across using the remaining oar. On reaching the drifting boat, I tied the dinghy onto the back and pulled myself on board, taking the oar with me, just in case. The cabin was sealed, but not locked, and I cautiously pushed back the hatch before reaching inside to open the doors.

Suddenly, there was a shout and something moved in the darkness. In a flash, a man in a cheap suit shot up the stairs and lunged towards me. I staggered backwards, tripping over my own feet and falling hard against the wheel. As I fell, the oar slipped from my grasp and skittered across the deck before dropping into the water, leaving me with no way of defending myself. Luckily, the man couldn't seem to work out how to get through the cabin doors and was repeatedly throwing himself at them; snarling and gnashing his teeth. The doors shuddered and shook, and it seemed like they wouldn't hold for long. I scrambled to my feet, glancing around, trying to find something else I could use as a weapon; just then, the wooden doors gave way, finally freeing the man from the cabin. I did the only thing I could think of and dived for the side of the boat, slipping through the guard rail and into the water just as he reached where I'd been standing.

I surfaced, wiping the water from my face; the man stood above me, his face contorted with anger. I stared at him: he was perhaps a couple of years younger than me, hair receding slightly more. His pale blue eyes bored into me, never once blinking, an intense rage burning deep within them. As I swam back to the dinghy, grabbing the oar from where it floated as I passed, he followed my progress along the side of the boat, growling as he paced back and forth. I tossed the oar into the dinghy and pulled myself out of the water before reaching up to untie the rope from the cleat on the deck. The infected man lunged at me again, just missing the tips of my fingers. I jerked my arm away and, with my hands shaking, I decided to untie the other end of the rope from the metal eye on the dinghy instead. Once it was free, I lay back as I drifted away from the yacht, breathing heavily and thinking about what had just happened. It was the second time in two days an infected had almost got me. That was when I realised I'd need to start being a lot more careful. I sat up, and using the oar, I paddled slowly back to the boat where Daz, Claire and Sophie were watching me, shocked expressions on their faces.

Daz helped lift the dinghy back out of the water. 'Man, when he came out of the cabin like that, I was sure you were a goner.'

I straightened up. 'You're not the only one.'

Daz put his hands on his hips. 'How the hell did he get in there?'

'I guess he must have been injured by an infected, but got away and managed to make it to the boat. He probably turned when he was in the cabin and couldn't work out how to get out again.' I shivered, both because I was soaking wet, and because I was reliving how close I'd come to being caught. 'At least until I was stupid enough to open the hatch for him.'

Across on the other boat, the man was still stalking the deck, screaming with frustration and hammering on the roof of the cabin. Daz shielded his eyes with his hand. 'Is there no' a way we can knock him off into the water? That way, you could go back on board an' see if there's any food an' medicine an' that.'

I shook my head. 'No, it would be too dangerous. What if he's not the only one on board?'

Daz gulped. 'I hadn't thought of that.'

'Yeah,' I let out a low sigh. 'This whole survival thing's going to be one hell of a learning curve.'

We left the boat with its infected passenger, and carried on southwards. By six that evening, I could make out the dome of Ailsa Craig in the distance. Once we were past that, we'd be free, but there was something else there, too, which meant this might not be as straightforward as it would otherwise seem: the grey and distinctive outline of a frigate. A dilemma started to form in my mind. I could steer a course which would take us well clear of the warship, meaning we'd finally be free of the Firth of Clyde, or I could steer for it and ask for help. They'd almost certainly have antibiotics on board and they might be willing to give us some, but they would then know we were there and it was unlikely they'd let us past.

Before I could make my mind up either way, the decision was made for me. Two large black rigid-hulled inflatable boats appeared from the general direction of the frigate and it was pretty clear they were heading straight for us. As they neared, I could see that these ribs were about thirty feet long and each had a large calibre machine gun mounted on its bow. I could also see that they were crewed by two teams of heavily armed men. Not knowing what to expect, I sent Daz and Sophie below, but Claire, unwilling to be ordered around, remained alongside me in the cockpit.

I heaved the boat to and waited for them to approach. Soon, there was one on each side, standing about twenty-five yards off, their weapons trained on us.

A loudspeaker mounted on the right-hand rib crackled into life. 'Remain where you are, and state the purpose of your voyage.'

I tried to work out which of them was speaking. 'We're just trying to get to safety.'

The voice boomed out across the water again. 'You're in a controlled zone and you need to stay within it until the situation's resolved.'

'When's that going to be?' Claire shouted back. I shot her an angry look; nothing good could come from provoking them.

'As soon as the outbreak's brought under control.' The voice was stern and authoritative.

Claire was about to say something else when I quickly stopped her.

'What should we do, then?' I waited for a response.

'We've set up a holding area. We'll escort you there. How many do you have on board?'

'There are five of us: four adults and one child.'

'Have you got any medicines?' Claire had stepped forward again. 'We've got someone on board who's badly injured and he needs antibiotics.'

Suddenly, the atmosphere changed; the men stood up straighter and adjusted their guns.

'What sort of injury?' There was an edge to the voice now. 'Were they bitten?'

'No.' I hurriedly explained. 'We were up by the Erskine Bridge when Glasgow was bombed. The explosion knocked us down, and he ended up with a burst lung.' I nodded to my right. 'Claire here's a doctor. She managed to sort it out, but the wound got infected. We need antibiotics or he'll die.'

'What antibiotics d'you need?' The voice was softer now. I ran my eyes over the boat again, and finally spotted the one with the microphone in his hand. He was slightly taller, and a good deal older than the rest, and he was the only one not carrying a machine gun. He was also dressed differently: while the others wore the green berets of Royal Marine Commandos, he was wearing the black and white cap of a senior naval officer. This was an odd combination to have on what was little more than a patrol boat.

Claire responded. 'I'd prefer Doxy, but I'll take anything you've got.'

There was a brief discussion on the rib before one of the men put down his gun, took off his backpack and started rummaging through it. There was another brief discussion before the voice spoke again. 'We've got Amoxicillin and Tetracycline.'

'Tetracycline's close enough.' Claire called back.

The rib manoeuvred slowly towards us until it was within throwing distance. The man lobbed a plastic tub in a gentle arc across the water that separated us from them. Claire caught it with ease. 'Thanks,' she yelled back before turning to me. 'I should go and start him on these right away.' With that, Claire disappeared down the companionway.

Once the rib was back in position, the voice came again. 'If you drop your sails and start your engine, we'll escort you to the holding area.'

'We don't have any fuel. The sails are all we've got.

'Okay, leave them up.' The man's voice sounded resigned: it would undoubtedly be a much slower passage than he'd been hoping for.

Just as the sun was going down, we arrived at the holding area immediately to the north of Ailsa Craig, and within view of the frigate. There were five boats there already:

three sloops; a double-masted ketch, like ours; and a powerboat. They had their anchors set and were tied to each other, side by side, making it easier for the people on the different boats to speak to each other and giving more space to move around. We dropped our anchor, manoeuvred ourselves alongside the one on the nearest end and tied our boat to theirs in a similar fashion.

Once we were in position, one of the ribs roared up and turned sharply, sending a wave crashing against our left side. The men had their weapons slung across their chests, clearly not anticipating trouble. The loudspeaker crackled into life again. 'This is the designated holding area; you're to stay here until we tell you otherwise. If you try to get past the blockade, we won't hesitate to use force to stop you.'

'How long are you going to keep us here?' I yelled back.

There was no reply; they simply shifted the engine into gear and sped off.

'So they got you, too, did they?' I turned to see a man leaning on the guard rail of the neighbouring boat. He spoke with a friendly, northern accent and there was a half-full beer bottle dangling from one hand. 'Where were you headin'?'

'South.' I rubbed the increasingly-long stubble on the side of my face. 'We were trying to get to the other side of Hadrian's Wall.'

'Yeah, that might work.' He took a swig of his beer. 'I was thinkin' St Kilda m'self. Ain't no infection goin' to get there in a hurry. You can live on it, too. People used to you know, right up until the thirties. I need to go get ma family first, though.'

His words were slightly slurred, but given what was

happening to the world, I couldn't really begrudge him a drink or two.

'Nice vessel. Yours?' His eyes lost focus for a moment, then he smiled. 'Or d'you borrow her, like I borrowed mine?'

'No, she's mine.'

'Very nice.' There was a pause as he examined the boat more closely. 'Is that a satellite TV receiver you've got there?'

'Yes.'

'Does it work?' He sounded eager.

'Yes.' I was beginning to wonder where this was going.

Suddenly, he got serious. 'Can I come across an' watch the news for a while? I want to be able to see what's happenin'. I want to see if ma family's safe. They're in Liverpool, staying with ma wife's mother while I've bin away workin' on the rigs. I've bin tryin' to call them all day, but ma mobile phone's not workin'. The news on the radio's just not sayin' anythin'. I need to see pictures.'

'Okay,' I beckoned to him. 'Come on over.'

'Great.' The smile returned to his face. 'I'll bring a couple of beers.'

'It would be better if you could bring some food.' I didn't know whether he'd have any to spare, but I thought there was no harm in asking. 'We've not eaten all day.'

'That's a deal!' He started to go down into his cabin, but then stopped and turned. 'How many of you are there?'

'Five.'

'Right.' He ducked inside and reappeared a couple of minutes later with some cans of soup, a loaf of slightly stale bread and a six pack. Soon, he was climbing over the guard rail and onto our boat; he was halfway into the cabin when he saw Tom and froze.

'What's up with him?' There was a touch of panic in his voice. 'Did he get attacked by one of *them*?'

'No, he just got injured. We got knocked down when they bombed Glasgow.'

His mouth gaped in shock. 'They bombed Glasgow?'

'Yeah, they pretty much incinerated it. I doubt there's much left. There's certainly no one alive.'

'They never mentioned *that* on the radio. They said they were doin' everythin' within their powers to stop the outbreak, but they never said they'd done *that*.'

'What do you think "everything in their powers" meant?' Claire snapped back.

'I don't know.' The man carried on down the ladder. 'I didn't really think about it, but I never thought it meant *that*.'

Before Claire could launch into another attack on the military and their tactics, I cut her off. 'Sorry, I forgot to ask, what's your name?'

The man waved, 'I'm Bob.'

'Bob has kindly brought us some soup in return for us letting him catch up on the news on the television. So if you'd like to join me in the galley, we can get it heated up.'

Daz and Sophie were on their feet almost immediately, and Claire wasn't far behind. Tom was already looking a lot better, but he was still too ill to do little more than sit up.

I called across to him. 'Tom, you want some as well?'

'Yeah,' he shifted his position and winced, 'that'd be great.'

As we ate, we caught up on the latest news. It was only as

I watched Bob as he saw many of the images for the first time that I realised that no matter how shocking they were, we were already becoming immune to them. Infected were now being reported throughout Scotland and it seemed like the attempts to contain them in the north had failed. The defensive line to the south, along Hadrian's Wall, seemed to be holding, but there were persistent rumours of people slipping through: there just weren't enough troops to guard every inch of it.

In the meantime, the military had given up any pretence that the politicians were still in control and had assumed command of the country. They were also continuing to move in on the media and most of the news broadcasts were starting to sound more like public information films than journalism. The main message seemed to be 'Stay inside and stay safe'. An emergency number was being displayed along the bottom of the screen which people could call if they saw any infected, or if they thought they might have become infected themselves. A curfew had been introduced and the army was now patrolling the streets of the major cities alongside the police, halting the slide towards anarchy which had been gaining momentum over the last couple of days. Scotland might have been lost, but at least it seemed like they were managing to maintain some sort of control in the rest of the country. This pleased Bob, and he passed round bottles of beer in celebration. Claire relieved Sophie of the one she'd been given before she could even take a sip and, much to his annoyance, she took Tom's, too, telling him he shouldn't really drink while taking the antibiotics.

Chapter Eight

The following morning, we met the others who were tied up in the holding area; there were seventeen of them in all, and they stopped by in ones and twos to check up on what was happening on the television. Word had clearly got round that we were happy to trade food for news, so when they came, they didn't arrive empty handed and we soon had enough food to last us for several days.

All day the news was improving; it seemed the tide was finally turning, and England and Wales might yet be saved. The military was now running every game in town, including all the television channels. No matter which one we switched to, they all showed the same pictures: some were live; others pre-recorded; all suggested things were being brought under control, and our spirits started to rise.

Only Claire remained sceptical. 'Look, we can't trust what they're saying. They want us to believe they've got it all sorted out; they haven't: they can't have.' She paced back and forth in the cockpit. 'There's no way they can get a grip on this, not this quickly. Look at what's happening elsewhere; if the Americans can't get things under control after Miami, we sure as hell can't after Glasgow. They're just saying what they need to say to keep people off the streets.'

'Oh come on, Claire. Surely you can't really be that paranoid, can you?' Tom was sitting with his back against the cabin watching her. 'Can't you give them the benefit of the doubt, even for a moment or two?'

'You don't know these people; I do. It's what they do. It's their job.' Claire stopped. 'I've seen it before.'

Daz was leaning on the wheel and this caught his attention. 'Where've you seen anythin' like this before?'

Claire gazed into the distance. 'Sierra Leone. Sudan. Rwanda. The Congo. The military always thinks it's doing what's best, even when it's doing the worst.'

I felt the need to interrupt. 'But this is nothing like any of that. This isn't a civil war; it's a disease.'

'It's not the cause that's important; it's the way those with power react when their way of life is threatened.' Claire was staring straight at me. 'You can't understand it until you've seen it.'

I could tell from her eyes she was keeping something back. I wondered if it was because Sophie was listening, but before I got a chance to ask, there was a shout from our left; the large black ribs were approaching, towing an empty wooden rowing boat. In one of the ribs, there were two men dressed not in uniforms, but in civilian clothes. They both looked young — early twenties at the most — and sat huddled together, surrounded by the heavily armed marines.

As they came closer, I could see that one of them had a black eye and was holding his arm delicately. He wasn't the only one who was hurt; one of the marines was sporting a series of ragged scratches across his cheek. Once they were close enough, the naval officer we'd spoken to the previous day hailed us. 'Hey, can you take these guys for us? It's against orders to take anyone back to the frigate and they'll end up dead if we leave them floating around in that.' He pointed to the rowing boat.

'I don't know.' I eyed the two men suspiciously. 'Are they okay?'

'Yes. There was just a bit of, er ... resistance, shall we say, when we tried to pick them up.' He glared at the man with the scratched face who, in turn, was doing his best not to catch anyone's eye. 'They really shouldn't be out here, but it's not like we can take them back to shore. The land's not safe anymore; at least, not around here.'

'I've got plenty of room. They can stay on my boat.' I looked up to see who was speaking. I'd talked to the man earlier in the day, but I couldn't remember his name. He was on his own on a thirty-foot yacht tied up at the other end of the line of boats, but when the ribs had arrived, he'd been sitting on Bob's boat, chatting to us as Bob cooked them some food down below.

The rib with the civilians on board came alongside and the marines helped the two men out and onto our deck. I watched as they moved unsteadily onto the next boat and then followed the man as he led them across to his yacht.

'They look like they've never even been on a boat before.' I turned back to the rib. 'What the hell were they thinking?'

The officer leant on our guard rail. 'I guess they were just trying to survive, and when you're desperate you'll try anything.'

He let go of the guard rail and rubbed his face with his hands, clearly exhausted. 'How's your man doing? The one with the infection.'

'Ask him yourself. He's sitting right there.' I pointed towards Tom.

Tom smiled. 'I'm happy to say, the antibiotics have pretty much got it under control.'

'Good. Here, catch,' He tossed a small package to me. 'A few extra, just in case. I ... eh-em ... liberated them from the ship's doctor.'

'Thanks.' I opened the bag and peeked inside: it contained several bottles full of capsules. 'But won't you get into trouble for this?'

He chuckled. 'Seems unlikely; I'm the first officer.'

I looked at him curiously: it seemed odd that someone so far up the chain of command would be running around in a rib, herding up strays trying to flee by sea.

'I know what you're thinking. It's just that there have been a few *incidents*.' He scowled at the highest-ranking marine, who adjusted his stance and stared back defiantly. The other marines suddenly took an intense interest in their boots in a bid to avoid making eye contact with either man. 'And the Captain thought there'd be a better chance of it not happening again if someone more senior went out on patrol with them.' He took off his cap and ruffled his hair. 'I was happy to volunteer; it's nice to get off the ship now and then, and it's not like we'll be getting shore leave any time soon.' He replaced his cap and adjusted it. 'Anyway, we'll leave those two,' he nodded to where the two men were now sitting on the boat at the far end of our little flotilla, 'in your capable hands.'

As the rib started to leave, there was a shout behind me. 'Wait! I want to speak to you before you go.' I turned to see Bob scrambling up his companionway. 'Hey wait! When're you goin' to let us go? I need to find ma family. Hey! Come back!'

Ignoring him, they left. As the boat disappeared off into the distance, Bob crumpled on to a seat in his cockpit, 'Shit! I don't think they're ever gonna let us get out of here.'

'I don't know about you guys, but I don't plan on staying here for much longer.' I'd finally found out that the name of the man who'd taken the two newcomers onto his boat was Pete, and he was addressing a group of us who'd gathered in the cockpit of Bob's boat; we were doing our best to make a dent in what seemed like an endless supply of beer which he had on board.

Bob opened another bottle and threw the cap into the water. 'What're you goin' to do?'

'One night, when there's no moon up, and it's nice and dark, I'll pull up my anchor and see if I can slip past the blockade.' He sipped the beer he was holding.

Bob pointed his beer bottle at Pete, slopping some of its contents onto the deck. 'You won't stand a chance! I got here before you guys; I saw what it was like before they put that officer on the ribs ... when it was just the marines. There was another boat here, an' it tried to sneak past the blockade on the first night.' He took a slug of beer. 'But they were spotted an' when they caught up with them, they didn't even try to turn them back; they just opened fire. They were pretty much right beside them an' they used the big machine guns, the ones mounted on the ribs themselves. The boat was riddled in seconds an' started sinkin'.'

I thought about how much damage the bullets from the Erskine Bridge had done to our bow, from 500 yards away. Up close, they'd have ripped holes the size of dinner plates in the fibreglass hull of a yacht: they wouldn't have stood a chance.

Bob carried on. 'There were eight of them on board. Some of them made it out of the cabin, but before they could launch their life raft, they were machine-gunned, too. All of them.' Bob's voice started to waver. 'Even the kids.'

The cockpit went quiet as everyone digested this new information. Daz was the first to break the silence. 'How'd they know they were tryin' to sneak past? You know, if it was dark an' all?'

Bob took another slug from his bottle. 'Radar: I'm guessin' that's how they're keeping an eye on us, and how they found us in the first place. I mean, it's the only way one ship could monitor the whole channel. The moment we move, they'll know about it.' He looked towards Pete, 'Even if it's pitch-black.'

I played with my empty beer bottle. 'Maybe we need to start talking to them; make them see us as something more than collateral damage. If they start seeing us as people and not just prisoners, or whatever we are to them, they might start listening to us, giving us some information. Maybe they'll even let us go.'

'That's not going to happen.' Claire took a mouthful of beer. 'Not if they are as trigger-happy as Bob says they are.'

Tom picked up a bottle, and Claire glared at him. He shrugged back at her. 'One beer can't hurt.' He reached for the bottle opener. 'That first officer seems pretty decent. He's already given us antibiotics and he seemed happy enough to talk to us earlier. From what Bob said, he's the one keeping the marines in line. Maybe he's someone we can work with.' There was a slight hiss as he opened his beer and took a swig.

'Maybe.' Bob scratched the side of his head thoughtfully with the top of his beer bottle. 'The only trouble is, they won't answer when we call them on the radio, an' they only come close enough for us to speak to them when they're bringin' new people here. The rest of the time they just watch us from a distance.' He drained his beer and tossed the empty bottle over his head; there was a splash as it landed in the water. 'Wouldn't hurt to give it a go, though, would it?'

'Daz. Lines!'

I'd been woken in the middle of the night by the sound of screaming. Rushing up on deck, I saw a commotion on Pete's boat. I grabbed the spotlight and shone it into the darkness, revealing a horrific scene: Pete was grappling with one of the young men the marines had left with us that afternoon, trying his best to fight him off as the man clawed and tore at his face; blood pouring from the jagged wounds. Pete backed away, trying desperately to escape, but he tripped over a winch, landing heavily between the cockpit and the guard rail. The man fell on him, ripping through his clothes and into his belly, sending long coils of his intestines spilling across the deck and over the side. They hung there, jerking back and forth, smearing blood across the white side of Pete's boat, as the man buried his head into his abdomen, Pete's mouth slowly opened and shut as bloody bubbles emerged from it. Somehow, despite his wounds, he was still alive.

The deck lights of the neighbouring boat came on, flooding the area with light and the young man's head snapped up. As the blood dripped from his face, I could see he had the unmistakeable stare of an infected. He leapt to his feet and lunged at a woman just emerging from the cabin of the next boat. Before she knew it, the infected man was on her, but he didn't attack her for long: people were appearing on the decks of all the boats, distracting him. Back on Pete's boat, the other young man sprang into view and leapt over onto the neighbouring boat where the woman was pulling herself back to her feet; yet he ignored her. The reason for this became clear when her young daughter appeared and was instantly set upon. The girl screamed as her mother pinned her to floor and bit into her neck, sending blood spraying across the cockpit. By this time Daz and Claire were on deck, while Sophie and Tom were coming up from below.

I shouted at Daz again. 'Lines! Now!'

'What d'you mean?' Daz sounded confused.

I yelled at him. 'Get those lines off. Now!'

'Why?' Daz's eyes darted around frantically until they settled on Bob, who was wildly swinging a winch handle at the first infected as it climbed over his guard rail. 'Shit! What d'we do?'

'Untie the lines holding us to the other boats!' I screamed, then changed my mind. 'No. Forget it! We don't have time.' I grabbed the small hatchet I kept strapped to the helm in case I ever had to cut any ropes in a hurry, and leapt forward, slicing through each line in turn. Almost immediately, the currents started to move us away from the other boats, and it was just enough to keep us out of reach of the infected. We watched helplessly as those left alive struggled with the infected, but it was clear they weren't going to win.

Daz shivered with fear. 'What now?'

'I don't know, but we can't stay here.' My eyes drifted across to where the other boats were still tied together, their deck lights shining down, illuminating the scene below: the fighting had stopped and the infected were feeding on those they'd killed; the ones who hadn't died had turned and were feasting alongside them. I could see Bob tearing the flesh from the throat of a teenage boy, leaving a gaping wound. Blood oozed slowly from it, adding to the congealing pools that were already seeping across his deck and soaking deep into the wood.

'Yeah.' Tom shuddered as two of the infected snarled and growled at each other as they fought over the body of a little girl. 'Let's get out of here.'

'What are we going to do about the navy?' For the first time since I'd met her, Claire sounded really scared. 'If we move, they'll think we're trying to get away.'

'We'll just have to explain what happened and hope they understand, but we can't stay here. At the moment, the tide's keeping us away from the other boats, but when it turns, it's going to push us back up against them.' I glanced at my watch, 'and that's going to happen in about ten minutes.'

'But how're we goin' to let them know?' There was concern in Daz's voice.

'I don't know.' If Bob had been right, they wouldn't respond to a radio call. I wondered how else we might be able to alert them, yet every alternative I could come up with required it to be daytime so they could see us. I glanced nervously at the other boats. The infected could sense our presence and some were already pacing along the nearest guard rail, searching the darkness, as they tried to work out where we were. 'But we can't stay here; we need to move away.'

'Are you sure that's goin' to be okay?' Daz shifted back and forth nervously. 'You know, with them navy guys?'

Before I could answer, there was the sound of a distant explosion and a fireball leapt into the night's sky somewhere to our south.

'What the hell's that?' Tom had sprung to his feet and was standing on his tip toes, trying to get a closer look.

'I don't know, but ...' I stopped when a thought

occurred to me. The only thing I'd seen in that direction was the frigate, but surely it couldn't be that, could it? I turned round to find everyone was looking at me, waiting for me to finish what I was saying. I wasn't ready to tell them what I thought: there was no point until I knew whether I was right or not. 'I think we need to go and check that out.'

'What if they catch us?' Sophie was white as a sheet, and clearly terrified, not only by what had just happened, but also by what might happen next.

My eyes returned to the flames leaping high into the distant sky. 'I don't think they will.'

The sun was creeping over the eastern horizon as we neared the source of the explosion. It revealed the frigate, flames leaping high into the air from its bow. At the other end, we could see huddled groups of figures battling each other. The fighting was intense and brutal, and I had little doubt that we were seeing the last of the sailors trying to fight off the advancing infected who had once been their colleagues.

Daz stood beside me, his eyes wide with shock. 'What d'you think happened to it?'

Before I could reply, there was a shout.

'Ben!' Tom was staring not at the frigate, but at a point a short distance ahead of our boat. 'There's something in the water.'

'Where?' I scanned the sea, searching for what he'd seen.

Tom craned his neck, trying to get another glimpse of what he'd seen. 'It seems to have gone.'

'No, I see it, too!' Daz was leaning over the right hand guard rail. 'It looks like there's someone in the water.'

'I can't see them.' I weaved my head from side to side. 'Where exactly?'

'There!' Daz was pointing frantically at the water just ahead of the boat and finally I saw him: a man, his head being kept above the water by the life jacket he was wearing. Yet, something didn't quite seem right.

Claire cried out. 'Quick, we've got to get him on board!'

Daz ran forward to where the man was just coming alongside the boat, with Tom following after. As they were reaching through the guard rails, hanging as far over the side as they could to try to grab the back of his life jacket, two things happened almost instantaneously: first, I realised the man had a deep bite mark on the side of his face; second, he began to thrash frantically just as Daz got a hand on to his shoulder.

'No! Daz, don't!' Too late, I'd finally put two and two together. 'He's infected!'

Tom reacted instantly, struggling to get away from the man's grasping hands, but Daz was slower and the infected marine grabbed onto his outstretched arm. Daz screamed as he started to slip towards the water. I scooped up one of the boathooks and shouted. 'Tom!'

Tom deftly caught the boathook and leant over the side, swinging it wildly from side to side. I heard it make contact with something, and Daz yelped in pain. Tom swung again, this time he must have hit his target because a second later Daz was wriggling his way back onto the deck.

'Fuck, that was close!' He lay there for a moment, his chest heaving as he tried to catch his breath, before pulling back his sleeve and inspecting his arm closely for any sign that he'd been injured by the infected. Once he was satisfied he was unhurt, Daz sat up and looked at Tom, who was still standing over him. 'Thanks. For a minute there, I was sure I wasn't goin' to make it!'

Tom ignored him, and instead slumped on to the top of the cabin, holding his right side, his face contorted with pain. Between his fingers, I could see blood starting to seep through his shirt. Claire must have seen it, too, because she ran forward and helped Tom back to the cockpit, where she started to examine him.

Daz pulled himself to his feet and adjusted his clothes. 'What the hell's goin' on?'

'I think the frigate's been overrun; I think that's why it's on fire. He must have fallen into the water after he was infected; we'll need to keep an eye out for oth ...'

Before I could finish, Sophie shouted: 'There's another one!'

We all turned towards where she was pointing and sure enough there was another man floating in the water; despite the fact he was infected and clearly couldn't swim, his life jacket was keeping him alive.

'And another!' By the time Daz cried out, we were sailing through what seemed like a sea of infected sailors and marines, all kept afloat by life jackets. We could hear them growling and snarling as they clawed and hammered at the side of the boat, trying desperately to get on board. The sides were slick and the gunnels well out of their reach, but still, in the dimness of the early morning light, it was a terrifying sight.

While the others stared at the infected, transfixed by their frantic, but fruitless, efforts to get on board, I looked ahead to the frigate itself. We were much closer now and I could see only one group still fighting: they were holding a position towards the stern where two black ribs were being lowered towards the water. Back on deck, I saw an orange tongue of fire engulf all the infected within thirty feet of the few who remained unturned. Despite the fact that the nearest were instantly incinerated, the rest of the infected still pushed forward. It took me a few seconds to realise the survivors must be using flame-throwers to keep their attackers at bay, and buy them enough time to get the ribs into the sea. Another ball of fire leapt towards the infected, but again it had little impact beyond frying the nearest ones to a crisp; they were immediately replaced by more.

As soon as the ribs were safely in the water, the last of the men clambered down the wires attaching them to the boat, the large packs of the flame-throwers visible on their backs. The moment their feet touched down, the wires were released and the ribs sped away from the burning frigate. Soon, they'd disappeared from sight and we were left watching the decimated vessel as it continued to burn.

Daz stared, aghast. 'How d'you think the infection got on board?'

Claire looked up from where she had just finished tending to Tom. 'Remember how that man they'd dropped off yesterday had been fighting with one of the marines? He scratched the marine's face: I'm guessing he was a carrier.'

Daz frowned. 'What's a carrier?

Claire explained it to him. 'It's someone who's been infected, but hasn't started showing any symptoms yet. It's common in quite a lot of diseases. Carriers can still infect other people, but they can look completely normal; they might have been attacked and thought they'd got away unscathed; it's even possible that they don't even realise they have the disease, not until they start to turn.'

I shot Claire a glance. 'How long would that take?'

She shrugged. 'I don't know. With this disease, I'm guessing a few hours; maybe a day at the most.'

Sophie scratched her head. 'Why do some people end up being carriers, but others turn right away?'

Claire shrugged again. 'It could be any number of things. It might be that some people just have better immune systems and they manage to hold the disease off for longer; it might be to do with how badly they're injured by an infected — a small injury might mean the initial viral load is lower, and that it might take longer to build up to a high enough level in their blood system to overwhelm them; it might even depend on where they're injured by the infected; it's possible that it takes longer to affect you if you're bitten on your ankle than on your neck.'

What Claire said made a lot of sense. If the young man had been a carrier, he'd have infected the marine without anyone realising. The man himself hadn't turned until late in the night, and the marine had presumably done the same. Once he'd turned, there'd have been little chance any of them would be able to escape, not in the confines of the ship, and it would have spread like wildfire. It was amazing any of them managed to get away unscathed.

'At least we're free to leave now. Sorry, that came out wrong.' Claire took a moment to marshal her thoughts. 'What I meant was, despite everything, at least we're still alive; at least we've got a way out. It's not much, but it's something.' She hesitated briefly. 'And I really need something to hold onto at the moment, otherwise I'm going to lose it.'

She glanced over to where Sophie and Daz were still staring at the burning ship. She spoke quietly. 'I've got to keep it together for her. I know she's trying to act all tough, but inside she's petrified by all this, and I don't blame her; I'm just as terrified as she is. I mean, how on earth are we going to survive? Where are we going to go?'

I turned to Claire and saw she was close to tears. Tom and I exchanged uncomfortable glances: even though the world as we knew it was rapidly falling apart all around us, like most men, we still didn't know quite what to do when faced with a crying woman. I'd assumed Claire was doing okay, but now I realised how much it was just a front she was putting on for the sake of Sophie. Inside, she was as scared as the rest of us.

I took a deep breath. 'Now we can get out of the Clyde, I think we have a chance.' Both Tom and Claire looked at me disbelievingly, but I carried on. 'No, I mean it. I was thinking about this last night. There are lots of islands out there where there aren't any people; they've been deserted for years, decades even. No people means no infected.'

'But what happens if they get there?' Claire still sounded upset. 'I mean look at that island you were on the other day? The infected got there, didn't they?'

'That's different. They were carried there from Glasgow because that was only a few miles away. If we can get out to the islands further west, they're miles from anywhere. It's like Bob said about St Kilda, there's no chance of infected getting all the way out there. If there's anywhere we can avoid them, it's out there.'

'I thought we were heading south?' Tom stood up and stared off into the distance. 'You know, get beyond Hadrian's Wall where we can go ashore. They seem to be holding back the infected so far.'

'I've been thinking about that, too. I can't see it staying that way for long. All it takes is just one person carrying the infection to slip past and that's it. Once it gets into England, there's going to be no way they can stop it. It's only a matter of time,' I looked at the burning warship, 'I mean look what happened with the frigate. I think we have to accept we're on our own now, at least for the foreseeable future. That means we'd be better off heading out to the islands and finding somewhere we can hole up until we get an idea of just how bad this is going to get.'

Tom was sceptical. 'That's all fine and well, but what are we going to do for food and things like that?'

'I know these waters, Tom. I've spent years out here each summer. I know where we can catch fish; I know where the seabirds nest. We can get food off the shores, like we did the other day. There'll be sheep and seals, and porpoises too, if we want something a bit different. The islands out west have supported people for thousands of years. Trust me, getting enough food for five people isn't going to be a problem. I'm not saying it's going to be easy. We're going to have to work hard, but we can survive, I know we can.'

Tom was surprised. 'Where the hell did you learn all this stuff?'

We might have known each other for years, but in all that time, he'd never seen me out here before; he'd only ever seen me on shore, and when we worked together he was the more experienced one; he was the one in charge. Out on the water, it was different: this was my world, my element, and out here, for once, it was me who would be teaching him. In fact, I'd be teaching all of them.

As we made our way past the still-burning frigate I considered my companions. The four of them, Claire, Sophie, Tom and Daz, each represented very different parts of my home city; not just physically, but socially as well. Claire and Sophie were very much the epitome of the West End, or at least the middle-class part of it: the types who shopped in Waitrose and sent their kids to private schools. They dressed well and were the ones the City Fathers wanted you to think of when they came up with the slogan *Scotland with Style* to promote the city.

Tom represented the West End too, but the alternative side: the artists, the musicians, the writers, the performers. They inhabited the bedsits and shared the rented top-floor flats. In the summer, you'd see them lounging around the parks, hanging out and subtly smoking a spliff, while chatting with friends and strumming on guitars. They might live off Social Security from time to time, but by choice rather than by necessity; they always had a family somewhere to fall back on if they really needed it.

This was all a world away from the Glasgow where Daz had grown up. His was a world of crumbling 1960s high-rises and housing schemes. People lived on Social Security there, too, but because they had to rather than because they wanted to. This was a life you were born into, and it was difficult to get out of; it could be done, but it was something few managed. After all, it was hard to know what to aim for when you had no one to show you the way. While it would be presumed from birth that Sophie would go to university, for Daz, just finishing school would have made him more educated than almost everyone else he knew; this wasn't because of a lack of intelligence, it was more a lack of expectation from those around him.

The ironic thing was that when the world suddenly

changed, Sophie, with all her advantages, education and parental encouragement, was just as unprepared for it as Daz: neither lifestyle had readied them to survive in a world which was rapidly being overrun by the infected. It was the same with Tom: this was the first time in his life when he'd been faced with a situation where he no longer had a safety net to fall back on; there were no longer any parents to go home to, or Social Security for when he didn't feel like working. He was out of his depth, and pretty much all he was facing was far beyond the realm of his experience.

Claire was different: she'd undoubtedly seen a lot, and in many ways she was better prepared than the rest of us, but there was still a lot which was new to her. For the first time when she was in a dangerous situation, she had Sophie to worry about, and that was a whole different ball game from the times when she'd faced adversity in the past. There was also the loss of Jake which, while she kept it hidden, I was sure was eating away at her. With both of these weighing heavily on her mind, I wondered just how well she was really coping compared to the front she presented to the rest of us.

I was lucky, if anyone could really be called lucky in a world where all this was happening: I'd lived much of my life in this part of the world, and I knew it like the back of my hand. I'd also picked up some useful skills over the years. I'd like to have been able to say it was because I could see the signs, and knew what was coming, but I couldn't: I had been taken as much by surprise as everyone else. It just happened that the skills I'd picked up were the ones which were turning out to be useful. This didn't mean I wasn't scared — I was petrified — but it meant I could keep us alive out here on the water. That gave us our best chance of surviving until this disease was finally brought under control or burnt itself out ... or at least that's how I hoped it would end.

If it didn't, if it kept on going, then no matter what skills I possessed, there was little chance of us surviving in the long term; not the five of us all alone in a world ruled by the infected. For that to happen, I knew we only had one option: we needed to find other survivors. This was an opinion I was keen to keep from my companions for as long as possible.

Suddenly, Daz called up from below. 'You guys need to come see this.'

While Claire, Tom and I had been discussing what we were going to do next, Daz and Sophie had gone down into the cabin to get something to eat. Daz had turned on the television to get the latest news about what was happening back on shore, and it wasn't good.

We climbed down into the saloon, where Sophie had her eyes locked on the television, an untouched mug of coffee going cold in front of her. When she heard us coming, she turned and spoke. 'Mum, oh god this is awful. I thought there was hope, I thought if we could just get south of Hadrian's Wall, we'd be okay, but we won't be; they've broken through.'

As Claire went to comfort her, Daz sank down onto one of the seats by the table and stared at the television, ignoring the rest of us; his eyes wide; his mouth open. I moved to where I could see the screen: it seemed that the media had finally broken ranks with the military, and were now reporting what was really going on. The rolling text along the bottom of the screen was listing all the places where outbreaks had been reported in the last few hours: Carlisle, Newcastle, Manchester, Liverpool, even as far south as Birmingham and Hull.

When it had just been Scotland, there had been a possibility of controlling the outbreak, but now there was little anyone could do. The military knew this and they'd pulled the army back to try to protect London. The reason they gave was that if they could keep London safe, it would give them a base from which they could work to try to take back the rest of the country. However, I suspected their true motives might be something different; that it was more an act of self-preservation. They were no longer protecting the people. Instead, they were doing everything they could to protect themselves. Those already in London would be lucky, as they'd be protected, too, but the rest of the country was being left to fend for itself, and given the current situation, this was tantamount to a death sentence. Tom turned to me. 'Looks like you were right.' He sounded despondent. 'I guess going south isn't an option anymore.'

'Where are we going to go instead?' Sophie's voice trembled as she spoke.

'Don't worry, honey, Ben's got a plan.' Claire avoided Sophie's eyes and I wondered how much she believed my plan was feasible. 'We're going to go west instead.'

Sophie stared at me. 'But where?'

I looked down at her, trying to sound self-assured. 'I don't know exactly, but we'll find somewhere where we'll be safe.'

'D'you think they'll manage to save London?' Daz was still staring at the screen and not really listening to what anyone else was saying.

'No.' I spoke without thinking. Daz glared at me, shocked by my bluntness. Yet, this wasn't the time to be giving people false hope. After a second or two, he went back to staring at the screen.

After an hour of watching the news, I'd had enough. There was nothing new, apart from the ever-growing list of places where outbreaks had been reported, and we needed to be getting underway. I glanced round the cabin. Claire was holding Sophie while Daz sat a short distance away. Tom was leaning against the sink in the galley. All eyes were glued to the screen, hypnotised by the gruesome images which were being shown and reshown.

Over the last few decades, Britain had become the most watched nation on the planet and CCTV networks could be found in almost every town and city. They'd been installed to improve public safety, but now they were providing live feeds of just how fast the country was succumbing to the infected. The footage was grainy, monotone and silent, but somehow this made the scenes they were witnessing even more graphic and disturbing, and watching them wasn't doing us any good.

'I think I've had all I can take for the time being. We need to be getting on. The sooner we get out of the Clyde the better, and I'll need you all out on deck for this.' I didn't, but I thought they'd have less time to dwell on how bad things were getting on land if I got them working.

Daz and Tom both headed for the companionway while Claire remained holding Sophie. 'Come on, you two, I'll need your help as well. I can't sail this thing on my own, not without the engine.'

Claire smiled at me, knowing this was clearly untrue as I'd just sailed the boat single-handedly from the Canaries, but also knowing I was trying to make them feel useful.

Sophie disentangled herself from her mother and without saying anything followed Daz and Tom into the cockpit. Claire carried on watching the screen. 'Mind if I stay here for a bit?'

'How're you doing with all this?' I knew I sounded anxious, but that's because I was. I could tell Claire was close to the edge, and I couldn't let anything tip her over. Suddenly I realised I desperately needed Claire; I needed her cynicism to keep me sane; I needed her medical skills in case anyone else got injured; and most of all I needed her to be there for her daughter. While Daz was only a few years older than Sophie, he'd been used to having to fend for himself for a very long time, which gave him a certain resilience to anything life could throw at him, even this. Tom, by contrast, wasn't a natural survivor; however, his innate positive attitude meant that even when the world was at its darkest, he always presumed it would eventually get better, and I knew this would keep him going. Sophie was different: up until now, she'd led a sheltered life; whatever she'd done, she'd never been truly on her own, and she'd always had her mother to look to for support and comfort, even now. Without Claire, and alone for the first time in this frightening new world, I suspected Sophie would fall apart, and if that happened, I had no idea how that would affect our ability, as a group, to survive.

Finally, Claire answered. 'I'll cope. I just need some time to get my head round all this.'

I could tell from her tone that Claire was growing both angrier and more resentful about how those in charge were reacting to the rapidly deteriorating situation. She continued. 'I know I've been pretty down on the military, but even I didn't think they'd go this far.' She buried her head in her hands. 'They've just abandoned everyone.

They're not even making a pretence of trying to do anything other than protecting themselves. I can't believe they'd do that.'

I glanced at the screen one last time. 'Maybe they're not doing it on purpose; maybe they're just as scared as the rest of us. After all, this isn't something they could train for; it's not something they could ever have prepared for. Maybe they're running from it, just like the rest of us; maybe all they're doing is trying to survive, just like we are.' I started to climb the steps up to the cockpit, not sure if what I'd just said had done more harm than good.

I was halfway up when Claire spoke again. 'Ben?'

I stopped and turned.

Claire was no longer staring at the television. 'Thanks.'

I looked at her curiously. 'Why?'

'I hadn't thought about it that way before.'

Leaving Claire to consider this alternative view of the recent events, I continued up through the companionway and into the cockpit.

Chapter Nine

'Pull!' Following my instructions, Daz and Sophie hauled on the halyard, raising the main sail up the mast. Working together, they soon had it close to the top, but the wind was starting to fill it, making it difficult to finish raising it.

I looked backwards. 'Tom, keep it facing into the wind.'

'Aye, Aye, Cap'n!' He gave a mock salute and turned the wheel. The boat twisted to the left and the sail billowed out even further, threatening to yank the halyard from Daz and Sophie's grip.

'Other way.' I yelled towards the stern.

'Sorry,' Tom replied, apologetically, and turned the wheel to the right. The sail emptied and started to flap lazily.

Turning back to Daz and Sophie, I showed them how to wrap the halyard round its winch, making sure to keep their thumbs out of the way, and crank it tight using one of the detachable handles. 'Now, see if you two can work out how to put the mizzen up on your own.'

'Okay, cool.' Daz's eyes moved around the boat. 'What's the mizzen?

I pointed over my shoulder. 'It's the smaller sail on the mast at the back of the boat.'

'Oh, yeah.' Daz looked sheepish. 'You've told us that before, haven't you? Sorry, I forgot.'

I returned to the cockpit and sat next to Tom. Together we watched the two youngsters struggling to get the mizzen up, followed by the jib at the front, with me shouting instructions as and when they were needed. After ten minutes, they'd finished and came back to the cockpit.

'Okay, so now you know how to get the sails up ...'

Both Daz and Sophie were listening eagerly as I spoke. '…
you need learn how to bring them down again.'

The teenagers groaned, but did as they were told, and
soon the sails were back where they started. They were
even more annoyed when I got them to put the sails up
again, this time with absolutely no help from me
whatsoever. When they finally returned to the back of the
boat, they both looked very pleased with themselves.

Next, I showed them how to tack and how to heave to;
how to use the winches to tighten up the jib; and how to
reef the sails. I took them through a man overboard drill
and showed them how to tie a bowline and a reef knot. I
wasn't too sure how much they'd remember, but I had
the feeling they'd have plenty of time to practise, and I
felt they now knew enough for us to head out of the
sheltered waters of the Clyde and into the open sea.

Taking the wheel, I turned it until we were pointing
south. The dome-shaped outline of Ailsa Craig, with the
snow-white lighthouse, lay off to the west. Staring at it, I
realised it was a little over six days since I'd passed it on
my way to Glasgow; it hardly seemed possible that so
much could have happened in such a short space of
time. I looked north, back the way we had come, and
saw dense black smoke still spewing from the infested
frigate. Off in the distance, dark clouds hung over the
smouldering remains of the now-distant city. I thought
about all those who'd lived there: friends, family, people I
only knew in passing, ex-girlfriends, those I'd gone to
school with, but hadn't spoken to in years. Faces and
memories rolled through my mind. All of them were almost
certainly now dead: either killed by the infected or by the
military as they tried to contain the outbreak. One day,
they were all there, living their lives; the next, all that was
left of them were the memories locked away in my mind.

Yet, many of those killed in the city would have no one still alive to remember them; all trace of them would have been wiped from the face of the planet. It was as if they'd never existed.

Trying to push these thoughts from my mind before they overwhelmed me, I turned my attention back to Ailsa Craig. The lighthouse was the only building on the uninhabited island, but in the breeding season it was home to thousands upon thousands of seabirds. It was still a little early in the year, but many had already returned. While humanity was wiping itself out, nature was carrying on like nothing had happened. I watched gannets floating high above the cliffs, white crosses against the blue sky. Then my eyes were drawn to a small flock circling about half a mile ahead. Every few seconds, one would fold its wings and plummet, a fountain of spray shooting into the air as it sliced through the water and disappeared. This meant only one thing and I steered the boat towards them.

'Hey, Daz, can you open that deck locker there?' I watched as he lifted the lid. 'There should be some fishing lines in there. D'you see them?'

Daz leant inside. 'What d'they look like?'

'Like string wrapped round a wooden frame with coloured feathers on them.'

He reached inside and pulled one out. 'You mean this?'

'Yep, that's one. There should be three others as well.'

Daz rummaged around until he had found the rest of them. After closing the locker, he picked one up and examined it closely. 'D'you no' use rods to catch fish? My grampy took me fishin' once, down on the canal; we used rods then.' He fell silent, as if reliving the memory.

'We didn't catch anythin' though.'

'That's what you use when you're fishing for fun. This is a hand line; it's what people around here use when they're fishing for food.'

Daz turned it over curiously. 'How d'you use it?'

'You'll find out soon enough. See those birds up ahead?'

'Yeah.'

'They're feeding, and that means there'll be fish under them.'

'What sort of fish?' Sophie had been listening as Daz and I talked.

'It's a bit early in the year, but I'm hoping it's mackerel.' I glanced ahead. We'd almost reached the area where the birds circled 100 feet above the water. Daz and Sophie watched as one of the birds started its dive, following it down until it hit the water with an audible *whump*. Sophie ran forward and peered over the guard rail. 'Hey, you can see it under the water! It's almost like it's flying!'

The bird popped back to the surface and shook itself, before taking off in an ungainly manner. They watched as it climbed back to where the other birds circled before dropping into the sea once more.

Daz stared, open-mouthed. 'This is amazin'! I've only ever seen stuff like this on TV before.'

I smiled at him. 'It gets better.'

Daz frowned. 'What d'you mean?'

I pointed to where a large, dark object appeared out of the water, rolled slowly across the surface and disappeared again.

A look of confusion mixed with fear flashed across Daz's face. 'What the fuck was *that*?'

I did my best not to laugh at his reaction. 'It's a minke whale.'

Sophie squealed with delight as the whale surfaced again, this time alongside the boat. Daz joined her at the guard rail and together they watched the massive animal as it manoeuvred just below the surface.

'It's swimming under the boat!' Sophie glanced at me nervously. 'Is that safe?'

'Yeah. It knows exactly where we are.'

Tom stood up. 'You can see it coming out on this side.'

Daz and Sophie scampered across and draped themselves over the opposite guard rail. The whale's head broke the surface a few feet from the side of the boat. There was a loud *whoosh* as it exhaled, followed by a deep *phup* as it breathed in again. Its back appeared next, glistening like black glass in the morning sun, followed by the dorsal fin, just before it disappeared below the surface once more.

Sophie wrinkled her nose. 'Urrggg. What's that smell?'

I chuckled. 'Whale breath.'

Daz waved a hand in front of his face, trying to waft it away. 'Awww, that's mingin'.'

I looked round: we were now right in the middle of the feeding gannets. 'Time to get the sails down and start fishing.'

I steered the boat into the wind; Daz and Sophie dropped the main while I dropped the mizzen and Tom rolled in the jib. The boat came to a standstill, birds diving all around us. I passed out a hand line to each of the others and showed them how to dangle the twelve hooks — each covered with chicken feathers dyed bright and unnatural colours — into the water. As the line unfurled from the wooden frame, the weight at the end helped it sink out of sight.

'Once the hooks are down deep enough, you need to jerk them up and down like this.' I pulled my line sharply up and then let it sink before doing the same again. The others quickly got the hang of it and soon there was a cry from Sophie. I turned and saw her line was vibrating wildly. 'Looks like you've got something there.'

'What do I do?' There was a note of trepidation in her voice.

'Pull it in!'

Sophie pulled up her line until one of the brightly coloured lures broke the surface.

'Lift it out of the water and see what you've caught.'

She grabbed the line just above the first hook and lifted the rest clear of the water: two mackerel were flapping from the lower hooks as she held the line out at arm's length. She stared at them. 'What now?'

As I showed Sophie how to deal with the fish, there was a shout from Tom, shortly followed by one from Daz, indicating they, too, had hooked some. I went back to my own line to find I'd caught some as well. Within twenty minutes, we had enough fish on the floor of the cockpit to feed us for several days and I decided it was time to stop. We brought the lines in for the last time and turned our attention to our catch.

Sophie picked one up. 'They're beautiful.' She moved the fish back and forth, watching as the sun glinted off the electric blue stripes along its side. 'Look at the colours! It's a shame we killed them.' There was a hint of regret in her voice.

I took one of the fish in my hand. 'You're right, they are beautiful, but we've got to eat something.'

Tom picked a fish up, too. 'What do we do with them

now?'

I went down into the galley and came back with some chopping boards and sharp knives. I showed Tom, Daz and Sophie how to fillet and skin the fish before casting the bones and the innards over the side. When we were finished, we raised the sails again and continued our journey south.

Leaving the others to wash the blood and scales from the cockpit, I took the fish down into the galley. I wanted to keep what little power we had left in the batteries for running the television. That meant we could no longer use the refrigerator to keep things fresh. Cooking the fish immediately would stop them going off too fast and it would mean they'd last for at least a couple of days.

Claire was sitting in the saloon staring blankly at the screen as I heated up a frying pan and dropped the first of the fish in: within seconds they were sizzling away. I turned my attention to Claire. 'You okay there?'

'Huh?' Her eyes remained glued to the television.

'I said, are you doing okay over there?'

'Yeah. I mean, no ... I mean ...' She sighed deeply. 'I'm not really too sure what I mean.' She got up, turned the television off and came over to the galley. She leaned back against the sink; her forehead creased with worry. 'How the hell are we going to survive all this?'

'I don't know,' I flipped the fish over in the pan, 'but there must be a way. I think we're pretty well set for the short term; I mean, as long as we can keep away from the shore, we should be able to avoid the infected. I'm not too sure what we can do in the longer term, but something will work itself out.'

'Do you really think that?' Claire looked at me incredulously.

It was a couple of seconds before I answered. 'No.' I shifted the fish around with a spatula. 'But I keep telling myself I've got to at least try to stay positive.' I glanced at her. 'Right now, it's the only thing that's keeping me going.'

'Yeah, I know what you mean.' She watched as I shook the pan. 'Sophie keeps asking me when this is all going to be over; when things are going to start getting back to normal. What can I tell her? She's fourteen, and I've always tried to be honest with her, but what can I say now?' Her voice was quivering. 'I can't tell her what I really think: that it's quite possible we're all screwed.' She put her head in her hands. 'How the hell am I meant to tell her that?'

It was late in the afternoon by the time I went back up on deck. Claire and I had spent the last couple of hours trying to work out what we should do, but we hadn't come to any firm conclusions. The best strategy we could think of was to wait and see what happened once we got out to the islands. Until we knew the situation there, we wouldn't really know what we'd have to deal with. As we talked, I felt the sea change beneath us: the swell was getting stronger and the waves further apart, meaning we were starting to pass into open water.

Outside, I looked behind us; Ailsa Craig was little more than a speck on the horizon. For me, it had always been a marker of coming home, and it suddenly struck me that I'd never pass it again because I'd never be going home. A sense of sadness and loss settled over me, and I slumped, dejectedly, onto one of the seats in the cockpit. I sat there staring at the little dot on the horizon as it grew smaller and smaller. I thought about what it meant: I no longer had a place I could call home. Throughout all my travels, Glasgow had always been there for me to come back to: it was my anchor point; the place where all my journeys began and ended. Now, it was gone and I felt I'd been cast adrift, disconnected from the world I'd always known.

I let my gaze wander over those who had been set adrift with me. Daz was at the wheel, a look of intense concentration etched onto his face as his eyes moved continuously from the sails to the sea and back again. Judging by our wake, he'd finally got the hang of keeping us on a straight course; he might never have sailed before, but he was learning fast. Tom sat upfront, his legs dangling either side of the bow. He was looking down into the water, taking the occasional draw from a hand-rolled cigarette which I was sure would have something more than just tobacco in it. I wondered if Claire would tell him off if she spotted him, just as she had when Bob had given him a beer the night before. Claire sat on the opposite side of the cockpit with her arm around Sophie, as they both stared off into space. We were all from different worlds and it was only by chance we'd all been thrown together as everything fell apart around us.

Of all of us, I was the only one who knew how to survive at sea, and in that respect, the survival of the others was in my hands. Whether I liked it or not, I was stuck with them for the foreseeable future. The way I saw it, though, I'd been pretty lucky: there were a lot worse people I could have found myself with.

As the sun was going down, I set the sails so we were barely moving through the water. Now we were finally free, I needed to try to work out exactly where we should go. Until this point, I'd given it little thought, beyond the general decision to head up to the islands which lay to the north-west. I took a chart into the cockpit and spread it out on one of the seats so I could examine it. It covered an area from North Rona in the north to Northern Ireland in the south. Between these, lay islands of all shapes and sizes: some were inhabited, but I knew many weren't, and hadn't been for a very long time. While some lay close enough to the mainland, or neighbouring islands, to be linked together by bridges and causeways; others were far from the coast, and from each other. I tried to think about what we'd need in order to survive, both in the short and the longer term: food, water, shelter; and what we'd need to avoid the infected and the virus which created them: to be as far away from anywhere which had had a large human population when the disease broke out.

I considered the outlying islands first: North Rona, Flannan, St Kilda. There was virtually no chance of any one with the disease reaching such places, at least not under their own steam. There were seabird colonies and seals, shorelines to forage on, and there'd be fish in the surrounding waters, but they were remote and wild places; there'd be little chance of meeting other survivors, and I still thought we had a better chance of surviving if there were more of us working together. They were also exposed to the full wrath of Atlantic storms and pounding seas, and it would be unlikely the boat would survive being anchored there for any length of time, not when faced with 100-mile-an-hour winds, and waves which could be fifty or sixty feet high. This meant that if we made for one of these islands, once we were there, there'd be no going back. This I didn't like, as I thought it would be important to keep our options open.

I looked at some of the nearer islands. The large ones — Lewis, Harris, the Uists, Barra, Skye, Mull — were all well-populated and well-connected to the mainland by ferries and flights, and it was likely people fleeing from the infected would have carried the disease there before everything fell apart completely. The medium-sized islands — places like Coll, Tiree, Islay, Jura, Gigha, Raasay — were potentially different. Yes, they were inhabited, but they were more sparsely populated, and they weren't as well-connected. It was just possible the disease hadn't reached there yet. Even if it had reached some of them, it was unlikely to be able to spread between them. There were also islands like Iona and the Small Isles; home to small, tight-knit communities. If they hadn't yet been affected, would we be welcome if we suddenly turned up out of the blue? Or would we be seen as dangerous strangers; people who could bring the infection to them? Would this be an issue anywhere where there were groups who had so far survived the outbreak unscathed?

Finally, I considered the smallest islands, the ones where no one lived: places like the Shiants and the Treshnish Isles. All were capable of supporting communities, and had done for hundreds and possibly thousands of years before they had been finally abandoned in the twentieth century. Many were sheltered from the worst that the sea and the wind could throw at them. They, too, would have birds and seals to eat, as well as access to shorelines and seas to fish.

There were so many possibilities to choose from: which one was best? Any decision I made would affect not only my survival, but the survival of the others, too. I was used to being in charge on board, to making decisions which affected people's immediate future; not ones which would affect the rest of their lives. This was life or death, and getting it wrong would probably be fatal to some, if not all of us. Out of nowhere, a fear unlike any I'd ever felt before gripped me: what if I made the wrong decision? Before, we only had one aim: to get out alive. Now we'd finally escaped, there were a myriad of possibilities before us and I was paralysed by the choice.

Tom emerged from the companionway, a rolled-up cigarette between his lips. He sat down opposite me and lit it, before taking a long drag and exhaling the smoke into the growing darkness. He looked at the cigarette in his hand. 'I think it's about time I gave these up once and for all.'

Lost in my own thoughts, I wasn't really listening to him. 'What?'

'I said,' he took another long drag, 'I think it's about time I gave up smoking.'

I knew Tom had smoked since he was sixteen, and I'd seen him try to give up before: the longest he'd lasted was a couple of days. I looked at him curiously. 'Why now?'

'Haven't you heard? It's bad for your health.'

Despite everything, this made me laugh. 'In case you hadn't noticed, there are a lot worse things for your health going around these days.'

'That's just the point. I've run out of tobacco and it's going to be a real killer nipping out to the shops for more!' Tom took a final draw on his last cigarette and threw the end over the side. 'I feel healthier already.'

Again, I couldn't help but laugh. Tom glanced at the chart. 'So, have you worked out what we're going to do?'

Instantly, I felt my insides tie themselves in knots again as the fear returned. I couldn't get any words out, and all I could do was shake my head.

Tom smiled. 'Don't worry. You'll come up with something.' He'd always been able to read me like an open book and no matter how hard I tried, he could see what was really going on in my head. 'You always do.'

I said nothing. Instead, I just stared at the chart, and all the possible options, unable to find a way to choose between them.

Tom leant forward. 'D'you remember after Aaron and Jane died? D'you remember what you told me?'

Jane had been Tom's girlfriend since before I'd known him, and Aaron was born the year after I'd left to work in the Azores. When Aaron was eighteen months old, Tom had arrived home after working at a late-night event to find their flat in flames. Despite his frantic efforts to get inside, there was nothing he could do. His mother had been the one who'd called me, and I'd caught the first flight home. It was the only time I'd ever seen Tom lose his will to live, and it took months to bring him back. Later, he told me that it was something I'd said to him the morning after I'd found him slumped on the floor, having mixed too much vodka with sleeping pills, dried vomit streaking his t-shirt, that made him finally want to live again.

'You told me that as long as I remembered them, they'd always be with me, and that no matter what happened, I needed to live on to keep their memory alive. You said that if I didn't, then it was like letting them die all over again.'

I avoided looking at him. 'Yeah, I remember.' I'd had no idea if he'd meant to do it, or whether it was just an accident, but either way, I'd known I had to do something or he would slip away into a place he'd never be able to come back from. At the time, I didn't know if it would help or not, but it had turned out to be the push he needed to get his life back on track.

'Well, I'm going to tell you something similar now.' Tom

sat back. 'The only reason we're all still here is because of you. You've kept us alive longer than any of us could have survived without you. You've given us a chance. Anything you do from now on, no matter what, will still be better than anything we could've done on our own.'

He got up and walked over to the companionway, stopping before he climbed down. 'Just remember that, Ben. We all owe you our lives, but that doesn't mean we'll blame you if something goes wrong.' With that, he disappeared inside.

As I sat there, I felt some of the panic ease inside of me. I still didn't know what to do, but somehow it didn't matter quite so much.

***

'You doin' okay?' Startled, I looked up at Daz and then at my watch: it was one o'clock in the morning and we were still hoved to, drifting slowly in the darkness. After Tom had gone below, I'd spent another hour staring at the chart, considering every possibility open to us, but I'd still been unable to come up with a definitive plan of action. Instead, I'd put the chart away and left the decision-making until another time; I knew I'd have to do it at some point, but I figured that if I left it for now, by the time the decision had to be made, I might have some more information which would help me decide what was best.

Since then, I'd sat in the cockpit staring out at the sea, trying to get my head round all that had happened. My mind wandered back to thoughts of my friends and family again: had any of them managed, like I had, to get out? Were any of them still alive? If so, where were they now? Were they looking up at the same night sky, wondering the same about me?

Earlier in the day, I'd checked my mobile phone yet again, just as I'd done every few hours since we'd left the dock in Glasgow, but still there was no signal, meaning there was no way for me to even try to get in touch with anyone. I wondered if I'd ever find out what happened to them; it seemed unlikely and this uncertainty was starting to eat away at me like acid eating into my very soul.

I got up and stretched before finally answering Daz's question. 'Yeah, I guess so.' For some reason I didn't want to admit how I was really feeling: not to Daz; not to anyone, even though Tom had already guessed. 'Anyway, what are you doing up at this time of night?'

'Can't sleep.' Daz yawned. 'I'm absolutely knackered, but I just can't seem to get to sleep; no' even for a minute.' He sat down opposite me.

I watched him for a few seconds; even though he was only seventeen, at times he seemed so much older. 'It'll be the stress; your body's all keyed up, full of adrenaline. I think we all are.'

'Tom doesn't seem to have much of a problem; he's been asleep for hours.' Daz almost sounded jealous.

'He's been through a lot; more than the rest of us. It'll have taken a lot out of him.'

'Still ...' Daz leaned back and looked up at the sky. 'Wow! I've never seen so many stars before; they're amazin'.'

I looked up, too: I was so used to being far from the bright lights of human habitation that I was no longer surprised by the multitude of stars you could see when it was truly dark all around you.

I glanced at Daz. 'Have you never been out in the middle of nowhere like this before?'

Daz shifted on his seat, trying to find a more comfortable position. 'I went campin' once, out at Loch Lomond.'

I knew the place well: just half-an-hour's drive north of Glasgow; it gave many of its residents their first experience of the wilds of the countryside beyond the city. 'Didn't you see the stars there?'

'Naw. I was with some pals and we were all pretty drunk by the time it got dark.' Daz chuckled at the memory. 'To be honest, I was that out of it, I think I'd've struggled to see the moon properly.'

'D'you know anything about them?'

'What? The stars? Nah, not really. I always wanted to, though; just never got round to it. Don't suppose I'll ever get the chance now.' There was sadness in his voice.

'Did no one ever tell you about them? Not your teachers or your family?'

'My teachers?' Daz huffed dismissively. 'They took one look at my family an' where I came from, an' they gave up on me straightaway. An' Mum, all she ever cared about was where her next bottle of vodka was comin' from.'

'What about your dad?'

'Never knew him. I'm no' even sure my mum knew who he was.' Daz huffed again. 'I dunno why she ever had me if she didn't want to look after me.'

Daz sank down in the seat, arms crossed defensively; I wished I'd never asked and decided to change the subject. 'Maybe it's not too late.'

Daz frowned. 'No' too late for what?'

'For learning about the stars.' I pointed upwards. 'See those ones up there? The ones that would look like a saucepan if you joined them together?'

I watched as Daz's eyes flicked around for a few second before they locked onto the right set of stars. 'Yeah.'

'That's the Big Dipper; it's part of a constellation called *Ursa Major*, the Great Bear. Now, if you imagine a line connecting the two stars at the end and continuing across the sky, that takes you to another star; that one there, out on its own. That's *Polaris*; the Pole Star. It's directly over the North Pole and it's the only star in the sky which doesn't seem to move. That means you can use it to navigate and work out where you are.'

'Just from that one star?' Daz shook his head gently. 'That's fuckin' mental!' He stared at the sky for a few seconds before he carried on. 'How d'you know all that?'

The back of my neck was starting to hurt and I rubbed it gently. 'If you spend enough time out here, it's just something you pick up.'

'What else d'you know?' There was an eagerness in Daz's voice.

'See that really bright star there?'

'Yeah.'

'That's *Sirius*, the Dog Star. It's the brightest star in the sky, but its light takes eight and a half years to reach us, and that's with the light travelling at almost seven million miles an hour.'

Daz let out a long, low whistle. He cast his eyes back and forth across the sky and then they fixed on something. 'What about that one?' Daz pointed to a faint object which looked a little out of focus. 'That one's no' very bright. It must be a lot further away. How long does its light take to get here?'

'That's not a star. It's another galaxy: the Andromeda galaxy. There's something like 300 billion stars in it and it's two and a half million light years away; the light we're seeing now left there about a million years before anything we'd even vaguely recognise as human walked the Earth.'

'Mental!' Daz paused for a moment. 'Mind you, with this disease thing, it mightn't be very long before it's like that again.'

It was a depressing thought; that humans had evolved, spread to every corner of the planet, created great civilisations, fought great wars, and then wiped themselves out: all in less time that it took for light to travel between two neighbouring galaxies. In the history of the universe, we were a mere blip; a momentary flash worthy of little more than a footnote.

Chapter Ten

'Mum, I can't get the TV to work.'

I'd stayed in the cockpit all night, unable to fall into any sort of restful sleep. The worry of what we should do next gnawed away at me, keeping me awake. I'd dozed now and then, but only briefly and Sophie's shout woke me from one of these naps. I checked the sails and went below, presuming the batteries had finally run out of power, but I was wrong. In the saloon, Sophie was pointing the remote at the television as she stabbed repeatedly at its buttons: it was on, but there was no picture ... not on any of the channels she selected.

I went out and checked the alignment of the antenna, and then the wire which took the signal down into the cabin; they both seemed fine. Back inside, I took the remote from Sophie and made sure the right input was selected.

'What's up?' Claire came into the saloon, her hand covering her mouth as she yawned. From the bags under her eyes, it was clear she'd slept as badly as I had.

Sophie flopped onto one of the seats. 'The TV's broken.'

I unplugged the wire for the antenna, blew on it and plugged it back in. 'The television's fine; it's just that it doesn't seem to be picking anything up.'

'How?' Daz had come into the main cabin as well. Shortly after, Tom appeared, stretching and then grunting in pain. Instinctively, his hand went to his bandaged side.

'I'm not sure.' Then a thought struck me. I went over to the FM radio and turned it on, but I couldn't find any of my usual stations. 'Hmmm ...'

'What's going on?' By this time Tom had sat down

opposite Sophie and was watching me intently.

I reached up and turned the television off. 'It looks like nothing's broadcasting anymore.'

'Nothing at all?' Claire sounded incredulous.

I looked at her. 'Not on the television, or on the radio.'

'You sure?' Tom got up and started fiddling with the settings on the radio. 'Not even an emergency broadcast of some kind?'

'What does it mean?' Sophie's gaze shifted from Claire to me, and then to Tom.

'I don't know.' I turned to Claire, 'D'you and Tom want to come up on deck with me for a minute?'

'Hey, you're going to talk about it. That's not fair!' Sophie leapt to her feet. 'Me and Daz have a right to know what's going on. We're not little kids!'

The more time I spent with Sophie, the more I was beginning to realise I'd underestimated her. I'd thought, given her sheltered upbringing, that she wouldn't be able to cope with all that was happening, but she was holding up much better than I'd expected, and she seemed willing to meet our situation head-on. I glanced at Claire. 'Your decision.'

'I suppose she's right.' Claire sat down beside Sophie. 'After all, we're all in this together.'

'So? What does it mean?' Sophie looked at us all again.

I took a deep breath. 'We can't know for certain, but I think it means London's been overrun. I think it means there's no one left in charge.'

Daz's brow furrowed. 'What does that mean for us?'

Claire stared straight ahead. 'It means we're really on our own now. Britain isn't coming back from this. Not any time soon; possibly not ever.'

There was silence as Claire's words sank in.

After a few minutes, Tom spoke. 'So what's your plan?'

I felt every eye in the room fall on me. They were looking to me to make a decision and yet I couldn't. Then I remembered Tom's words from the night before and I felt a wave of relief wash over me. Suddenly my brain was no longer paralysed with fear and I knew what to do. 'I can lay out the options, but I think we should make any decisions as a group.'

Daz sat down at the table. 'So what're the options?'

'There are really only two: we can try to find an island which is uninhabited and set ourselves up there; or we can see if we can find other survivors and join up with them.'

'How likely is it that we can find an uninhabited island?' Claire was clearly leaning towards that option.

'Very. A lot of islands around here don't have anyone living on them anymore, especially the smaller ones.'

'But where're we goin' to get food from?' Daz was thinking with his stomach.

'There's plenty around, if you know where to look. It just might not be what you're used to.'

'What d'you mean?' Daz glanced at me curiously.

'Well …' It took me a couple of seconds to come up with a good example. 'We're a lot more likely to be able to find puffins than chickens.'

Daz looked startled. 'What the fuck's a puffin?'

'I think that's getting away from the point.' Tom leant forward, placing his elbows on the table and clasping his hands together. 'If we find other survivors, do you think they'll be happy to have us turn up?'

'I'm really not too sure.' I'd already given this some thought, but I had yet to come to any firm conclusions.

'Some might; some might not. Either way, I think our chances will be better in the long run if there's more than just the five of us.'

'Why?' Sophie was staring at me, eyes narrowed.

I wondered how to explain this, and settled for just being honest. 'Because if something goes wrong, there'd be more people to help out. Think about it: if something happened to me, if I got ill or got infected, would the rest of you be able to handle the boat on your own?'

Daz puffed out his chest. 'I could do it.'

His growing self-confidence made me smile. 'Daz, you've done well so far, but you've still got a lot to learn. Wait till we run into a decent bit of wind, then you'll see what I mean.'

'Can we trust other people?' I could understand Claire's concern. 'I mean, we won't know them or what they're really like.'

I turned to her. 'Until a few days ago, you'd never met Daz or Tom, or me, but you trust us, don't you?'

Claire looked flustered. 'That's different.' She was obviously worried she'd offended us. 'Anyway, I had no choice; it was the only way we were going to get out alive.'

I slowly scratched the side of my face, where the lengthening stubble was really starting to itch. 'I think it's going to be the same with other survivors, but we won't know that until we've met them.'

'How d'you even know there are other survivors?' Sophie stared at me solemnly. 'What if it's just us? What if we're the only ones left who aren't infected?'

That was something I hadn't even considered. I'd presumed that if we'd made it this far, there had to be others who'd made it, too. Suddenly, I realised I needed to know if there were others out there, or whether we were really the only ones who'd survived.

'Okay, here's a compromise. Why don't we see if we can find any other survivors. If we do, and if they'll let us, we can spend some time with them and then decide if we want to join up with them or not.' I glanced at Claire. 'That way we can at least see what they're like before we make any decisions. How does that sound?'

There was a general murmur of agreement.

Tom sat back in his seat. 'So where do we start looking?

I retrieved the chart I'd spent so much time staring at the night before and laid it out on the table. 'If there are any other survivors, it's most likely they'll be on one of the islands out here: the sea should have acted as a barrier to the infected getting to them. We can start here,' I pointed to a medium-sized island which lay about twenty miles to our north, 'and then work our way up from there.'

Daz peered at the chart. 'How're we goin' to know if there are people there, and if they're infected or no'?'

This was something else I hadn't really thought about. 'I don't know, but if we find people, I'm sure it'll be obvious, one way or another.'

As the day wore on, the wind shifted to the north and started to pick up. To make any sort of headway, we had to tack back and forth, slowing our progress to a snail's pace. As the wind strengthened, I handed out life jackets and safety harnesses, and insisted they were to be worn at all times when on deck. The strong winds meant it was more difficult for the others to both hear and follow my instructions, and it didn't help that as the seas increased, so did the movement of the boat. Tom succumbed to sea sickness early in the afternoon and went down below, quickly followed by Sophie, who'd started to look a little green.

By nightfall, we were still some five miles from our destination and the winds had built to a force ten. The waves, which had started the day as rough chop, had built into a sizeable rolling swell, lifting the boat high into the air as we passed over them and then dropping it into troughs so deep we could see nothing but water all around us. The mizzen had been reefed once, the main twice and the jib was little more than a pocket handkerchief. The rain which had started at lunchtime was moving almost horizontally as it rattled off the sails. Waves broke over the bow every few minutes and washed along the decks. It was rougher weather than I might have expected for the time of year, but it was by no means unusual.

Daz seemed to be enjoying the challenge of sailing in the harsh conditions. He'd quickly picked up the knack of steering through the swell and tweaking the sails to keep us as stable as possible. He still couldn't handle tacking, but that was hardly surprising, given that he'd only been at sea for such a short period of time. Claire sat in the cockpit with her legs pulled up to her chest, the hood of the waterproof jacket she'd taken from one of the lockers pulled tight around her head, and a pallid tinge to her face. Having thrown up continuously for about an hour, Tom was now lying on his back, with his eyes closed, on the floor of the saloon, at a point which he insisted moved the least. Sophie had bundled herself up in a sleeping bag and was wedged in the corner of one of the seats, looking dejected. She hadn't actually thrown up, but it seemed like it was only a matter of time.

Despite the darkness and the weather, I pushed on, knowing the others would feel better once we finally got into the lee of the island and by midnight I could feel the seas start to calm beneath us. Tom reappeared in the cockpit soon after, looking drained, but apparently feeling better. Daz took the helm and I went below to search the charts for a bay which would provide us with shelter from the wind and where we could anchor up for the rest of the night. Almost immediately, my eyes fell on Port Ellen. It wasn't an anchorage I'd used a lot, but I'd been there a few times: the seabed was firm, meaning there would be little risk of the anchor dragging, and since it was almost encircled by land with a south-facing entrance, it would provide the much needed shelter from the strong northerly wind. Being the largest community on the island, it would also be the best place to start our search for other survivors.

The decision made, I returned to the cockpit and gave Daz a new heading to follow. Since we were now going north-east, parallel to the island's coast, rather than north, there was no longer any need to tack and there were no hazards marked on the chart which we'd have to worry about until we reached the entrance to the bay itself. With this in mind, I left Daz at the wheel and went back into the cabin to make a snack.

Down below, Sophie was still wrapped in the sleeping bag, but she'd fallen asleep. I tried to be as quiet as possible, yet I managed to wake her as I opened the last of the cans of soup we'd got from the others in the holding area.

She stretched and yawned. 'What time is it?'

'Just before one. How are you feeling?

'Better.' She blinked blearily. 'I think.'

'Do you think you'd be up for some food?'

'That depends.' She got up, clutching the sleeping bag

round her like a cape, and shuffled unsteadily over to the galley. 'What is it?'

'I'm just warming up some soup.' I looked at the cans. 'Tomato and basil. It might help you feel better if you get something in your stomach.'

'Okay.' She shuffled back to the table and collapsed onto the seat. 'I'll have some.'

When it had been warmed up, I split the soup evenly between five mugs. I handed one to Sophie and passed three up to the others before taking my own and climbing back up to the cockpit. Claire blew on hers before taking a mouthful, while Tom sipped his tentatively, clearly worried it might come straight back up again.

Once I'd finished mine, I took the wheel to give Daz a chance to finish his unhindered. While the seas had dropped, it was only because we were in the lee of the island and the wind was still driving the rain horizontally, meaning the visibility was poor and I had to rely on the GPS receiver to measure our progress towards our destination.

Suddenly, there was a noise from below and Sophie shot out of the cabin. She made it to the left-hand guard rail just in time to throw up over the side. She wasn't wearing her waterproofs, her harness or her life jacket, and I was about to tell her to go and put them on when something loomed out of the darkness directly ahead of us. It took me a second to realise it was a fish farm, a series of massive floating cages anchored to the seabed. They must have been new as I'd never seen them here before and I hadn't marked them on the chart when I'd passed through the area the previous year.

Since we were under sail and they were so close, there was nothing I could do to avoid the nearest set of cages.

In a desperate attempt to avoid hitting them head-on, I spun the wheel sharply, bringing the nose of the boat into the wind. Sophie straightened up and turned just as we jibed. The boom of the mizzen swung across the width of the boat and smacked her hard across the forehead, sending her tumbling backwards into the water. Claire screamed, but before we could do anything, our right side slammed into the outer pontoon of the fish farm, stopping us dead and throwing us all to the deck.

Daz was the first to scramble to his feet. He ran to the guard rail. 'Sophie!'

Without thinking, he unclipped himself and leapt into the sea. The rest of us were up a second later, searching the inky waters, but we could see neither of them. I grabbed the spotlight, turned it on and shone it into the darkness.

Claire was yelling desperately, 'Sophie! Oh my god, Sophie!'

Tom held her back, preventing her from jumping over the side, too.

Then I found them: Daz, with his life jacket inflated, holding Sophie's face out of the water, blood gushing from a wound on her head. I grabbed the life ring and holding onto the end of the rope, I threw it towards them, but the wind blew it out of Daz's reach. I pulled it in and tried again. This time he managed to grab it with his free hand and as fast as I dared, I pull them both towards the back of the boat. As soon as they were within reach, Tom and I lifted Sophie from the water and placed her carefully on the floor of the cockpit. She lay there, unmoving; suddenly looking very small in the outsized clothes she was wearing.

Claire barged past. 'Out of my way!'

She knelt down beside Sophie, checking her pulse and her breathing. 'Shit!'

Working fast, Claire started pushing on Sophie's chest and breathing into her mouth. Daz climbed back onto the boat and stood next to Tom and me, shivering, as we stared down at Claire as she fought desperately to revive her daughter.

There was a noise behind us: I shone the spotlight into the night and saw a man running along the pontoon of the fish farm towards us. Behind him were two more: all three were dressed in the same yellow waterproofs and black boots.

'Infected!' My yell alerted Tom and Daz. Together the three of us tried to push the boat away from the fish farm, but it wouldn't budge. I ran the spotlight's beam along the side of the boat, revealing the point where our guard rail had become entangled in the metal framework of the cages. The men continued their charge, their boots rattling the metal walkway as they pounded towards us.

As I set to work trying get us free, the other two grabbed the boathooks. Tom was the first one to step onto the pontoon, with Daz close behind. Standing side by side, they waited for the infected to come within range; Daz trembling with cold and fear, Tom standing firm. Each held their boathook like a baseball bat, ready to swing. When the first was only a few feet away, Tom lashed out, grimacing as pain shot through his still unhealed body. He caught the infected across the side of its beard-covered face, sending it spinning into the water. It thrashed there, gripping on to the edge of the walkway and trying desperately to climb back out. The second arrived, younger and leaner than the first, and moving faster. This time is was Daz who struck out, catching it on the shoulder rather than the head: it stumbled, but didn't go down. Daz swung again, this time breaking the wooden handle of the boathook across the side of the infected's head: it dropped like a stone onto the pontoon.

Tom and Daz glanced down, wondering what to do with the body which now lay at their feet. The distraction was enough to allow the third infected, who was little more than a lanky teenager, to take them by surprise. He lunged for Tom; doing his best to get out of the way, Tom tripped over the body lying on the walkway and stumbled into the water, sending the first of the infected into a frenzy as it stretched its grasping hands towards him. The boy turned his attention to Daz. Left with only the broken handle, Daz thrust it deep into the infected's chest. The boy sank to his knees and Daz kicked him as hard as he could, sending him tumbling into the cage. As he slipped beneath the surface, I leapt onto the pontoon and grabbed Tom, pulling him out of the water just before the bearded man managed to reach him.

The three of us stood there, breathless and terrified; the wind whipping across our faces and driving the rain against our skin.

'D'you think there're any more of them?' Daz's eyes darted along the walkways, searching for signs of any further infected.

'I don't know.' Tom was breathing heavily. 'Let's just get the hell away from here.'

I slicked my hair back with one hand. 'It's going to take time to get the boat untangled.'

'How long?' Daz was soaking wet and his teeth were starting to chatter as he shivered and rubbed his arms, trying to warm himself up.

'I don't know; five, maybe ten minutes.' I jumped back onto the boat where Claire was still working away on her daughter. I glanced at Sophie: her face was grey and her lips were blue. 'Is she doing any better?'

Claire didn't stop, or even look up. 'No.'

'Is there anything I can do?'

'Just give me space; let me work.' Claire snapped back.

I swung myself down into the cabin and searched through my toolbox, looking for something that might prove useful. I had a hacksaw in mind, but my eyes fell on a pair of bolt cutters. Grabbing them, I climbed back onto the deck and, with a last look at Sophie, I ran forward to where Tom and Daz were trying to separate the metal work of the fish farm from the guard rail.

As I got there, another infected came screaming out of the darkness. I stepped onto the walkway and swung the heavy bolt cutters. It stumbled backwards, but it wasn't dead. Before it could get back to its feet, I fell on it, swinging the bolt cutters again and again until its face was barely recognisable. I stared at what I'd just done, and felt nothing but the rush of adrenaline pumping through my veins. I quickly turned my attention to the boat. Kneeling on the pontoon, I realised the situation wasn't as bad as I'd first assumed. I took the bolt cutters and cut through the guard rails on either side of where they were tangled and within seconds the yacht was free.

Almost immediately, the wind started to push it away, and the moment I realised what was happening, I leapt for the boat, landing half on the deck and half off. I struggled, knowing that if I fell into the water, the boat would drift away faster than I could swim, and with only Claire and an injured Sophie on board, there was no one who'd be able to sail it back. As we picked up speed, I could feel my feet dragging through the water and pulling me downwards. Using my elbows, I fought desperately to pull myself up and, on the third attempt, I managed to swing my left leg onto the deck. I hung there for a second, regaining my strength and catching my breath before dragging myself fully on board. The moment I was there, I jumped to my feet and looked back. Neither Tom or Daz had realised what was happening and were standing in their blood-streaked jackets, faces etched with fear, staring after the boat as it drifted ever further from them.

I ran back to the cockpit, stepping on the seats to avoid Sophie as Claire continued to pump her chest and breath for her. The blueness had disappeared from her lips and there was now a hint of pink to her skin: I hoped this was a good sign. Claire stopped for a moment and checked Sophie's pulse before carrying on.

As I reached the wheel, I spun it to the left, turning us away from the fish farm. I heard Daz and Tom shouting after us, scared I was leaving them behind, yet I had no choice: before I could have any hope of going back for them, I'd need to turn the boat through the wind. With the wheel hard over, the boat tipped sharply to the left as it turned.

Without even taking her eyes of Sophie, Claire screamed angrily. 'Keep the bloody thing stable!'

'I'm doing my best.' I straightened up the helm, 'but we need to go back for the others!'

Claire glanced round. 'Where the hell are they?'

'On the fish farm.' I turned the wheel again. 'There are infected there, too.'

Claire paused for a second, seeing the blood on my jacket for the first time and realising how dangerous the situation had become. 'Just try and keep us as steady as possible.'

The boat finished its turn and we were once again running north-east. I was aiming to steer a course which would take us along the side of the pontoon that was at a right angle to the one we'd previously hit. As we drew alongside, another infected, this time a woman, appeared out of the night, running at Tom and Daz. Weaponless, they'd stand little chance if I didn't get to them before the infected did. As soon as I thought we were close enough, I pulled the wheel to the left, but oversteered and the boat crashed against the pontoon. Luckily, we didn't become entangled again, and Tom leapt, landing heavily on the foredeck. Daz followed a moment later, but by then we were bouncing away from the fish farm and he only just made it across the widening gap. As he landed, Tom had to grab him to stop him falling backwards into the sea.

The woman drew level with us and screamed as she threw herself towards the boat. I turned the wheel to the right, taking us far enough from the pontoon to ensure she didn't land on the deck. Instead, her hands closed over the guard rail and she hung there, struggling to drag herself on board. I pulled the wheel to the left once more, aiming for the pontoon. As we glanced off it again, the woman was crushed between the edge of the fish cage and the hull. I watched as her grip loosened and she dropped into the water.

Beneath me, I heard a cough and a splutter, and I looked down to see Sophie spitting water onto the deck. I shifted my gaze to Claire. 'That was a long time to not be breathing for; will she be okay?'

A second later, Sophie's eyes opened and she tried to sit up. Claire hugged her, the tears streaming down her face. She looked up at me, 'I timed it. It was only three minutes.' She stroked Sophie's wet hair and smiled. 'She'll be fine.'

As Tom and Daz made their way back to the cockpit, I stood amazed at all that had happened in such a short length of time: to me it had seemed like hours.

Chapter Eleven

I woke the next morning to find I'd fallen asleep in the cockpit. After we were free of the fish farm, Claire and Tom had helped Sophie below, while Daz and I remained on deck. The rest of the trip had been uneventful and we'd finally pulled into the bay at Port Ellen just before three. As we dropped the anchor and brought down the sails, I looked round, but could see nothing in the darkness. The bay was sheltered, but the wind was still strong enough that I worried the anchor might drag in the night, so when Daz went below, I remained on watch, huddled in the cockpit in my waterproofs, alert to any unexpected changes in our position.

Despite my worries, I must have dropped off, exhausted from the day's events and glad to finally be out of the storm. Luckily, it had passed as I slept and the sun was now breaking through the wispy white clouds which covered much of the sky. I stood up, my limbs stiff from my awkward sleeping position. As I stretched, I surveyed my surroundings: the bay was tranquil, with clear waters and patches of golden white sand strung out along the shore. The small ferry terminal lay to our east, and around it stood a cluster of low stone buildings with white-washed walls and dark roofs. To the north, were buildings which looked industrial, but it was unclear what they housed. As far as I could see, it was deserted. I checked my watch; it was still early so maybe it wasn't too surprising.

Suddenly, there was a movement on the island. I grabbed the binoculars and focused them on the shore. It took me a while to work out what had caught my eye: it was an elderly woman shuffling along a street leading away from the shore in what looked like a nightdress. It seemed unusual, but not necessarily completely out of place in a small, tight-knit community.

'Hey, Ben, you want some breakfast?'

I glanced down the companionway and saw Claire looking up at me. 'Yeah, if you're making some. How's Sophie?'

'She's got a sore head and her throat's a bit raw, but other than that she seems fine. Pretty lucky really: it would have been an awful lot worse if Daz hadn't found her so quickly. I still don't know how he did it.'

I smiled faintly. 'Yeah, brave little bugger, isn't he?'

'He most certainly is!' Claire shook her head. 'You wouldn't think it to look at him, would you?

'No. I guess it's that whole thing about not judging a book by its cover.'

Claire shielded her eyes against the early morning sun. 'Anything going on up there?'

I turned my attention back to the shore. 'I'm not sure, yet.'

I lifted up the binoculars again and tried to find the elderly lady. It took me a few moments: she'd shuffled round in a circle and was now heading towards us, the front of her nightdress covered in what looked like dried blood, while her face and hands were stained with something dark. There was little doubt in my mind she had the disease. Yet she wasn't behaving like any of the other infected we'd encountered so far.

I swept the binoculars along the shore, stopping momentarily whenever I found someone. In all, there were about ten people visible, and while none of them were acting normally, neither were they acting like I'd grown to expect the infected to act. The few that moved, shuffled slowly and aimlessly, while most stood still, staring off into the distance. I wondered whether there was something different going on here; whether the virus had, somehow, mutated again; or whether this was just what happened once people had had the disease for a while. Maybe this thing wasn't going to last that long after all, and this was the first sign the disease was starting to burn itself out.

Claire interrupted my thoughts with a shout of 'Breakfast's ready!'

Down below, we ate a poor imitation of a kedgeree made from the last of the mackerel, most of our remaining eggs and what little rice we had left. While Claire might be a great doctor, it was clear her culinary skills left much to be desired. Regardless, we were all ravenous and cleaned our plates in record time. Daz even scraped what was left in the pan together to get enough for seconds.

'So,' Daz spoke between mouthfuls, 'what's it look like out there?'

'The weather's better.' I scooped the last of my kedgeree onto a fork. 'But I think the infection's here.'

'How d'you know?' Sophie was pale; her hair was tied back and there was a bandage where the mizzen boom had caught her the night before. Given what she'd been through, I was surprised she was back on her feet already.

'There are people out on the streets: not many of them,' I hesitated briefly, 'but they're acting very strangely. Not like any of the other infected we've seen so far.'

'What d'you mean?' Claire seemed intrigued.

'They're just standing around. They're all covered in blood, but they don't seem crazed or angry. They just look, I don't know ...' I searched for the most appropriate word. 'Lost.'

'Hmmm ... I wonder if it's some new phase of the disease.' Claire was thinking medically. 'I mean, we really don't know too much about it. Maybe there's an initial violent phase and things change once that passes. After all, nobody knows what rabies does to the brain in the long term. Until the virus mutated, everyone who started showing symptoms ended up dead.'

I took my plate over to the galley and wiped it clean before putting it back in its place. 'I wondered that, too. But what about those people on the fish farm last night? If there's a violent phase, they were clearly still in it.'

'Maybe they got infected more recently.' Daz's suggestion was certainly feasible and it would fit with Claire's theory.

'If that's what's going on, it changes everything. It means the worst of this could be over in a few more days.' I found the prospect strangely exhilarating. 'So how do we find out if you're right?'

Claire glanced round the cabin. 'We could go ashore.'

Daz looked at her disbelievingly. 'You've got to be fuckin' kiddin'!'

'No, I'm serious.' Claire stood up. 'I don't mean all of us and whoever did it would need to be very careful, but it's really the only way we can find out for certain.'

Tom handed the binoculars to Daz. 'How're we going to do this?'

The five of us were standing on the bow of the boat, staring towards the shore.

'If we get the dinghy in the water, we can go ashore on the beach, there in front of the road,' I pointed to the spot I was meaning. 'The nearest person I can see is over there by that big building. If they try to attack, we'll have plenty of time to get back out onto the water.'

'So who goes?' Claire glanced round.

'Only one person should risk it,' I took a deep breath, 'and I think it should be me.'

'Ben, you can't.' Tom was staring at me. 'You're the only one who knows how to sail the boat. If we lose you, we're screwed.'

'Yeah, but I'm also the only one who knows how to drive the dinghy.' I turned back to the shore and watched the people lurking there for a moment. 'Anyway, I'm planning on making damn sure I get back in one piece.'

'Here goes.' I started the little outboard on the dinghy. The beach I was aiming for was about a quarter of a mile from where we'd anchored the night before. Trying to make as little noise as possible, I puttered slowly towards my destination. Halfway there, I stopped and scanned the shore with the binoculars: none of the people I could see on the land seemed to have moved at all. I pushed on and soon the dinghy was bumping against the sandy beach with a soft scrunch. Hesitantly, I stepped ashore, pulling the dinghy just far enough from the water to stop it drifting away.

Remembering what had happened when we'd been foraging for food south of Brodick, I took the remaining paddle with me, just in case, and placing each foot carefully on the sand, I crept forward, expecting to be attacked at any minute. At the top of the beach, I paused. I could hear the blood pounding in my ears as my heart raced. I glanced around. I could only see one of the locals: the one near the big building. Now I was closer, I could tell it was a man. His back was towards me so I couldn't see his face, but he had a wiry frame and thinning hair; still he hadn't moved.

I pulled myself up onto the grass and stood there, my eyes darting around, waiting for something to happen, but everything remained still. Off in the distance an oyster catcher called shrilly, while gulls circled lazily overhead. I looked back at the boat, and could see the others gathered on the bow, nervously watching my every move.

After a minute of edging ever further from the water, I reached the road. I could see two figures now, the man nearer me and the elderly woman further off, still shuffling round in circles: neither appeared to know I was there. I wondered what to do next. I decided to get a little closer and then call out, but not wanting to be caught by surprise I kept my eyes glued to the man.

I'd made it about five yards when my foot landed in a pothole, sending me sprawling onto the tarmac. The paddle flew from my hand and clattered along the road. Almost instantly, I heard a roar and looked up to see the man racing towards me. Gone was the listlessness he'd had until that moment. Instead, his face was contorted with rage. I scrambled to my feet and leaving the paddle where it had come to rest, I turned and ran. When I reached the loose sand at the top of the beach, I stumbled, almost ending up on my hands and knees, but somehow I kept myself upright. I didn't need to look behind me to know that the man was gaining; I could hear his snarls getting louder and louder with every passing second. My lungs burned from the exertion and I could feel my heart pounding in my chest. I reached the harder sand near the water's edge and could run faster. I hoped he'd be slowed at the top of the beach, just as I'd been, but I knew I couldn't count on it.

I hit the dinghy at full speed, pushing it backwards into the sea and away from the shore. I carried on until the water was up to my knees and with one last push I leapt in. The momentum carried me further from the beach as I struggled towards the engine. I glanced back and saw the man was at the water's edge, growling and gnashing his teeth. Not knowing if he'd be willing to pursue me into the water itself, and if he did so, how far he would go, I started the engine, twisted the throttle and pushed it hard to the right.

When the dinghy was facing back towards the yacht, I straightened it up and looked back to the shore: the man was still there, pacing back and forth, but by the time I was back at the boat, he seemed to have lost track of me. He'd fallen silent and no longer stalked along the shore. Instead, he'd returned to his placid state, staring off into the distance. From what had just happened, it was clear Claire had been wrong: the violent phase, as she had called it, had not passed; instead, it seemed the infected were only active when they sensed prey were near.

'D'you think it's safe?' Sophie craned her neck to try to get a better look.

'I think so. The one we hit's over there,' I pointed to our left, 'it doesn't look like there's anyone on this one.'

As soon as we'd realised there were no survivors in Port Ellen, we'd decided to carry on northwards, but before we did, we'd returned to the fish farm, pulled there by the lure of easy food. Now it was daylight, we could see there were six groups of cages in all, separated from each other by 100 yards of open water. The night before we'd struck the southern-most enclosure, but now we floated near the cages at the northern end. There were no buildings here, meaning nowhere for infected to hide, and we could see the rest of the low-lying pontoons were clear. Inside the cages, salmon churned; each five to ten pounds in weight. If we could work out how to preserve them, we could get enough food here to last us for weeks. It would be monotonous, but it would at least be filling and nutritious, and given what we'd found at Port Ellen, it seemed we might need it.

I cast my eyes around one last time, just to make sure it really was safe. 'Let's see how many we can get.'

I stepped hesitantly onto the pontoon: after my last encounter with the infected I was nervous, even though I could see there was nothing to worry about. Daz and Tom followed, leaving Sophie and Claire on the boat to keep a look out. The three of us walked up to the edge of the cage and peered in. The water swirled as the fish moved just below the surface. Every now and then, a dark body would emerge before slipping from sight again.

Daz was entranced. 'How many fish d'you think are in there?'

'Ten, maybe twenty thousand.' I did a quick mental calculation. 'That means the fish in this cage would be worth about a quarter of a million pounds ... or at least, they would've been.'

Daz shook his head in disbelief. 'That much money just for some fish?'

'Fish farming's big business. Well, it was.' I turned my attention back to the cage. 'They're pretty much worthless now. They'll starve to death eventually 'cos there's no one left to feed them.'

'That's just cruel.' Daz peered into the water again. 'Can we no' let them go or somethin'?'

'They're not wild fish; they'd die if we did. They're pretty much doomed either way.' I looked away. 'At least if we take some, they'll die humanely.'

'How're we goin' to get them out?' Daz was still staring into the cage, mesmerised by the ever-moving shadows lurking just below the surface.

I glanced round and saw a large dip net leaning against one of the handrails, left there by a worker who no doubt thought they'd soon be back to retrieve it. They'd never returned, but now it would let us catch as many salmon as we could handle.

Grabbing the net, I plunged it into the water. When I pulled it out a second later, there were three large, silver fish flapping around in it.

'Whoa!' Daz's eyes widened. 'They're massive!'

I emptied the fish onto the walkway and held the first one down with my knee. Pulling out the hammer I'd brought with me for just this purpose I smacked it sharply on the top of its head: instantly the fish was still. I repeated this with the next two.

'What do we do with them now?' Tom was watching me closely. 'I mean, how are we going to stop them going off?'

I thought for a moment. 'I'm not sure, but I did wonder if we could dry them somehow.'

Daz nudged one of the fish with the tip of his shoe. 'How're we goin' to do that?'

I looked back at the boat and an idea came to me. 'If we fillet them, we can string them up from the rigging; they should dry out in the sun and the wind, and that'll preserve them.'

Tom folded his arms, unconvinced; he nodded up at the sky, which was now heavily overcast. 'I'm not so sure the sun's going to be much help.'

Two hours later, we'd killed a couple of hundred salmon. Working on the pontoon, we'd set ourselves up as a production line. Being good with a knife, Claire had taken the role of filleting the salmon. Beside her Sophie washed the fish in the sea before Daz poked a hole in the tail end and pushed a piece of fishing line through it. Tom then passed them up to where I was standing, ready to hang them from the rigging.

After thirty minutes, we were all covered in scales and fish juice, and Sophie was beginning to complain about the state her clothes were getting into. Another forty minutes after that, we were finally finished. I jumped onto the pontoon and looked back at the yacht. It was a somewhat surreal sight, festooned as it was with salmon fillets which swung slowly back and forth in the stiff breeze.

Claire cleaned her hands in the water. 'We're all going to stink if we don't do something to get all this crap off.'

'No problem!' With that Daz leapt off the pontoon, holding his knees tightly to his chest. He hit the water with a loud splash that sent water spraying over the rest of us. Sophie screamed and tried to hide behind her mother.

'Bastard! I'll show you!' Tom dived into the sea and a second later Daz disappeared from sight. He resurfaced coughing and laughing, followed shortly by Tom.

I turned to Claire and shrugged, 'well, if you can't beat them ...' I stepped off the side and dropped vertically into water that was colder than I'd expected. In the gloom, I could see the net of the fish farm a few feet away, and beyond it, the salmon packed tightly together, their sides glinting as they milled around in the confines of the cage. It seemed unfair that they would all soon be dead, but there was nothing I could do about it. I heard two more splashes and saw first Claire's and then Sophie's legs appear above me. I kicked back to the surface and joined the others as we scrubbed ourselves, and our clothes, clean.

After about five minutes, I pulled myself out onto the pontoon beside Claire and watched as Tom, Sophie and Daz splashed and played in the water.

Sophie had been distant from Daz, Tom and me at first, and I don't think she quite knew what to make of us. Each of us was so different in our own way from anyone she was used to dealing with. Daz, in particular, was someone she'd probably have crossed the road to avoid before all this happened: now they swam happily together in the cool waters around the fish farm. It seemed the collapse of civilisation was a great leveller, and just as it had swept away all of Sophie's advantages, it had done the same with all of Daz's disadvantages.

If I were being honest with myself, Daz wasn't someone I'd ever have mixed with before either, and certainly I'd never have invited him onto my boat, but now he was here, it turned out he was a bit of a natural, taking to sailing like a duck to water. I was amazed by how much he'd picked up in such a short space of time and he was rapidly becoming the one I relied upon to be my second-in-command. Without him, life in this suddenly changed world would be so much more difficult. I wondered if Tom was put out by this; after all, I'd known him for years, but it seemed unlikely. Both of us knew this wasn't his type of thing; he'd be glad he was alive, but unlike Daz, this wasn't an opportunity for him to learn about things he'd never have had the opportunity to do if the world hadn't changed.

Watching them now, I noticed that Sophie was spending much more time wrestling and splashing with

Daz than with Tom. She certainly seemed to look up to him and I wondered if there was the start of something else going on there. If there was, it wasn't surprising: if it wasn't for him she'd almost certainly be dead.

I nodded towards Sophie, 'I wouldn't have thought she'd be keen to get back in after yesterday.'

'Me neither. She doesn't remember any of it, though,' Claire waved to her and she waved back. 'Judging by how hard the boom hit her, she was probably out cold before she even hit the water.'

'But still ...'

'She's pretty resilient really. She always has been, even as a toddler. When she was learning to walk, she'd fall down and smack her head off the floor. I'd pick her up and hold her until she stopped crying, then the moment I put her down, she'd try it again.' Claire looked lovingly at her daughter. 'It was so different with Jake. He'd get put off by any set back. I remember when he was learning to ride his bike, he fell off and it took me a month to get him to give it another go ...'

Claire stopped suddenly. I glanced across and saw tears streaming down her face. I put my arm around her and she buried her head in my shoulder, her body heaving with each deep sob.

'Tom, pull in the sheet there; just a tad. That's it.' Daz turned the wheel slightly to the right and then straightened it. 'Sophie, tighten up on the jib a little. When I call out, let them go an' pull them in on the other side. Ready about?'

'Ready!' Both Tom and Sophie sang out in reply.

'Lee-ho!' With that, Daz turned the wheel sharply to the left. It was the first time I'd let him be in charge while we changed from one tack to another, and he'd started too soon. I could see he wasn't going to make it, but I was doing my best not to interfere: he'd learn much faster by making mistakes on his own than with me stepping in and taking over. Sure enough, the boat stalled halfway round, causing the salmon fillets to swing around wildly as the boat swayed back and forth. A moment later, the wind pushed us back onto our original course.

'Tom, Sophie, pull in the sheets on the right side again.' I watched the sails tighten up then I glanced across at Daz. He looked both frustrated and slightly embarrassed. I gave him a reassuring smile. 'Don't worry. It takes everyone a few goes to get the hang of it. You ready to try again?'

Daz nodded. I sat back and watched. Again he failed, but on the third attempt he succeeded and we were soon racing along our new course in the strong afternoon breeze. Daz raised his arms above his head in triumph and Tom, Sophie, Claire and I applauded. He beamed at me, pride written all over his face. For the rest of the afternoon, Daz stood happily at the wheel, ordering the others around and practising the same manoeuvre over and over again. By suppertime he was getting it pretty near perfect on almost every attempt.

While Daz was improving his sailing skills, I studied the charts with Claire, trying to decide where we should go next. To our north was a chain of islands of ever-decreasing sizes, which lay almost parallel to the mainland, separated from each other by narrow and dangerous channels.

'We've got two choices. We can go west through here.' I pointed to the channel between the island which currently lay to our left, and the next one up. 'And try this island here, which is Colonsay, or we could keep going north.' I ran my finger up the east side of a large island with the name *Jura* printed on it, 'and see if we can find anyone in any of these settlements.'

Claire examined the chart closely. 'It looks like there are more places to check out if we keep going north. That should mean a better chance of finding other survivors.'

'True, but if we do that we'll have to keep going north, and that means we have to pass this.' I stabbed my finger at the chart.

Claire leaned forward, squinting as she tried to work out what the strange markings on the chart meant. 'What *is* that?'

'*That* is the entrance to the Corryvreckan whirlpool.'

Corryvreckan wasn't a place for the faint-hearted. Years before, I'd sat on the hills above it when the whirlpool was in full flow and seen the maelstrom first-hand. It was a quarter of a mile across and I could hear it roar even though I was more than 500 yards away. I'd watched as three boats approached it and all turned back after being tossed around like corks on the eddies and the standing waves. If we ended up in conditions like that, the yacht would be torn apart and we'd all surely drown.

Claire shot bolt upright. 'A whirlpool?'

'Yeah, but it's only dangerous in some tidal states. As long as we time it right, it's not really that much of a problem. Anyway, we're not going to try to go through it, we just need to get past the entrance without getting dragged in.'

Claire sat back. 'Have you done it before?'

'Yes, loads of times.' I leant backwards, too, 'but always with an engine as back-up in case the wind suddenly changed, or a storm blew up.' I glanced up at the sky, trying to judge the weather and what might be coming over the next few days: it looked settled now, but you could never tell what might be just over the horizon.

'So as long as we're careful, it's not too much of a problem?'

I nodded. 'That pretty much sums it up.'

Claire considered this for a few seconds. 'And if we go north, we've got a better chance of finding people?'

'Yes.'

'Hmmm …' Claire stared at the chart. 'Okay, let's go for it; let's go north. You never know, we might even find other survivors before we get anywhere near the whirlpool.'

Chapter Twelve

So far, Jura had been a bust. After my close escape in Port Ellen, none of us had dared go ashore again, but every time we'd come near a settlement, even when it was just an isolated croft or a cluster of white-washed buildings, we'd seen evidence of infected. Either we saw them standing, staring off into the distance, waiting for something to happen, or we saw the remains of their victims scattered across the ground. Sometimes we saw both, with the infected picking over the carcasses of those they'd killed. It had been a long two days, sapping our hope with every new discovery, but before nightfall I wanted to push even further north.

To make matters worse, our attempt at preserving the salmon by drying it had failed. I'd emerged that morning to the stench of rotting fish. I guess the air was too moist and the sun not strong enough to preserve them properly. It had taken me a good hour to cut all the fillets down and throw them over the side. I watched as they drifted off into our wake, aware that we were back where we'd started: in need of food and with little option but to try to get what we could from the sea.

I'd kept my eyes peeled, but since we'd left the Clyde, I'd seen no more flurries of gannets, indicating fish feeding close to the surface, and since we had little left to eat, I was beginning to worry: what would happen when we ran out? I was just mulling this over when I spotted something which might solve the food problem, at least temporarily. 'Daz, see that red buoy there?'

'Yeah, I saw it.' Daz sounded put out that I thought he'd missed it. 'I'm keepin' clear of it, just like you told me to do with the others.'

I stood up. 'No, steer towards this one.'

'But I thought you said ...'

I cut him off. 'I know, but I've got an idea. Give me the wheel and then go up front; take Tom with you. When we get there I'm going to turn into the wind. Try to grab it and then pull it up and loop the rope it's attached to over the cleat on the bow.'

'But why?' Daz looked puzzled.

I smiled. 'You'll just have to wait and see!'

Five minutes later, we had the sails down and the rope from the buoy tied securely to the bow.

I rubbed my hands together. 'Let's see what we can bring up.'

'What d'you mean, "bring up"?' Daz frowned. 'What's on the other end?'

'Lobster creels!' I shot back.

Daz scratched his head, 'Lobster *whats*?'

'Creels: they're like traps.' I peered over the side, trying to get an idea of how far down they might be. 'Fishermen put bait in them to attract things like lobsters and crabs. Once they get in, they can't get back out again.'

Daz nodded, taking in this new information. 'And you can eat them?'

'You bet!'

Daz and I started hauling on the rope, while Tom coiled what we pulled on board into a neat pile. Within a few minutes, the first trap broke the surface and a moment later it was on deck. Unfortunately, with the exception of a few crabs which were too small to bother with, it was empty. I threw the crabs over the side and we hauled in the next one: it was completely empty.

Tom wiped his hands on the guard rail, trying to get rid

of the slime which had come off the rope as he'd coiled it. 'Is this really worth it?'

'Hopefully.' I reached up, stretching out my back. 'Even if there's nothing in them now, the creels themselves will be useful for catching food.'

We went back to work and brought up the next one. It was covered in a mass of writhing arms.

Daz watched as one of the animals drop onto the deck and wriggled across it. 'What the hell's *that*?'

I chuckled at his reaction. 'It's a brittle star. It's a kind of starfish.'

Daz knelt down and examined it. 'Mental!'

After a few seconds, he tried to pick it up, but its arm snapped off in his hand. 'Oh shit! I didn't mean to hurt it.' Then he noticed the severed arm was still moving and dropped it with surprise. It thrashed around on the deck. 'What the fuck?'

'Don't worry. It'll grow back.' I scooped up the brittle star and its dismembered arm, and threw then both over the side. 'It's something they do to distract predators.'

I opened the door of the creel and emptied the rest of the brittle stars over the side. Together, we watched as they sank from sight.

'What's that then?' Daz pointed to a round object about the size of a man's fist and covered in short spines which was wedged into a corner of the trap.

'That,' I carefully plucked it out, 'is good eating!'

Daz wrinkled his nose. 'You can't eat that, can you?'

'Not all of it, but some of it.' I placed the sea urchin in the bucket I'd put nearby in case we got anything worth keeping. 'Just the roe really: it's a bit of a delicacy.'

Daz remained unconvinced, and slightly disgusted, while Tom just laughed.

After an hour of hard work, we'd pulled up some thirty traps and had a bucket filled with shellfish of various descriptions, as well as three more large, spiny sea urchins: they'd make a nice change from the fish which had made up almost our entire diet since we'd left the Clyde. I put the bucket aside and tried to work out what to do with the creels which were now piled untidily on the bow. There was no way we could take all of them with us, but I was keen to take some. I surveyed the deck and figured we could probably store about a dozen on top of the cabin without them getting too much in the way. After I cut the rope, Daz and Tom threw the unwanted creels back into the sea while I tied the ones we were keeping securely into place.

'Now we get our reward for all that hard work.' I picked up one of the sea urchins and cracked it open before scooping out five plump orange lobes and throwing the rest away. I cut a small piece off one of the lobes and popped it into my mouth, savouring the texture and the taste. Daz and Tom watched curiously.

I cut off some more slices and held them out towards Daz and Tom. 'You want to try some?'

Tentatively, they took the orange morsels, examining them closely and then looking at each other. Daz spoke first. 'I'll do it, if you do it, too.'

'Deal.' Tom took a deep breath. 'On the count of three: one, two, three!'

While Daz swallowed his, Tom's was spat over the side. He wiped his mouth with the back of his hand. 'That's disgusting!'

'I dunno.' Daz was still undecided. 'It's an interestin' sort of taste.'

I cut off another piece and held it out. 'You want some

more?'

'Yeah,' Daz said noncommittally, 'but what exactly is it?'

I waited until he'd put the next bit into his mouth before answering. 'Gonads!'

This time Daz spat over the side rather than swallowing. 'Urgh! You mean like ...? Awww, that's mingin'.' He spat over the side again. 'Why d'you no' tell me that's what I was eatin'?'

I laughed at his reaction and cut off another piece for myself before carrying everything down to the galley. Once inside, I threw crab claws, langoustines and lobster tails into a large pan with some olive oil and a bit of paprika, and put it on the stove. Tom sat at the table, while Daz filled a glass with water and used it to rinse out his mouth. The other two came through from the front cabin and Claire sniffed the pan. 'That smells good.'

'You want some of that?' I pointed to where the orange lobes from the sea urchins lay on a plate.

Daz turned round. 'Don't fall for that. They're sea urchin gonads. You know like ...'

'*Uni!*' Claire and Sophie called out in unison.

I smiled at them. 'Freshest you'll ever get.'

A confused expression spread across Daz's face. 'But ... What's *uni?*'

'It's what the Japanese call it: it's great. We had it when Mum took us to Tokyo last summer. Jake wouldn't even try it though ...' Sophie stopped suddenly and her face dropped. A moment later, she turned and walked quickly from the room.

I looked at Claire. 'Sorry.'

'It's not your fault. You couldn't have known, could you?' Claire got to her feet. 'I'd better go after her.'

That evening, Tom, Claire and I sat in the cockpit, while Daz and Sophie sat up by the bow, dangling their legs over the side and chatting. Tom was fidgeting, and I could tell he was missing his cigarettes. I decided I'd see if I could take his mind off it.

'Hey, Tom, I've been meaning to say, thanks for what you said the other night, it really helped.'

'I thought it might have; you seem to be doing better now.' Tom replied distractedly. 'You know I was only returning the favour.'

Claire raised a curious eyebrow, but didn't say anything. I figured I owed her an explanation. 'I got a little overwhelmed by everything the other night, and Tom helped me put it all in perspective.'

'The way I see it,' Tom glanced at each of us in turn, 'we're all going to struggle from time to time, and we'll all need to be there for each other when that happens.'

Claire nodded, and we fell back into silence. I looked towards the bow and remembered something which had been niggling away since the first day. 'Claire, can I ask you about something Sophie said? You don't need to answer if you don't want to.'

Claire frowned. 'What?'

'Remember on the first night, when the infected was trying to drag you over the side?'

'How could I forget!'

'Well, Sophie said she couldn't lose you, too, not after losing her father. What was she talking about?'

Claire shifted uncomfortably and said nothing.

Realising it was something Claire didn't want to talk about, I quickly apologised. 'Sorry, I shouldn't have asked.'

Claire cleared her throat. 'No, it's okay.' She stared down at her hands. 'Dan, my partner, and I had been together since our late twenties. We met when we were working in the same refugee camp; just two people from Glasgow who found ourselves a long way from home.'

She smiled sadly as she relived the memory. 'Anyway, we hit it off right away, and when I found out I was pregnant a few years later, we both decided to go back home so we could have a proper family life.'

Claire swept her hair back and looked off into the distance. 'When Sophie was ten, Dan started to get ill. It took a while for the doctors to work it out, but it turned out to be leukaemia. He didn't respond to chemotherapy and a bone marrow transplant was the next step. When no one else in either of our families turned out to be a suitable donor, Sophie insisted she should be tested, too, and she was a perfect match. We both said she didn't have to do it if she didn't want to, but she did it anyway. She was so brave about it.'

Claire wiped the corner of her eye. 'It seemed to work at first, and he went into remission, but after a couple of years it came back. They tried another transplant, but this time it didn't work. Sophie was so close to her dad; in many ways closer than me and her ever were, and it was awful to watch her have to go through it all again only for it not to make any difference.'

Claire's voice dropped to almost a whisper. 'He died just over a year ago, and Sophie was so lost without him. Somewhere deep inside, she blames herself for the transplant not working the second time; she thinks there was something more she could have done.' Claire swallowed. 'Losing Jake, and then almost losing me, brought it all back again, just as it seemed like she was finally starting to get over it.'

Claire glanced towards the bow. 'Sometimes, I don't know how she does it. She's so young and she's been through so much, yet she just keeps on going. And now all this: if it wasn't for her, I think I'd have given up by now. The only thing that's keeping me going is knowing I can't leave her on her own. I think that's her biggest fear: having no one left and being all alone in the world.'

I thought about this. The way the world was now, we all needed something to keep us going. For Claire and Sophie, it was to be there for each other; Tom and I knew each other inside out, we had our shared past to help us keep each other from falling apart, but, I wondered, what was keeping Daz going? Then I realised: Daz kept going for himself; with his upbringing, if he hadn't learned how to do that as a kid, he'd never have made it as far as he had in life.

****

The next morning we were up early: our passage would be a tricky one as we'd finally be passing the entrance to the Corryvreckan whirlpool. I checked my watch; we'd have the tide with us for the next six hours, which was just as well. The currents were so strong in the channel we were aiming for that we'd have no chance of getting through it under sail if they were flowing the other way. The only problem was that this would mean the tide would also be pushing us towards the whirlpool.

I checked the wind: it was blowing from the south-west; that would at least help keep us away from danger. I turned to the others. 'You all need to be on deck today, and you need to do whatever I say as soon as I say it. If you don't hear me or understand what I said, let me know immediately. Put your life jackets on now and keep them on.' I looked at Sophie. 'No matter what.'

Claire leant forward on her seat. 'Ben, just how dangerous is this?'

'Don't worry, it's not *that* dangerous, at least if everything goes to plan. It's just that if things do go wrong, they could go very wrong, very fast, and we won't have much time to sort it out.' I glanced at Claire. I didn't seem to have eased her concerns. I pointed to the north. 'We're aiming to go through the channel between those two islands up there. We just need to make sure we don't get drawn into that channel there.' I pointed to the north-west.

'Why no'?' Daz enquired.

I shifted nervously. 'Because that's the entrance to a bloody great whirlpool.'

'A whirlpool?' Sophie sounded worried. 'Isn't that dangerous?'

'It will be if we get pulled into it, but we're going to stay well clear. Daz, you want to get the anchor up? Claire, can you deal with the main sail? Sophie, the mizzen, and Tom, will you be able to handle the jib?' I looked round. 'Everyone ready?'

'Just one question,' Tom scratched his head in an exaggerated manner, 'which one's the jib again?

'It's the one at the front!' Daz cried out in exasperation. 'How can you no' remember th—?' He turned to find Tom grinning at him. 'You're just messin' around, aren't you?'

I surveyed the waters ahead of us. 'I think we need to go a little further east.'

In the hour since we'd left the previous night's anchorage, the wind had picked up and turned into an easterly. Now both it and the tide were pushing us steadily towards the whirlpool. While we were making good headway, without a motor we'd be at the mercy of the currents if anything went wrong.

Originally, I'd planned to take a relatively straight route north, but now I wanted to position us further away from the dangers which lay immediately to our west: this meant we needed to tack our way into the strengthening wind, costing us time, but it was only prudent given our situation.

I called out. 'Ready about?'

'Ready!' The others chorused back.

I glanced round quickly to double-check everyone was in place. 'Lee ho!'

We were halfway through the turn when the jib crashed onto the foredeck. With no head sail, the turn stalled and we were pushed back towards our previous course. As this happened, the wind took hold of the fallen sail, blowing much of it over the side and into the sea.

'Tom, take the wheel. Just keep us pointing into the wind as well as you can.' He jumped up and took my place. 'Daz, Claire, Sophie, come with me.'

I ran forward with the others following closely behind. On reaching the foredeck, I leant over the guard rail and started pulling in the wayward sail. 'Daz, see if you can get hold of the sheet there. Claire, Sophie, help me here; just grab any of it you can get hold of and pull it on board.'

For five minutes we fought with the sail until it was finally back on the boat. While the others recuperated, I inspected it: the metal loop which connected the jib to the halyard that was used to pull it up to the top of the mast had snapped, leaving nothing to keep the sail in place. I went into the cabin and returned with the spare I carried for just such an eventuality, knowing that, with a bit of luck, I could have the sail back up in a matter of minutes. I undid the jib halyard from its cleat on the mast and I looked up. Even though it was now free the other end stubbornly remained at the top of the mast. 'Shit!'

'What's up?' I turned to find Daz standing beside me.

I pointed upwards. 'That is. We can't get the sail back up until we get the other end of the halyard down.'

He looked up. 'How the hell're we goin' to do that?'

'One of us is going to have to climb up there.'

'How?' Daz sounded incredulous.

'See those things on the mast? They're mast steps: they'll take you right up to the top.'

Daz's eyes widened. 'Me?'

'Yeah. I've got to stay down here in case anything else goes wrong.'

'But what if he falls?' Sophie had come up behind us. 'He'll get killed!'

'No, he won't. There's a harness we can clip to the main halyard to keep him safe.'

'But it's a long way up.' Sophie seemed dubious.

'Don't worry. I'll be fine.' Now Sophie thought it was dangerous, Daz seemed more willing to take on the task.

'Okay then,' I slapped Daz on the back. 'Let's get on with it.'

As Daz struggled into the harness, I dropped the main sail and clipped him onto its halyard. Daz stared up the mast, suddenly unsure of what he was about to do.

I put a hand on his shoulder. 'Don't worry. You'll be fine once you're up there.'

With that, he started to climb and I pulled in the slack in the halyard. Every time he took a step upward, I did the same; not enough to lift him up, just enough to stop him falling if he should slip. At the halfway point, Daz paused to catch his breath.

I craned my neck upwards. 'You're doing fine. Just don't look down!'

Almost immediately, that's what he did. I saw him tighten his grip on the mast and close his eyes. He took a deep breath before opening them again and carrying on. When he was within reach, some fifty feet above the deck, he took one hand from the mast and pulled at the end of the jib halyard, but it wouldn't move: he tried again but still it wouldn't budge.

I shouted up to him. 'Try using both hands.'

Shakily, he took his second hand off and grasped the end. He pulled tentatively at first, then harder. Finally, he leaned back, putting his full weigh on it. After a second, it came free, causing Daz to fall backwards and swear loudly. Bracing myself, I pulled on the main halyard, and stopped him before he'd fallen more than a few feet. I watched as he swung back and forth, doing his best to avoid hitting the mast. Slowly, I lowered him down to the deck, with the end of the jib halyard gripped firmly in his right hand. He was shaking as he started to remove the harness. 'Jesus! I thought I was a goner there!'

I bent over, attaching the top of the jib to the end of the halyard with the spare loop. 'Ach, you were perfectly safe; you were never going to fall *that* far.'

Daz gave me a look that told me he didn't appreciate my flippant response.

Working with Claire and Sophie, we had both the jib and the main sail back up in a matter of minutes and we all returned to the cockpit. For the first time since it happened, I looked around to see where we were.

'Shit!' I leapt towards the wheel and took it from Tom

and turned it so we were heading north-east. The sails filled, but the currents were so strong that they were pulling us backwards.

'Guys, we're in trouble.' I adjusted the course, trying to increase our speed. 'Daz, pull on that sheet there; Sophie, crank the jib a bit tighter with the winch.'

It made no difference. I decided to try the other tack.

'Ready about!' Then without even waiting for their response, 'Lee ho!'

The practice Daz had given the others paid off and we completed the manoeuvre flawlessly. The only problem was we were still getting slowly and inexorably drawn closer and closer towards the narrow passage between the two islands. Without an engine, there was nothing I could do to stop it: we were going to go through the whirlpool.

I gathered the others in the cockpit. 'This is going to get really hairy. You need to get your safety harnesses out; if we end up in the water, try to swim for the shore.'

I glanced round to find them all staring at me. Tom was the first to break the silence. 'Is it really that bad?'

'Yes. Go!'

As they raced off, I turned the boat and adjusted the sails until we were pointing directly towards the whirlpool and then considered our options. I'd seen it worse than this, but still it was going to be rough: very rough. I tried to remember what I knew about navigating this channel. The only advice I could bring to mind was that it was best to do it at slack tide and to try to keep to the southern edge. We couldn't do anything about the first, but at least we could try the second. I changed course again and headed for the coast of Jura to our south. As the others returned to the cockpit, I could already feel the waters starting to buck and churn beneath us. Ahead, waves were rearing up and breaking almost everywhere.

I pulled on the harness Daz had brought up for me. 'Everyone clip on to the safety lines and stay clipped on, no matter what.' I looked at the sails: we wanted enough up to keep us stable and moving forwards, but not so much we'd lose control: at the moment, we had too much up. 'Daz, Sophie, get the main sail down. Claire, loosen the jib off a bit, while Tom winds it in. A bit more than that; that's it.'

We were now as far to the south as I felt safe to go without risking running aground. It was keeping us out of the worst of it, but we were still being tossed around like a cork. I could feel the eddies pushing and then pulling at the hull as we passed through them, while the bow was rising and falling as we crashed into standing waves. I glanced round: Claire was gripping onto the side of the boat with one arm while her other was tightly wrapped around Sophie; Tom and Daz sat on the other side, hanging on and ducking whenever a wave crashed over the side. They all looked terrified and I couldn't blame them.

Suddenly, a movement on the nearby land caught my eye. I turned and saw three figures tracking our progress. With the strength of the currents, we were moving at six knots, but they were easily keeping up despite the rugged shoreline. Their clothes flapped loosely in the wind as they moved, yet they didn't seem to notice. Instead, all their attention was focused on us. One slipped and fell, but quickly sprang to its feet again and had soon caught up with the other two. Given their actions, I had no doubt they had the disease and a realisation settled over me, leaving me cold: if anything happened to the boat and we were lucky enough to make it to shore before we drowned, we'd almost certainly be torn to pieces by the infected that waited for us there.

I surveyed the surrounding land, trying to judge our position. As far as I could work out, we were only a third of the way through and had yet to reach the worst of it. Off to our right I saw a standing wave, some six feet in height. It wasn't breaking; instead, it was milky green with a sheen like glass. On the other side, it dropped into a trough which boiled and foamed like the water in a washing machine. If we hit something like that, we'd be lucky to get out in one piece. In an instant, I came to a decision. 'Daz, take the wheel.'

His jaw dropped. 'What?'

'Take the wheel.' I stepped to the side.

Daz gaped at me. 'But I can't handle it.'

'Yes, you can.' I tried to look at him reassuringly. 'All you need to do is follow my instructions.'

There was a moment's silence before Daz finally responded. 'Okay.' He stood up and stepped behind the helm; tentatively at first, then with more certainty, he put his hands on the wheel. I unclipped myself and ran forward to the foot of the mast. I climbed up to a point where I could see as far ahead as possible before clipping my safety line onto the metal mast step just above me. While the movements on the deck were rough, they were many times worse near the top of the mast and I had to grip on tightly with all my strength to avoid being thrown off.

I scanned the waters ahead of the boat and saw a boiling mass of water about fifty yards from the bow. 'Daz, to the right.'

The boat lurched beneath me. I shouted again. 'Now

straighten up.'

We narrowly missed the worst of the seething mass of water, but the bow still rose and then plunged deep beneath the surface. The sea swirled and washed across the deck below me before it broke the surface again. There were a few yards of what looked like calm water and then a swirling eddy about twenty yards across. Before I could call out, we hit it. Glancing down, I saw Daz and Tom fighting with the wheel, trying to keep us straight, but they were losing and the boat spun round. The mizzen's boom crashed across as our position relative to the wind shifted. Now broadside to the current, we were spat out only to immediately hit a wall of water. We rolled as we were lifted to the top of the standing wave where the boat hung momentarily before dropping over the other side. I slipped from the mast and swung wildly on my safety line as the boat heeled over, almost onto its side, and I was dunked into the sea. I surfaced to see water filling the cockpit: Sophie and Tom had been swept off their feet and were only saved from being washed over the side by their harnesses, while Daz and Claire somehow managed to keep themselves upright.

On the shore, the infected stalked back and forth, driven wild by the screams and shouts emanating from the boat. Above them, another appeared over the brow of a low hill, drawn by all the commotion. This was quickly followed by another and another. Soon, there were so many of them that I could hear their roars and snarls even above the noise of the water and the wind. They milled around, jostling for position at the water's edge, frustrated that uninfected humans were so close and yet still beyond their reach.

For what seemed like an age, we lay there half under the water, half out of it. Finally, the currents pushed us free and the boat started to right itself again, throwing me upwards towards the mast: I hit it hard and was sent spinning across to the other side. Below, Daz and Tom fought with the wheel again as the water drained from the cockpit. Finally, they started to win and soon the boat was pointing in the right direction once more. As I scrambled to regain my footing on the mast, I glanced across to the island. We must have finally moved beyond the range at which the infected could sense our presence because they were no longer pacing, following our every move; instead, they stood staring out to sea after us, before gradually drifting away from the shore, some on their own, others in small groups.

Looking ahead, I could see we were through the worst of it. Satisfied we were now safe, both from the dangers of the whirlpool and from the infected on the shore, I unclipped myself and climbed back down to the deck. Returning to the cockpit, I surveyed my fellow crew: they were soaked to the skin, but were clearly relieved to have survived. I bent over and shook my head, trying to get as much water out of my hair as possible, and then straightened up. I gazed back at the maelstrom before turning to the others. 'Well, that went better than I expected.'

They glared at me, but said nothing.

Chapter Thirteen

We were anchored out of the wind on the west side of the island which lay to the north of the whirlpool, recovering from our ordeal, when I heard the sound of a distant engine. Grabbing the binoculars, I scanned both the water and the land, but found nothing. As the noise grew louder, I suddenly realised it wasn't coming from the sea, or the nearby island: it was coming from the sky. Craning my neck, I finally found it: a dark speck moving against the clouds.

Tom stood beside me, shielding his eyes with his hands. 'Is that what I think it is?'

'It sure looks like it.' I lowered the binoculars.

Tom stared at it. 'I wonder what it means.'

Claire stepped forward and leant on the guard rail. 'It means someone knows somewhere where it's safe to land a plane!'

Sophie leapt enthusiastically to her feet, scrunching up her eyes, trying to get a better look at the aircraft. 'Can we follow it?'

I turned back to the plane and tracked it for a few seconds. 'Not at the speed it's flying.'

'What about attractin' their attention?' Daz waved his hands back and forth above his head. 'If they know we're here, maybe they can let us know where they took off from, or where they're goin'.'

Sophie started waving, too, as did Tom

'Good idea, but they'll never see you from that distance.' I ducked into the cabin and rifled through the chart table, looking for my flare gun. Back on deck, I slotted a cartridge into the chamber, held it above my head and pulled the trigger. The flare arched high into the sky before slowly drifting back towards the water: the plane didn't respond. I reloaded the gun and fired again. For a moment, I thought that this one hadn't been seen either, but then the plane slowly banked, only straightening up again when it was heading directly towards us. Wanting to make sure they didn't miss us, I grabbed one of the smoke signals I kept in a waterproof canister by the helm and pulled the strap to ignite it; it burst into life, sending a bright orange flame several feet into the air and red smoke billowing out across the water.

Within minutes, the plane was directly above us. I moved the smoke signal back and forth, indicating our presence and wondering what they'd make of us: our decks still grubby from the ash which had fallen on us after Glasgow had been bombed; lobster creels strapped to the top of the cabin; and Claire and Sophie dressed in mismatched and outsized men's clothes. The plane circled round once and then started to descend. At first, I wondered what it was doing, but then I spotted the floats hanging below the fuselage; it was a seaplane and it was coming into land. That's when it struck me: if it could land on the water, maybe Claire was wrong and there wasn't any safe place to land on the shore after all; the sense of hope its appearance had kindled within me vanished in an instant.

The plane's floats hit the sea's surface, sending white plumes into the air; it bounced, leaving the water for several yards, before coming down again. I watched as it slowed to a crawl and then taxied over to us, a sense of trepidation bubbling inside me: this was the first time we'd seen another living soul since we'd left the Clyde, or at least one that wasn't infected. The seaplane came to rest some ten yards from where we were clustered in the cockpit. For a minute, it just floated there; then the door swung open and a figure stepped out onto the left-hand float. As the person emerged, I saw a leg clad in tight black trousers tucked into a leather motorcycle boot, followed by a body wearing a camouflage jacket; then, as the person turned, I saw a shotgun held loosely in one hand. Finally, they straightened up and we could see them clearly for the first time.

'It's a woman!' Daz exclaimed in surprised.

Sophie punched him in the arm. 'Don't sound so shocked. Women can be pilots too, you know.'

A broad grin spread across my face. 'Mitch! Well, aren't you a sight for sore eyes!'

Tom turned to me, confused. 'You know her?'

'Hey, Ben; I thought I recognised the boat!' Mitch took off her sunglasses, looking serious for a moment. 'Sorry, but I've got to ask; you're all okay, aren't you? None of you are ill or anything?'

'No, we're all fine.' I replied

Relief spread across her face. 'Good!'

I smiled at her. 'Well, are you going to come over and say hello properly, or are we just going to stand here shouting at each other all day?'

She smiled back. 'Throw me a rope, then!'

'I was lucky, I guess. I had a charter trip booked for two, and I was running through my usual pre-flight checks. Suddenly, this guy appeared out of nowhere, running flat-out. He kept looking back over his shoulder and I couldn't understand what was going on. Then I heard them: this mass of people, yelling and screaming, all chasing after him. The man saw me and the plane, and turned in my direction. He was shouting something, but I couldn't hear him above the noise of the people who were following him.

'He was about twenty yards away when he slipped and went crashing to the ground. As he struggled to get back to his feet, the crowd finally caught up with him, and they just tore into him. He tried to fight them off, but it was pointless and within seconds he'd been ripped limb from limb, right there in front of me. That's when I realised what must be happening. I was frozen with fear, but I knew I had to force myself to move before they noticed I was there and attacked me, too. As quietly as possible, I crept over and undid the lines holding the seaplane to the dock, and then I slipped into the cockpit.

'I started the engine, and that's when they realised I was there. They flew along the dock as I pulled away, not even stopping when they reached the end as they threw themselves towards me. They gripped onto the float and the side of the plane, and I knew I'd never be able to take off with all the extra weight. One of them, this big muscular guy, was hammering on the window and I knew it was only a matter of time before he broke through. I had no option but to open the door and slam it into him again and again until he finally fell off into the water. Then I pushed the throttle forward, and the plane started moving faster. This dislodged more and more of them until there was only one left, yet no matter what I tried it clung on. The plane lifted from the water, but with the extra weight of the infected hanging from the float I struggled to get enough height ...'

'Wait a second.' I remembered our near miss when we'd first taken to the Clyde. 'That was you? You were the one who just about flew into us?'

'Oh, so you're the boat that got in my way! I didn't recognise you. I was too distracted, what with having some mad Weegie bastard trying to kill me!'

Despite everything, I laughed. It was the type of casual banter Mitch and I always shared whenever we got together: her ragging on me for being from Glasgow, and me making fun of her for being from the islands. A few years older than me, we'd met the first summer I started running my own whale-watching tours on the west coast of Scotland and we'd stayed in touch ever since. We each had our own business — hers running a seaplane service between Glasgow and the islands — so we didn't get together much, but whenever we ended up in the same place, we made a point of spending time together, usually over a few drinks in the nearest bar. I looked at the plane, wondering why I hadn't recognised it as Mitch's immediately. Then it occurred to me. 'That's not the one you were flying last year, is it?'

'No, it's a new one. I've only had it a couple of months: business was so good last summer, I thought I'd invest in a bigger one for this year.' She glanced at it and sighed. 'Shows what I know!'

Considering the circumstances, Mitch was looking in good shape and I was keen to find out how she'd been surviving. 'So, where did you go after you left Glasgow?'

'I went to Loch Lomond first, just to regroup and check the plane hadn't been damaged. Once I heard how bad it was getting I headed out this way; I ended up in Tobermory. It took a few days for the disease to reach there, and this meant they had enough time to get prepared. They got together and set up barricades to keep the place safe, well some of it. A lot of people still died, or got infected, but there are about fifty of them left, hanging on. It's where I've mainly been basing myself. We've always kept a fuel dump there, so I've been flying around trying to work out where there are survivors and which communities have been overrun.'

I leant forwards. 'How many are there?'

'I've found ten groups, so far; maybe a couple of hundred people in all; mostly on the smaller islands and further north. I've found nothing south of Mull.'

That fitted with what we'd found at Port Ellen and on Jura.

Mitch continued. 'Everyone's just so shocked at what's happened, but we're hanging in there, y'know. Some of the groups are more friendly than others, but there's only one I know about which I haven't been able to speak to at all and that's on Iona. They just won't let me near, and I can't really blame them: it's a risk letting strangers come ashore now.'

She paused for a moment. 'That's how it was at first, then this group of naval personnel showed up in a couple of large ribs. They set themselves up on Rhum, and they've been throwing their weight around ever since. For some reason, they think they're in charge, and that we should all do what they say. It's a bit of a pain, but we're hoping if we ignore them for long enough, they'll take the hint and just leave us to it.'

I wondered where these naval people had come from and whether they were in some way connected to the frigate from the blockade. It was possible these were the survivors we'd seen escaping in the ribs, but they could just have easily come from somewhere else entirely.

Mitch interrupted these thoughts. 'So how did you end up here?'

I gave her the potted account of what had happened to us: how we got out of Glasgow, of seeing it being bombed; about the outbreak in the holding area; about the storm; the incident at the fish farm; what had happened in Port Ellen; and at the whirlpool.

'Sounds like you've had it rough.' She shook her head. 'I can't believe they bombed the city; they kept that out of the news.' She rubbed her hand across her forehead. 'I guess they didn't want everyone to panic.'

'Yeah, right!' Claire joined the conversation. 'More likely they wanted to cover up how much they screwed up their attempts to contain the outbreak.' Claire snorted derisively. 'All they did was make it a hell of a lot worse!'

'Sorry, I should introduce you.' I turned to the others. 'This is Michaela McDonald, better known as Mitch.' I turned to Mitch and pointed to my right. 'This is Claire: our resident doctor, cynic and anti-militarist.'

Not appreciating my description, Claire scowled at me before turning to Mitch and holding out her hand. 'Nice to meet you.'

While Claire's greeting was outwardly friendly, I detected a hint of reticence. I wondered if she was still concerned about mixing with strangers, and what that might mean for her survival, and more importantly, that of her daughter.

I carried on with the introductions. 'This is Sophie, Claire's daughter; Daz, someone we picked up along the way; and finally, Tom.'

'Tom?' Mitch eyed him carefully. 'As in the guy you used to work with when you were a juggler?'

'The one and only!' Tom grinned at her. 'So what's he been saying about me? You know he lies, don't you?'

Mitch shook the hand he held out. 'If even half of what Ben's told me about you is true ...' She smiled, looking him up and down as she did so. 'Well, let's just say I'll need to keep an eye on you.'

Daz and Sophie looked enquiringly at each other and then at Tom. So far, they'd only seen Tom on the boat, where he was out of his depth. This new information got them wondering about what he'd been like before the outbreak started.

For the next hour, we sat in the cockpit and chatted, trying to talk about anything other than the fact that the world had fallen apart. Tom was getting on with the new arrival like a house on fire, and they spent much of the time exchanging stories about me: Tom telling her about some of the things I'd got up to in my days as a performer; Mitch telling him about drunken nights out in various remote island bars. Both left me feeling rather embarrassed, but it was the first time that I'd seen Tom like this with a woman in a very long time, not since Jane, so I couldn't help but be happy for him.

Finally, reality reasserted itself and the first moment of normality we'd had since the start of the outbreak came to its inevitable end. Mitch glanced at her watch and stood up. 'I guess I need to be heading back: the others will be wondering what's happened to me. Where're you guys heading?'

'We haven't really decided yet.' I leaned back and put my hands behind my head. 'We were just scouting around to see if we could find any other survivors.'

'Why don't you come on up to Tobermory? There'll be a few faces you'll recognise there and they've got a pretty good set-up.'

Tom's face lit up. 'That seems like a good idea.'

'We should make our decisions based on something beyond your hormones,' Claire muttered.

Tom shrugged his shoulders. 'If there are other people there and they've got an area that they've managed to keep secure and free of the infected, they're doing better than the army. We'd have a much better chance of surviving with people like that around than we would on our own.' Tom's tone was matter of fact. 'I imagine they'll also have better resources than we have, and access to things we don't: like food, drinking water, weapons, medicines; stuff we're going to need.'

Claire opened her mouth to say something, but thought better of it. Tom winked at me and I sniggered: this was a side of him that Claire hadn't seen before; his more intelligent side. Many people took one look at Tom and the way he dressed, and presumed he was some brainless stoner, but you needed to be able to think on your feet if you were to survive as a street performer; to be able to read a situation and make the right decision in an instant. In this case, Claire could see Tom's assessment of the advantages Tobermory offered us was spot-on, but I suspected that Mitch's presence made Tobermory an even more attractive proposition for him.

***

It took us a couple of days of pretty hard sailing to reach Tobermory. We'd taken the outside route, round the south-west corner of Mull, rather than going up the sound on the northern side. It meant we'd avoided areas with strong currents, but I'd also wanted to check out the survivors on Iona that Mitch had mentioned.

As it turned out, I shouldn't have bothered. I'd always been welcome there before, but this time we were met with warning shots when we'd tried to approach the ferry dock. I didn't see where they came from, but the message was clear. I couldn't blame them really; if the island was still free of the disease, the best approach to keep it that way was to stop anyone from bringing it

229

ashore. In this new world, it made sense for once welcoming communities to cut themselves off from outsiders. Strangers now posed a danger beyond belief, I'd already seen this first-hand in the holding area: both those of us on the boats and the naval personnel had trusted the two men they'd picked up to say whether they might be infected or not, and when it turned out one of them had been a carrier, it had very nearly killed us all.

We finally pulled into Tobermory Bay on the evening of the second day, shortly after the sun had dropped below the horizon. Mitch must have warned the surviving residents we were coming, and that we were safe, because almost immediately two small motorboats emerged out of the darkness and directed us to a place where we could drop anchor. They obviously weren't completely trusting as this was set away from the other vessels in the anchorage, and from the main settlement itself. Rather than coming alongside, they shouted across that they'd leave it until the following morning before they welcomed us properly. Just before they left, one of the motorboats came close enough to toss a large package into our cockpit and one of them yelled: 'A welcome present from Mitch!' Before we could say anything, they zoomed off into the night.

Sophie picked up the bundle, 'I wonder what it is.' She quickly untied it.

The first thing that fell out was a packet of Tom's favourite tobacco and some cigarette papers. He instantly grabbed them, and within seconds was leaning back on one of the seats, taking in large lungfuls of smoke with great gusto. I looked at him and raised an eyebrow; he laughed. 'You know I've never been good with will power!' He took another long draw. 'Remind me to tell Mitch how much I love her for this.'

Before I could reply, Sophie yelped with pleasure. 'Clothes! Proper clothes!' She held up a top, her face beaming with delight. 'And they'll actually fit!'

Claire picked up a note which had fallen onto the deck, reading it silently.

'What does it say?' Daz was curious.

Tom took it and read it aloud. 'Claire and Sophie, as I've told him many times, Ben has very little taste when it comes to clothing. I think these will suit you better than any of his. I hope they fit. Welcome to Tobermory. Mitch. PS. Tom, have a smoke on me. You deserve it for getting this far!'

I could tell by the look on Claire's face how much she appreciated Mitch's gesture, not just for herself, but also because of how it lifted Sophie's spirits. She wasn't as keen, however, on the fact that Tom was smoking again.

Chapter Fourteen

'Oh my god! It's Balamory!' It was early the following morning and I was studying the surrounding land with the binoculars, so I hadn't noticed Sophie come out on deck.

'I used to watch it as a kid: it was my favourite programme.' She seemed excited. 'I never knew it actually existed. I thought it was just a made-up place.'

'It is.' I looked towards the brightly coloured cluster of traditional stone houses which lined the shore. At one end was the distinctive outline of the local distillery, while at the other was an impressive stone building topped by a tall spire. 'But much of it was filmed here.'

I put the binoculars down and turned to Sophie; she was dressed in denim jeans, and a blue and white Nordic jumper: both fitted perfectly. 'How are the clothes?'

'They're brilliant!' She grinned widely. 'No offence, Ben, but your clothes aren't really my kind of thing. It's so great to have something nice to wear again.'

I smiled, glad to see her happy for the first time since I'd met her. I knew it wouldn't last, but since the world had changed, any moment of happiness, no matter how brief, had to be fully enjoyed.

A few minutes later, Daz came out and we had a similar conversation about Balamory to the one I'd had with Sophie; Tom and Claire commented on it, too. It seemed that even though it was a programme aimed at pre-schoolers, everyone was familiar with it. Me, I'd spent a lot of time in this part of the world as a kid: summer holidays; Easter breaks; the occasional New Year. This meant I always thought of it as Tobermory first and Balamory second.

The older parts of the town occupied a narrow strip of

land between the sea and the hill that loomed over it. Bales of straw had been used to build barriers on the main street about seventy yards on either side of where the quay projected out from the shore. Each barrier was some fifteen feet high and three bales thick, and they'd been extended far enough into the water that there was no way round them, even at low tide. While I couldn't quite see for myself, I presumed the alleys and lanes leading between the buildings had been blocked in a similar manner.

Islanders who had the disease gathered on the outside of the makeshift barricades, aware there were uninfected nearby. I wondered about the infected, about how much of their humanity they retained. I'd not really had time to study them before and now that I did, they intrigued me. Humans, real, uninfected humans, could have climbed over these barriers, yet the infected seemed unable to work out how to do this, or that they could swim around the ends where they reached into the sea: it seemed that while the infected had desires, they couldn't think for themselves; they couldn't reason or work things out. Maybe this gave us an advantage, maybe it didn't; ether way I thought it was something worth knowing,

As I was eating breakfast in the cockpit, an off-white open motorboat drew up nearby, but not alongside as would usually have been the case. Two men were on board, one of whom I recognised as Mitch's cousin, Hamish. I didn't know him well, but he worked on one of the local fishing boats and often called me on the radio if he saw anything which he thought might be of interest to the tourists who came on my whale-watching trips.

Hamish called out. 'Hey, Ben, good to see you made it out in one piece.'

'Good to see you guys made it, too. How's the town doing?'

'We've lost a lot of people, but at least some of us are still here.' I could tell from his tone that he was struggling to see this as something positive. 'From what I hear that's better than most places.'

I put my plate down. 'Yeah, I guess.'

The two men glanced at each other and shifted nervously from one foot to the other and back again.

'Ben,' Hamish looked everywhere except at my face, 'before you can come ashore, we need to ask something.' He was staring down at his boots now. 'Are you all ...? Have you had any ...?' He hesitated as he tried to think of how to ask the question he needed the answer to. Eventually, he just blurted it out. 'Is there any chance that any of you are infected?'

Before, I'd always been greeted with warm and open arms whenever I'd arrived in Tobermory, and it felt strange to be treated this way now. I guess it was a measure of how much the world had changed in such a short space of time. People arriving from elsewhere, even ones you already knew, meant the possibility of the infection being brought into areas which were still disease-free; and this was something those already there wanted to avoid at all costs. Being wary of outsiders was no longer rude; instead, it was a vital survival strategy. As we'd already found at Iona, once open communities had now closed themselves off. I suspected the only reason they were even considering letting us into Tobermory was a mix of Mitch putting in a good word, and the fact that I wasn't a complete stranger to at least some of those who'd survived this far.

I did my best to reassure them. 'We're all fine. Not even

a chance. We haven't been anywhere we could've picked up the disease in days, so if any of us had it, we'd know by now.'

The sense of relief in the other boat was clear. Hamish shifted the engine into gear and finally pulled up alongside. The other man held it in place and looked across. 'So where'd you come in from?'

They both stared, open-mouthed as I gave him a quick summary. Finally, Hamish spoke. 'Sounds like you've been pretty lucky.'

'I guess so.' I glanced over to the shore, and the barricades which had been erected to protect the survivors. 'What happened around here? How've you guys managed to hold out so well?'

Hamish snorted. 'Fifty of us left? I'd hardly say we're doing well.'

'You're doing way better than anywhere else we've been.'

'Yeah, I suppose.' A pained expression crossed his face. 'I guess these days everything's relative. You want to come ashore; have a look around?'

'Definitely.' We'd been cooped up in the boat for almost two weeks, and I longed to be able to stretch my legs. 'Have you got room for a few more?'

Hamish nodded.

I yelled down the companionway and Daz, Sophie and Tom scrambled into the cockpit, all as eager as I was to get off the boat, even if it was only for a short while; Claire appeared a few seconds later, with somewhat less enthusiasm, and I guessed she'd rather stay on the boat and catch up on her sleep now we'd finally found somewhere safe. Yet, she also wanted keep a watchful eye on her daughter, so she joined the rest of us when we climbed into Hamish's boat.

As we motored towards the shore, Hamish filled me in on what had happened in Tobermory since the outbreak began.

'We'd been hearing the news out of America for a couple of weeks, but we didn't really pay much attention to it: it was all so far away; none of us could see how it could possibly get anywhere near us. Then we heard about the outbreak in Glasgow. That was when we started to worry, but still we felt it was a long way off.' As he spoke, he manoeuvred the motorboat round an anchored fishing boat.

'Mitch arrived the following morning and told us first-hand what she'd seen. The morning after that, we started hearing about people turning up at the ferry terminal over on the east side of the island. Most were locals who'd moved away, but some were strangers, who thought Mull might offer a safe haven from all that was happening on the mainland. I guess it was the same with other islands. We worried about them bringing the disease with them, but we didn't feel we could turn them away.' He turned the boat sharply and shifted the engine into neutral as we bumped against the end of the stone quay. The other man jumped ashore, a rope held in his hand which he tied to a metal ring set into the stone.

Hamish turned to me. 'That's not the type of people we are around here; it's not in our nature: maybe it should've been, though, because soon we heard about the first infection on the island, over on the east coast, just up the road from where the ferries come in. Mitch flew down to check it out and what she told us wasn't good: it seemed the disease was spreading fast.'

One by one we climbed onto the quay as Hamish continued. 'We knew it was only a matter of time before it got here and we felt we needed to do something, so we set to work trying to make a secure area where we could all hole up when the disease finally reached us. We knew we couldn't protect the whole town so we worked out which parts we could secure and which we couldn't. When we looked around, we found the only area we could hope to do anything with was the middle of Main Street.'

Before Hamish could continue the other guy jumped in. 'It was Hamish, here, who came up with the idea of using straw bales to build the defences. That's what saved us; it's what's been keeping us safe ever since.'

Hamish's face turned as red as his hair, embarrassed at being given so much credit. 'I used them to build my house; got the plans off the Internet. It works better than you'd think, and there was no reason I could see why it wouldn't work just as well for building walls to keep out the infected; you just need to know how to secure them all together properly. The bales won't last forever, but they should hold back the infected until we can get something more permanent in place. We're thinking shipping containers, if we can find them and work out how get them into place.'

We walked slowly along the quay; Sophie and Tom were swaying gently, while Daz had stumbled twice already. After the second time, he was getting frustrated. 'How come I can't walk properly? It's like I'm drunk or somethin'!'

'It's called "sea legs". Your body's got used to being on a moving boat.' I grinned, amused by the confused look on his face. 'Don't worry. It'll wear off.'

Daz stumbled again, grabbing onto Sophie for support. 'When?'

I stifled a laugh. 'In about half an hour or so.'

By then, we'd reached the point where the quay met the road which ran along the shore. In front of us, was a row of stone houses, each several storeys high. While most were jammed tightly together, some were separated by narrow lanes. Many of the lower levels housed shops, while some were occupied by pubs and cafes. In effect, these buildings acted as a vast pre-existing barrier between the small stretch of land in front of them and the rest of the island, and all the residents had needed to do to secure it was board up any rear-facing windows, close off the alleyways and block the road at either end. It was still a mammoth task, but the local architecture had made it possible for them to hold back the infected rather than being overrun. I turned to Hamish. 'So where'd you get all the bales from?'

'From various farms on the island; it didn't take as long as you might think to get the safe area set up, not with all of us working together. The only problem was we weren't fast enough and the infection arrived while we were still trying to gather all the supplies we thought we'd need.'

He paused and looked off into the distance. 'I still don't know how it happened. One minute, we were unloading cases of canned food from the back of a Land Rover, and the next it seemed like there were infected everywhere, and all we could do was run. That was when I realised I'd screwed up when I designed the barricades. I'd aimed to make them as impregnable as possible, but it never occurred to me that we might have to get over them in a hurry. We were pinned against the wall by the infected and we didn't have any weapons. Anyway, these weren't strangers; they were people we recognised; people we'd known all our lives; people we went to school with ...' His voice faded away for a moment.

'We all just huddled there with the infected whittling us down as those on the outside of the group got attacked and killed, or worse, got turned into more infected. Our only option was to try to get over the barrier we'd built, but there weren't any footholds and nothing to grip onto so it was difficult. I'm not proud of it, but it was everyone for themselves. It was the only thing we could do to survive. Only those of us who were fit and able enough made it. The old people, the kids, they didn't stand a chance. You couldn't carry anyone; you couldn't pull them up behind you. All you could do was climb. I remember sitting there once I'd reached the top, looking down. The infected were everywhere, tearing into people, people I knew, people I loved.' Hamish shook his head. 'If only I'd thought about how we were going to get in when we built the walls rather than just how we were going to keep *them* out. At the start of that day, there were almost 800 people here. Within ten minutes of the first infected showing up, there were only fifty of us left.'

The loss of life was small in comparison to what had happened in other places, like Glasgow, but for a small community like Tobermory, it would have been as devastating as the loss of hundreds of thousands in some distant city. The fact that the infected who now lined their makeshift walls, desperate to break in and kill those inside, were people they knew, or were even related to, made it all the more heart-wrenching.

Hamish continued. 'Those of us who survived that first day have been working hard to try to keep the community together, to work with people on the other islands which are still disease-free. Mitch has been great for that. She's been able to check out places which it would have taken us days to get round to visiting. It's helped us maintain some of the connections we had before all this happened.'

I remembered something and broke in. 'Mitch mentioned about navy people turning up.'

'Aye.' Hamish rubbed the back of his neck. 'They arrived a couple of days after the infection. They were looking for somewhere to set up a base. The one in charge was nice enough, but they seemed to feel they had some right to order us around. They were talking about bringing survivors together, thinking it would make it easier for them to protect us. They didn't seem to appreciate we were doing just fine on our own and that we could damn well protect ourselves. They weren't here when we really needed them, and I can't see how they can do any better than we're already doing.' There was a great deal of bitterness and anger in Hamish's voice. 'They might have their machine guns and their training, but there's more to staying safe than that, isn't there? I mean, you've done pretty well without any guns, haven't you?'

I started to reply, but Hamish carried on before I could answer. 'Anyway, they clearly didn't think this place would make a particularly good base and they moved on almost as soon as they arrived. Next thing we know, Mitch was telling us they'd taken over the Big House on Rhum. There's no infection there and even though it's a big island, only about twenty people live there so the residents couldn't put up much resistance against thirty-eight heavily armed men.'

I was keen to find out more. 'Any idea what they've been doing since then?'

'Going round the various surviving communities, trying to persuade them to relocate to Rhum, so they can protect them more easily. So far, they've not had much luck. People around here are used to doing things for themselves. We don't like outsiders coming in and telling us what we should be doing.'

The other man chimed in. 'From what I hear, they've also been fortifying the Big House.'

Daz frowned. 'What's "the Big House"?'

'It's where the island's owners used to live. It's a mansion really, but everyone calls it the "Big House" because it's much larger than anything else on the island.'

Claire nodded. 'Makes sense. And you said they're fortifying it?'

'It's pretty much built like a castle, anyway, so it's not exactly difficult, but they've been blocking up the windows on the ground floor and stuff like that. I guess it's in case any infected get onto the island, but I can't see how that's going to happen. Rhum's too far from the mainland.'

'Aye,' Hamish nodded before looking round. 'So you want the tour?'

'Sounds good.' I followed as Hamish led off, with the others trailing after us.

Our tour of Tobermory was both illuminating and horrifying. It was clearly secure, at least for the time being, but the infected were never far away. Almost everywhere we went, I could hear their snarls and moans as they clawed on the barricades and hammered on the boarded-up windows and doors at the backs of the buildings, which separated the safe area from the rest of the town. At one end, there was a ladder leading up onto the top of the straw bales. We climbed up and found ourselves looking down on more infected. Our presence enraged them, and they started to screech and scream as they threw themselves against the bales below us. Despite the anger which burned in their eyes, they looked so normal; like people you might meet every day.

While the rest of us stared, Hamish turned away.

Daz was watching him. 'What's wrong?'

'What's wrong?' He turned back and pointed angrily to a man about his own age with closely cropped hair. 'That's my best friend down there. I've known him since I was eight.' He pointed again, this time to an elderly woman who, despite her years, was pounding violently against the barrier. 'That's my aunt; and that ...' He couldn't even look at the woman wearing a bloodstained jacket, slowly healing bite marks visible on her throat and neck. 'That's my wife.'

Daz let out a low sigh, the full impact of what Hamish had just said quickly sinking in. 'Shit!'

I gazed at the infected, seeing them in a new light, and then I recognised one of them. I turned to Hamish. 'Is that ...?' I almost couldn't get the words out. 'Is that Big John?'

Hamish nodded.

Big John had worked at the fuel dock in Tobermory for as long as I'd been sailing these waters, and he was always happy to share a story or pass on a snippet of information. It wasn't that he gossiped, he just let everyone know what was happening. You'd spend five minutes filling up and by the time you left, you'd have a better idea of what everyone else was doing than if you'd spoken to them all yourself.

Now, there he was, his beard flecked with grey, his hair dishevelled, still wearing his trademark yellow oilskin jacket. Gone was the usual friendly grin, replaced by a look of intense rage: I'd never seen such fury in the eyes of another human being.

I climbed down from the barricade, deeply affected by what I'd seen, and what the survivors in Tobermory had to endure each and every day. The infected we'd encountered before were unknown to us; they were strangers; we had no prior knowledge of them: we knew nothing of what they'd once been. Here, in Tobermory, they knew many of the infected that surrounded them; they'd lived with them, laughed with them; they'd grown up with them; and now, all those with the disease wanted to do was to attack those who remained uninfected.

'Why don't you do something about it?' Sophie was staring at Hamish.

He looked confused. 'What d'you mean?'

Sophie kept her eyes locked on him. 'Why don't you put them out of their misery?'

'How? We don't have the guns or the ammunition to kill them all.' Hamish gazed off into the distance. 'Besides, everyone in here knows almost everyone out there. Who do we decide to kill first? Who's going to do it?' Hamish stared at Sophie. 'Could you do it to someone you loved? If you could, you're a better person than I am because I'd give anything to be able to put them out of their misery, to be able to bury them, to mourn their loss, but I can't. I know; I've tried. I've sat up there with my hunting rifle, but I just can't bring myself to do it. So they live on, hollow husks of the people they once were. Whenever I see one that I used to know, it's like someone stabbing a knife into my very soul and twisting. Yet, I can't help it, because they're always there, waiting for us to slip up so they can tear us apart.'

Sophie didn't say anything, but the look on her face suggested she was thinking about Jake, and about what her mother had done. Finally, I think she realised how much courage it had taken for Claire to kill him before he turned, and why she'd had to do it.

Just as we finished our tour of what was left of Tobermory, there was a shout from our left, and I turned to see Mitch striding towards us. 'So you finally made it. Great! Sorry I wasn't here when you arrived.' She looked at Sophie and Claire. 'I see you got my welcome present.'

'Yes!' Sophie twirled round, showing off her new clothes. 'They're brilliant! Where did you get them from?'

'They belong to a friend's daughter who's about your age.'

'Cool. I'll need to thank her for letting me have them. Can I meet her?'

There was an awkward silence.

'What?' Sophie's eyes narrowed. 'Where is she?'

Mitch turned away to avoid making eye contact.

Sophie suddenly looked very serious. 'Where is she?'

Seeing Mitch was getting upset, Claire stepped forward and put her hand on her daughter's shoulder. 'Just leave it, honey.'

Sophie shook off her mother's hand. 'No, I want to know. Where is she?'

'It's okay.' Mitch's voice sounded flat; she took a deep breath. 'She's gone. We lost her when Tobermory was overrun.'

'And you thought you could just take her clothes and give them to me?' Sophie's face clouded with anger. 'They're not yours; they're hers. You've got no right to do that!'

Claire grabbed Sophie and pulled her back. 'Don't speak to Mitch like that!'

'But she's got no right!' Tears welled up in Sophie's eyes. 'Don't you see? Their stuff ... it's all that's left of them: it's all that there is to remember them by.' A single sob escaped from her. 'If I'd died, would you just give my things away? What about Jake's? Would you give Jake's stuff away now he's gone?' Sophie turned and stormed towards the quay. As she did so, she yelled back to us. 'Someone needs to take me back to the boat. I need to get out of these clothes. Now!'

Daz frowned. 'Why's she so upset?'

Claire watched Sophie walk away. 'I think all this has reminded her about Jake and her friends, and how they're all gone. And how many kids just like her are now dead ... or worse. I'd better go after her.' She glanced at Mitch. 'Sorry. It's not your fault. She's not dealing with all this very well.'

Daz, looked at Claire. 'I thought she was doing okay.'

'She's not; she just hides it well: she always has. It was the same when her father died.' Sophie was now standing at the end of the quay, staring out towards the boat. 'I really need to go after her.'

'I'll go.'

We all turned and stared at Daz as he carried on. 'I know how she's feelin' an' I'm closer to her age; she might find it easier to talk to me about it.'

Claire considered this. 'Maybe you're right.'

This was all the encouragement Daz needed and he set off down the road. We watched as he reached Sophie; they talked for a couple of seconds and then sat down on the quay, legs hanging over the end; Daz tentatively put one arm round her and in response she let her head fall onto his shoulder.

I turned back to Mitch, and saw her wiping her face. 'Who's clothes were they?'

'My god-daughter's.' She cleared her throat. 'She was

so great: I used to take her up in the plane all the time. She loved it; she loved how everything appeared so different when you were looking down on it. She wanted to be a pilot, just like me.'

Tom stepped forward to comfort her. 'How did she die?'

'That's the worst thing.' Mitch sniffed and wiped her face. 'She didn't, but she might as well have. She got infected; I know because I've seen her, attacking the barricade, trying to get in. This sounds terrible, but I wish with all my heart she had died: it would've been painful, but at least I'd know how to deal with it. I mean how do you deal with something like this?'

Chapter Fifteen

Within a week of our arrival in Tobermory, we'd settled into a routine of sorts. Since we could sail, rather than having to rely on our engine, we didn't have to waste precious diesel, which could be better used in generators and other equipment, when we travelled around. We were also the largest sailing vessel which was at the disposal of the local communities, so we could carry the most. This meant we were quickly engaged to run food and other supplies, between the different communities of survivors. With no other options, Claire's skills were also in great demand, and wherever we went, she'd set up a temporary clinic to deal with any medical problems which had arisen since our last visit.

We also took part in foraging expeditions. Together with Hamish, Mitch and the other locals, we fished for mackerel, raided seal haul-outs for meat, and seabird colonies for eggs. I staked out the creels we'd pulled up off Jura and was able to provide a regular supply of crabs, lobsters and other shellfish. This meant that while we only retained the slightest of toeholds on the land, we were never short of food.

For the most part, Tom, Daz, Claire, Sophie and I stayed together, but if it looked like it wouldn't be a difficult trip, I'd leave some of them behind so they could get a day off to relax ... as much as anyone could relax given all that was happening around us. This also gave me a break from them, and every now and then, I couldn't resist taking the boat out on my own just to be alone. After all, on a forty-five foot boat with five people living on board, it was difficult to get any sort of personal space. Out on the sea, all on my own, I could pretend — at least for a short while — that everything was the way it used to be before the virus entered our lives.

It was while we were returning from a raid on a fish farm, which had netted us several thousand fresh fish that would be smoked or dried over fires to preserve them, that we finally ran into the naval personnel Hamish had complained about when we first arrived. Daz was the first to spot them. 'Hey! What does that remind you of?'

I took the binoculars and saw a familiar-looking black rib cutting through the sea towards us, the silhouette of a large gun near the bow clearly visible. My first instinct was to avoid them, but when I changed course, the rib changed its course, too: there was no doubt they were specifically heading our way. Knowing we couldn't out-run them, I turned the yacht into the wind and prepared for their arrival. 'Daz, you'd better go and get the others.'

A moment later, a sleepy looking Tom climbed through the companionway, rubbing his eyes, followed shortly by Claire and Sophie: all three had been making the most of their time off watch to catch up on some much needed sleep.

'What's going on?' Tom stretched, 'How come we're not mov—?' His eyes came to rest on the rapidly approaching rib. 'Is that who I think it is? What do they want?'

That was what I'd been wondering, too. So far, we'd only heard rumours about what the naval personnel were like from the communities we'd visited and the reviews were, at best, mixed. Now, it looked like we'd get to find out for ourselves.

'Ahoy there! I thought I recognised the boat.' The rib was now pulling alongside and the first officer from the frigate was hailing us, smiling as he did so. 'Good to see we're not the only ones who made it out of the Clyde in one piece. We'd have come back for you, but I thought if we'd been overrun, you lot would've had no chance.'

I crossed my arms, annoyed that they'd simply given up on us and saved themselves. After all, they were the ones who'd brought the person carrying the infection to the holding area in the first place, and I felt they owed it to us to have at least tried to see if we needed help rather than just abandoning us.

The first officer took off his cap and ran a hand through his hair. 'We only made it out by the skin of our teeth.' His voice sounded flat, as if he still couldn't quite believe what he was saying. 'We were up on deck preparing to go out on patrol when a strange noise came echoing up from below. At first, it sounded like animals, but I knew that couldn't be right. Then, all of a sudden, there were people everywhere, but they weren't people anymore; they were attacking everyone they could get their hands on. We had to fight them off, kill them, but no matter what we tried, we couldn't hold them back, not for long. In the end, we did the only thing we could, which was get the ribs into the water, and get the hell away from there.' He hung his head.

I regretted jumping to conclusions before I knew the whole story. They'd been struggling to keep themselves alive, just like we had, and who was I to judge them? We'd abandoned the others in the holding area just as readily as the first officer and the marines had abandoned us. I pushed these thoughts from my mind and surveyed the men on the rib. Despite all that had happened, they looked well-rested and well-fed. Unlike Tom and me, they were also clean-shaven, and had maintained their short, military hairstyles. The uniforms they still wore were clean and the first officer's looked freshly pressed. I couldn't help but think that whatever they were doing, given the circumstances, they were doing it well.

'What about the others who were there with you?' The first officer seemed genuinely concerned. 'Did they get out too?'

I thought back to that night and all who'd died. 'They weren't so lucky.'

'Damn!' There was a moment's silence. 'Look, since we've run into you, there's something you might be able to help us with. I'm sure you've heard we're trying to set up a safe zone on Rhum, and to get as many of the other survivors there as possible. That way, we can protect them better, but it seems the locals aren't too keen on the idea.' As he spoke, he replaced his cap on his head and straightened it. 'I can kind of understand their point of view. They think we're just coming in and ordering them around, but we've been on the front lines, we know what we're dealing with, and we think getting everyone in one place is by far the best way to protect them until ...' He hesitated as he tried to think of what until might be. Eventually, he gave up. 'Well, until what, I don't know, but it's our duty to do all we can.'

There was a derisive snort from behind me: I turned and glared at Claire. It seemed to work because she didn't say anything further.

Nonetheless, the first officer must have heard her, 'Okay, so I can see you're sceptical, and you've got every right to be. All I wanted to do is to invite you to come up and see what we've been doing, and judge for yourself. We can't even get the locals to come and take a look, and I think that's the biggest stumbling block. Once they see how well we have it set up, I think they'll see we're right. What do you think? Would you be up for checking it out? If you think we're doing some good, you can let the locals know, and maybe that will help get them on side. You've managed to fit in in a way we haven't. From what I hear, people around here respect you; they might listen to you if you say it's a good idea.'

I tried my best to look noncommittal, but he could clearly tell I wasn't sold on the idea. He continued anyway. 'You don't have to decide right now. Maybe just drop by sometime if you happen to be in the area. There's no pressure, honest. We're just trying to do our bit.'

'Okay,' I shifted uneasily. 'We might be able to do that.'

With that, the rib circled round and disappeared in the direction it had come, the first officer waving to us as they disappeared off into the distance.

'Ever get the feeling they weren't just passing?' I looked at Claire. Her cynicism got to me sometimes, but on this occasion I was pretty sure she was right.

'Rhum's not going to be that much out of our way.' I pointed to a loose cluster of islands on the chart I'd laid out on the table. 'All I'm saying is that we could swing by and take up that invitation before we come across to Canna to pick you up.'

It had been four days since we'd run into the rib and we'd got word from Mitch that there was a woman on Canna who was about to give birth. Mitch was going to fly Claire up there and we were going to follow the next day to pick her up and bring her back. In the meantime, I was trying to persuade the others we should at least check out what the navy personnel had been up to on Rhum.

'You never know, they might be onto something.'

Claire and Mitch both gave me withering looks. 'Well, okay, what I mean is we should at least keep our options open. You never know when we might need them.'

It looked like I was facing a losing battle until Tom chimed in. 'You know, I think I'm with Ben on this one. Claire, you're judging them based on your past experiences in completely different situations, and I know you've been right a lot of the time, but you've not been right every time. I mean look at Port Ellen; what you thought there almost got Ben killed.'

Claire started to protest and Mitch shot me an enquiring glance, but Tom didn't let either of them get a word in. 'And Mitch, what's your biggest problem with them? That they're outsiders? So what? So am I, and Daz, and Claire and Sophie, and even Ben for that matter. Yet, you're quite happy for us to help you out when you need it. When you really think about it, how different are they? They're just trying to stay alive, the same as the rest of us. The way I see it, we need all the help we can get to keep things running in the face of everything that's happened. If they're able to help in some way, shouldn't we let them?'

Before Mitch could say anything, Daz joined in. 'I think you need to at least give them a chance to explain what they're up to, an' see what they have to say for themselves.'

'You know, Mum, he's got a point.' Sophie was now standing next to Daz. 'You're always telling me I shouldn't judge people before I get to know them properly.'

Mitch and Claire looked at each other, and then at the rest of us: they knew when they were outnumbered.

'Okay you win. I'll head off to Canna with Mitch now and you can visit Rhum on your way to pick me up tomorrow,' Claire hesitated for a moment. 'But Sophie comes with me.'

'Mum!' Sophie whined as she crossed her arms.

Tom jumped in before the spat could develop into an argument. 'Look, Claire, we're not going anywhere near any infected, so it's not as if we're likely to run into any trouble, and there are going to be three of us with her all the time,' Tom smiled at Claire. 'You do trust us, don't you?'

Claire gave a resigned sigh. 'I suppose so.'

'Yes!' Sophie punched the air in delight: it would be the first time since we'd fled Glasgow that she'd be spending time away from her mother and she was clearly relishing the possibility of a little freedom.

***

At first light the next morning, I stood at the helm as Daz pulled up the anchor, and Tom and Sophie set the sails. We were soon slipping out of Tobermory Bay and into the sound between the island and the mainland. By breakfast time, the seas were starting to build as we moved out into open water.

With the winds picking up out of the south-west and all the sails raised, we started making good speed, clipping along at four knots. As Tom fried up some eggs and bacon we'd traded for lobsters the day before, Daz took the wheel, and I went below to the chart table. I marked out our route for the day and worked out how long it would take. If we could keep up our current pace, we'd reach Rhum by three in the afternoon. From there, it was only another twelve miles or so to Canna, meaning as long as we left Rhum by five, we'd arrive at our final destination before dark.

I was just putting the charts away when there was a shout from outside. Back in the cockpit, I found Sophie scampering along the side of the boat. I shouted after her. 'Hey! I've told you before: no running on deck!'

'But, Ben, dolphins! Look! They're all round us: they're everywhere!' By then, she'd reached the bow and was leaning as far out as she dared. 'I can hear them! This is amazing!'

I glanced across at Daz and saw he was split between dashing forward to join Sophie and his responsibilities at the helm. I nodded towards the front of the boat. 'Go.'

'Thanks!' With that, Daz sprinted along the deck.

'Don't run!' I called after him.

'Yeah, yeah.' He didn't even slow.

At that moment, Tom's head appeared in the companion way. 'You lot ready for food?'

'I am,' I looked towards where Daz and Sophie were now jockeying for the best position to see the dolphins, 'but I think those two will be a while.'

Leaving their food below, Tom brought mine and his up and joined me in the cockpit. He surveyed our surroundings. 'This is some place.'

Off to the east, on the mainland, lay a squat lighthouse surrounded by a cluster of white-washed buildings. To the west was the island of Coll, its northern tip marked by another lighthouse. Ahead, rising up over the horizon, I could already see the distinctive outlines of Rhum and its neighbouring islands. In the waters around us, the school of dolphins played, a pale hourglass pattern visible on their sides each time they surfaced. Looking round, I found it hard to find anything which had changed since the infected took over. While almost all the land had been lost, the sea was like it had always been, and I couldn't see any reason why it wouldn't continue that way forever. Out here, I felt safe. After all, there was little chance of running into any infected this far from the shore.

With breakfast finished, Tom turned to me. 'So, how are you doing these days?'

I smiled. 'A lot better now we've found other people; I think we've got a real chance. I don't mind saying it now, but there were times when I really thought we weren't going to make it.'

'I thought you were doing better. There's a lot less pressure on you now, isn't there?'

'Yeah.' I nodded in agreement 'What about you? How are you doing?

Tom leant back. 'Not bad … all things considered.'

'How's your shoulder?'

He lifted his arm and rotated it backwards. 'It's almost as good as before. The chest wound gives me a bit of trouble every now and then though, especially if I try to lift something that's a bit too heavy, or if I turn over too fast in my bunk.'

Tom took out the tobacco Mitch had given him as a welcome present when we'd first arrived in Tobermory, and carefully rolled his single cigarette for the day, making sure nothing was wasted. He was doing his best to eke it out; making it last as long as possible, knowing there'd be no more once this packet was gone. It reminded me of something I'd been meaning to ask him. 'By the way, how are you and Mitch getting along?'

Tom grinned sheepishly. 'You noticed then?'

'It's hard not to. She's the first woman I've seen make you happy since …' I didn't really want to bring Jane up, not now.

'You mean since Jane?' There was a pause as he thought about this, then he smiled. 'Yeah, you're right.' He looked off into the distance. 'I don't know. There's just something about her; it's … it's like we just clicked.' He lit his cigarette and took a draw. 'Who'd have thought, after all these years, the only thing it needed to make me finally move on was the world coming to an end!'

I reached out and patted him on the shoulder. 'It's good to see you like this again. It's been a long time.'

'Looks like I'm not the only one, though.' Tom nudged me and tilted his head towards the bow. 'Those two seem to be getting rather friendly.'

At the front of the boat, Daz and Sophie were pressed closely together, Sophie leaning over the guard rail, the ill-fitting clothes she was wearing flapping in the wind. I shook my head: despite all attempts to change her mind, Sophie still refused to wear the clothes Mitch had given her, and had reverted to wearing mine. As I watched, Daz put his hand on her shoulder and whispered something into her ear. I couldn't hear what he said, but I saw the look she gave him in return. I chuckled and turned to Tom. 'I wonder what Claire's going to make of that when she finds out.'

For the next hour, we sailed with our new-found escorts keeping pace. By then, Daz had got bored with watching the dolphins and had come back to eat his now cold breakfast, but Sophie remained on the bow, transfixed by the animals playing a few feet below her.

We reached the dolphin's destination, marked by a flock of several hundred gannets diving into the water from high in the sky and almost instantly, they deserted us. Sophie skipped back to the cockpit. 'That was amazing!' She was wearing a grin almost as wide as her face. 'I always thought you had to go somewhere tropical to see dolphins. I never knew you could see them in Scotland.'

I smiled at her. 'You get killer whales here, too.'

Daz perked up and started to look around. 'You get killer whales in Scotland?'

'Yeah, not often, but they're around from time to time.'

Daz frowned. 'How come I never heard about that before?'

Tom laughed. 'Because it wasn't featured on the Discovery Channel?'

Right on time, we slipped into a narrow bay on the east side of Rhum. The shoreline ahead was dominated by a large and imposing sandstone building; the one Hamish had referred to as 'the Big House'. To the north, was another small cluster of buildings, but other than these structures, the bay was uninhabited. On the beach in front of the main building, one of the large black ribs was pulled up beyond the high tide line, its heavy machine gun causing it to lean to one side. We might have dropped by out of the blue, but at least it looked like someone was home.

As we neared, I scanned the shore with the binoculars and I could see that they'd been busy. All the windows on the lower floor of the Big House had been boarded up, and barbed wire had been strung out along the grass in front of it. Between the building and the foreshore, men in military fatigues moved between piles of what looked like machinery and supplies, carrying things back and forth. To the left, three makeshift corrals had been set up and filled with sheep and goats, and several cows were tethered to stakes which had been hammered into the ground.

I lowered the binoculars and handed them to Tom.

'You know, they seem to be doing pretty well around here.'

Tom took the binoculars and after a few minutes handed them to Daz. 'Where d'you think they got all that stuff from? D'you think they've been going ashore in places where there are infected to get it? If they have, you've got to give them credit for having guts.'

'It helps when you have some pretty heavy duty fire power to back you up.' Daz had the binoculars raised, but not towards the shore: rather, he had them pointed back out to sea. I turned and saw the second rib had just rounded the headland on the north side of the bay. As it neared, I could see what Daz was talking about. Each marine had a machine gun slung across his body, while one also had a large pack on his back from which hoses protruded, linking it to what looked like a spray gun of some kind. I thought back to what we'd seen as the frigate was overrun and wondered what they'd been up to that needed a flame-thrower. In addition to these weapons, all the marines carried a pistol in a holster strapped to their waist, and I had no doubt there were other weapons stowed in the compartments which lined each side of the rib.

As soon as they saw us, the rib changed course. As it neared, Tom and Sophie dropped the sails while Daz went up front and released the anchor. Once we were at rest, all we could do was wait to be boarded.

The rib bumped hard against the side of the yacht as many hands reached out to hold it in place. The man at the helm was the first to speak. 'So, you finally decided to take up Bucky's offer? He'll be glad to see you.' His accent was southern English, almost cockney. He leaned forward and reached out his hand. 'I'm Nick, by the way.'

I shook it. 'Ben. This is Tom, Daz and Sophie.' Each waved in turn.

'That doctor woman not with you? Bucky won't be pleased. He's got all his hopes pinned on her putting in a good word for us. Me,' he shrugged, 'I'd take a different route, but Bucky's the one in charge.'

As I wondered exactly what he was talking about, Sophie piped up. 'She's over on Canna helping someone give birth. We're just on our way over to pick her up.'

I scowled at Sophie, feeling she shouldn't have given away this information after what Nick had just said. I half-expected the rib to go roaring off, but instead Nick put his hand back on the wheel. 'You lot want a lift ashore?'

Before I could say anything, Daz and Sophie were clambering over the side and into the rib. Knowing it would seem impolite to object, I did the same, followed shortly by Tom. As we skimmed over the water towards the shore, I could see Daz eyeing up the weapons and I wondered how long it would be before he asked if he could fire one of them. Sophie, meantime, seemed to be casting a critical eye over the marines themselves, while Tom looked to be enjoying the feeling of the wind rushing through his hair.

Within minutes we were at the beach, and the marines were jumping into the shallow water. Tom, Daz and I followed suit, but Sophie hesitated; Nick noticed this and stepped back towards the boat, holding out his arms. 'You want a lift ashore, ma'am?'

Sophie giggled. 'If you're offering.' With that, she flung one arm around his shoulder and climbed into his arms. Daz shot Nick a look which said he'd wished he'd thought of that rather than just leaping into the water and leaving Sophie behind.

On reaching the shore, we stood around, not quite sure what to do, while the marines busied themselves unloading gas canisters and other items they'd scavenged from god knows where. These were added to the heaps of similar items on the grass above the beach. After a couple of minutes, the first officer came striding towards us. 'Sorry about the mess. We're still getting everything sorted out. If we'd known you were coming, we could have been better prepared.'

I didn't tell him that this was exactly why we'd turned up unannounced. 'We were just passing and had a couple of hours to kill.'

'No matter. The important thing is that you're here.' His hand shot forward. 'We haven't been formally introduced, yet. I'm Commander Buchanan-Smith, but you can call me Gordon.'

I shook it and introduced the others.

'Hmmm, no doctor then?' He looked disappointed and I wondered why he was so keen to get Claire here. After a second, he clapped his hands together. 'No matter. D'you want to take a look around?'

Tom peered at a cluster of what looked like farming equipment. 'Where'd you get all this stuff?'

Gordon smiled. 'From all over. We've been raiding all the buildings and settlements we can. Mostly we've been concentrating on farms, but there are also a few small factories we've been able to get to.'

Daz looked at him in amazement. 'Is that no' dangerous? I mean, aren't there infected everywhere?'

'They're around, but we've been specifically targeting places where there's not going to be more than we can handle.' He nodded to where a number of the marines were messing around, two of them throwing a hat back and forth, while a third tried to get it back. The rest watched and laughed. 'They might not always look it, but they're a pretty tough and well-disciplined bunch when they need to be. I really couldn't have ended up with a better group of men.'

All the time he'd been speaking, Sophie had been keeping her eyes trained on Gordon. She crossed her arms. 'Why are you so interested in my mother?' Her tone reminded me so much of Claire I almost laughed.

The first officer drew himself up to his full height and started what I soon realised was a well-practiced speech. 'As far as I see it, I'm still a serving officer in the Queen's navy and, as far as I know, the country's still under martial law: that means I have a duty to do everything I can to keep people alive and safe. We're trying to get in touch with London, or whoever else might still be out there, but until then, we're on our own, and it's up to us to do the best we can.'

Gordon glanced at us, trying to read how we were taking this. Daz seemed impressed, but both Tom and Sophie looked less convinced, and I had to say I felt the same way. He pressed on. 'I'm under no illusions. I know this isn't going to be easy, but with this island, I think we can really achieve something. Think about it: it's isolated, so there's little chance of the infection reaching here; it has a very low population for its size and plenty of resources. The Big House there,' he pointed over his shoulder, 'is built like a castle already and it's been quite a simple job to fortify it. So far, we've been finding it remarkably easy to pick up the supplies we need, and I think we have a chance of having a pretty good life here, at least in comparison to anywhere else, until all this blows over.'

'You think this is going to blow over eventually?' I watched him closely and saw the slightest flutter of his eyelids which suggested that he didn't, but that he wasn't ready to admit it openly.

'I have to stay positive, otherwise what would be the point of trying to do anything? Anyway, if we all work together, I think we can get a real community going, and even if we end up here in the long term, we'll still be safe. There's space to grow things around here, and we've been picking up farm animals as and when we come across them.'

I eyed him sceptically. 'You know how to deal with animals?'

'Well ...' There was an awkward silence. 'No. And to be honest, we don't really know much about growing things either, but this is where the locals come in. If we can get them to move here, we can protect them, provide them with a level of security they can't get anywhere else, and in return, they can help us by doing the farming and helping to maintain everything. It's a fair trade, isn't it?'

I considered this. 'I can see how it's beneficial for you, but I can see why you're struggling to convince anyone else.'

'Yes, we are rather.' He let out a sigh. 'I think we really messed up when we first arrived. Nick slipped back into his old habit of throwing his weight around, and it just annoyed everyone. We lost a lot of goodwill because of it. That's why I've come up with a new plan; something that will really benefit everyone.'

Despite all he'd said, I couldn't help but notice he still hadn't answered Sophie's question about why he was so interested in Claire and this left me feeling uneasy. 'So what's your new plan?'

He swept his arm towards the building behind him. 'Come inside and I can tell you all about it.'

I figured I had nothing to lose by listening to what he had to say. 'Okay.'

Gordon turned to the others. 'Nick should be around here somewhere. If you can find him, tell him I said he should show you around. That okay with you?'

Daz grinned. 'No problem!'

He was clearly looking forward to exploring the marines' settlement. Tom and Sophie seemed pretty keen, too. I, however, wondered why they'd been dismissed. It had been very subtle, but it was clear that I was the only person Gordon wanted to discuss his plans with.

'Just make sure you stay together.' I looked at my watch, 'and be back here in an hour. We'll need to be heading off to Canna soon after that if we're going to get there before it gets dark.'

'Will do, Cap'n!' Tom gave a playful salute as he turned and walked off, following Daz and Sophie who were already halfway across the grass, heading for the animal enclosures.

Gordon waggled the now half-empty whisky bottle at me, 'You want a top-up?'

I stared down at my glass and swirled the dregs of the previous round. 'I should probably leave it at that. I've still got a few hours of sailing to go tonight.'

I might only have known him for less than an hour, but I'd quickly warmed to Commander Buchanan-Smith, or 'Bucky' as he was known to those who served with him. His hair was thinning, with a smattering of grey, but he was still well-built. He'd served in the navy for almost twenty years, reaching the rank of commander before all this happened. Since arriving on Rhum, he'd put his time, and his extensive experience, to good use, and they were well on their way to establishing a very reasonable facsimile of a fully functioning settlement capable of supporting a sizable population, complete with electricity, and hot and cold running water. They were still using diesel generators for the time being, but they'd already gathered a large number of solar panels and a couple of wind generators, which Gordon hoped to have up and running before they finally ran out of fuel.

'Go on. Another little bit won't do you any harm.' He leaned forward and poured a splash of whisky into my glass. He did the same to his own, then picked it up and rolled it between his palms for a second before taking a sip. 'So, you're no doubt wondering what my new plan is, and why I'm so interested in your doctor friend.'

I settled back in my chair, feeling the effects of the whisky warming my blood. 'I most certainly am.'

'Well, as I see it, there are three things we can offer people.' He ticked them off on his fingers as he spoke. 'Security, food production and medical help. From what I've seen, the locals don't feel they need our protection, and they're probably right about that, at least for the time being, and they can probably handle the food side of things better than we can because they know the area. But there's one thing they can't really provide for themselves, and that's the medical help. If we can set up some sort of medical facility here, with a proper doctor in residence, then we'd have something which would make it attractive for people to come here, wouldn't we? Something which they can't really do for themselves, or get elsewhere.'

Definitely.' I drained the last drops of whisky from my glass. Suddenly everything had become clear. 'But I should warn you, you'll struggle to get Claire to agree: she's a pretty independent person and she's not exactly big on the military.'

'Yes, that was the impression I got when we ran into you the other day.' He scratched his chin thoughtfully before looking up. 'Any ideas how I can go about getting her onside?'

'I don't know.' I mulled this over. 'Probably by getting her equipment and medical supplies. Providing antibiotics when Tom needed them really helped get you into her good books back at the blockade.'

Gordon put his now empty whisky glass on the table that separated us. 'I can see I'll need to put some more thought into this.' He glanced at his watch and I did likewise. He stood up and pulled on his cap. 'We should be getting you back to your boat so you can be on your way.' At the doorway he stopped and held out is hand. 'Thanks for coming, and for hearing me out. You've given me something I can work on, and as far as I'm concerned, that's a big step forward.'

'Man, those guys are so cool!' We were all in the cockpit having left Rhum half an hour before. The winds were fair and we were on time to reach Canna by ten. Daz was at the helm while Tom and Sophie sat opposite me on the lee side of the boat. Daz was filling me in about their time on the island. 'We ran into them up in the woods behind the house an' Nick, he's a lieutenant y'know, he's second-in-command after Gordon, an' he's in charge of all the marines, he showed us how to use his assault rifle.'

'He even let us fire it!' Sophie was jubilant, then nervous. 'Whatever you do, don't tell Mum. She doesn't like guns much.'

'It's just a pity you couldn't hit a barn door from two feet away.' Daz needled her.

'It's harder than it looks!' Sophie punched him playfully on the arm. 'Anyway, it's not my fault I'm not a natural, like you.'

I shot Daz a questioning look. He smiled, 'Nick said I must have a natural instinct for shootin' an' that I was really good for someone who'd never even fired a gun before.'

Sophie folded her arms, scowling. 'It must be all those computer games you played.'

I glanced at Tom. 'So what about you?'

'He was too chicken to even give it a go!'

Tom stuck his tongue out at Sophie in response. 'It wasn't that; I'm just not that into guns. Anyway, I had other things on my mind.'

I raised an eyebrow. 'Oh yeah, what was that?

'I'm not really too sure,' Tom leaned back in his seat, 'but there was something odd going on there. There's a path behind the Big House through the trees, and we were walking up it when we saw a bunch of the marines up ahead. They were crowded around what looked like a hole in the ground, all laughing and joking with each other. They were pushing one another towards the edge. I got the impression there was something in there, something alive, but before we could get close enough to see anything, Nick spotted us and shouted at the others to get back to work. That's when he came over and offered to show us how to fire his gun.'

'So what d'you think was going on?' I was curious to hear Tom's views.

'I don't know.' Tom's forehead furrowed. 'Nick said it was just an old septic tank that had collapsed in on itself, but, I don't know ... that didn't seem right. I could've sworn I heard something moving around in it.'

I turned to Daz and Sophie. 'What about you two? Did you see anything unusual? Anything which seemed odd?'

They looked at each other and then shrugged.

Daz spoke first. 'I didn't see anythin'.'

'Me neither.' Sophie swiped a stray hair away from her face. 'And anyway, Nick seems really nice. Why would he lie to us?'

Chapter Sixteen

'So how did you get on?' Claire and I were in the cockpit drinking a couple of the beers she'd been given as a thank you for helping out with the birth. Although she hadn't been keen on us going to Rhum in the first place, she now seemed very eager to hear about what we'd found there.

'Pretty good, actually. Gordon seems to have his head screwed on the right way, and if they can really achieve half the things he's planning, it'll be very impressive. I'm just not too sure he can actually do it though, or even if he can get enough of the people around here to go along with him.' I sipped my beer. 'Oh, and I might have dropped you in it .'

Claire looked concerned. 'What d'you mean?'

I took another mouthful of beer. 'He's very keen to get all the survivors around here together on Rhum and set up a community there, and he seems to think the key to doing that is to offer them something they can't get anywhere else.'

'Like what?' Claire was eyeing me suspiciously.

'Like some sort of medical facility, complete with its own doctor.'

'And by that, you mean *me?*' Claire took an angry swig of her beer. 'I hope you told him where to shove it!

'Well,' I rubbed the back of my neck, 'no.'

Claire glared at me. 'What did you tell him?'

I picked nervously at the label on my beer bottle. 'I told him that his best chance of getting you on his side was to get you medical supplies: equipment, medicines, and so on.'

Claire slammed her bottle down onto the seat beside

her, sending beer foaming out over the top. 'You told him *what?*'

'It's true, isn't it?' I replied defensively.

'I suppose,' she conceded.

'And if he can get you stuff like that, then you'd be able to do much more for the people around here, wouldn't you?'

'That's true.'

'So if he made you an offer, would you take him up on it?'

Claire picked up her beer again and drained what was left. 'If it means I can treat people better, then I might. There's only so much I can do with what I've got with me, and I've already run out of almost everything useful. We've been lucky so far; there's not really been anything I haven't been able to handle, but our luck's got to run out some time, hasn't it?' She got up and leant on the side of the boat. 'I don't know. I'd need to think about it. I wouldn't want to get stuck there, and I'm not too sure I'd want Sophie to be around those marines all the time either, but I can see the benefits of having somewhere with proper equipment in case of emergencies.'

*****

'What's that over there?' We'd left Canna early that morning and we were just getting ready to turn into the sound between Mull and the mainland when Daz called out. 'Over there. You see it?'

I stared in the direction Daz was pointing, but with the wind blowing at a steady twenty-five knots, it was difficult to spot anything amongst the swell and breaking waves. 'What did it look like?'

'Dunno. It looked big, though, six, maybe eight feet long.' Daz craned his neck, trying to find the object again. 'Might've been a whale or somethin'.'

'It could've been a leatherback turtle. I've seen them out here before.' I glanced up at the sails, checking how they were set. 'We need to come about.'

I watched as the others scuttled around the deck, dressed in their waterproofs and life jackets. The seas were rough, but they weren't so bad that safety harnesses had to be worn. Nonetheless, care needed to be taken. 'Daz, one hand for yourself and one for the boat.'

'What?' Daz sounded confused.

'I mean, always hold on with one hand whenever you're doing anything outside of the cockpit.'

He gave me a double thumbs up. 'Gotcha!'

Tom and Sophie laughed.

'Daz, stop messing around.' I gave the boat, and the sea, a quick once-over, then I picked a spot between the approaching swells. 'Ready abou …'

'WAIT!' Daz was standing on his tip toes, peering into the distance.

'Daz, I told you to stop messing around!' I was beginning to lose my temper.

'No, I saw it again! The thing I saw before: it's a boat!'

I searched the waters around us, but saw nothing. 'What sort of boat?'

'A little one; a rowing boat or somethin' like that.' Daz's eyes were sweeping back and forth across the sea. 'I've lost it again, but it was definitely a boat, an' I think there're people in it.'

'Where?'

Daz pointed off the right-hand bow. 'Over there somewhere. No' too far away.'

'And you're sure it was a boat?'

'Definitely!'

I made a quick assessment of the situation: if there was a small boat out here with people on it, then they were in trouble, especially in these seas. Instead of turning to the east, I turned until we were heading in the direction Daz had indicated. 'Daz, go up front. See if you can spot it again. If you do, call out, but keep your eye on it; don't lose it. Point at it and keep pointing. Sophie, Claire, stand by the mast; you can relay any instructions between Daz and me. Tom, I need you to stay back here and adjust the sails.'

Within moments, everyone was in position and the boat was cutting as close to the wind as I dared. The waves were now crashing over the bow on a regular basis, and Sophie squealed as a particularly large one drenched her. I heard Daz call out from the bow and saw him point.

'Claire, what did he say?'

'He says he can see it now. Straight ahead, about 100 yards.

Daz called out again and Claire relayed it back to me. 'Fifty yards. I can see it now, too.'

Another few seconds and I caught a glimpse of it myself. Daz was right; it was a small rowing boat, no more than six feet long. Two people were huddled towards the stern. Neither of them had realised we were there; instead, they were concentrating on something lying on the bottom of the dinghy that I couldn't see.

'Claire, I can see them now. Tell Daz to get back here, we're going to have to do some pretty tight manoeuvring to get them alongside.'

Claire arrived back in the cockpit. 'What d'you mean get them alongside?'

'We'll need to take them on board. We can't just ignore them. That boat won't last much longer out here in this weather, and if they end up in the water, they'll drown.'

'But what if they're infected? Remember that man back at the blockade? The carrier? Remember what happened when Pete took him on board?'

That hadn't even occurred to me and the possibility distracted me momentarily.

'Ben, look out!' Daz leapt into the cockpit, grabbing the wheel and turning it sharply to the left. The yacht heeled steeply onto its side and we narrowly avoided smashing into the wooden dinghy.

'Shit! Thanks, Daz.' I took a few seconds to compose myself, not believing I'd almost run them down. 'We'll turn up into the wind and heave to. Then we can work out what we're going to do.'

With the others following my directions, we soon came to a halt some twenty yards upwind of the dinghy, rising and falling each time the heavy swell passed under us. Unsurprisingly, since we'd very nearly run them down, the people on board had finally noticed our presence and were waving frantically.

'So what do we do?' I turned to find the others looking at me enquiringly.

I scanned the dinghy. 'They don't look like they're infected.'

Claire scowled. 'But that doesn't mean they're not carriers, does it? They could have been bitten or injured in some way; if there's even a small risk of that, it's too great.'

Sophie was holding on tightly to the guard rail as she swayed back and forth with the movement of the yacht beneath her feet, eyes fixed on the tiny boat. 'But, Mum, we can't just leave them here, can we?'

'Yeah,' Daz chimed in.

Tom did his best to avoid making eye contact with me, 'Sorry, Ben. I'm afraid I'm with Claire on this one.'

'But if they're not infected and we leave them there, they're going to die.' I looked from Claire to Tom and back again. 'You want that on your conscience?'

'No, I suppose not,' Tom mumbled noncommittally. 'But still, it's a risk; isn't it?'

I glanced at the rowing boat: the two people were now calling out to us, but their words were being whipped away by the wind before they reached us. 'They don't seem sick right now. Claire, d'you think you'd be able to tell if they're carriers or not?'

'If they are, they'll have an injury of some kind, and I should be able to find it if I examine them.' It was Claire's turn to look at the dinghy, which was now only about ten yards away. 'That's if they'll let me.'

'Okay, so how about this? We'll pick them up for now. You can examine them, and if you're sure they're not infected, we can take them back to Tobermory. If you think there's even a chance of them being infected, or if they won't let you examine them, we'll drop them off on one of the uninhabited islands nearby; then we can wait and see what happens. Does that sound like a plan?'

There were nods all round.

'Fuck!' Daz was peering over the side of the boat. 'What happened to him?'

The wooden dinghy was now alongside the yacht, inside were two women, one in her late twenties, the other probably in her thirties; neither were dressed in waterproofs and their clothes were soaking wet. Both looked terrified and exhausted. Now the rowing boat was beside us, we could see a third person lying, unconscious, in the bottom. He was young, maybe only a couple of years older than Daz and from the colour of his skin, he looked close to death. The reason for this was clear: his left arm ended in a mass of blood-soaked rags just above the elbow.

'He got bitten by one of *those* people.' It was the younger of the two women who spoke first. 'He didn't have a choice, he had to cut it off.'

Claire's eyes narrowed. 'How long?'

The woman stared blankly, seemingly confused by the question. 'What?'

'How long between when he was bitten and when he cut his arm off?' It took me a few seconds to work out what Claire was thinking.

'I don't know, maybe two or three minutes.' The older of the two women answered this time. 'Why? What does it matter? Are you going to help us or not?'

'Was he the only one who got bitten?' Claire was observing the women closely; their clothes were stained with blood, but neither had any visible injuries.

'Only him,' the younger woman gestured to the man lying in the bottom of the dinghy. 'They attacked us out of nowhere.' She shook her head, 'I just don't understand where they came from.'

'When did all this happen?'

The women looked at each other and shrugged, then the older one answered. 'I don't know; five hours ago, maybe six at the most.'

Claire straightened up. 'Okay, get him on board and I'll see what I can do.'

'He's not going to make it.' Claire and I were down in the cabin; on Claire's orders, the others had remained in the cockpit. Claire continued. 'He's lost too much blood, there's nothing I can do. What he really needs is a blood transfusion and there's no way we can do that out here, not without the right equipment.'

She moved over to the sink and washed her hands. 'Probably just as well really. Feel his forehead; he's burning up.'

I reached out and put the back of my hand against his skin. Sure enough, he was hot to the touch; sweat was starting to bead and roll down the sides of his head. 'What does that mean?'

'It most likely means he's infected.' Claire dried her hands. 'They said it was a couple of minutes between when he got bitten and cutting his arm off. Given how quickly the virus seems to affect most people, I doubt that would be quick enough. Once it got into his blood stream, it would have been pumped round his body in seconds.'

'So how long before he turns?' The thought of having someone infected with the disease on board terrified me.

'I don't know. I guess it depends on how much of the virus got into the rest of his body before he did the amputation, but I don't think it really matters.' We both looked at the man. His breathing was shallow and erratic, his skin pale, almost grey. Claire turned away. 'With the amount of blood he's lost, he'll be dead in minutes.'

I glanced towards the companionway. 'We need to get him off the boat as soon as possible.'

'So how did you end up all the way out here?' Tom was sitting with Sophie and Daz on one side of the cockpit, while the two women sat opposite. 'I mean, where did you come from?'

It was the older woman who answered. 'We're from Iona. We've been doing pretty well there, really. Then yesterday, these two people with the disease appeared out of nowhere. I didn't recognise them. I don't know where they came from. We haven't let anyone near the island since we heard that Mull had been overrun, and none of us have been off it other than to fish.' She shook her head. 'Before we knew it, we were running for our lives; I think some of the others made it back to their houses, but I don't know for sure. We ran for the boats. They chased us though.'

'Just the two of them?' Daz was clearly wondering how this had happened.

'No, there were others by then.' The younger woman interjected. 'People who'd been attacked, lots of them. People I've known all my life: friends, relatives ...' Her voice tailed off into silence.

The older woman picked up where the younger one left off. 'We got there just in time and jumped into the first boat we found, only Ruairidh stayed on the dock to untie it and that's when he got bitten. There was a fish knife tucked under the gunnels. He grabbed it and cut off his arm: I don't know how he could do it. He had to snap the bone once he'd cut through the skin and muscle.' She looked up as Claire and I climbed into the cockpit. 'How is he? Is he going to be okay?'

Claire took a deep breath, 'No, I'm afraid he's ...'

Before she could finish, there was a roar from behind us. Instinctively, I pushed Claire out of the way as I turned to see what was happening, but something hit me before I was even halfway round, sending me sprawling face-first onto the deck. I heard screaming and shouting above me as I tried to free myself, but I was pinned by the weight of the man on my back. I kicked and thrashed, expecting to feel his teeth sinking into my neck at any moment, his hands ripping into my flesh, but before any of that happened, I heard the sound of a heavy blow and he went still. I pushed up with my arms and felt him slip to the side. Not knowing what I was going to find, I leapt up, my eyes darting round the cockpit.

For an instant, everything seemed frozen: Claire was scrambling to get back to her feet; Tom and Daz were standing on the seats on one side of the cockpit where they'd jumped to get out of the way; the two women on the other: all were staring down at the man, who was now lying, lifeless, on the deck. His head had been shattered, and fragments of his skull mixed with hair, blood and brains. Standing over him was Sophie, shaking, a heavy winch handle gripped tightly in both hands.

'That's us here. Let's see what we can see.' Mitch adjusted the throttle and turned the seaplane to the left, bringing it low over the shoreline.

We'd arrived back in Tobermory an hour after unceremoniously dumping the lifeless body of the young man over the side, and alerting the others on the radio. By then, Mitch had offered to do a fly-over to find out more about what had happened on Iona. I was keen to find out too, so I volunteered to go with her.

It took a little over twenty minutes before the island came into view and we started to descend. Almost immediately, we saw two people shuffling slowly along an otherwise deserted road.

'There!' Mitch pointed and brought the plane around

in a tight circle. Below us, a knot of infected surrounded a two-storey house which stood slightly apart from a small group of other buildings. A man leaned from one of the upper windows, waving frantically up at us. Mitch took the plane in low, momentarily distracting the infected which crowded round the homestead, trying desperately to break in. Iona had undoubtedly been overrun, but it seemed that at least some had survived.

In the ten minutes it took to fly the length of the island and back, we'd found three houses which, judging by the infected clustered round them, had groups of survivors inside. We were debating what to do next as we flew over the island one last time just to make sure there weren't others we'd missed on the first two passes.

'Mitch, I agree we can't just leave them like that, but we can't really do anything about it either. We can't take on that many infected. We're not equipped for it.'

'So what are you suggesting instead?'

We flew over one of the besieged houses again, causing the infected to look skyward as they searched for the source of the noise. As soon as we'd passed, they returned their attention to the building, and renewed their assault.

'I know you're not going to like it, but how about we ask Gordon? The marines could be down here in a couple of hours. They've got the guns and they're trained to do just this sort of thing.'

'I'm really not sure about that. Isn't this something we should be handling ourselves?'

'They're not as bad as you think. Gordon realises they screwed up when they first arrived: they misread the situation.' I looked down as the last of the island slid below us and we headed back out to sea, the white caps of the wave shining against the deep blue. 'All he wants to do is work with us, not against us, and if they're willing to risk their lives to help rescue people, then I don't think we should hold that against them.

'I guess not.'

'So where are the survivors trapped?' Gordon was poring over a map he'd spread out on his desk while Nick stood beside him. Mitch and I had arrived at the Rhum community a few minutes before and as soon as we'd explained the situation, Gordon had offered to mount a rescue mission.

Mitch pointed to the map. 'There's one here, another here, and the third's further up the coast, here.'

Nick examined the map closely. 'How many infected did you see?'

'There's maybe eighty or ninety in all, mostly around the buildings where the survivors are, but there are others scattered across the island.'

Nick straightened up. 'That shouldn't be anything we can't handle.'

'We'll fly down with you. We can keep a look out and tell you where the infected are.'

Gordon smiled at Mitch. 'That'd certainly be useful.'

Nick seemed less keen on the idea. 'I'm sure we can manage on our own.'

Gordon glared at him. 'We might as well take the help if it's there. Now, go get the men ready.'

'Yes, *sir*!' With that Nick turned and left the room, slamming the door behind him.

Mitch stared after him. 'Was it something I said?'

'Don't worry about him,' Gordon replied dismissively,

'he can be a bit prickly sometimes. He just doesn't like civilians telling him what he should be doing.'

Mitch snorted. 'He doesn't seem to have a problem trying to give us orders.'

'Yes, I've had a word with him about that; well, with all the men. I've told them they need to start thinking of everyone else who's survived this far as their equals and not as people they can order around.' Gordon stood up. 'Come to think of it, that might have something to do with his attitude, too.'

I pressed the transmit button on the plane's VHF radio. 'Gordon, there's a small group of infected coming along the road from your left.'

'Roger that.' There was a burst of static, followed by 'How far?

I hit the transmission button again. 'About half a mile or so.'

'We should be out of here before they arrive.'

Mitch tapped me on the shoulder and pointed off to the north where a larger group of infected were now heading towards the house below where we were circling.

We'd been over Iona for almost an hour, watching Gordon, Nick and the rest of the marines as they took on the infected. So far, things had gone well and a total of ten survivors had been rescued from two of the houses surrounded by infected. It was amazing to watch the marines in action. They moved with efficiency and ruthlessness, dropping those with the disease in a hail of bullets before they even knew the marines were there. The survivors had been led down to the shore and taken out to a fishing boat which was tied to a mooring in the main harbour. One of the marines had got the engine started and they'd chugged off along the coast after the ribs, heading for the last building where survivors were holed up.

Gordon and the remaining marines were now approaching the third house. This had the largest number of infected crowding round it, and to make matters worse, we could see more streaming towards them.

I picked up the mike again. 'Gordon, there's a group of five coming in from the north and ...' I twisted in my seat so I could see over my shoulder. 'And about twenty coming up from the south.'

'Roger that.' There was a shout in the background. 'Keep us updated on their movements.'

'Will do.' I let go of the transmission button as Mitch circled the plane back round and we watched the first of the infected fall as the marines moved in, but this time things didn't go quite as smoothly as before. With a greater number of infected, it wasn't as easy to shoot them all before they realised the marines were there, and within a few seconds, infected were racing towards them: mouths wide, screaming and roaring. With unfathomable speed, the first of the infected crossed the ground between the house and the dry stone wall which the marines had been using for cover, but they didn't panic. Instead, they systematically targeted whichever infected were closest at any given moment. Although some fell instantly, it was harder to hit targets which were moving so fast and most took several shots to bring them down.

Below us, I saw one of the marines take his assault rifle from his shoulder and desperately pull at the bolt, fighting frantically to unjam it. There was a shout, audible even above the sound of the plane's engine, and the struggling marine looked up as a skinny man leapt onto the wall in front of him. He dropped the machine gun and grabbed for his pistol, but before he could fire, the man was on top of him. Suddenly, the infected's head exploded, and the marine pushed the now lifeless body to the ground. I watched as he put his hand to his neck, then inspected it, staring disbelievingly at the bright red liquid dripping from his fingers. He put his hand on his neck again as first comprehension and then terror spread across his face.

A stillness descended across the battlefield, and now all that moved were the marines as they stood up slowly, examining their surrounding for any hint of further danger, but for the moment, there was none. Spotting the injured man, Nick lowered his machine gun and strode over to him. He crouched down beside him, and patted him on the shoulder before picking up the man's pistol from where he'd dropped it. At first, I thought Nick was going to hand it back to him, but I was wrong. As Nick pushed it against the injured man's forehead, the young man realised what was about to happen. He struggled backwards desperately, trying to get away, but before he got more than a few feet, there was a flash from the muzzle and he went limp.

'Jesus!' I swallowed hard. 'D'you see what Nick just did?'

'No, I was too busy watching them.' Mitch pointed ahead, where infected were racing towards the house in ever-increasing numbers; the first were only 100 yards away. Pushing what Nick had just done from my mind, I grabbed the mike. 'Gordon, you've got to get out of there. There's a whole heap of infected coming your way. You need to get those people and get out of there!'

Gordon must have heard me because I saw him signal to two marines, who rushed forward towards the house. Even before they got there, the door opened and people started pouring out. Leaving their dead colleague where he lay, the rest of the marines guided the shocked survivors towards where the ribs floated a few feet from the shore, ready to ferry them out to the waiting fishing boat. The distance they needed to cover wasn't great, but some of the survivors were elderly, others were children, and this slowed their progress. With the infected closing in, there was little we could do but watch. Occasionally, one of the marines would turn and fire, but for the most part they just ran.

I looked, horrified, at Mitch. 'They're not going to make it. We've got to do something.'

Mitch stared at the scene unfolding below us. 'What?'

'I don't know,' I shifted in my seat, trying to get a better view, 'but we've got to do something.'

'Hang on, I've got an idea.' Mitch pushed the stick forward, and almost immediately we were diving towards the ground. The moment before impact, she levelled the plane, and we sped, just a few feet above the ground, towards the infected.

Bracing myself against the back of my seat, I turned to Mitch. 'Just what exactly is this plan of yours?'

'You'll see.' She tensed up. 'Hold on!'

I felt the heavy floats hanging below the plane smash into the infected with a series of sickening thuds. Glancing down, I saw them sprawled across the ground: some struggled back to their feet, but others were clearly dead, heads smashed beyond all recognition.

Mitch pulled back on the stick as we turned. I tried to keep an eye on what was happening below, but I was forced back into my seat as we climbed almost vertically. A second later, we were heading for the ground again. Mitch pulled back on the stick and we skimmed towards the infected once more. We'd taken them by surprise the first time, but this time they knew we were coming; yet they didn't try to escape: instead they sprinted towards the speeding plane, drawn by the noise of the engine, giving those on the ground the few extra seconds they needed to escape.

I felt the plane judder as we made contact for a second time; sending infected flying in all directions and blood spraying across the windows. As we climbed again, this time more slowly, I saw the survivors clambering into the ribs as the marines pushed them away from the beach. I looked back at the scene of devastation we'd left behind, amazed that despite all the infected, only one of the marines had been lost. At first, the remaining infected ran as fast as they could after the rapidly departing plane, but gradually they slowed, and then stopped; my last glimpse was of them standing amongst the low, scrubby vegetation, almost motionless, gazing blankly after us.

With everyone now safely off the island, Mitch brought the seaplane down onto the water and taxied over to the fishing boat, reaching it just before the ribs. I flung the door open and stepped out onto the right-hand float, trying not to slip on the blood and gore spattered across it. I greeted the approaching marines. 'That looked pretty hairy.'

'Nothing we couldn't handle.' Nick stared at me, fists clenched, bristling with anger. 'Just as well your little stunt didn't get in our way.'

This wasn't the reaction I'd expected and I didn't know how to respond. If it hadn't been for Mitch distracting the infected, there was a good chance a lot more of them would have ended up dead.

'Nick, this is not the time or the place. Keep it civil.' Gordon turned to me. 'Sorry about that, Ben. We lost someone back there and everyone reacts in their own way when that happens.' Gordon reached out a hand. 'Thanks for your help.'

I shook it and then watched as the fishing boat, accompanied by the ribs, headed off into the distance. As I climbed back into the seaplane, an uneasy feeling settled over me. The way Nick had killed one of his own men, seemingly without a second thought, and his response to Mitch's actions made me glad that it was Gordon, rather than him, who was in charge of the Rhum community.

Chapter Seventeen

'I know you don't like it, but they really put themselves on the line to rescue those people on Iona, and I think it's the least we can do.' I glanced at Claire. 'Anyway, it'll give you a chance to hear what Gordon has to say for himself.'

When we got back from Iona, Mitch and I had filled the others in about what had happened. While everyone was pleased the rescue mission had gone so well, there was a lot of concern about how the disease had got onto the island in the first place. It seemed the sea hadn't acted as the impregnable barrier we'd always assumed it would, and suddenly everyone felt less secure, even in the most distant island communities.

However, there was also much less resentment towards the naval personnel, and what they were trying to do on Rhum. The survivors from Iona had already moved there and there were mutterings amongst other communities that perhaps this wasn't such a bad idea after all.

In order to make the most of this easing of tensions, Mitch and I had arranged for Gordon and some of the marines to come down to Tobermory that evening for some much needed socialising. We thought it might be a way to bring everyone together and put the initial friction between the locals and the naval personnel to rest, once and for all.

Gordon readily agreed, both because he, too, thought it would help to bring our two groups closer together, and because it would give him the chance to speak to Claire about his idea for creating a well-equipped medical clinic, to encourage the remaining survivors to relocate to Rhum.

Claire, needless to say, was dubious about the benefits

of getting everyone together, and she was particularly against the idea of having to listen to Gordon and his plans. 'I'm just saying that I can't think of anything Gordon could say that would change my mind.' She stood up and leant on the guard rail. 'I know it would be good to have access to some proper equipment and drugs, but I don't think it's something worth giving up our independence for.' She turned back to face me again. 'If we decided to set up camp there, and then we change our minds, do you really think they're going to let us just get up and leave?'

'After what Gordon and the marines did on Iona, can't you at least give him the benefit of the doubt, and listen to what he has to say?' Mitch was sitting beside me in the cockpit and from what she was now saying, it seemed she was coming round to my point of view. 'I'm not saying you have to like it or go along with it, all I'm saying is that you should at least hear him out.'

'Okay, okay.' Claire could see she wasn't going to win. 'I'll listen to what he has to say, but I really think it's going to be a waste of time.'

'Here they come!' Sophie's excited voice drifted down the companionway. She'd been up on deck for the last hour, keeping an eager eye out for the appearance of Gordon and the marines.

I looked up at Daz. 'Are you okay taking the others ashore in the dinghy?'

Daz nodded, his mouth full with the last of his supper.

'In that case, I might hitch a ride ashore with Gordon and show him around a bit.' I turned and made my way up to the cockpit, where I found Sophie with the binoculars trained on the approaching boat. I cleared my throat, and she jumped. 'Sorry Ben, I was just, ummm ...'

Her voice trailed off.

'Checking out who was on board?' I ventured.

A tinge of pink spread across Sophie's cheeks and I laughed at her embarrassment. 'You'd better not let Daz catch you looking at other men. You might make him jealous.'

A grin leapt on to her face. 'Really?' Then she realised quite how much she'd given away, 'I mean ...' The pink on her cheeks turned into a deep red. Cringing slightly, she turned and headed for the companionway. She paused when she got there and glanced back. 'D'you really think Daz would be jealous?'

'Yeah,' I nodded slowly. 'I think he probably would.'

Sophie smiled and disappeared inside.

I leant forward. 'So what d'you think about this place?'

Gordon, Claire and I were sitting round a small table near the back of the one pub which was still at least partially operational. Sophie and Daz were next to us, lost in their own conversation, while Tom was over at the bar where he alternated between flirting with Mitch and chatting with Hamish and some of the other locals.

I looked around the bar; there were about forty people in the small room: sixteen marines; the rest locals. At first glance, it was no different than it had been on any Friday night before the disease swept across the island, and, for a moment, I was transported back to how it used to be.

A braying laugh from one of the marines brought me back to reality with a thump: uniformed men, armed with pistols, were certainly something you'd never have found here before. The two groups were keeping themselves to themselves for the time being, but there were signs that with a little help from the lubricating effects of alcohol, the tensions between them might ease.

I turned my attention back to the conversation at our table as Gordon finally answered my question. 'You've got a pretty good set-up here, given the circumstances; better than I'd realised.' He took a mouthful of whisky from his glass. 'But it's still vulnerable. There are infected just beyond your barricades. All it would take would be one little slip and they'd be inside.' He put his glass carefully on the table. 'All in all, I think Rhum's much safer.'

Claire swigged her beer. 'But how would the infected get in? The walls might be made of straw, but have you seen how thick they are? There's no way they're coming down accidentally.'

'I suppose.' Gordon picked up his glass again, 'but look at Iona. There's clearly some way of infected getting across water. What if that happens here?'

'But we don't know what happened there.' Claire was waving her bottle in Gordon's general direction. 'So there's no way you can say for sure whether Rhum's any safer than here.'

Seeing the conversation starting to go in circles, I intervened before it descended into something less pleasant. 'So what d'you think happened on Iona?'

Gordon put down his drink again. 'I really don't know, but it's rather worrying. I'd always assumed that the water would keep us safe.'

Claire took another mouthful of her beer. 'Then don't you think we should be trying to work that out?'

Gordon nodded. 'Yes, but with only one incident to go on, there's not much we can do. D'you have any ideas?' He looked round the table.

'Well, as a matter of fact, I do.' Claire turned to me. 'Ben, remember what happened when Glasgow was bombed? Remember all those infected clinging to the debris? What if it's as simple as that? The infected can't swim, we've seen that, but they can hang onto things, can't they? What if one was just drifting around out there, clinging onto something, and it just happened to come ashore on Iona?'

I pondered this possibility; it would certainly explain what had happened, but if it were true, then nowhere was really safe. I shuddered at the thought.

Gordon was clearly worried by this possibility, too. 'You think it could have come all the way from Glasgow? That was weeks ago. Could they survive in the water that long? Surely, they'd die of exposure within hours.'

'That's just the point.' Claire set her beer firmly on the table. 'We don't know what this disease really does to people. Maybe it changes their physiology in some way; maybe they don't need to stay warm like us. Anyway, I'm not saying that it was necessarily someone from Glasgow, but there are other places much closer where they could've come from. We ran into some on a fish farm just outside Port Ellen. Maybe they came from somewhere like that, and they'd only been in the water for a few hours.'

Suddenly a thought struck me. 'Maybe they weren't even in the water at all.'

Claire looked at me questioningly. 'What d'you mean?'

'Well,' I took a gulp of beer. 'Think of what would've happened if we hadn't found those people in the rowing boat when we did: the man would've turned and attacked the others. Chances are they'd have ended up dead and he'd have been left on his own, drifting around in the dinghy. Something like that would be a floating time-bomb, just waiting to come ashore somewhere.'

Gordon stared through the window and out into the gathering darkness. 'If there are things like that drifting around out there, we could be in big trouble.'

'There can't be that many, though, can there?' We turned to find that Daz and Sophie had been drawn into our conversation. Daz continued. 'In all the time we've been out here, we haven't come across anythin' like that, no' an infected just floatin' around on its own, an' Mitch hasn't mentioned seein' anythin' either.' Daz looked at Gordon. 'Have you seen anythin' like that?'

Gordon shook his head. 'That's a good point. If none of us have run into that sort of thing, then it can't be too much of a threat, can it?'

'But it's still a possibility, isn't it?' There was a warning note in Claire's voice.

'Yes, and we'll need to keep it in mind, but I think there are more pressing matters for the time being, like setting up a clinic, and that's what I really want to talk to you about.' Gordon must have seen Claire's face change. He held up his hands. 'I'm not saying you have to move up to Rhum, or anything like that. All I'm saying is that if you tell me what would be useful, I'll see if I can find it and give you a room to set it up in; that way, if you ever need it, it'll be there waiting for you.' He took a sip of his whisky. 'You have to admit, it would be useful to have a place like that at your disposal … just in case.'

I could see the cogs turning in Claire's head as she considered the offer. There was clearly a part of her which could see the advantage of what Gordon was offering, but there was also a part of her that didn't trust him because of his military background, and her experiences with such people in the past.

Gordon saw this, too, and carried on. 'How about this

as a compromise? You draw me up a wish list, with no strings attached. I'll see how much of it we can find, and then, maybe, we can discuss it further. Would that work for you?'

Before Claire could answer, we were interrupted by the sound of raised voices. I turned and saw Nick standing just a few inches from Hamish, jabbing his finger into his chest. 'Don't tell us what we can or can't do, and who we can or can't do it to. We'll do whatever we fucking want. We're in charge around here, not you.'

Hamish was bristling with anger. 'Says who?'

'Says the fact this country's under martial law, and like it or not,' Nick swept his arm across to where the other marines were standing, tensely watching the situation, 'it seems we're all that's left of the military. That means we're in charge.'

'Country? What fecking country?' Hamish spat back 'There ain't nothing left of your precious country.'

'Yes, there is.' Nick was swaying slightly as he yelled at Hamish. 'There's here. You might not want to admit it, but you won't be able to survive for long without our help.'

'Ach,' Hamish waved his hand derisively at Nick, 'why don't you just feck off back to wherever you came from. We don't need your help; we're doing well enough on our own. And anyway,' Hamish's face was turning a deep, angry red, 'where were you when we really needed you?'

'What d'you think?' I glanced at Gordon. 'Should we let them sort it out between themselves?'

'Yes.' He nodded. 'Hopefully they're just letting off steam. You never know, it might help clear the air if they can get it all off their chests.'

Across the room, Nick jabbed Hamish again, this time hard enough to force him to take a step backwards. Nick advanced. 'We were fighting on the front line, protecting sorry arsed people like you.' He jabbed Hamish once more. 'You don't have a chance in hell of surviving around here without us.'

Hamish stepped forward until his nose was almost touching Nick's. 'We've been surviving around here since before fecking Sassenachs like you ever even knew places like this existed.'

'What the fuck's that supposed to mean?' Nick looked confused. 'What is it with you people? How do you expect to be able to run things when you can't even speak proper English?'

Hamish sensed he was starting to get the upper hand. 'If you don't like how we do things around here, why don't you go back to your precious London? Oh, because you can't, can you?' This time is was Hamish who poked Nick in the chest. 'You fecking Sassenachs couldn't even save your own capital, what makes you think you can help us any better than we can help ourselves?'

The room held its breath as it waited for Nick to react. Unsurprisingly, he exploded. 'You fucking prick! My family was in London. I'd rather have been there, protecting them than trying to stop you fucking diseased Jocks killing each other. The moment it happened, we should have just walled the lot of you off and left you to it.'

Tom put his beer down on the bar and stepped forward, standing beside Hamish. 'Don't forget they tried that. It didn't exactly work, did it? And I'd hardly say fire-bombing a city of half a million people's trying to stop us killing each other.'

'We should have bombed the whole damn country back to the Stone Age. We should have done it years ago.' Nick stopped, looking around in an exaggerated manner. 'Oh wait, how would anyone have been able to tell the difference?'

The other locals watched intently, trying to get a read on where the situation was going before making a decision as to whether or not to get involved. The marines were doing likewise. To my left, I heard Daz make a move to get up and I put my hand on his arm, 'This isn't our fight.' He shot me a look of disdain as I carried on. 'Not yet at any rate. We'll only get involved if we have to. Otherwise, it's best to just let them sort it out between themselves.'

Daz settled back onto his seat, but he didn't seem 100 per cent convinced.

Suddenly, Hamish lunged at Nick, but Nick stepped back and pulled out his pistol, pushing it into Hamish's face as he tumbled onto his hands and knees. The room froze, no one quite sure what to do next.

Keeping the pistol pressed against his cheek, Nick leant forward and growled into Hamish's ear. 'Not so brave now, are you?'

Tom stepped forward and Nick turned the gun on him. 'You stay where you are!'

Tom held his hands up. 'Look, let's just cool it. I get it, we're all pretty stressed; it's no big surprise; we've all got to let off a little steam, but it's over now. You won the argument, everyone can see that. Why don't you put that away and I'll get you another drink?'

Nick straightened his arm and pressed the barrel against Tom's forehead. When he spoke his voice was cold. 'Don't you tell me what to bloody well do!' He adjusted his grip on the gun. 'Just remember that around here, I outrank you.' He pointed back to the other marines. 'We all do. In the pecking order, we're up here,' he held his other hand out parallel to the floor at shoulder height, 'while you ... you're all the way down here.' He dropped his hand to waist level. 'And don't you ever forget that!'

Tom remained stock-still. 'Sorry, what did you say? I wasn't listening.'

A look flashed across Nick's face and there was a click as he cocked the gun.

The last time I'd seen Nick like this, he was preparing to execute one of his own men and I had no intention of letting him do the same to Tom. I moved to stand up, not quite knowing what I was going to do, but Gordon beat me to it. In a firm voice, he called out across the bar. 'Nick, stand down.'

Nothing happened. Gordon took a step forward. 'Nick, I think you've had enough; I think we all have.'

Nick remained where he was, staring furiously at Tom.

'Lieutenant!' Gordon stepped forward again. 'Since you seem to be so keen on who outranks whom, you'll remember that I'm your commanding officer, and I outrank *you*.' He kept walking slowly across the room as he spoke until he was standing next to Nick. 'This is a direct order.' Gordon wasn't shouting; instead, his voice was quiet and authoritative. 'Stand down. Now!'

Nick finally took his eyes off Tom. 'Oh for fuck's sake, Bucky, I'm just having a bit of fun.' He lowered the gun and uncocked it before shoving it back into its holster. He glowered at the locals. 'None of you are worth the fucking trouble!' With that, he turned and stormed out of the bar; the other marines filed out silently after him.

Gordon returned to the table and smiled apologetically at Claire and me. 'I guess this didn't do as much for improving relationships as I'd hoped it would.'

He looked towards the still open door. 'I should go after them, just to make sure they don't cause any more trouble.' He picked up his drink and finished it in one gulp. 'Maybe this whole idea of bringing everyone together in one place just isn't going to work. Maybe we should just leave you to get on with it.' He sounded a little sad and deflated. 'After all, now the world's changed, who says we really know any more about surviving around here than you guys do?'

Gordon put down his glass before walking to the door and disappearing into the night.

At seven the next morning, I heard the sound of the rib's engines starting up. Gordon and the marines were leaving early, not even waiting around for breakfast. The previous evening, which was meant to have built bridges, had clearly failed; instead, it had only served to further sour the already strained relationship between the locals and the naval personnel. I went up on deck to see if I could get a word with them before they left, but they were already heading out of the bay. On board, I could see Nick yelling at Gordon and gesticulating wildly. I wondered if this was all about last night, or whether it ran deeper. The argument continued as they disappeared from sight a few minutes later, leaving me with a growing sense of unease in the pit of my stomach.

****

Over the next few weeks, we saw Gordon and the marines in their ribs off in the distance from time to time, but we had no direct contact with them. They weren't obviously avoiding us, but neither were they going out of their way to speak to us. Maybe I was just imagining it, and it might just have been that they, like us, were feeling the strain of how things were changing. Infected were now turning up regularly in communities spread across the islands, and one by one they were being overrun. To give them credit, the marines were doing their best to help out wherever they could, and on more than one occasion they'd been lucky enough to be in just the right place at the right time to save many lives when this had happened.

An infected had even turned up in Tobermory early one morning, and it was only by chance that it had been spotted as it staggered up the shore, seemingly sluggish after its time in the water. Hamish had managed to dispatch it with his hunting rifle before it got much further and we gathered around the body as Claire examined it.

After a few minutes she stood up. 'This doesn't make any sense. It doesn't look like he's been in the water for more than a few minutes. Look at his hands.' She pointed at the body. 'They'd be all wrinkled if he'd been in the sea for any longer, and they're not.'

Hamish bent down and stared closely at the man's face. 'I know him.' He looked up at me. 'You do, too.'

I knelt down beside Hamish. The man did seem familiar, but the disease had changed him: he'd become gaunt, his cheeks hollow from lack of food. 'I don't thi— Wait! That's Martin Gallagher!'

Martin was well-known locally, although most people simply referred to him as 'The Professor', both because of his eccentric looks and because of how he'd ended up on Mull. He'd taken early retirement after selling some energy saving gadget he'd invented to a big multi-national, and had used the money to buy a long-abandoned farmhouse on the south coast of the island. He'd rebuilt it from the ground up and made it completely self-sufficient by installing wind turbines, solar panels and even a small tidal power generator of his own design. Much to the bemusement of the locals, this resembled a gigantic duck whose head dipped in and out of the water as the tide rose and fell.

Both Hamish and I straightened up. I glanced at the man again. 'How the hell could the Professor have got here? If he went into the water anywhere near where he lived, the currents would have been against him all the way.'

Hamish shrugged. 'I don't know. None of this makes any sense.'

***

By the end of the month, the only community where no infected had appeared was the one on Rhum, and the result was that the number of people living there was swelling rapidly as more and more of the locals chose to relocate: some forced from their own homes by the rapidly spreading infected; others doing so by choice, believing that the naval personnel could offer far better protection than they could provide themselves.

The infected were certainly a growing threat, but it was still unclear why they'd suddenly started turning up with such regularity, or where they were coming from. The morning after Canna had been overtaken, Mitch and Hamish came out to the yacht, and together we tried to work out what was going on.

'Ben,' Mitch pressed her temples in frustration, 'I know you think there could be infected drifting around out there, and while I agree it's possible, the fact is, in all the time I've been flying around, I haven't seen a single one. And neither have you.'

'I know, but how else can they be getting onto the islands?' I blurted out exasperatedly. 'It's the only way that seems remotely feasible'

'There've been eight attacks in the last week, including when the Professor turned up here. With Canna gone, we're the only place, other than Rhum, where people are still holding on.' Hamish shook his head. 'For this to be happening so often, there'd have to be a lot of them out there ... and there just aren't.'

'Maybe you're missing them somehow,' Tom interjected.

Mitch turned on him. 'Are you saying I don't know what I'm looking for?'

'No, it's just ...' Tom fumbled around, trying to put his thoughts in order. 'Maybe we're just not out there at the right time of day. Haven't you noticed? The infected always turn up late at night or first thing in the morning, like the Professor did. Maybe that's got something to do with it.'

I hadn't noticed the pattern before, and now I thought about it, I saw Tom was right, but I struggled to work out what it meant.

'Maybe it's something to do with the way they behave.' Sophie looked quizzical. 'Could they be doing it on purpose?'

Claire leant forward. 'There's nothing we've seen so far which would suggest they're capable of anything other than basic functions like running and biting: all they seem to care about is attacking uninfected. The disease seems to burn out everything else in their brains. I don't think they can do anything which isn't innate. That would rule out them using a boat, or even swimming, so I don't see how they could be doing it on purpose.'

'But they're doing it somehow!' Sophie retorted.

I could see the discussion was getting us nowhere and that tensions were beginning to show. We badly needed to work out what was going on so that we could protect ourselves, but there seemed to be no logical explanation.

Letting out a deep sigh, Claire sat back in her seat. 'Maybe we should think about moving up to Rhum after all.' She glanced round nervously. 'As far as we know, it's the only place which hasn't been affected yet, and even if infected make it there, they're better prepared to deal with it than we are: they've got the guns and the training, and there's the Big House to hole up in until the infected are dealt with.'

Tom stared at her. 'That's quite a change of attitude.'

Claire shrugged. 'Sometimes you've got to be pragmatic about these things. If Rhum really is safer, then maybe it's our best option.'

'Aye, but how do we know if it really is?' Hamish glanced round the group. 'Maybe there have been attacks there and they've just kept it quiet. They're keeping pretty tight control of the place nowadays, not letting anyone off once they move there.' He turned to Mitch. 'When was the last time they let you visit?'

Mitch nodded. 'True, but even if they have had infected turn up there, they haven't been overrun, have they?'

'So are you saying we should leave here?' There was anger in Hamish's voice. 'After all we've done and all we've been through?'

'No.' Mitch looked down to avoid making eye contact with Hamish, 'but I think we should at least consider it if we can't work out what's going on.'

Chapter Eighteen

The sun was just about to drop below the horizon when a black rib raced around the headland and into Tobermory Bay. Daz was the first to spot it, but by the time it was clear they were making a beeline for us, we were all up on deck. As the rib turned sharply and bumped alongside of the yacht, I could see Nick was at the wheel.

He wasted no time in announcing why they were there. 'We've got a badly injured man. We need Claire.'

Claire stepped forward. 'What happened?'

'We were trying to get supplies for the clinic Bucky was setting up for you when we got jumped by some infected. Things got messy and one of our men got caught in the crossfire.' Nick looked to Claire. 'He needs your help. Please.'

'Okay, I'll get my bag,' Claire turned just as she reached the companionway, 'Where is he? Has Gordon taken him back to Rhum?'

'Bucky's dead.' Nick spoke in a perfunctory tone as he kept his eyes locked on Claire. 'An infected got him. I told him it was too risky, but he was hell-bent on getting supplies for the clinic. He just wouldn't listen to reason.' We looked at each other, shocked and not quite knowing what to say.

Claire was the first to speak. 'But I never even gave him a list. I never agreed ...'

'I know, but he thought he could make up for the trouble I caused in the bar by putting the clinic together for you anyway.' Nick shook his head. 'I feel so responsible.' He looked down for a moment and then quickly back at Claire. 'Anyway, what's done is done, and I don't want to lose anyone else.'

This stirred Claire back into action. 'I'll just be a minute.' With that she disappeared below. As we waited, I watched the marines: despite their loss, they seemed to be holding up well.

A moment later, Claire reappeared. 'Sophie, you're coming with me.'

Sophie protested for a moment, but then saw the expression on her mother's face and ducked into the cabin, grabbing her waterproof jacket and pulling it angrily over her head. Just as Claire was about to climb into the rib, Tom stopped her. 'Wouldn't it be faster to fly up with Mitch?'

Claire quickly scanned the anchorage. 'She's not here, and we don't know when she'll be back. If someone's been shot, I'll need to see to them as soon as possible. I don't want anyone else dying if they don't have to.' Clearly, she was rattled by the fact that Gordon had lost his life trying to find supplies so she'd be able to treat people better in just this type of situation.

I could see where Claire was coming from, but something was niggling at me about the whole situation; I just couldn't work out what. I glanced at Tom and could see he was troubled by similar thoughts. In the meantime, Sophie was already in the rib and Claire was about to follow.

'Wait, I'll come with you. You never know, I might be able to help out.' Before I could stop him, Tom leapt into the rib, too.

Nick smiled. 'It's okay with me; any of the rest of you want to come?'

Daz made to move forward, but I stopped him. 'I need you here.' I looked at Claire and then Tom. 'We'll sail over in the morning and pick you up.'

'Sounds like a plan.' Tom waved over his shoulder as the rib turned and sped out of the bay. I stared after them, trying to work out what was causing the odd feeling deep in my stomach. The fact that Gordon was dead had a lot to do with it, but there was something else I couldn't quite put my finger on.

Just then, I heard the sound of Mitch's seaplane off in the distance. Searching the sky, I saw it coming in from the west. Within minutes, it had dropped onto the water and come to a halt a few feet from the back of the boat. Mitch climbed out onto the pontoon and nodded in the direction the rib had just disappeared in. 'What did *they* want?'

'They wanted Claire. They were attacked while trying to get supplies for the clinic.' I stared off into the distance. 'Gordon's dead, and one of the marines was shot in the confusion. Claire's gone to see if she can fix him up.'

Mitch's brow furrowed. 'That can't be right. I've spent most of the afternoon trying to see if I could find any infected drifting around out there and I saw the ribs over at the Suil Ghorm Lighthouse on my way out; the thing is, they were still there when I passed it again an hour ago. They can't have been trying to get supplies there, and the lighthouse was automated years ago so there's no one on the island; infected or otherwise.'

Now I was worried. 'Could you see what they were doing?'

'I didn't really pay them much attention, I just noticed they were there and moved on.' Mitch's eyes narrowed. 'Why?'

'Because if that's the case, then Nick must've been lying about what happened.'

'Why would he do that?'

'I don't know.' I glanced around uneasily: night had fallen as we spoke, but I knew the waters well enough to handle the passage in the dark. 'But I think I need to see if I can find out.' I leaned into the companionway, 'Daz, get up here; we need to head up to Rhum right away.'

'Daz, pull in the sheet there,' I pointed to the left, 'and tighten up the jib.'

We were a couple of hours out of Tobermory, and with stiff winds, we were making good progress. Yet, I wanted to go faster. Daz wasn't listening to me; instead, he was staring back the way we'd come.

'Daz, sheets!'

He pointed over the stern. 'Ben, is that no' Mitch?'

I turned to see the seaplane flying low over the water towards us, flames spewing from the engine compartment.

'Yes, and she's in big trouble!' I steered the boat into the wind, trying to work out what to do next. As I watched, the seaplane stuttered and dipped towards the sea. Somehow, Mitch was managing to keep it in the air, but it didn't look like she'd be able to continue to do so for much longer.

A realisation of what was about to happen swept over me. 'Daz, pass me the spotlight.'

Daz reached into the cabin and pulled it from its bracket before handing it to me. I pointed it in Mitch's direction, clicking it on and off several times. Mitch must have seen my signal because she changed her course and headed directly towards us.

Daz's eyes widened. 'What're we going to do?'

'Get the dinghy ready!' I pulled the boat round, trying to shorten the distance between us. 'She's going to end up in the water, and when that happens, we'll need to get her out as soon as possible.'

Within a couple of minutes, we had the dinghy over the side and ready to go. Just then there was a loud crash, and I glanced up to see the seaplane had finally hit the sea some 200 yards away. I turned the boat into the wind once more before jumping into the dinghy; cranking the engine as far as I dared, I sped across the choppy waters. It was only a few minutes before I reached the stricken aeroplane, but it felt like an age.

As I neared, I could see flames licking up the left-hand side towards the wings as it tilted sharply to the right. Inside, Mitch was lying, unmoving, across the controls. Bringing the dinghy alongside, I climbed onto the pontoon and pulled on the door; it didn't move. I banged it hard and tried again: this time it opened; Mitch stirred, lifting her head and looking around, a dazed expression on her face.

'Mitch, over here! You need to get out of there!'

Mitch stared at me, as if trying to work out where I'd come from.

'Mitch, the plane's on fire,' I beckoned to her. 'You need to get out!'

'Oh, right ... Yeah.' Mitch turned her head, but remained in her seat. The heat from the flames was becoming unbearable and the plane's cockpit was rapidly filling with thick, acrid smoke. Knowing there wasn't much time, I leaned into the cockpit and punched the release button on Mitch's seatbelt before pulling her towards the door. This seemed to be the jolt she needed to bring her round, and she scrambled into the dinghy behind me. I gunned the engine; we made it about twenty yards before the fuel tank in the wing finally exploded, engulfing the plane in a fireball that rose thirty feet into the air. By the time we got back to the boat, the plane had sunk from sight, leaving nothing but an oily slick on the water and the lingering smell of burnt kerosene.

'That was close. Mitch, are you okay?' Daz was peering into the dinghy.

Mitch ran her fingers through her hair, flinching as she reached the point where it was stained with blood. 'Yeah, I'm fine. Just a bit banged up.'

Daz and I helped her onto the boat; other than the shallow gash on the side of her head and badly bruised ribs, she'd got away lightly.

'So what happened back there?' Then another thought occurred to me. 'What were you doing flying at night? Were you looking for us?'

Mitch dabbed at the cut on her head with a wad of tissues. 'No. It's Tobermory; I don't know what happened. Somehow the straw bales at the north end caught fire. We tried to put them out, but the fire was too well set in. I realised it was only a matter of time before it burnt through and the infected could get in. We wouldn't be able to hold them off on our own and I thought our best chance was to get the marines to come and help us, so I got out to the plane and took off.' She took a deep breath. 'I spotted them almost immediately, sitting in the water as if they were waiting for something to happen.

I was confused. 'Spotted who?'

'The marines; in one of the ribs; they were just up the coast from Tobermory. I circled round to get their attention, only when they realised I was there, they opened fire.'

An incredulous expression flashed across Daz's face.

'They shot at you?'

'Yeah.' Mitch frowned. 'It was like I caught them by surprise or something. Once they saw I was hit, they sped off towards Tobermory.'

I paced around the cockpit. 'What the hell's going on?'

I'd assumed the other rib had taken the injured man back to Rhum, but it couldn't have made it all the way there and back again in the little over two hours which had passed since Nick had come to get Claire.

'Ben,' Mitch glanced at me, 'you don't think they could have had something to do with the barricade catching fire, do you?'

'I don't know, but we'd better go and see if we can find out.' With that I turned the boat sharply and headed back the way we'd come.

We saw the flames from Tobermory well before we finally pulled into the bay. The straw bales which had kept the inhabitants safe for so long were now nothing more than ashes and many of the houses which formed the barrier at the back of what had once been the safe area were ablaze. By the light of the fires, we could see the infected: they clustered around the bodies scattered along the road; pulling and tearing at the flesh of those they'd just killed. Close to the shore, a young girl, about the same age as Sophie, was silhouetted against the flames as she chewed at the face of a man I no longer recognised. I shone the spotlight on her and she looked up: blood dripping from her pale face, her long, blonde hair matted with the red liquid. Her eyes searched the darkness, burning with anger. She stood up and took a step towards the water; now she could sense that the living were near, she was no longer interested in the dead.

'Turn it off! I don't want to see her like that.' Mitch looked away, unable to watch any more, and I realised who the girl was, or at least who she'd once been. I switched off the spotlight. 'Sorry, Mitch.'

'You couldn't have known.' Mitch wiped her face. 'She was so beautiful, and now look at her … what's left of her.'

'I don't understand it. How come none of them tried to get away?' Daz stared in disbelief. 'They could've just swum out to any of the boats in the harbour an' been safe. Hamish an' me talked about it when we first arrived; what would be the best chance of escapin' if the infected somehow got in.' There was a pause before he spoke again. 'How come they just stayed on the shore an' let the infected get them?'

I stared back towards the remnants of the town which had felt like our last semblance of normality, wondering, like Daz, how it was possible that no one had escaped. There must have come a point when they knew the infected were going to get in: yet, it looked like none of them had even tried to get away. Knowing we wouldn't find the answer here, we turned and headed back out of the bay; after all, with everything gone, there was little reason to stay.

'Wait, what's that?' Daz was pointing ahead of the boat. I clicked on the spotlight again and played it across the water where it illuminated a man's body floating face down, arms out to the side.

'Daz, wheel!' I ran forward and as the body came alongside, I reached down and grabbed the back of the man's jacket, pulling it up until I could reach through the guard rails and grip him properly. 'Mitch, can you give me a hand?'

Between the two of us, we managed to manhandle the body onto the deck. By then, Daz had turned the boat into the wind and we were no longer moving. I rolled the body over and Mitch gasped. 'Oh shit!'

It was Hamish. There were no signs he'd been attacked by the infected; instead there were three large holes in his chest.

Daz stared, wide-eyed. 'He's been shot!'

Mitch slumped down onto the roof of the cabin, looking lost. I looked grimly at Daz. 'That explains why no one managed to get away.'

'We need to work out what's going on.' I paced back and forth; Daz was at the helm, while Mitch and I were in the cabin. 'Why would the marines attack Tobermory?'

'I don't know, but Nick's had it in for us right from the start.' Mitch shook her head. 'You heard him in the bar the other night. Maybe with Gordon gone, he thought he'd get his revenge.'

'Yeah, but it doesn't really make sense.' I stopped and stared up the companionway, watching Daz for a few seconds as he adjusted the wheel to keep us on course. 'I mean, if the other rib was waiting outside Tobermory, then it can't have been taking an injured man back to Rhum, and from what you said, they spent most of today at the Suil Ghorm Lighthouse, not out looking for supplies for the clinic.' I rubbed my forehead. 'So how did Gordon end up dead?' A coldness suddenly rushed over me. 'You don't think Nick had anything to do with that, do you?'

'I don't know, but I think we need to find out.' She pointed west. 'The lighthouse is just over there, we could be at it in a couple of hours; it's not that far out of the way. If we can work out what they were doing there, it might help us understand the bigger picture ... whatever that might be.'

'You're right.' I strode across the cabin and climbed into the cockpit, taking the wheel from Daz. He looked at me curiously as I turned it left until we were on a new heading, taking us straight towards the lighthouse which, thanks to automation, still blinked its signal out into the night's sky despite everything that had happened.

I stared downwards, scuffing my foot through the loose earth. 'What d'you think?'

We'd reached the island on which the lighthouse perched and had lost no time in setting the anchor before going ashore. From there, it had been a short, but difficult, climb up to the small cluster of buildings which nestled at the top. Once there, I scanned the ground with the spotlight, illuminating evidence of a struggle by the door of the lighthouse itself, and marks that suggested someone had been forcibly dragged inside: it was the only trace we'd found that anyone had been on the island any time within the last few weeks.

Mitch knelt down and ran her hand across the dirt, before picking some up and rubbing it between her fingers. 'This looks fresh.'

Suddenly, there was a loud bang; Mitch jumped to her feet as Daz and I took a step backwards. For a moment, there was silence and we stood stock still, eyes searching the darkness which surrounded us.

'What the hell was that?' Daz hissed, his eyes wide with fear.

'I don't know; I think it came from in there.' I nodded towards the lighthouse door, training the light on it as I spoke.

'D'you think there's one of *them* in there?' Daz whispered.

'I can't see how an infected could have made it up here; it's too steep.' Mitch whispered back. 'And no one's lived here in years.'

'D'you think it's him, then?' Daz's eyes were locked on the door.

'I don't know,' I whispered to the others; then slightly louder, 'Gordon?'

There was no response. I inched my way forward, and put a hand on the door; then an ear. I called out a second time, louder than before. 'Gordon?'

Something hit the other side of the door hard enough to make it shudder; I leapt away. 'Are you sure an infected couldn't have made it up here?'

Mitch nodded. 'I'm certain. They'd never make it up the rocks. If they could do that, they'd have been able to climb over the barricades in Tobermory, and that never happened.'

Daz glanced at me. 'What if he's been tied up an' gagged or somethin'.'

'Only one way to find out.' I reached out, grabbing the handle and twisting it before pushing the door open. 'Gordon, is that you?'

There was a snarl as an arm shot through the gap between the door and its frame, and a bloodstained hand fastened onto my wrist. Instinctively, I pulled the door back towards me as hard as I could, but despite using all my weight, I couldn't get it closed again. I felt the infected tighten its grip and start to drag me towards the gap. I dropped the spotlight and tried to prize its fingers off, while my attacker did its best to wrench the door open with its other hand.

Suddenly, Daz was beside me, kicking out at the arm; I heard bones shatter, yet still the infected held on. Daz kicked again and again until finally I was released, but its arm remained sticking through the gap between the door and the frame as the infected fought to get it open from the inside. I held onto the handle with both hands and leaned back, doing my best to stop it succeeding.

'When I say, let go of the door.' I turned to see Mitch standing beside me, a large rock raised above her head.

I stared at her, incredulously. 'You mean let it out?'

'Yes. I should be able to get it as comes through the door.'

'You sure?' Daz had backed off and was standing a few feet behind me. 'Have you seen how fast they can move?'

Mitch shifted her grip on the rock. 'I don't see what other option we have: we can't get the door closed again, not with its arm sticking out; we can't stay here holding on to the door forever; and if we let go and try to run, then it'll definitely get us.'

The door shuddered and shook as the infected tried to force its way through, and with my strength already fading, I knew I wouldn't be able to hold on much longer: Mitch's plan, risky as it might be, was the only thing we could do.

'Okay. On the count of three: one, two.' I took a deep breath.

'WAIT!' Daz's outcry almost caused Mitch to drop the rock.

'What?' I hissed.

'What if there's more than one in there?' He hissed back.

'Trust me, there's only one.' The door trembled as the infected clawed at the gap between the door and its frame.

Daz looked petrified. 'How d'you know?'

'Because if there were more, they'd have got the door open by now!' I glanced at Mitch, she nodded. 'Three!'

I let go of the handle and threw myself away from the door as a large, muscular man wrenched it open and bolted forward: mouth open; teeth bared. Mitch swung the rock, catching him on the shoulder and sending him sprawling to the ground. As he struggled to right himself, Mitch raised the rock again, this time finding her mark and I heard his skull crunch beneath its weight. Finally, he was still. Leaving the now bloodied rock where it had come to rest, she straightened up, breathing heavily. 'I told you it would work.'

'Just as well …' I replied, relieved that Mitch's plan hadn't gone horribly wrong. I picked up the spotlight and ventured towards the door, wondering how an infected had got in there in the first place. I flashed the light around the small room at the base of the lighthouse, blood was splattered across the walls and the floor, while the air was fetid and smelt of death. Holding a hand over my mouth and nose, I stepped further inside. Behind the door, I spotted what, at first glance, I though was just a pile of old rags, but approaching it, I realised it was all that was left of a body. Swallowing hard, I knelt beside it and examined it closely: the infected had torn it apart and it was almost unrecognisable, but enough remained of the face that I could tell it was Gordon.

'So Nick wasn't lyin' when he said Gordon was killed by an infected.' Daz was looking over my shoulder as Mitch lingered by the door.

'Yeah.' I reached out and turned what was left of Gordon's torso, 'but it wasn't the whole truth either, look.' His hands had been fastened behind his back with a thick black cable tie.

'Awww fuck!' Daz kept his eyes trained on Gordon's body as he spoke. 'What do we do now?'

'There's nothing we can do, not for Gordon at any rate.' I could feel myself starting to hyperventilate and despite the smell, I forced myself to take a slow, deep breath. 'But we need to get out of here; we need to get up to Rhum and get the others away from there as soon as we can.'

As I turned to leave, I spotted a small metal tube with a tuft of yellow fibrous material protruding from one end. I pulled the sleeve of my shirt over my hand and carefully picked it up before sliding it into my pocket so I could examine it properly later; if it was what I thought it was, it would do a lot to explain what had happened to Gordon.

'So,' Daz turned the wheel to keep us pointing in the right direction, 'what d'you think went on back there?'

We were back on the boat and heading for Rhum. It would be a good few hours before we got there and we had plenty of time to discuss what we'd just found.

'I think there's little doubt that Nick killed him.' I stared out into the darkness. 'I don't know how much the other marines know, but I don't think he could have done it alone.'

Mitch was sitting opposite me in the cockpit. 'But what I don't understand is how they could have got him in there with an infected. You saw how it went for us when we tried to get in.'

'Because they used this.' I took an old rag from one of

the deck lockers and gingerly pulled the small metal tube out of my pocket, making sure I kept my fingers well clear of its razor-sharp tip. Daz leant forward to pick it up, but I stopped him. 'Careful. If I'm right, that's infected blood on the end of it.'

He recoiled instantly. 'What is it?'

I held it up and ruffled my thumb across the yellow fibres. 'It's a tranquilizer dart: the kind vets use to knock out large animals.'

Daz frowned. 'What's that got to do with anythin'?'

I examined it closely: it was about half an inch wide and five inches long, with a thick hypodermic needle sticking out of one end. 'I think they used it to knock out the infected so they could put it in the room with Gordon. It's the only way they could have done it safely.' I glanced across at Mitch. 'It would also explain why they waited around for so long; they wouldn't have known how long it would take for the infected to recover and they wouldn't want there to be a chance of Gordon getting away.'

Mitch stared at the dart. 'But why go to all that trouble?'

'Think about it; if they'd just shot him and we'd stumbled across Gordon's body, then we'd have known what they'd done.' I stared at it. 'This way, if he was ever found, it would look like he'd been killed by an infected, just as they said.'

'But what about the cable tie?' Daz was watching me closely, 'is that no' a bit of a giveaway?'

I carefully wrapped the dart in the rag and tucked it into a safe place beside the helm, just in case we needed the evidence later. 'My guess is they forgot about it until it was too late, and when they realised, they couldn't exactly go back in and take it off.'

'You don't think they saw me, do you?' Mitch was concerned. 'You don't think that's why they attacked Tobermory?'

I rubbed my hand along the side of my face, feeling the thick beard which now grew there. 'There's certainly a good chance that was part of it. But it could also have just been good, old-fashioned revenge. Or maybe it was because we were the only other group left and they knew we were unlikely to give into them. Other than us, they've got pretty much everyone under their control now. They're saying it's for protection, but I think there might be more to it than ...'

A thought popped into my head and it was so startling that it stopped me in my tracks. If they'd managed to knock out one infected with a tranquillizer gun, why couldn't they have done it to others, too? Nick had made it clear in the bar that he thought they were in charge and that everybody should be doing exactly what they said. What if he'd worked out a way to persuade people he was right? It was only after that night that we'd really started having problems with communities being overrun, and we hadn't worked out any possible way for the infected to be getting to the islands on their own. What if someone had given them a hand?

It wasn't unusual to see lone infected loitering near the shore on the mainland or the islands they infested, and with a tranquilizer gun, the marines could easily immobilise one. Once they'd done that, it would be simple enough to pick it up and drop it into a community under cover of darkness. All they'd need to do then was wait for it to recover and start attacking people; they could then ride in, all guns blazing. It would be the perfect demonstration of why people needed them, and why they should be allowed to take control. Once the marines had saved the day, people would feel indebted to them, and would do what they said. It was a simple strategy, yet the very idea of it was horrifying.

I wondered if Nick had got the idea from Iona, because I was pretty sure he wasn't behind that attack, but the others after that, the ones we'd had so much difficulty trying to explain, they all fitted with the pattern rapidly coalescing in my mind.

Maybe Gordon had been getting suspicious, and that's why he'd had to die; or maybe he'd simply out-lived his usefulness. It was Gordon's friendliness and leadership that persuaded people to leave their homes and move to Rhum; not Nick's strong-arm tactics. Now all the other communities had been forced to move there by the infected, and Tobermory had been destroyed, maybe Nick felt he didn't need him anymore. If that was the case, things on Rhum were likely to take a turn for the worse with a man like that in charge. It wouldn't be a democracy, it would be a dictatorship, with Nick reigning supreme, while the other marines took their places in the upper echelons: everyone else would be treated little better than slaves.

If I was right, and still I wasn't yet certain of that, then we were in real trouble, because the last thing Nick would want would be us turning up at Rhum, trying to take Claire, Tom and Sophie back to Tobermory. There was just too much evidence there of what they'd done, and they had too great a need for Claire and her medical skills if they wanted to survive in the long term.

Chapter Nineteen

'Are we agreed that this is the best plan?' I looked at Daz and Mitch, and they both nodded. I examined my watch and then the sails. 'We'll reach Rhum in about twenty minutes. Are you both clear about what we're going to do?'

They nodded again.

'Any questions?'

Daz moved nervously on his seat in the cockpit. 'You think this'll work?'

I avoided giving a straight answer. 'I think it's the best chance we have.'

'That's no' really answerin' the question, Ben.' Daz glared at me. 'Is it?'

'If we're careful, yes, I think it'll work.' I picked at my nails. 'The biggest question's what they're going to do once they find out we're gone.'

Mitch stood up and stretched her back. 'What d'you think they'll do?'

'My guess?' I chewed on the inside of my lower lip. 'They'll come after us, but they're going to assume we're heading for Tobermory: that should give us enough time to get away.'

Daz stared down at his feet. 'If we're no' goin' back to Tobermory, where are we goin'?'

I shook my head. 'I don't know. Somewhere north would be best; see if we can find somewhere that's beyond their reach.'

We'd delayed our arrival as long as we dared. It would need to be dark before we tried to make our escape, and the less time we spent on the island, the less time there'd be for our plan to be discovered. We finally pulled into the bay in front of the Big House just before five in the afternoon, with Mitch taking care to keep out of sight: our plan would only work if they didn't suspect that Daz and I knew about what had happened in Tobermory. Even before we'd dropped anchor, one of the ribs was speeding from the shore towards us with Nick at the controls, flanked by two other marines, both carrying their assault rifles.

Nick smiled as he pulled up alongside. 'Glad to see you made it. We were beginning to wonder where you'd got to.' While his voice was calm, there was an edge to it and his expression was forced.

I smiled back, hoping I was doing a better job of faking it than he was. 'I thought we'd take our time. After all, there's no rush, is there?' I searched his face, trying to work out if he believed me or not. 'Did Claire manage to get your man sorted?'

This seemed to throw him. 'What? Oh, yes. Turned out it wasn't as bad as we first thought; it wasn't really an emergency after all.'

'That's good to hear.' I paused briefly, suddenly getting cold feet about our plan, but as far as I could see there was no other way: it was this or nothing. Yet, once we'd started to put it into action, there'd be no going back. Mentally, I steadied myself and then took the plunge. 'You want to give us a lift ashore then?'

Nick looked nonplussed; he'd obviously not expected us to go with them voluntarily, and without our own dinghy as that would mean we'd have no way to get back to the yacht. He took a couple of seconds to answer. 'Yeah, okay. Climb in.'

Daz and me jumped into the rib, and moments later we were skimming across the water towards the beach. Just above the high-tide line on the shore, I saw the distinctive shape of the Professor's home-made tidal power generator lying on its side. It hadn't been here the last time we'd visited, and its presence here now seemed to confirm my suspicions that Nick was behind the infected suddenly appearing out of nowhere, both in Tobermory and in so many other communities.

Once we got to shore, it took us almost half an hour to find Claire and Sophie, mostly because Nick was keen to interrogate us about what we knew, but he was careful to make it seem casual and friendly. Eventually, he must have decided that we really didn't know what was going on, and he let us head off in search of the others. We found them in the room which Gordon had ear-marked for the clinic. It had already been well-stocked with equipment and supplies, and a number of beds had been set up at one end. Claire and Sophie were standing round the nearest, changing the dressing on the shoulder of the marine who'd been shot the previous day. Given what we'd discovered in the last twenty-four hours, I'd half-expected there to be no injured man at all, but then I realised there'd have to have been if Nick was to have any chance of getting Claire on side.

There was a yelp of pain from the marine.

'Hold still.' Claire's voice was firm and authoritative. 'Sophie, hand me the new dressing.'

Sophie passed Claire a white square, which she slapped unceremoniously onto the marine's shoulder, causing him to yelp again. There was the sound of Elastoplast being ripped from a roll before Claire spoke again. 'That's you finished for now, but it'll need changed again in the morning.'

The marine grumbled and rubbed his shoulder as he slid off the bed, and headed for the door. That was when he spotted Daz and me. He froze, a look of complete surprise on his face that suggested we were the last people he'd expected to see there. After a second, he seemed to come to his senses, barging past us and out into the corridor, slamming the door behind him.

I stepped forward. 'You were a bit rough with him, weren't you?'

Claire spun round, a look of relief spreading across her face. 'You got here safely then? I was starting to get worried.' She went over to the door, opened it, glanced outside and then closed it again. 'Just wanted to check we're not going to be overheard.'

She beckoned us over to the far side of the room. 'There's something very odd going on around here. For a start, that marine wasn't shot by accident in a fight with the infected.'

Daz frowned. 'How d'you know?'

'Powder burns around the wound. By the looks of it someone took a bullet, removed most of the charge and then fired it into his shoulder at point-blank range. It looked bad, but it was never going to do him a serious injury. I think they were just trying to get me up here.'

My eyes drifted to the window. Outside I saw the injured marine talking to two others. He was pointing first out to where our boat was anchored and then up at the window where we were standing. Claire continued. 'And I think a lot of locals are regretting ever coming here. I ran into one of the women from Iona that we picked up in the dinghy, and she gave me the impression that she feels trapped here, like they're being held prisoner. No one's allowed a boat except the marines and they seem to expect the locals to do all the hard work: like they're little more than servants.'

I turned my back to the window. 'Did she actually say that?'

'No, it's just the impression I got from speaking to her. She was being very careful about what she said. I think she was scared one of the marines might hear her. I don't quite know what, but there's something really wrong here.'

I let out a sigh, 'Claire, you don't know the half of it.'

'Why?' Sophie chimed in. 'What's happened?'

Before I could say anything, Daz leapt into the conversation. 'We found Gordon.'

Claire's eyes widened. 'Gordon's alive?'

'No, Gordon's dead.' I was uneasy about speaking when I didn't know if I could be overheard or not, but Claire had to know. 'And I'm pretty sure Nick killed him.'

Sophie was shocked. 'But I thought Gordon was killed by an infected? That's what Nick told us, wasn't it?'

'He was killed by an infected alright,' Daz shot back, 'but Nick set it up.'

'How?' Understandably, Claire was incredulous.

I told Claire and Sophie about what we'd found at the lighthouse and what had happened at Tobermory; I told them about Mitch's seaplane and how we thought the infected had been getting onto the islands … and why.

Both Claire and Sophie looked horrified. I kept my voice low. 'It's really important that you don't let on that you know any of this. If they get even a hint of it, I think we'll be in big trouble.'

'But we can't stay here.' Claire hissed back.

'I know, but they're not going to let us just walk out of

here, are they? You, in particular, are too important an asset for them. They need your medical skills.' I checked once again that no one was listening. 'We're going to have to wait until it's dark and then try to sneak out. We'll have to be very quiet, but I think we can make it. They brought us ashore, so at the moment they're going to assume we don't have any way of getting back to the boat. I'm hoping that means they won't keep too close an eye on us for the time being. I've arranged for Mitch to bring the dinghy ashore at midnight, so if we can just get down to the beach to meet her, we should be able to make it out of here.'

'Okay, but what are we going to do for the others? We can't just leave them here, not living like this.' Claire was adamant.

'I know,' I rubbed my temples with the thumb and fore finger of one hand, 'I know, but the first thing we've got to do is to get ourselves off the island; then we can work out what we can do to help everyone else.'

'Speakin' of gettin' ourselves out of here,' Daz was now standing by the window looking down at the marines. 'Where's Tom?'

'I don't know. I've been in here all day.' Claire looked at her daughter. 'Soph, you were with him after lunch. When was the last time you saw him?'

Sophie shrugged. 'When he dropped me off here.'

Claire glanced at her watch. 'That was about four. Any idea where he was going?'

Sophie thought for a moment. 'He said he wanted to check something out while we were here.'

Daz turned to face her. 'D'you know what?'

Sophie shrugged again. 'I don't know. We saw a couple of the marines going up the path into the woods, the one that only they're allowed to use, and Tom suddenly said he'd drop me back off here because he wanted to take a look at something while we were here.'

Claire seemed puzzled. 'Who told you the path was out of bounds?'

'One of the girls I was speaking to last night while you were fixing up the marine.' Sophie nervously twiddled with her hair. 'They showed me round a bit, remember?'

I thought back to what Tom had told me after our last visit to Rhum; that he thought there was something going on in the woods. 'I think I know where he was going. Daz, let's go and see if we can find him.'

At that moment the door opened and Nick strode in. He smiled. 'So, are you all caught up?'

A jolt went through me and I wondered whether he'd been listening at the door, and, if so, for how long. Claire was the first to break a silence that was starting to get awkward. 'Yes, not much to tell, though. When you've heard Ben go on about one sailing trip, you've heard them all.'

Nick was clearly relieved to hear that this was apparently all we'd been talking about. 'You want to join us for supper? We can't offer you much, but we do okay.'

Looking for Tom would have to wait. I rubbed my hands together, 'I could certainly do with some food.' I glanced at Claire, 'and it would be good to have some company that I haven't already bored to tears with all my sailing stories.'

Claire scowled back as she followed Nick and me out of the room.

All things considered, the dinner was a civilised affair, with the locals serving us food and wine. I watched them as they moved around the room; they appeared happy enough when they were at the table, but the moment they thought they were out of sight, their masks slipped, revealing how tired and frightened they really were. The way the marines treated them was also illuminating: they expected to be waited on hand and foot, snapping their fingers and beckoning the nearest local over whenever they wanted something. Altogether, it was painting a very unpleasant picture of how the marines saw their role in the Rhum community.

As we ate, Nick discussed the clinic with Claire. 'You know, I think Bucky was right, we really do need a doctor around here, and you need somewhere you can run your clinics. Let's face it, people are going to get hurt, and they can't work if they're injured.' He forked more food into his mouth. 'And we can't afford to carry anyone who can't work; not for long at any rate.'

'I suppose that's one way of looking at it.' Claire leaned forward. 'So, what are you proposing?'

Nick picked up his wine glass and drained it before waving it around above his head. One of the locals scuttled over with a bottle and refilled it before returning to their place by the back wall. 'Well, you're not like these people,' he swung his arm in the general direction of the locals huddled near the door, 'are you? You're more educated; you've been places; you know how the world works. We can't exactly expect you to live like them, can we? If you're willing to stay and help out, then you can stay in this place, rather than outside in the tents with that lot.' He waved an arm at the locals again.

Daz butted in. 'All of us?'

Nick took another swig of wine. 'As long as you're willing to play by the rules, I don't see why not. I'm sure you've all got skills we can use.' As he spoke, he glanced round at us, his eyes lingering a little too long on Sophie.

Daz saw this too, but before he could say something which Nick would certainly not consider to be 'playing by the rules', I jumped in. 'So have you got somewhere for us to stay for the night? No point in going back to the boat if you can offer us proper beds.'

Nick smiled, happy that we seemed to be seriously considering his offer. 'I'll show you myself.'

I looked at my watch: it was almost eleven and there had still been no sign of Tom; I was really starting to worry that he'd got himself into some sort of trouble. I hadn't wanted to ask Nick where he was over dinner in case it alerted him to Tom's absence, but then again, he hadn't mentioned it either, which I felt was distinctly odd.

'Daz, are you awake?'

We'd been lying in the dark since ten, listening to the noises of other people moving around the house, hoping the marines would assume we were asleep after the heavy supper.

'Yeah,' Daz whispered through the darkness.

I sat up. 'I'm going to see if I can find Tom; I'm not leaving here without him.'

I heard Daz start to get up, too. 'I'm comin' with you.'

'No,' I hissed back. 'I need you to stay here in case something happens to me. You need to make sure Claire and Sophie get down to the beach on time, and if I'm not there by midnight, you need to get in the dinghy, go back to the boat, and then you need to leave.'

'But ...'

'No buts. Remember: my boat; my rules.'

'I'm no' leavin' you behind.' Daz was indignant.

'Daz, you have to. You need to get Claire and Sophie

away from here; this is our only chance. I think Claire managed to persuade Nick that she's seriously considering his offer, so their guard's down: it's now or never.'

'But I can't leave you here.' There was fear in his voice. 'If Nick catches you, he'll kill you.'

The same thought had occurred to me. 'Daz, if I'm not on the beach with Tom by midnight, get on the boat and take it round to the far side of the island. There's a point there; you can't miss it. Wait there until six o'clock tomorrow morning. If Tom and I are still alive, we'll meet you there: six hours should be more than enough time for us to get there. If we're not there by then, it means we're dead, and you need to leave. Take the boat and get as far north as you can as quickly as possible. Head for an island called Handa. It should be beyond their reach and no one lives there so there shouldn't be any infected either. Mitch will know where it is, and you'll be able to find it on the charts. If somehow we're still alive, we'll know where to find you, but they won't.'

Daz said nothing.

'Daz, promise me, please.'

'Okay.' There was a pause. 'But you'd better make sure you're there, because I'm no' too sure I can sail the boat without you.'

'Daz, you'll be fine. Just remember what I've taught you. You've really got the knack for it in the last few weeks. You know what you're doing, you just need to have a little faith in yourself.'

There was another silence. Then Daz spoke again. 'Thanks, Ben.'

'For what?'

'For givin' me a chance.'

'What else could I do?'

There was a rustle as Daz shifted his weight on his bed. 'I know, but still … Thanks.'

'You know, you're a good kid. None of us would ever have lasted this long without you.' I glanced at my watch again, it was now five past eleven. 'I've got to go.'

I crept over to the door and listened: there were no sounds outside. I reached out and turned the handle slowly before easing open the door. 'I'll see you on the beach, Daz.'

'Promise?'

'I promise. Just make sure you get Sophie and Claire there on time. Until then, just sit tight.' With that, I slipped through the door and into the empty hallway.

It took me twenty minutes to get out of the Big House undetected and make my way across the uneven ground to the wooded area which Sophie had told me was off-limits to anyone but the marines. I'd only gone a few yards up a path that weaved between the trees when I saw the glow of arc lamps off in the distance. I crept cautiously forward until I saw a small group of marines in a clearing lit by portable lights set up around its perimeter. As I crouched down, trying to make sure I remained hidden, I realised the men were standing around something I couldn't see. One of the marines said something I didn't quite catch, but it made the others laugh. I shifted to my left, trying to get a better look, and glimpsed a figure lying on the ground, a black hood over its head. I recognised the clothes instantly: it was Tom. Panic bubbled up inside me as I watched him try to get to his feet, but he was hampered by the fact that his hands were secured behind his back with a thick, black cable tie.

Suddenly, Nick stepped into the light and strode towards Tom. Without even stopping, he kicked him hard in the chest, sending him sprawling backwards. 'So, you're finally awake ...'

Nick lashed out again and Tom yelped in pain as Nick's boot smashed into his ribs for a second time.

He walked round to Tom's other side. 'What were you doing sneaking around in the woods? You trying to spy on us?' Nick gave him another well-aimed kick before leaning down and pulling off the hood. I saw Tom's face, and recoiled in horror: both eyes had been blackened and there was blood running down one side. Nick grabbed Tom's hair and yanked him up onto his knees, yelling into his ear. 'You think you're tough? Well, we'll see about that.'

He pushed Tom to the ground and dragged him by his tied arms across the ground. I heard a pop as one of Tom's arms separated at the shoulder joint and he screamed in pain. As the marines moved aside to let Nick through, I could see the opening of a large pit. He pushed Tom's head over the side. 'This what you were looking for?'

Tom recoiled and from within the pit I heard the unmistakable sounds of infected. Tom tried to pull himself away, but Nick pushed his boot hard between Tom's shoulder blades, forcing him back onto the ground. Hands reached up towards him, grasping the air just inches from his face. Around him, the marines laughed.

Nick knelt down beside Tom. 'You know, I might have let you live if you hadn't got so bloody nosy.' He put his hand on the back of Tom's head and pushed it downwards. Tom fought hard, twisting his head from side to side as fingertips brushed against his cheeks, trying their best to tear into his flesh. The infected in the pit screeched and howled, yet Tom remained just beyond their reach.

Nick let go and stood up before walking a few feet from the pit. Tom squirmed away from the edge and wriggled onto his back before trying to get to his feet.

Nick turned to face him once more, 'Just as well Samo had the tranq gun when he saw you. If he'd had to shoot you properly, the noise might have got people asking questions, especially that bitch of a doctor. She's another one that's been sticking her nose where it doesn't belong; asking questions she shouldn't. She'll get what's coming to her soon enough, and that daughter of hers, too.' Nick took a step forward and kicked Tom hard in the side of the face. He fell and his head lolled over the side of the pit, his long hair dangling within reach of the infected, they roared with anticipation as they latched onto it. I watched as Tom struggled desperately, but no matter what he did, he couldn't stop himself being pulled slowly towards the edge of the pit.

Suddenly, Nick grabbed Tom's legs and pulled him away. 'Not so fast! I'm not finished with you yet. Don't think for a minute that you're not going to end up in there eventually. It's just not quite time yet.' He turned and pointed towards where one of the marines was cradling a long-barrelled gun. 'That tranquilliser gun turned out to be pretty useful really. It was Bucky's idea, you know, to use it to knock out infected. The pit was his idea, too, only he wanted to study them, learn more about them and the disease.' Nick laughed coldly. 'He just couldn't see that there was a much better use we could put them to. You fuckwits were never going to listen to us unless you thought you had no other choice, so we had to give you no choice.'

Without warning Nick dropped down onto his knees, landing hard on Tom's chest, knocking the wind out of him. Tom struggled to breathe, but I knew there was nothing I could do, not with so many heavily armed men around him. I had to look at the situation logically: there was no point in me getting caught, too, and I had to make getting Daz, Sophie and Claire off the island my top priority. Yet, Tom was my closest friend, and I couldn't just leave him, not in the hands of someone like Nick. I hovered indecisively, knowing what I should do, but also knowing I couldn't leave Tom like this.

Nick climbed back to his feet and Tom took a huge gulp of air. 'That's something they don't teach you in basic training, but it's really effective when you want to get someone to talk. Means they can't breathe, and just when they think their lungs are about to explode, you get off, and then,' he dropped onto his knees again, causing Tom to exhale sharply, 'you do it again. You can keep it up all night if you need to and it doesn't leave a mark.'

Tears of pain streamed down Tom's face as the marine got up once more. Nick watched as he struggled to get air into his lungs. 'You lot have to learn I'm the one in charge now; I'm running this game; I'm the one in control.'

Nick's attack had opened Tom's old wounds and blood was starting to seep through his shirt. Breathing heavily, Tom struggled onto his knees and spoke for the first time. 'Fuck you, Nick! They're not going to let you get away with this, you know. People will come looking for Claire, Sophie and me. Ben will be here anytime now, and once he finds out, you're in trouble. There are more people in Tobermory than you can handle.'

A cruel smile crept across Nick's face. 'Oh, sorry, did I forget to mention? Ben's already here, him and that lanky Glaswegian twat who follows him around like a lap dog. They're up at the Big House right now, thinking all's fine and dandy.'

Tom's face fell as he struggled to work out if Nick was telling the truth or not.

'That's right. It doesn't look like Ben's too bothered about you after all. He hasn't even asked where you are.' Nick stepped forward and kicked Tom in the stomach, causing him to slump forward. 'And don't even think about anyone from Tobermory coming to rescue you. You see, I'm the Big Bad Wolf: I might not have blown down their house of straw, but I certainly burned it to the ground. They're all dead: I made sure of that. They had to go, just like Bucky and his fucking morals. I'd love to have seen the look on his face when that infected we locked him up with finally came round. He was looking pretty damn scared when we left him in that lighthouse, tied up and all.' Nick peered down into the pit causing the infected to growl and snarl, their hands clawing at the edge. 'Getting a bit low on numbers now. We need some more, or maybe the ones we have are enough; maybe they just need to be fed.' He turned to face Tom. 'Either way, you won't last long down there: not as you at any rate!'

I'd seen all I could take; Tom had always been there for me, and I'd never have got this far without him: I couldn't let him think I'd abandoned him when he needed me most. Not quite knowing what I was going to do, I stepped out of the trees and into the light. Tom spotted me immediately and a broad grin spread across his face.

Nick looked confused. 'What the fuck are you smiling about?'

Tom nodded towards me. 'You might not have it all your own way!'

As Nick turned, Tom lunged, sending him sprawling backwards towards the pit. He came to rest with his upper body hanging over the edge. For a moment, everyone froze, staring, then two of the marines bolted forward and dragged Nick to safety. Almost immediately, he leapt to his feet and strode over to Tom. He pulled his pistol from its holster. 'You little fucker!'

Tom took one look at the gun and yelled. 'Ben, run!'

I remained rooted to the spot as Nick aimed at Tom and fired repeatedly, not at his head, but into his stomach until Tom was rolling on the ground screaming in pain. Only then did Nick turn to his men, waving his pistol at me. 'Well, don't just stand there, grab him!'

No one moved.

Nick stared angrily at them. 'What the fuck's wrong with you? I said get him.'

Still, there was no movement.

Nick's face was red with anger. 'What the hell are you waiting for?'

One of the marines stepped forward, 'Nick, you're bleeding ...'

Nick glanced down and saw the ragged wound on his left hand. 'It's nothing; I must have caught it on something.' The colour drained from his face as he stared at it. 'Can one of you go get that smart-arsed doctor? Drag her up here if you have to; she'll know what to do.'

There was no reply. Nick looked up just as one of his men tried to draw his gun but before he could get it out of its holster, Nick had his pistol levelled at him. 'No you don't. I'm not going out like that. I can beat this. I just need the doctor up here now.'

Another marine made a move, but Nick swivelled and fired before he could get his machine gun into position. Instantly, he dropped to the ground, blood oozing from a large hole his forehead. Nick stared at the remaining marines, a wild look in his eyes as he swung his pistol back and forth. 'After all I've done for you, this is how you repay me? Are none of you going to help me?'

The marines glanced at each other nervously, unsure of how to deal with the situation. Then, one by one they started backing away, slowly at first, then faster and faster, until they were racing down the path to the Big House.

Nick stepped forward, yelling after them. 'Come back, you fucking cowards!' He glanced down at his hand again. 'Shit! I'll just have to get the bitch myself.' He spoke more to himself than to anyone in particular.

While Nick was distracted I crept forward, trying to get to Tom, but before I could, Nick remembered I was there. In a single movement, he raised the pistol and pulled the trigger, but there was no shot, just a hollow click. At first, Nick looked surprised and then he smirked. 'Don't think you've won.'

Before I could react, Nick threw away the empty gun as he bent down and rolled Tom onto his side. Then, with one last kick, he sent him over the edge of the pit before sprinting off into the darkness in search of Claire. I ran forward, hoping against hope that I still might be able to save Tom, but I heard his terrified screams even before I was close enough to see the infected pull his intestines from his open belly. I looked down into the pit, as they screeched and snarled, fighting over Tom's still-moving body. He stared up at me, pleading with me to do something to end his pain, yet there was nothing I could do, but stay there with him until he was finally gone.

For what seemed like an age, I stood, staring into the pit, unable to believe what had just happened. Then something snapped deep inside and an anger like I'd never felt before washed over me. Wiping the tears from my face, I turned and ran after Nick, not knowing what I'd do when I caught up with him, but knowing I was going to make him pay for all he had done.

Back at the Big House, Nick was nowhere in sight, but people were running in every direction. Then Daz appeared in the main doorway, with Claire and Sophie close behind. The sight of them standing there, eyes moving back and forth as they tried to work out what was going on, brought me back to my senses: Tom was gone, there was no point in trying to seek revenge. He'd already seen to it that Nick was finished anyway. Instead, I needed to concentrate on getting the others back to the safety of the boat and then away from the island. I glanced at my watch, it was now ten minutes to midnight, and we needed to get down to the beach as quickly as possible to meet Mitch.

Then I realised that it wasn't just people who were running, there were infected, too: Nick must have turned and attacked others. Suddenly, our escape was much harder and more vital than ever.

'Daz!' I shouted and waved. 'Over here!'

Relief spread across his face and he ran forward, dodging between people and jumping over a body which lay bleeding on the ground. Behind him, Sophie screamed as the body reached out and grabbed her ankle, pulling it towards its mouth. In an instant, Claire threw herself on the newly turned infected, punching and kicking it. It dropped Sophie's leg and turned its attention to Claire. For what seemed like a lifetime, but must have only been seconds, they struggled before Daz stepped forward and kicked the infected as hard as he could in the head, sending it spinning across the ground. Claire leapt to her feet and grabbed Sophie. 'Let's go!'

She ran forward, Sophie stumbling behind her. Daz and I followed, and within minutes we were on the beach. The dinghy was where it was meant to be, but there was no sign of Mitch. I stared nervously into the darkness, wondering where she'd gone. I could hear the snarls of infected mixed with panicked screams and the sound of automatic gunfire echoing around the bay.

Suddenly, a figure raced out of the darkness. Daz stepped forward, clutching a heavy lump of driftwood he'd hurriedly grabbed from the beach. Then the figure came within striking distance, I realised who it was. 'Daz, it's Mitch!'

He let out a relieved sigh. 'Where the hell've you been?'

'Just making sure they can't follow us.' She tucked a knife from the galley carefully into her jacket pocket. 'What's going on up at the house? Have they realised you're trying to get away?'

'Infected!' I hissed, hearing the fear in my own voice. 'We need to get out of here.'

'Where did they come from?' Mitch glanced round, horrified. 'Where's Tom?'

'Mitch,' I fought back the tears I could feel building inside me, 'Tom didn't make it.'

'What happened?' Mitch asked, shocked and dismayed.

From behind us came the sound of running and three marines emerged from the darkness, firing over their shoulders, before heading in the direction of the ribs. I watched them disappear. 'I'll tell you later, we need to get out of here!'

Wasting no time, Claire and I pushed the dinghy into the water as the others climbed in. By the time we were in waist-deep, Daz had the engine started and I signalled to Claire to climb in.

She looked away, avoiding my eyes. 'I'm afraid you're going to have to go without me.'

Sophie stared at her. 'Mum, what're you talking about?' She grabbed Claire's arm and pulled. 'Just get in.'

Claire resisted. Sophie tried again, this time pleading with her, not understanding what was going on. 'Mum, please, before the infected get here, before they get you.'

'No.' She said it so quietly, I barely heard it above the commotion going on behind her. Claire pulled the neck of her jumper aside. 'I'm sorry, honey. They got me, already.'

The blood drained from Sophie's face as she stared at the wound. 'Wh—? When did that happen?'

'I got bitten back there.'

'When you pulled that infected off me? You ... You mean it's my fault?'

Claire reached out for Sophie's hands and held them in hers. 'Honey, it's not your fault; it's no one's fault; it just happened.'

'But there must be something you can do?' Sophie looked desperately at each of us in turn. 'There must be something one of you can do. Please!'

Claire stroked the side of her daughter's face. 'There's nothing anyone can do, you know that.' Her eyes glistened as she did her best not to cry. 'You need to leave me here. You need to go. You know you do.'

Tears welled in Sophie's eyes, 'But, Mum, you can't. You can't leave me. You promised. You promised you'd never leave me. You're all I've got left!' she sobbed. 'You can't be infected. I can't lose you, too.'

'But I am; I can feel it.' Claire put her arm round her daughter's shoulder, pulling her towards her and kissing her forehead. She held Sophie's face in her hands, wiping away her tears with her thumbs, and stared into her eyes. 'Remember when Dad was ill? Remember what we talked about then? About how someone's never really gone if you've still got them in here.' She tapped the side of Sophie's head. 'As long as you've still got memories, I'll always be with you, no matter what.'

I glanced at Claire and saw tears streaming down her face. I swallowed. 'Are you sure you're infected?'

'Yes.' Claire sniffed. 'I'm certain. You've got to leave me here.'

For a moment, we just stared at each other.

'I don't have much time.' There was an urgency in Claire's voice. 'You need to get out of here. Now!'

I pulled myself into the dinghy and turned to Claire, not quite knowing what to say to her.

She leaned forward and kissed Sophie on the top of her head one last time. Sophie lunged towards her mother. 'But you said you'd never leave me. You promised!'

Daz pulled her back.

Claire called out after us. 'Just promise you'll look after her for me.'

Daz and I answered in unison. 'I promise.'

As Daz held Sophie, I grabbed the throttle and slammed the engine into gear. Within seconds, we were skipping over the water back to the yacht. I glanced back to where Claire was wading back to shore. When she got there, she sat down, waiting for the inevitable to happen. Not wanting to watch, I turned away, barely able to see through the tears which filled my eyes and rolled down my face. Yesterday, it had seemed like we were doing so well, and in just a few short hours it had all fallen apart: Tobermory was gone; Tom was dead; and Claire was infected.

I was pulled back to the moment by the sound of heavy machine gunfire. I turned and saw tracer rounds streaking through the darkness towards the dinghy and felt the spray as they landed in the water just to our left.

Instinctively, we crouched as low as we could despite the rubber sides of the dinghy offering little protection.

Mitch looked across at me. 'I think they might've discovered what I did.'

Keeping as low as possible, I turned and searched the shoreline, trying to work out where the shots were coming from. 'What was that?'

'I slashed the ribs so they wouldn't be able to follow us.' Mitch looked guilty. 'It seemed like a good idea at the time.'

There was another burst of gunfire followed by a shout in a scared voice I didn't recognise. 'Come back! You've got to take us with you. You can't leave us here.' Then, with more anger than fear, 'We won't let you leave without us.'

By this time we'd reach the yacht and had climbed on board. I set Daz to work lifting the anchor as Mitch and I readied the sails; Sophie sat in the cockpit sobbing and hugging her knees tight against her chest.

There was a cry from the bow. 'It won't budge. I think it's …'

The last of what Daz said was lost amongst the sound of another barrage from the machine gun. I ran forward, leaving Mitch at the helm, but even with the two of us pulling on it, we couldn't get the anchor to move.

I glanced at Daz. 'Time for more drastic measures.'

I ran back to the cockpit and down into the cabin where I rummaged frantically in my tool kit. Grabbing my hacksaw, I climbed back onto the deck just as another shout rang out from the shore. 'Don't leave us here, you bastards!'

When they heard no reply, they fired again. This time the last of the bullets hit the side of the yacht, sending fragments of fibreglass flying across the cabin. I ran forward and thrust the hacksaw towards Daz. He wasted no time in grabbing it and set to work on the chain while I returned to the cockpit.

There was another burst of gunfire, this time ripping through the sails, leaving dark circles in the white cloth.

'You're not going to leave without us. You've got to help us.' The cries from the shore now sounded desperate and panicked.

Then, out of the darkness, came the sound of splashing. A second later, a hand appeared over the left side of the boat, followed by an arm with a deep, red wound carved across it, then the upper half of a body. I picked up the hatchet from beside the helm, but before I could strike out, there was a shout from Daz and I felt the boat finally start to move: I had no choice but to turn back to the wheel. The injured marine managed to get his leg over the side just as the next barrage of bullets hit, cutting his body in half and splintering the hull along the waterline.

I wondered how bad the damage was, but there was no time to investigate. I tightened the sails and we finally began to move in earnest. Another round of bullets smashed into the back of the boat, showering us with water and fibreglass. I glanced back and saw the dinghy deflate and sink under the weight of its outboard engine. Knowing it was now useless, I reached up and untied it from its cleat. Daz returned to the cockpit and wrapped his arms protectively around Sophie as I adjusted the sails, trying to wring every possible ounce of speed from them, knowing it was all that stood between us and certain death. Yet, finally, it felt like we had a chance.

After ten minutes, we rounded the headland at the entrance of the bay and were finally out of range of the machine gun. It didn't matter, by then it had already fallen silent as the last of the marines had been killed, or worse.

Leaving Mitch at the wheel, I went to inspect the damage. As soon as I entered the cabin, I knew we were in trouble. The water was already several feet deep, but it was unclear where it was coming in from. I swore loudly.

'What's wrong?' Daz poked his head through the companionway, and his jaw dropped. 'Shit!'

I scrambled back onto the deck and opened the hatch which led down to the engine.

Mitch remained at the wheel, but she watched me closely, a worried look spreading across her face. 'Ben, what's going on?'

'I don't know yet.' I stuck my head into the engine compartment and instantly spotted the problem. There was a series of bullet holes below the waterline, and water was pouring through them, but worse than that, there was a crack connecting them which flexed with every movement of the boat, letting in bucketfuls of water each time it opened up.

I pulled my head out of the hatch and looked up at Daz and Mitch. 'We're in deep trouble. The hull's damaged and we're taking in a lot of water, more than we can cope with for longer than a few minutes.'

Mitch stared at me, her eyebrows knitted with worry.

'Can you fix it?'

I could feel the panic building within me. 'I can try, but there's a hell of a lot of water coming in.'

'Well, get goin' then!' Daz urged me on.

I ran down into the cabin and waded through the water looking for anything which might help. The first thing that came to mind was an old oilskin that had floated out of one the lockers. I grabbed it and ran back outside. With Daz holding the spotlight, I snaked my way into the engine compartment, and started forcing the waterproof jacket into the crack each time it opened up. At first the amount of water coming in slowed, but it put too much strain on the already weakened fibreglass and, with a sound like a gunshot, the crack raced along the side of the boat, sending a torrent of water streaming into the hull. I felt the boat list and settle deeper into the sea with every passing second, and I knew there was nothing we could do.

I reached up my arms. 'Help me out.'

Daz and Mitch dragged me up through the hatch and we stood, staring at each other as we felt the boat tip ever further to the left. Daz gasped as the first wave washed over the side and spilled into the cockpit. 'We're goin' down, aren't we?'

With those words, the reality of our situation sank in. We were about to lose the only thing which had kept us alive since the outbreak started, our only source of transport and protection. How we'd survive without it, I didn't know.

'Daz, we need to get the life raft into the water; Mitch, grab whatever food and water you can from the cabin, Claire ...' I stopped abruptly as I remembered Claire was no longer with us. I tried to ignore the pain that shot deep into my heart. 'Sophie, grab the life jackets and make sure everyone has one on.'

Sophie didn't move.

'Sophie! Life jackets!'

The order seemed to break through her sorrow, and she looked round as if seeing us all for the first time.

I knelt down beside her. 'Sophie, we're sinking; you need to get the life jackets.'

She stared at me blankly for a moment before the realisation of what was happening struck home, and she leapt into action.

Within minutes, the large hexagonal life raft was floating alongside the rapidly sinking yacht and we were loading it with as many supplies as we could. Daz helped Sophie into it, before he followed and then Mitch climbed in. I took one last look round, seeing if there was anything else useful I could grab. That was when it occurred to me that the fishing lines might prove invaluable. I opened the deck locker and grabbed the first one I saw. As the boat started to slip beneath the waves, I threw it across to Daz before lunging into the life raft, just as the yacht finally disappeared in a swirl of inky black water.

***

'What're we going to do?' Fear and despair were etched deep into Sophie's face.

We'd been in the life raft for three days, enclosed by the orange, tent-like sides which came to a point above our heads, unable to do more than drift with the winds and the currents. I had a rough idea of where we were, but little more than that. We were already running low on food and water, and the constant movement of the thin rubber floor of the raft meant we felt sick most of the time. Ever since the yacht had sunk, I'd been wracking my brains, trying to work out what to do, but I could think of nothing.

After what had happened to her mother, I couldn't look at Sophie; I couldn't look at Mitch, either: I'd yet to explain to her what had happened to Tom, and I still wasn't ready to say out loud what I'd witnessed in the woods, and how I'd been unable to do anything to save him.

I slept fitfully from time to time, but I usually woke feeling worse than when I'd fallen asleep. It was the dreams; whenever I closed my eyes I saw vivid fragments of everything that had happened: Iliana's head exploding; Jake on the bench in the cockpit as his life drained away; Hamish's body floating face down in the harbour at Tobermory; what was left of Gordon lying in the darkness of the lighthouse; Tom being torn apart by the infected in the pit; and Claire sitting on the beach, waiting for the inevitable, as we left her behind.

For a brief time, we'd had people around us, we'd had a plan, and I could see a way of surviving in a world which, only a few weeks ago, I could barely have imagined. Now we had nothing. There were just the four of us, trapped in the life raft, at the mercy of the tides and the elements. Eventually, we'd either drift out into the open ocean or onto the shore, and I didn't know which was worse. The land had infected, but they weren't everywhere; we might get lucky and wash up somewhere uninhabited, but then again we might not. In the open ocean, there was no chance of encountering any infected, but there was also no chance of life, not in the long term. We might last weeks, maybe even months, but eventually death would creep up on us, taking us one by one as the others could do nothing but watch.

When we'd had the yacht, we'd at least had a

chance, but now I couldn't help but feel the final roll of the dice had been cast: we just didn't yet know if we'd got lucky or not. I thought back to the morning the outbreak had started in Glasgow, how the problems in Miami had seemed so far away. Now Tom was dead and the yacht, my home for the last five years, was gone, I'd lost my last connections to the world as it was before. I felt the final separation as deeply as if it had torn my soul in two. It was the last straw, and one from which I felt I might never recover.

I knew Sophie was still waiting for an answer to her question, but I didn't have one. I'd promised Claire that I'd look after her, that I'd protect her, but now I was powerless to do anything. All I could do was sit in the twelve square feet of rubber and stale air that was now our home; existing rather than living, waiting to see what further horrors life had to throw at us in the frightening new world we found ourselves thrust into with little warning or preparation. I wondered why it had all happened. Why had the biotech company pushed ahead with the vaccine trial when its technology was still unproven? Why hadn't they foreseen the consequences? I'd never know. But whatever the reason, it was humanity that had paid the ultimate price.

A shout from Daz brought me back to the present. He'd raised the flap on the side of the life raft to let in some fresh air and was now staring through it. 'There's land right beside us!'

The currents must have finally carried us close to shore, yet we still didn't know if this was good news or bad. I lay there, unmoving, finding it difficult to care one way or the other. The world was now ruled by the infected and there was nothing I could do about it. That was when I realised I'd finally given up. After weeks of fighting to stay alive, I was physically and emotionally spent. I no longer cared if I lived or died.

I heard Mitch scramble onto her knees and move over to the opening. 'Ben, I know this island: it's Soay. No one lives here; not anymore.' She bent over the side and started paddling frantically with her hands. 'It's close; really close: maybe a hundred yards at the most. Ben, I think we can make it.' She stopped for a moment and turned to the rest of us. 'Come on!'

First Daz, then Sophie joined her, and I could hear their arms splashing through the water, throwing spray against the side of the life raft. Yet, still I couldn't bring myself to act. Instead, I closed my eyes and lay there, unable to move.

'Ben, come and help!' Sophie paused and I realised she'd stopped paddling. 'Ben?' She sounded concerned.

The next voice I heard was Mitch's. 'Don't just lie there, Ben. You need to help us. We won't make it if you don't.' I heard her shuffle across the life raft. 'Ben?'

Still I didn't move; I couldn't.

'Ben, are you okay?' Daz had stopped paddling, too.

I felt Sophie's small hand on my shoulder. 'Ben, we need your help. We can't make it to shore without you.'

I opened my eyes and saw them all looking down at me, worried expressions on their faces. I thought about Tom, and what he'd say to me if he was still here, and I realised I couldn't let the infected win so easily. I held out my hand. Daz grabbed it and pulled me up.

I looked at him, barely recognising the skinny teenager I'd met only a few weeks before. 'Thanks.' I turned to the others. 'All of you.' I stared towards the nearby island, a steely determination now burning within me. 'Let's do this.'

Together, we scrambled to the side and, with all the

strength we had left, we paddled furiously. I watched the island gradually draw closer and closer, and for the first time in days, I smiled. Soon, I knew, we'd be safe, at least for the time being.

347

About the Author:

Colin M. Drysdale has worked as a marine biologist for almost twenty years. During this time, he has travelled extensively and spent much of his professional career on or near the sea. He is also a keen sailor and has sailed in Scotland, the Bahamas, Florida, Newfoundland and Labrador.

When writing *The Outbreak*, he drew on his experiences both of living in Glasgow, where the novel starts, and from sailing amongst the islands of north-west Scotland. This allowed the story to be tightly woven into the landscapes in which it is set.

He now lives in his native Glasgow, where he runs a small business providing mapping advice to ecologists and marine biologists. While he is the author of countless academic papers and a number of technical books, this is only his second novel. He is currently working on the third book in the *For those in Peril* series, which will bring together the characters from the first two books. This is scheduled for publication in summer 2015.

If you would like find out more about the world of *The Outbreak*, and the *For those in Peril* series in general, visit:

TheOutbreak.ForThoseInPeril.net